The Most Happy

Holly-Eloise Walters

Churchill Publishing
October, 2019

This book is dedicated to my nan, Susan Walters, who carried me and raised me up every single day of my life. I would have never been able to write this without her voice guiding me. She held my hand through whatever storm I had to face, and even though she is no longer physically here, she has left a handprint on my heart for eternity.

It is also dedicated to my Auntie Pam who was there for me at the hardest time in my life. I survived because of her influence and love.

And finally I would like to dedicate it to Anne Boleyn. She inspires me each and every day. She faced each and every challenge thrown her way and she survived.

Three strong women who have made me the person I am today. Thank you all for helping to shape me.

PROLOGUE

18 May, 1536
London, England

Tonight I sit alone in my cold, dark room with nothing but my ramblings for comfort. Tonight I breathe in the cold night air, and feel every breath as the gift that it is. I feel each with a new appreciation for the life it sustains.

Tonight I look upon this room for the last time; I stare out of my small window and at the night sky for the last time. I will never again see the darkness of the evening, never see the moon light up the sky again.

Tonight I will not sleep, I will not eat, and I will have not one moment of rest, for my mind is alive with the memories of my short time. Tonight is my last night in this tower, it is my last night in London, my last night as queen, and it is my last night in this world.

Tomorrow I will die.

Tomorrow they will come to me early; I will wash and be dressed as I am every day. I will hold my head high and let my ladies ready me. Then, when the time comes, I will be led out of my room and to the scaffold. I will leave this room behind, never to look upon it again. I will leave my books, jewels, and all of my worldly possessions.

I will leave my daughter to this harsh world, and to the mean-spirited people who live in it. I will leave my Lizzie with the men who sought to destroy me, the men who did destroy me. She will be left with no motherly guidance, left with no help to navigate the evils that lie ahead of her.

I can only pray that after I am gone she is loved by her father, and by the people who are left behind with her. I hope that she knows how I have loved her. I hope that her life will be longer and fuller than mine, and that she is shown more kindness and care than the people before her.

I know that one day she will become the woman I believe she can be. It pains me to know I won't be here to watch her grow; I won't be around to influence her or to teach her. She will not know me. I will be nothing more than a distant memory from her childhood. She may not remember what I looked like or how I spoke. She won't remember me singing her to sleep at night, holding her tightly to my chest. She won't know the way she made me smile, and the way her presence made my heart sing. She will not know that when she was born, I felt a love I had never known before. She will not know her mother at all.

I no longer rant and rave as I did before; there is no one to listen. I do not plead that I am innocent and that I should be set free. There is no point. It would do no good. I would be wasting the precious time I have left on useless words. It is too late for that. The decision has been made.

Instead, I sit. I sit, and I sob. I despair for the misery of my existence and the wretchedness that has become my life. Then I remind myself that I am a queen and I should always remain dignified. Even now I must appear in control of my emotions. I accept my fate for a while, coming to terms with what must and will happen. I live in a vicious circle of acceptance, fear, and denial for the foreseeable future.

It is exhausting, arguing with oneself, thinking up different scenarios for how this could have played out. I think of ways that I may still be set free, and then admonish myself for thinking of the impossible. I may refuse to shout my innocence, but that does not mean that a part of me does not still hope that someone will come to save me.

Thirty-five! I am thirty-five years old. Thirty-five short years I have been in this world, no more, no less. I am not a young maid, but I still had the possibility of years ahead of me, and now those possibilities and my life are to be cut short. They will be taken from me. Without my permission, my years will be stolen. Death will come to me like a thief in the night, in search of the years that I have left to give. I have not had many years, but my life has been so full. From my time on French soil to the greatest love of my life, a love that has given me my beautiful Lizzie, a greater love than any other person may experience.

I have lived through a whirlwind; it has brought a storm and left chaos in its wake. However, I will never regret the love that I have felt, no matter what it has come to, or what it has destroyed. No one will ever hear me say that I regret one moment of my love for Henry. If I could change how it had ended, of course I would; if I could remove the damage it has done, I would not think twice.

Do I sometimes think that I would have been happier without him? I do. I often think of how my life would be had I married another, but Henry brought my heart to life and opened up a universe of possibilities. He made me want things that I did not know I could ever want, he made my life mean something. And now that it has all been taken away, I feel so cold and empty. Oh, how I love him still. It is wrong for me to love him still. I should hate him, cast him from my heart, and detest his name.

But even after he has ordered my execution and kept our daughter from me, I still love him with such passion. There is a small part of me that believes he may come barging through my door at any moment, with his mighty presence and booming voice, smile at me, and ask for forgiveness. He might say that he wants me to go home with him and that this was just a test of my faith in our love; I am to return to my rightful place as queen, and we will have more children. Boys. We will have boys, and I will be the queen of England forever. We will be in love, and no one could ever take my place. For a moment I believe it. It will not be the last time that I believe it. I will imagine Henry coming to my aid one hundred times over and feel the crush of pain as reality strikes me again.

What am I thinking? How can I say that I still love him? I am here in this place because the man who is supposed to love me wants me dead. He has removed me so that he can replace me, and I dream of him still. He wishes to marry again so that he can have sons, and my Elizabeth will be displaced. He will put his future children above ours, just like he did with Mary, his daughter with Catherine. He will make Elizabeth nothing more than a bastard to please whoever follows me. He tossed Mary aside like she was nothing, and he had been married to her mother for over 20 years; why would he not do exactly the same thing to Lizzie? He did it to me, and he will do it to whatever whore replaces me. I bet it will be that Seymour slut. Well, I can promise one thing, she will never sit comfortably in my place, and she will never be the queen that I am...was.

> "Remember me when you do pray that hope doth lead from day to day."

A sentence that I inscribe into my book of hours, knowing that one day Henry will see this passage, and he will remember me. He will not be able to shake me as easily as he thinks. Jane will know that whenever he is in bed with her at night, it is I he thinks of. She will know that when he screams from some unspoken terror, it is my face that haunts his dreams. I will be with him for the rest of his days, never letting him forget the sins he has committed, and never allowing him one moment of peace. He will be tormented with his deeds until the end of his days. And after he is dead, I will be there to greet him. Jane will know that she never truly has his whole heart; she will know that she will never be as good as me, and the crown will not sit on her head as easily as it has on mine.

When I was first imprisoned, I wrote Henry a letter. I, first of all, wanted to approach him about the ridiculous notion that I would ever confess to something of which I am not guilty, especially not to such a man as Thomas Cromwell. I had also hoped that he would feel once more connected to me. I imagined that my words would call to somewhere deep within his soul, to where he may love me still.

When we first found each other, he would write me letters of love. He would write to me of his deepest feelings, of his hopes for our future. I wished to stir some memories in him, of long ago when we had nothing but hope in front of us. I hoped that the man who fell in love with me so quickly would find that he was unable to destroy me.

At the very least, part of me imagined I could plead for the lives of the men accused with me. If it was useless to beg for my own forgiveness, then I could at least try to obtain their pardon. For they are free of any guilt and I cannot go to my grave knowing that I did not at least try to help them.

Of course, it did absolutely nothing to help. I never received any sort of reply. I doubt that the letter ever made it into Henry's hands at all. I imagine that someone would have stood in the way. Cromwell probably intercepted it and disposed of the evidence. He would do anything to keep Henry and me separated. He had such a hatred for me that to see me die tomorrow will bring him the greatest pleasure.

I look upon the night sky and feel a stab of pain that I will never be able to look upon it again. I will never again see the stars in their beauty, shining down on me in the darkness. This is the last time that I will be under the moon, its glorious glow illuminating my room—the air that I breathe is only mine but for one more night. In the morning I will hear the birds chirp a final time, I will have my last conversation, say my last goodbyes. Then I will stand on the scaffold and see my subjects once more.

They will look to me to deliver my final words of wisdom. They will call to me, some with love and sorrow at my death, some with taunts and hateful words, but they will all be there for one reason: to watch their queen die. They will listen as I say my final piece, as I speak my final words, and they will watch me take my final breath. They will look on as the swordsman takes his swing, and then they will gasp as my head is…

I cannot bear to think of it — the thought that tomorrow, I will draw my last breath. Will the sun be out? Will the sky darken, and rain thunder down on us? Will God show his displeasure at such a task? Will it hurt? Am I to feel the pain as the sword hits the back of my neck or will it be just like going to sleep? Will I feel the blow at all or will it be so quick that in one moment I close my eyes and in the next, I open them in heaven?

I cannot help but worry about what it will be like afterward. Will everything go all black, and that be the end of me? I am a very pious woman. I have been taught to believe that God will be waiting for me and I will be welcomed into the Kingdom of Heaven. It was all so certain before death was in my sights. Now I find myself questioning everything I believe. What if everything we think we know is wrong? And afterward there is nothing at all, just an empty void that stretches on for all eternity. What if I am to go to the other place, trapped in the fires of hell to pay for the awful misdoings in my life. Or I could be left to roam the earth forever, seeing and hearing but never being able to touch or talk to the people I love. How will I cope if I am to be stuck in the tower for all of time, never allowed to leave its walls, bound to this place that has been both a joy and a terror to me?

I was supposed to die today. My death was set for early this morning, but by a stroke of luck the swordsman that Henry has ordered from France was delayed, and I was told that I had a while longer to live. Nothing but a few hours at first, and then I was gifted another night.

I found myself wondering if this was meant to happen, that maybe God was stepping in to postpone my death. He knows that I am guilt-free; perhaps He wants to give the king a little time to reconsider. Maybe Henry could yet realise he is wrong and turn on Cromwell, the man who orchestrated this whole mess. Why can Henry not just realise that he loves me and choose to forgive me for whatever I have done?, Or realise that he already knows I am not capable of such things.

For a moment I allow the hopefulness to wash over me but I am wrenched back to life as it crashes away again. It cannot happen, for if Henry were looking to change his mind, then why is my younger brother dead? Why Mark and Norris? Weston and Brereton? Because there is no mercy in this world, and once you are condemned, you are condemned for all of time.

When people think of me, Queen Anne, they will think of the lying, cheating adulteress of Henry VIII. The one who fought her way to the top only to be cut down again. The one who imagined good King Hal's death, who used witchcraft to lure a king to her bed, and displace his beloved wife. They will say that I destroyed a family, took one woman from her place and put myself in it. A woman who took their beloved queen from the throne and replaced her with herself.

They will not speak of the love that I felt and gave, the good things I did as their queen. The princess I gave them, or of the sorrow I faced. They will speak only of hate. This will be seen as Catherine finally receiving her justice.

Poor Catherine. She would laugh if she could see how the tables have turned, and my fortune has changed. Is this why I am being punished now? Is it possible that the reason I now find myself in despair is for what I did to her? I treated her infernally, and she did not deserve any of it. She was a good queen and a good woman, who found herself tormented because she was no longer loved. Is God angry with me for taking a rightful queen's place? He gave Catherine no male children, so surely He smiled on her no more than He did on me.

If He had then, she would still be married to Henry and I to Henry Percy. Maybe if I had married Percy I would be happy. We would have lived at court, and we would have been content with our three children. Elizabeth would have been ours, and we would have had two healthy boys to follow. They would have carried on the Percy name, and that would be enough for me. We would have lived a long life, and I would have been happy. Happy. The most happy.

Why could I not have a son? Just one living son. Was that too much to ask? A queen to have one son to save her life. Can I blame God for this? Or perhaps Henry is at fault. Maybe it is because I was not made right; I had one fatal flaw that meant I could not bear a son for my husband.

Why did God feel that He should rip my young boys away from me? My precious boys who never even took one breath. They never felt their mothers love, never had any idea of how much I loved them, never slept soundly in my arms as I rocked them gently. They had no idea of the greatness for which they were destined. They would be two little princes. One day the elder would become king of England, and all would be right with the world. If only they had lived, Henry and I would go to our graves old and happy in the knowledge that we left the country in safe hands.

Lizzie would marry a far-off prince and become queen of her own country. She would write to me of her own life and her children, and we would visit whenever possible. I would have many royal grandchildren, and they would call me "Lady Grandmother." I would spoil them with gifts and sweet treats. Henry and I would be responsible for a long line of Tudor kings and queens, and through them we would live on forever.

I can picture the both of us as an old couple, still as strong and steady as ever, just as in love as we were at the very beginning. Henry and I ruling over England side by side, and nothing could part us. Our children would surround us, watching as we grow old. And when we did die, they would be there to see us off together, and they would weep for us. But Henry and I would have lived a full life, content with the path we took. We would go into the next world hand in hand and be together for the rest of time. I would not die at 35; I would die an old lady in her marital bed. I would die the greatest queen of England. I would not leave behind my daughter to fend for herself, to be forgotten and bargained with, I would leave behind a King, and I would be the reason that the Tudor dynasty continued. Everyone would know that I was the mother of a Tudor king. I would not be forgotten. I would live on in the generations of Tudors to come.

I think we would have named our first son Edward, like many great kings before him. Our other boy I would have liked to call Henry, after his father. How I long for those boys. Will I see them again? Now that I am to join them in heaven, will I be able to cradle the boys that I was never able to nurse? Will they still be the beautiful babes that I lost or would they have aged like people in the living world and now be strong young boys? Maybe they have grown and are waiting patiently for their mother to join them; I will sweep them up into my arms and never let them go again, raining kisses down on them to make up for all that they have missed. I picture them looking the image of their father, bright red hair, broad shoulders but the softest delicate blue eyes. They would have my gentleness and determination, truly little princes in every way. If they are what awaits me afterward, then I welcome death with open arms. I will be with them happily and leave the tragedies of this world long behind me.

I let myself drift off into a peaceful sleep for the briefest of moments, I dream of the small red-haired boys, waiting for me up in the clouds far away from this dreadful prison.

* * * * *

The last image I remember before I wake is of Lizzie asleep in her cradle. I wake in a state of panic; I find myself clinging to life, remembering that I would be trading my living child who is kept not far from here, to be with the children who I have not seen grow. She needs me in this world, they are with God, safe and sound in His kingdom, while she is here in this living hell. There must be some way that I can escape this? Surely there is some hope even at this late hour, is it too late for the truth to be revealed? Even if it were, could I ever forgive Henry for killing George? My sweet brother.

I want to live; I have so much life left within me, so much more that I can give to this world. I want to see Elizabeth become a woman who knows that she is loved. I long to see Henry one last time. Perhaps if he could see me, he would be convinced to send me to a convent to live out my remaining days in solitude. A convent far from London and the court that has strived to bring me down from the start. It is too late for him, this I know, but maybe he would be content to let me suffer in silence. But I know that even as I think this I would never be happy on the outside. I could never bear to sit back in the shadows and let life go on without me. Knowing that Henry lived with another woman and life went on, that the court worshipped a new queen would be too much to bear. The court is a place of egotistical men and deceit. It had built me up, broken me, chewed me up and spat me back out again when it was finished. It will do it all over again to the next woman.

I do not want to die. I really do not want to die; please, dear God, do not let me die, hear my plea in my last hours and do something to keep me from this ordeal. The thought of standing on the scaffold sickens me; I cannot do this, I am not strong enough; God, this is unbearable.

Why has all of the air left the room? The small window is doing nothing to help; it is suffocating in this place. My bodice is so tight that I cannot breathe, the walls close in on me as the room seems to shrink smaller, and I can feel death's gentle tick nearing closer and closer. I stand and go to the window, trying to fill my lungs with the cold night air. I call one of my ladies, Madge, to loosen my bodice. It is as if I can already feel the cold steel of the sword on the back of my neck as its final stroke prepares to end me. Madge tries to comfort me, but I shrug her off. I do not want anyone to touch me. I want the room to myself; I want only the sound of my thoughts.

I sit at the window, weeping into my hands. I find that the words are no longer only in my head. I whisper them as if God were in this very room and able to answer me. They hang in the air, unanswered questions that will never receive a reply.

"Why do I deserve this fate? Am I guilty of too many sins?" I cry. "Did I take my sisters' place too easily?" I wait as if there were someone to answer.

"Wolsey, are you punishing me for his death, God? A man of God, a cardinal. Or perhaps my sins against Catherine? Is this of my own doing?" I had played a massive part in both Wolsey's and Catherine's downfall; had I offended God in this? To destroy a man of the cloth? I ruined a man who had pledged his life to God. Wolsey was not a good man, but did he deserve to be brought so low after his service to the king? Or could I have stepped in and saved him from Henry's wrath?

I let the silence stretch out for a moment, feeling more alone now than I had since I was first imprisoned.

"Well? Answer me." I screamed. Nothing, there was nothing. What did I think would happen? God had never answered me before so why would He now?

I sat in silence for a while, thinking about all the things that I would do differently if given a chance. I wish that I had never left the French court. I wish that I never caught Henry's attention, or that instead of allowing him to sway me, I turned on my heels and ran from the court the moment he showed me any affection. I like to think I am an intelligent woman, so how have I managed to get into this mess. I knew that it might not end well, but I allowed myself to be overcome with the excitement of new love. Henry is a hard man to say no to, and I really did try for a while. But eventually, I let his love completely consume me. I could see nothing else, could think of nothing but him. He was my very first thought in the morning and my very last at night. I could concentrate on nothing but him. Every moment I could not be with him was like torture; I needed him to survive. If it were possible, his love could have been the only thing to sustain me. When I was not with him, his face was in my mind. I thought about what he might be doing every moment of the day; who he was talking to and what they spoke of. I would picture him sitting with Catherine or in her bed, and I allowed myself to grow jealous and then to hate. Every time I pictured Catherine by his side, I would turn sick with grief. Her face made me ill with envy. I allowed myself to become cruel, to taunt her, all for the love of a man. I treated her with such contempt because I wanted her husband. I resented every moment that she had with him, but now I realise that both of us were victims in the world of men, both treated unfairly by our husband and used by our families.

At first, I did everything that I could to avoid Henry and his affections. But after a little time in his presence, I realised that I was in love with him and that I wanted him fully. He would have been happy to keep me as a mistress, a bit on the side for his pleasure. But I did not want to be nothing more than his whore, always playing second fiddle to Catherine. I wanted to be his everything, for him to have no other in his life. I wanted him to be as consumed by me as I was by him.

At first I told Henry that he already had a wife and had no choice but to be loyal to her. I rebuked his advances, not wanting to be the middle woman in a marriage. But as we grew closer, I cared less and less that he was already married. I wanted him, and I would go to the ends of the earth to have him and to be his. I was stupid and naïve; stupid to let myself fall in love in a world where love was never going to be enough. And because of this I am going to lose my life. I am going to be killed tomorrow because I chose to fall in love with a man who should never have been mine in the first place. I strove to obtain the unobtainable, and now I will pay the ultimate price.

My mind is brought back once again to my impending doom, and I find that this time, I am wondering about my earthly body and what will become of it afterward. I do not know what order has been given for what will be left of me. Will they bury me with the honour I deserve as the queen or if I will be left to rot in a ditch somewhere, separated from my head? I worry that this will stop me from finding peace, having one's body separated from its other part, going to my grave incomplete. Will being put into an unmarked grave stop me from entering heaven? Will I be condemned and sent down to hell as a sinner? Surely Henry will allow me the dignity of being placed in a church. Even though he destroys my mortal body, surely he would not want my soul destroyed. Will he display my head as a traitor, as is the fate of all other traitors? Will he allow all of London look upon their dead queen's face in disgrace? I know not the boundaries of his cruelty and hatred for me now.

* * * * *

I have had my clothes ready for days. I have known since my judgement what I will wear on the day that I am to be executed. I was dressed in it just a few hours ago, as I waited to be led out of my room and prepared to face the crowd that built up below my window to watch their queen face her fate. I was wearing my dark grey gown, with ermine mantel, my head covered with a headdress, over my linen coif. I wanted the colour of my clothes to match the darkness of the morning ahead, dressed in black to mourn my own death.

It is a funny thing to be able to choose the thing you will die in; many do not have the option. Many do not know when death will come to them. It usually gives no warning; it comes when we least expect it, and we have no time to fear its coming, I am not granted that kindness. I have to prepare for my own death.

I was prepared. I had come to terms with it. I was ready to die then. I was content with the idea of meeting my maker. I simply waited, knowing that there was no way to get out of it. I would die, as my dear brother and those poor other men died but a day ago. I would face my fate, as the brave woman I am. But, since being told that my execution was delayed, and then delayed again, I found that a hope rose in me. A hope that maybe Henry himself was stalling, and that he did not want me dead; he wished only to teach me a lesson. A harsh lesson. I knew that I was wrong, deep down I knew, and realised that my wishes were useless. But now that my death has been delayed, I do not feel ready to face it. I do not feel strong. I feel like my legs will buckle beneath me and that I will have to be carried to the block. Laid upon it, not even able to show one last defiance of queenly pride. I will be dragged out and humiliated one last time. People will watch as my last act is that of a coward, shying away from the inevitable. At least the men were able to stand and stare death in its cold face.

14

I pray for those men. I pray that God knows in all of His wisdom, that they are as innocent as I am. I pray that they have found peace, that they are reunited, and they are ready to accept me and to forgive. For they only died because they had the misfortune of knowing me. If they had never met "Queen Anne Boleyn" they would be alive now. If my brother had stayed far from court, with his wife, he would have children and be unconcerned with my life at court. If Mark Smeaton were not friends with me, he would be alive. He would not have had to face the terrible torture that he was subjected to. He would not have died for nothing more than an unlucky friendship with a woman always on the edge—always battling to stay on the right side of the King and court. Their names haunt me now, and I am reminded that in every way, these men would be alive if they were never caught up in my life. Mark, George, Henry Norris, Francis Weston, and William Brereton. Five men. Five men, dead for totally fictitious crimes manufactured by the crown to dispose of the "problem."

The whole world will be speaking of "the whore queen," "the King's concubine" who proved them all right when she took five lovers, including her own brother. I will not forget the way those men looked at me as their verdict was delivered. George, who remained a loyal brother until the end, forgave me; he never blamed me in the first place. He knew that this was the king's doing. Mark was full of sorrow, beaten and battered. He had been worn down until there was nothing left of him, black and blue from the torture to which he had been subjected.

Henry Norris and Francis Weston looked upon me with hatred. They knew that it was my fault that they were put on trial. They had been caught up in a mess that had nothing to do with them. William Brereton did not look at me at all. He would not meet my eye, and I cannot blame him. Those poor men, added to a long list of victims caught up in the massacre by Henry and me. We destroyed many lives together and committed unforgivable crimes against innocent people. Catherine, Mary, and Thomas More, who were dear to Henry. I should have known that if he could kill a lifelong friend then he would stop at nothing to get what he wanted.

Am I one of his victims? Or is my fate deserved? Have I asked for this in my deeds? The fate that I am meeting death is not much different than the fate that I have helped to inflict onto others. My wickedness has come back to me threefold, and I must bear the consequences of my actions. I know I am not totally innocent of evil, but I did try to lead a good life. I never wanted to hurt anyone. It is almost as if I can see their blood staining my hands. I feel their presence in this tower as I feel the presence of the other souls that fill this now-dreadful place. The prisoners that have been locked here, tortured, and then executed. Their spirits cry out as the anguish of their death marks the very foundations of this tower.

* * * * *

I have been working on what I will say. I have practised it over and over again in my head. I always start off angry.

"How dare the king, whom I have loved more dearly than anyone before, accuse me of such disgusting, vulgar crimes…he is no king at all…he is a weak man, who kills a Queen of England…"

And then I am reminded that I left Elizabeth and my family to this man's mercy. And that my last act of defiance will leave them to suffer the consequences. Sometimes I simply weep and beg for forgiveness.

"I am sorry for all the crimes that are believed of me. Please forgive me. I love the king with all my heart. Please do not let me die, I beg. I can do better, I swear." But I am no weak woman who will plead in her last moments.

Again, it is a wonderful and strange thing to be able

to plan out the very last words that you will say in this world. I want it to be just right for it to leave a lasting mark on the people willing to listen. I want the things I say to be remembered. I want my voice to ring in their ears for years to come, and I want them to know that I. Am. Innocent. Innocent of the crimes of which I have been accused, and innocent of ever even looking at a man other than the king.

I have decided on a few words, and I feel the rest will come to me when the moment is right, I believe that God will fill me with some wisdom, He will guide me on the right things to say and help the words to spring from my lips. It will start something like this:

"Good Christian people, I have not come here to preach a sermon; I have come here to die. For according to the law and by the law, I am judged to die, and therefore, I will speak nothing against it…"

I know now that I will tell the world of how I love the king, he will know that he kills a good and loyal wife, who would not turn from him even after his sins against me.

"I pray God to save the King and send him long to reign over you, for a gentler nor a more merciful prince was there never, and to me, he was ever a good, a gentle, and sovereign lord."

Part of me feels compelled to say this so that he knows even in my last hours; I was a loving, caring wife. I also hope that this will aid the family I leave behind. But most of all, It is true I still love him. And some of me does not want him to carry the guilt of this forever. I hate him in one brief moment, I curse him, and I wish him dead and love him in the next, I forgive him, then I despair at what he has done to me.

Why can my mind not be quiet? I just want a moment of silence, just to be still, and not constantly flickering between acceptance and fear, hatred and love, hope and despair. I find myself at first sobbing as the agony of my last few years takes over my body; and in the next, I am

17

doubled over laughing at the absurdity of the fact that no one else really prepares this much for their own death.

Who else gets such a say in how they will die? It is comical to me that I am, in part, the choreographer of my own end, even down to choosing the man who will do it. The fact was that I was able to request the man who will murder me. I am literally going to walk out and thank a man for killing me and pay him for his awful deed. How silly is it that I will pay someone for removing my head as if they are doing me some act of kindness. Then I am going to lay my own head down and let it happen, with no fight, I won't try to stop him from butchering me. I am going to let him do it, and there will be a crowd of people just watching, no one will try to save me, or fight for me. They will cheer as my head lands in the basket, or rolls onto the ground. They will laugh as my blood spurts out at them. They will relish it if it happens to hit them, and then they will go and tell their friends that they watched the queen die.

Have you ever heard anything so ridiculous? It is insane, is it not? The whole thing is like a story, a play put on for people's entertainment. It might take a few swings, and I will just bear it. I will just lie still while this man hacks away at my neck. Ha! You could not make it up. I get lost for a moment in my own laughter as the whole situation suddenly becomes humorous to me, like a comedy rather than a tragedy.

Tears prickled my eyes, as the laughter escapes me into the silent night air. It causes the guard to bang on my door to check on me, as a prisoner condemned to die filling the Tower with her cackles of humour. They will think I'd gone mad; maybe I will be saved by my own insanity. Maybe they will think I have lost my faculties altogether, and they cannot possibly execute a crazy woman. It goes against the law. They would have to keep me alive, and I would have narrowly escaped death's dark flag.

The laughter turns into sobs and the sobs turn to heaves as I run to the door screaming to be let out.

"Let me out! I do not want to die." I banged on the door. "Let me out, let me be free. Let me live," I bellowed. "I am your queen. I command you to free me."

It was useless, as I already know. I collapsed against the door, and finally I felt nothing as I stared into the open space of my room, emptiness finally filling my heart. It takes over, like a wave crashing and washing away all of the anguish in my soul. Perhaps I am already dead; maybe this is my personal hell. To be trapped in the place that once brought me so much happiness. Just three years ago, I was here the night before my coronation. How happy I was. I was pregnant and married, and about to become the queen of a country I loved so dearly. And now the irony is that the place that started my life as queen ends my life altogether.

The place that I slept in before my coronation is now my prison cell. A place that had been done up especially for me to stay in was now a place of despair. It had once been a place of love, a place that held hope for the future. But now that turned to dust, just as I will. When I first stayed here, my future held nothing but promise and joy. I looked out of my window, and at the country that I would rule, knowing that I had everything I could ever want in the palm of my hands. Now I look out, and I see the place where my future will come to an end, where all of my dreams die. Tomorrow a man will lose his wife in that spot, a daughter will lose her mother, a woman will lose her sister and parents lose their child, another child. It is a place of death; it holds evil within its walls.

I refuse to think on this any longer, I do not have a lot of time left, and there is something I want to do. I have chosen to use my time in the Tower to tell a story. To write down once and for all my own feelings on the occurrences of the last few years. I began a few days ago and would like to finish it tonight. There is a need for myself to feel that I can one day be vindicated. That one day the people of England will know my tale as a tragedy and not as crime and punishment. Not as the black and white story that the king wants everyone to know, but as a story of ups and downs, of tears and unbelievable joy.

I felt the need to have someone, anyone, whoever has the chance to know that I was a good woman, a good wife, mother, and friend. And then they may tell another, and another. Long after I am gone, people will talk of Anne Boleyn. Some will be kind, some will not. They will say I was unfairly judged, or they will say that I got what was deserved. They will see that the world I lived in destroyed the ambitions of a young woman, whose hopes and dreams were plenty. They will see how my own family turned from me in my hour of need: An uncle who betrayed me and passed the judgement that ended my life; a father who saw me only as a pawn; a mother who, in her quest for power, allowed both of her daughters to sleep with a man; a brother who is now gone from the world because of heinous lies and the crimes of his family; and a sister betrayed. I want them to know that my world was cruel and unkind.

I played the hand I was given and in the end that hand failed me. I sit in my chair, at my table, with quill and parchment in hand. I write this, the last thing I will write. This is for anyone willing to read, who has the time to hear my story. This is the tale of how I ended up here in this cold place with no love left within its walls; the story of my life. It is the truth of my romance with a man destined to be great and fated to be cruel — the truth of the choices I made and the options I was given. This will be the real story.

Henry knows all of this, he knows the truth, and I hope that one day everyone else will. To whoever reads this, if it is ever found, please stay until the end of my tale. It is not a long one. It is sad, and it is unfortunate, it has its horrors, but also its share of joy. Please read with a kind heart. Please do not let my death be the end of me. Please remember me as Anne Boleyn, Queen of England, the innocent woman, innocent mother, sister, daughter...wife. The girl who lost her life to the passions of men. One that once burned through the sky like a shooting star, only to crash and fall to earth in a fit of fiery agony, to be brought so low and fall so far.

CHAPTER ONE

I was born on 22 July, 1501 at Blickling Hall, to parents
Thomas Boleyn and Elizabeth Howard. I was the middle
child of three. I had an older sister, Mary, and a younger
brother, George. We spent most of our childhood years at
Hever Castle in Kent. It was a beautiful place surrounded
by the stunning English countryside, and it is still the one
place that I will always be able to call my home. Now as I
sit in the tower, I long to be back there, roaming free in the
gardens or sitting in my adolescent bedroom. Dreaming of
the handsome gentleman I would like to marry, talking into
the night with Mary about the things we expected from our
lives, or climbing a tree with George. How simple things
were then. I had no idea of what was to come. I had no clue
that my life would take such a disastrous route. The most
important part of my day back then would be to choose
which sibling with whom I would spend it, and what
trouble we would get into. The hours of the day seemed so
much longer. We would have all the time in the world to
play and be free, and the world around us did not matter. It
made no difference who sat on the throne or who sat beside
him. I miss the days when my biggest problem was
choosing a dress for the day, when politics made no
difference to me. I look back on them now with a smile on
my face, fondly remembering the days I took for granted.

I would say that my childhood was perfectly happy;
neither my siblings nor I ever lacked a thing. Mother and
Father provided us with anything we could want or need —
everything but their affection. That was one thing that our
parents never heaped on us. Mary, George and I were each
others' constant companions. We relied on each other for
the love that should have come from our mother and father.
When we cried, it would be Mary who soothed us. When
we were excited we would share it with each other; we
looked after one another throughout our whole lives.

George never left my side, still standing with me years later, even when he had his wife to look out for. Mary and I would love nothing more than singing and dancing together. We would put on a show for George, and he would usually sit laughing at us and tease us for our girlish fancies. He was so mischievous. He could be the most loving child in the world, or he could be a little brat, teasing us and making us chase him around the grounds. When we did finally catch up with him, he would give us his cheekiest grin, and we would forgive him instantly.

He was always such a joyous person, and even as we grew up he would never lose his boyish charm. The ladies at court were infatuated with him. Jane Parker was the most hated lady at court when she managed to catch him. Still he enjoyed flirting and keeping them on their toes. He was very handsome. From a young age you could see his good looks. He was such a sweet little boy, chubby and cute as a button.

As he went from child to adult he grew taller, and his shoulders widened into the set of a man. He had the structure in his face that was almost that of a woman, his cheeks drawn in, and jaw set into a perfect line. His dark brown eyes would dance with humour, his childish personality coming through; this is what drew in the ladies. The charm behind his smile allured them. He stood with confidence, towering above most people, a Boleyn family trait.

He was always such a loving person; he was the greatest friend and brother that anyone could ever ask for. When he was little he would cuddle us and make Mary and me little gifts, whether it be a sketch or flowers from the garden. His sweet side totally balanced out his naughty side. He would hold Mary's hand whenever we left Hever, keeping a tight grip on her hand, afraid to lose us. Whenever he was frightened at night, he would creep into my room and beg to sleep at the foot of my bed. He particularly disliked the thunder; he would run into my room and bury himself under the covers. I would sing him to sleep, rubbing his back gently to soothe him.

As an adult he would become the one person I could not live without. The idea of being separated from him was agony. We spoke almost every day, and if we did not, I would feel completely lost. He always knew exactly what to say to make the bad things go away, or at least to make them less of a burden. He was so kind and gentle; not a bad bone lay in his body. He made me smile whenever we were together, just being in his presence brightened the darkest of days.

Mary could not be more different; she was always the typical overbearing older sister. She loved the idea that she was in charge and could tell us what to do, in whatever way she saw fit. She was a very emotional child; where George and I were made of sterner stuff, she would cry over the smallest of things.

Mary and I were not only completely different in personality but we looked completely different as well. I was always tall, my limbs too long for my body. I was all arms and legs and had not one touch of grace about me; Mary was short and stout. She was round and plump, as a child should be, while I was thin and gangly. She walked as if floating, her head held high, back straight, I ran and tripped over thin air, I was so uncomfortable in my own body.

Where she was fair, I was dark. I would grow into my looks, thank goodness. As I entered my 14th year I would start to look more the part of a proper English lady, my body finally stretching to fit around all of its parts, my face finally holding a fuller structure, and my appearance less awkward.

I have always said that if Mary is the day then I would be the night. We were so different. Where my charms lie in my mind and my speech, hers were in her looks and her sweetness. Her personality changed as she aged, she went from being a quiet nervous little thing to a woman whose name was on everyone's lips. At first she would shy away from being the centre of attention, never stepping a foot out of line and being practically invisible to anyone around, but then she became aware of her sexuality and how it could be used to her benefit.

When she became the mistress of King Francis in 1515, she realised that she could have power and wealth from sleeping with powerful men. So it only made sense that when she returned to English court our family would place her in the sight of the king. It pains me to know that my sister and my husband once knew each other intimately, but it is something I have learned to accept.

My mother and father were always kind enough to us. They were never unnecessarily cruel or unfair, and I truly believe that in their strange way they did love us. Just not as much as their ambitions. From the moment we were born they would devise a plan for how we could further the Boleyn name. With each child they had, they knew that one day we would do their bidding and hoped that we could bring about the family's good fortune. We were not hard done by in any way. If anything we were very well off. Father had made sure that we were a family of great reputation, but he always wanted more in his quest for power.

My mother's brother, Thomas Howard was a constant fixture in my early life. At that time, we believed that the purpose of his visits was to bring us gifts and spend time with his nieces and nephew. But as I grew older, I realised that he and my father would lock themselves away to scheme about our prospects. They would plot and plan what they could do with each of us, where we would be sent, how we would be educated, even who we would one day marry.

Father never had much of a personality. He was the person from whom Mary got her soft fair features, gentler in his looks than in his attitude. He was a bit of a weaselly looking man, his outward appearance showing exactly what lay on the inside. My father never held himself very well, a bad back making him slightly bent over. He had the stature of someone lower than his class. He never held himself in the way most men did, puffing their chests out and squaring their shoulders. He faded into the background, making it no wonder that he would use his children to further himself in the world.

I only saw my father laugh genuinely two or three times in my whole life. One of those times was after my wedding, he was so overjoyed to be part of the royal family. He told me that he loved me that day, a first for any of the Boleyn children. I would never hear it again and would feel his disappointment every time I tragically lost a child.

My mother was cold both inside and out. She had a cruel look about her; she was stern and unkind. Not one look of kindness ever crossed her features. Both she and my uncle Thomas Howard had the same look about them, strong set with a quiet control behind their eyes. He was broad and towered above everyone, and she was small and petite. But their features were so alike, both having long faces and that look of superiority. I believe that she may have been the backbone that my father did not have.

She was the person in the family to drive him onwards, forcing him to constantly further his position, along with my uncle who would prove to play one of the biggest parts in my fall. Both of them hungry for power and caring little for who they stood on. Mother never smiled and was not a loving woman; she believed that children should be seen and not heard. While we played in one part of the castle she would be at the other end, her door tightly locked.

She refused to see me in my last days as a free woman. She would no longer be associated with a woman in disgrace. She who knew the pain of losing children never bothered to visit me when my babies died. She stayed tucked away at Hever reaping the rewards of the income collected by her children.

* * * * *

I got into a lot of trouble when I was young. Where Mary enjoyed dressing up and learning how to become a lady. I enjoyed running free and returning to my home caked in dirt. I ruined many of my pretty dresses, much to my father's disappointment. George would always do his best to tease us, stealing our ribbons or our playthings, and I would chase him up trees and over hills, through muddy puddles and into the lake. Mary would sit and cry until he was forced to return them.

I remember on one particular day George had crept in and stolen my new pair of blue lace slippers. Uncle Norfolk had brought all three of us a present on his latest visit, he had given Mary a pink ribbon, which George also took. He had taken them and climbed to the top of the highest tree, where he left them to dangle off of a branch. I can still picture him now, sitting on top of the tree, laughing wildly. When I discovered him, I simply laughed, hiked up my skirt, and began to climb the tree. Mary, however, took the whole thing much more to heart. At the sight of her pretty new ribbon dangling from the tree, high out of her reach, she began to cry her eyes out.

"George, you are such a horrid little boy!" she shouted up at him.

I, who had made my way to where George was now sat, decided that I liked it up there and would sit with him a while, taking in the views of Kent. I could not help but laugh at Mary's sorry appearance, as she stood at the bottom of the tree, stamping her feet in anger.

"Anne, will you please bring down my ribbon," she pleaded.

"Why can you not just climb up, Mary? Are you scared?" I giggled at her.

"I cannot climb so high! What if I fall?"

"Oh just climb up Mary. I am here, should you fall," I promised her. I knew she would never do it. She would ruin her perfectly placed hair.

George nearly fell from the tree with laughing. "Come on Mary. your little sister will protect you."

At this point, Mary had had enough of our teasing and was bright red in the face; she looked as if she would burst from crying. She picked up a stone that lay on the ground and aimed for George's head. It missed by a long mile and this only made her madder. She turned and started to march back to the house, shouting all the way.

"I am telling Father," she raged. "You better get down Anne, or Mother will never let you out of doors again," she threatened.

With that, she disappeared inside, off to find Father and cry about her awful siblings.

I made my way back down the tree, dragging George with me. We left her ribbon up there, to teach her a lesson for being such a baby. Father came out and gave us a good telling off for making our sister cry. He was madder at me than he was at George. I was supposed to be a lady and should be sitting inside reading or practising my music, not acting like a "wild little devil."

At other times, it would be Mary and me in cahoots, and George left on the outside, much to his dismay. He and I both knew that whatever I felt for Mary, I felt one hundred times more for him.

We were all well-educated; father believed that girls should be given the same education as boys if they were to be of any use to their family. Mary and I studied alongside George sharing the same tutor and missing out on nothing. I enjoyed my education very much; there was nothing I did not want to learn about. I could never get too much information, and I soaked up everything that was taught to me. It was because of this that my days at Hever with my brother and sister were all too short. I was the smart one, you see, and even from a young age father sought to use that to his advantage. He had been working for some time as an envoy to Maximillian I and had spent some time in the court of Margaret of Austria where he had become fast friends with her.

Margaret was known for educating some of the most intelligent girls at the time, her court being a magnet for the arts, music, and culture. Every family in Europe, be they royalty or nobility fought for the chance to have their children educated there, and many were not given the opportunity. I was lucky enough to be offered a place, and in the year of 1513 at just 12 years old I was shipped off to Austria.

I hated leaving my family home, but it would turn out that I enjoyed my time in Mechelen very much. It was the beginning of my formal education, and although I was only there for one brief year, it set me on the path to the life I lead now. It gave me the skills and knowledge that I needed in order to run within the higher class circles in this world. However, sadly it was only a year and before long I was moving on to bigger and brighter things...in France. My father had sent me a letter explaining that I was to leave Mechelen and go to France where I would become a lady to Mary Tudor, who was about to marry the French king.

CHAPTER TWO

In December of 1514 I left Mechelen and made my way to France. Mary Tudor and her entourage had already been there for a little while, and my sister was amongst them.

After I had arrived and settled into my new accommodation there was a tap at my door, and I opened it to see a woman standing on the other side. She was very radiant as she smiled from ear to ear, elegance seeping off of her. I stood in awe of her for a moment. There was the scent of familiarity there, but it was not until I looked into her eyes, and saw the round brown eyes of a Boleyn gazing at me, that I realised that it was my sister who stood before me.

She had shot up, not as tall as myself, but not the short stocky girl I had left either. She had lost most of her childhood padding and was now slim and shapely. Her face had taken on a structure, and she now looked like a woman. Her hair flowed loose, curling slightly at her shoulder before continuing down in light waves. She was now fifteen years old, and that whole year had done her a great service. She had left all traces of the child she was behind her, and now stood in front of me a lady. I did not realise just how much I had missed her.

Seeing her familiar, smiling face brought tears to my eyes. It had been well over a year since I had seen any family at all. I had spoken to them briefly in letters, but I had not had any home comforts for such a long time, and it was overwhelming to be in the company of a sibling once more.

The memories of our childhood together came flooding back, and in her eyes I could see the children we were not so long ago. We held each other for a long while, not wanting to let go, as if we may separate again. I took in every last inch of her; she looked so well, her waist drawn in perfectly by her gorgeous pink gown, her cheeks the perfect rose blush, she was like an oil painting of a graceful princess, stood tall and confident. She was only a year older than me, but her maturity shone through, so changed from just a year ago when she was making dances, and stomping her feet in fits of childish anger.

"Well, will you not invite me in sister?" she asked after a moment.

I moved into the room and gestured her inside where she took a seat, and I poured the both of us some wine. We sat for just a moment staring at each other. It seemed that not only had she changed to me, but I also looked very different to her. I had grown to fit my body finally. My arms and legs no longer being in my way. I stood tall and graceful, the slouch now gone from my posture. My face had matured and now I looked to people somewhat beautiful. Not in the same way as Mary, but I held it in my own way. It was the way I looked upon one and held my gaze with the confidence of someone sure of their own attractiveness. I believed I was attractive, and so I was to the outside world.

Suddenly the year apart seemed like such a long time, and I realised that although I had enjoyed my time at Mechelen, Mary and I had missed seeing each other grow and change into young adults. It was a year that we would never get back. We spent the evening talking about everything that we had missed in each other's lives. She spoke of George and reassured me that he was still the same sweet boy that I had left. She told me that mother and father were also unchanged. They were still self-obsessed and cold.

We also spoke of what we wished for our time in France. She expected that she would find a husband there. Some rich Frenchman to settle down with and move here permanently. Marriage was always so important to Mary. She wished to use her time in France to find a suitor. She told me that it was her duty as a woman to always be on the lookout for an advantageous marriage.

I, however, had different views. I hoped to pursue art and religion while I was here. Our idea of how best to live our lives were so very different. We spoke the night away and when the early hours crept up on us Mary readied herself to leave. Not before wrapping her arms around me. I hugged her back relishing in the feeling of being reunited with a loved one. It felt good to be in the presence of someone so important to me once more. I hoped that we would never be separated again.

* * * * * *

My time with Mary Tudor is not worth much note. She never liked me and I never liked her. No particular reason on either part. Just a mutual distaste. From the moment that we laid eyes on each other, a bitterness grew. We would avoid each other wherever possible and I am sad to admit that it brought me great joy to have her leave me behind in France.

Mary Tudor was a small woman, both in size and personality. She had little features, almost like that of a rodent, her face appeared pinched and snotty. She looked like she had eaten something foul and could not keep the bad taste from showing on her face. She was so thin, her size and height making her look like a child. She had long dark hair, not very different from mine, and she was rather plain.

Nothing about her shouted great beauty. There was nothing to her. She was not the type who inspired sonnets or songs of love and beauty, but she was not ugly either. She was what I would call adequate. She was always someone who could make my blood boil just from a look. She vexed me with her proud look and blunt way of talking.

I would only serve as lady to Mary for a short time...thankfully. Her husband would die soon after her coronation, meaning that she was no longer queen of France. She left as soon as she could. After it was safe to assume that she was not pregnant, she boarded a ship back to England. She and Charles Brandon got married somewhere along the way, showing how little respect she had for not only her recently deceased husband but her brother as well.

I would not see her again until years later when she was one of the main opposers to my marriage to Henry; she tried to convince her brother many times to abandon me. It never worked of course. She was nothing more than a bitter woman in a marriage that had become loveless.

In the meantime I stayed on in France with my sister so that we could serve the new Queen Claude, wife of Francis I.

* * * * *

Both Mary and I found that being a lady to Queen Claude was much better than when we had served Queen Mary. She was much nicer for a start, and although she did still have a temper, it was mainly reserved for use on her husband. She was very relaxed and had a lot of time for the women who surrounded her. She was always lending an ear or offering guidance if we needed it. Claude and I would often share our private jokes, mainly over the fact that I towered over her. She was a short, stout woman and envied my height and slimmer waistline. She would joke that with each child she bore her hips would grow outwards while I kept my figure in perfect condition. We were good friends. She was a little over a year older than me and I feel that because we were so close in age it meant that we understood each other.

I enjoyed every moment that I spent in her company. I never felt like I was her inferior. She treated us all as if we were part of her family, and she always had a kind word for anyone who may have needed it. She was an extremely pious woman, and took her religious devotions very seriously, something that I appreciated very much. I would go along on a pilgrimage with her to see the tomb of Mary Magdalene and found it to not only be an eye-opening experience but something that only strengthened my faith in God.

Serving a woman who devoted so much of her life to our Lord taught me the importance of always keeping faith, to trust in our Creator and to know that no matter how hard things may get, He always has a plan for us. He knows where our lives are going, and we can count on Him to guide us in the right direction. Even now I keep that faith with me as I hold my book of hours to my heart and pray that He leads me into the light. France changed my views on religion and it was here that I learned that Catholicism was not what I had thought it was.

* * * * *

My time with Claude would not always be good. Unfortunately, early in 1515 Mary had decided that she would no longer merely flirt with the men at court, she would go one step further and lay with them as well. She saw no problem with using her body for her own gain, and could not see that there may have been consequences for such a thing. Worse still is that she went for a man who should have never been available to her: The king. It had started with a harmless back and forth; Francis complimented her and she batted her eyelashes. This annoyed Claude to no end, but there was not a lot that could be done about it. Women had no right to tell their husbands what to do, and whether she was queen or not, she would simply have to put up with it.

Mary was not the first person who had shared a bed with Claude's husband, and she would not be the last. Still it was obvious that in private Claude broke her heart over her situation, hating that while she lay pregnant, the king would be having his fun with whichever lady he had chosen on that day.

It was Claude's steely determination that would help me with my own situation years later. I watched her hold her head high every single day, and never once would anyone at court have suspected that she was breaking her heart because of the treatment she was subjected to by her husband. My heart went out to her; I held her as she cried in private. I saw how she would dry her eyes, stand up straight and walk out to face the court, never breaking her composure for even a moment. I looked up to her and was completely struck by the way she behaved and held herself, hoping that I too would become a woman who was broken by no man.

Francis tried her patience again and again. He was an unkind man who wanted whatever he could take for himself, caring little for whoever he hurt in the meantime. He abused her both physically and emotionally. Hitting her when she did not comply to his order. Shouting profanities at her when she did not agree with him. He would make her pregnant and abandon her until she had had the baby and was ready to conceive again.

This was my first real taste of what was expected of one as a wife and in all honesty, it scared me. How could a woman be expected to continue on through so much adversity? Watching her birth child after child. Going through terrible agony each time and never receiving any thanks or appreciation for the heir that she bore the king. She was treated as if she were there only as a vessel to carry life and then be disposed of.

She was, at times, not even treated like a human, thrown about by a man who saw her as a toy to do with as he pleased and then picked up again when he had a use for her. Her job was to be quiet and obey. She had no rights, no voice or any opinion that mattered. I listened as she would argue back with Francis, defiant at first, arguing her point and standing her ground. I would think about how proud I was of her to tell him that he could not treat her as he did. But then you would hear a loud thud, followed by complete silence, then sobs and finally Claude would return to us, a black eye beginning to show, or a swelling on her lip and she would have no fight left in her.

She seemed ready to give in and accept the deal she had been given. But then, when we believed all hope was gone, she would rise again stronger than ever and show us all exactly what it meant to be a queen. She was an inspiration and a magnificent queen, and if I could, I would thank her now for bestowing on me the strength to face any situation. I once asked her how she managed it, how she survived through all of the heartache and sadness that filled her life. She replied to me in such a simple way, and I will always hold on to it.

"Because I am queen. God has chosen me for this role, and I trust that God will guide me to my destiny." That would be my answer years later when a friend named Thomas would ask me why I accepted the treatment bestowed upon me.

Mary would leave France after just a few years. She was disgraced after her affair with Francis finally and abruptly ended. She returned to England in shame.

I would stay with Claude for seven years and quickly became one of her closest allies. I held her hand as her children were born and wiped her eyes when she cried. I was there in her highest points and lowest points. I celebrated the birth of her beautiful children and wept with her as she took blow after blow from Francis.

I really grew into myself whilst with Claude. I learned about the person I wished to be and the life I wanted to lead, going from a girl with childish ideas of love and life to a woman who understood that life and love were painful. I learned that in order to survive, one had to be a strong woman. Life was unfair and unjust, and the only thing to do was to grab it by the horns and refuse to let it push me down. I saw as a woman I loved was beaten and abused by both friends and family. I watched as my sister went from innocent to adulteress in a heartbeat. She had stepped on a woman who she had claimed to love like family and betrayed her, all in the quest for personal gain.

My time taught me many things, good and bad, such as if you wanted something, then you must go for it, as Mary did. You would need to hold your head above the damage you had caused and refuse to take note, never stopping to look at the people you have hurt. Loyalty was useless; everyone is loyal to one's self and one's self alone. They would push and ruin others to get ahead. A person could trust no one, let no one in; even one who has taken vows and sworn to be true would take advantage of their position. And as a woman it was even harder to lead a good, happy life.

France did prepare me for the darkness in this world, but it also showed me that there may be some light. One can choose to be kind to others, can decide to make a promise to the people closest to you, and refuse ever to hurt them. You may choose to refuse to let your enemies beat you, and you can be kind to the people who are less fortunate, like the poor and deprived, who are born without the luxury of money or health.

I watched as Claude would give out money to the lower class. She would offer food and warm clothing to those who had little to their name, she had an ear for anyone and would help as much as she could. Her people loved her, they adored her, and saw her as a savior. She led the country with her love of God and her total trust in His master plan.

I became strong and unbreakable because of her. She would be the biggest influence on my life. It is she whom I conjure in my mind in my darkest moments. While Henry was with Jane Seymour, it would be Claude's spirit that I would allow to fill me, to get me through the heartache. As I birthed my children I wished she were by my side. Wiping my head and reminding me that I was strong and capable of facing anything that God sent my way.

I can almost feel her presence, and in a way I know she will be there with me tomorrow, whispering in my ear that I was one of the lucky ones, to be taken in to live with our Lord early. To be able to meet our creator sooner. I had been devastated when the news of her death reached me. She was so young and full of promise, and had had such a troubled life. It seemed cruel that God had decided to take her so young. He had allowed her to face terrible trials and punishments and then had ended her life before she was able to experience much joy.

She was younger than I am now, 24 years old. She had become exhausted. Forced to bear so many children in such a short time, when she miscarried her final son, she had followed him, unable to stand the grief and pain any longer. I wept for her, saddened by the idea that I would no longer be able to turn to her, that I could not write to her and share in all that life may hand us. But she herself gave me strength in her death as the words she had repeated many times echoed in my head. "This is God's plan for me." it was as if I could hear her tell me. "Do not weep Anne. For I am going to be with God." and I had felt a small amount of peace at this.

It is exactly what I remember while I despair at my losses. As I face my trials I remember that God is in control and He will do what is best. I have Claude to thank, not only for my strength, but for my understanding, for my will to carry on. For the knowledge that even when times are hard, God is by my side. I do hope that when I die, I will join her in heaven.

* * * * *

After many years in France I was ready to return to England. I missed my siblings. I missed Hever. I wanted to start the next part of my life. I was ready to go home and begin my life as a lady at the English court.

CHAPTER THREE

I made my way back to England. I was a little excited
and nervous to see my family and home again. It had been
a long time since I was within the walls of Hever; the place
which I had once called my home was nothing more than a
distant memory. I wondered whether I had forgotten
exactly how it had looked, if the images in my mind were
what I had conjured up. Would it be totally different from
the picture I had clung onto for all of these years? When I
had first moved away I would think of it when lying in my
bed at night, homesick and lonely, imagining myself back
in my bed in my own room.

It had been years since I had looked upon George; he
was now 18 years old. I had left a boy behind and would be
coming back to a man. Maybe the childish image of my
beloved little brother was no longer relevant, and he would
stand before me as a man who I did not know.

We had written to each other over the years. Telling the
other about our life experiences and updating each other on
our opportunities, our happiness, and our troubles. Within
our letters we would also talk of our feelings. I could share
anything that I wanted to with George, and he is still to this
day the only person who knew every last thing about me.
He knew of all my secrets, of all my wrongdoings. He
knew of the deepest feelings that lay within my heart. I
have allowed him to share in a part of me that no one else
could ever reach, and he has taken that to the grave with
him, having never shared a word with any other.

Mary was now married, and in typical Mary fashion was
not satisfied with that alone. She had to have more. So she
was having an affair as well. With Henry. The English
king.

As my carriage pulled up to Hever I took in the look of
the place. It was still as beautiful as I had remembered, set
a little back and surrounded by the greenery that had once

been my playground. It seemed smaller somehow, not the giant place that it had been when I left, towering well above me and looking like the safest place in the world. Compared with the palaces I had seen and the wonders of foreign countries, it appeared minuscule and unimpressive. As I gazed, the childhood I had left behind seemed to come flooding forward, as I could almost see myself and the others rolling down the hills or running after each other.

A great sense of belonging washed over me, as if this were exactly where I needed to be, as if I had never left in the first place. It was as if it were calling me back to it, welcoming me inside where I would again feel the warmth and security that can only come on a return home after a long journey. I knew that inside its walls it held the people who I held dear, it held a part of me, my young self who had escaped to a new world, only to return wiser and stronger than ever.

This place would be my solace. Whenever I would need to escape and feel any comfort I could bury myself within, locked away from the things that wished to cause me harm. It is the place I go to in my mind when I want to feel safe. When I am in this tower, Hever is the place I pretend to be, home and secure, where no one can ever hurt me.

My family were waiting in the courtyard. All five of them, including Uncle Thomas, had come to greet me on my return. My father opened my door and offered his hand to help me out. There was no hug of greeting, but he did plant a kiss on my cheek. My mother was unchanged and she stood with no emotion at seeing her daughter after so many years. My uncle formally kissed me on my hand and stood back out of the way. He at least gave me a warm smile in greeting, appearing to be happy at my return. Mother noted that I had finally grown out of my unattractive stage; this was about as good a compliment that I could ever expect. Father nodded along, apparently having no words for the daughter from whom he had been separated for so long.

Then my gaze turned from them, and I was looking upon my brother and sister. I first took note of Mary, who I hugged graciously, happy to see her again. When she stepped back, behind her stood a young man, tall and broad, handsome and charming. He beamed at me, and I would have recognised that cheeky smile anywhere. It was my George. My sweet little George now stood in a man's body, towering over both of his older sisters. He was changed in so many ways, as his baby fat had fallen off of him and had been replaced by lean muscles. His chubby cheeks had slimmed down, showing a stunning structure hidden underneath. He now had the beginning of a beard, which only aided in making him look older.

His childish grin had gone and been replaced by the gorgeous smile of a handsome young man. I could not believe my eyes, as I was totally taken over with pride at the adult that had replaced the baby of the family. My George was a man. He took two strides and within an instant was lifting me off of the ground and kissing me on the forehead. My eyes began to fill as I held on to him tighter and tighter, never wanting to let go again. I was finally back with my baby brother, and I did not want to lose him for even a second.

"Anne, you are more beautiful than I remember, sister." George smiled at me, his eyes gleaming with barely contained joy as he held me at arm's length to inspect me. "I can scarcely believe you are in front of me again." He touched my cheek with his thumb in a comforting gesture.

"I have missed you so much, brother." I held onto his arms. "You are so handsome and so grown up," I beamed, as I let the emotion of the moment overcome me.

After my things were unpacked, I bathed and dressed. Then I prepared to make my way to the dining room where a meal had been laid out to celebrate my return to England.

I had picked out my red dress, trimmed with gold, and had placed on my head one of the fabulous French hoods that I had brought with me. I wanted to appear perfect, for my parents to see that I had grown out of my immaturity and into someone of whom they could be proud. I needed them to see that I no longer slouched, or behaved like a little boy. I was a lady who had experience and knowledge on her side. It was important to show them that I had learned how to behave properly. I wanted them to be fascinated by the stories I had to tell, to take an interest in my time in France, Most of all I wanted them to notice me.

We sat down to eat. I was next to Mary, and George sat across from us with mother at his side. My uncle and father each took one end of the table. It started quietly, just like the many family meals we had had in the past. No one had any interest in anybody else. We each chewed our food with our faces turned down to the table. Awkwardness was as apparent as ever. It was George who finally spoke up, a grin on his face.

"So sister, tell us of your time in France. What was it like serving Queen Claude? I hear she is ravishing." a playful smile spreading across his face as he wiggled his eyebrows at me from across the table.

"It was magnificent, George. I met many wonderful people. Have you heard of an artist, da Vinci? Oh, he is fabulously creative." I was happy to be able to talk about my experience finally, had wanted to since the moment I had gotten back. I had kept it inside of me, waiting for the right moment. I was glad that it was George who had asked.

"Oh yes, he is rather talented, I hear. What's he like?" George asked.

"He's moody and terribly glum." I sighed, and we both laughed. "But I guess that great talent comes at a price. You cannot expect to be both a master of art and a master of conversation," I giggled.

"Father, why don't you tell Anne all about King Henry?" George prompted.

Father looked up from his food and stared at George as if annoyed to be brought into the conversation.

"The king...he is fine. A very nice man..." father mumbled out before returning to his meal.

George practically snorted his wine out as he erupted with laughter. "Fabulous description, Father." he clapped. "I hate to think how you would describe someone you love."

Mary and I both joined in with his laughing, trying and failing to contain it, as father continued with eating as if nothing had been said. He had grown used to blocking out our "insistent noise."

"Mother care to have a crack?" George continued, looking at mother with his boyish grin, knowing full well that she would not be best pleased with his continued attempt at conversation.

"George, will you be quiet and eat your food." mother scolded. She also had little patience for our chatter. "And leave your father be. He is a busy man and would like to enjoy his meal in peace."

Each of us sank back just like we had when we were children and mother had raised her voice at us. It was unbelievable that at our age we still acted like naughty children in trouble with their strict mother. But George was not done with his teasing.

"Mary can tell you all about the king..." George started, raising his eyebrows. He looked at Mary innocently, as she clearly had no idea how to reply to him, gobsmacked at his lack of tact. I imagine that she could already sense where this was going.

"...She can even tell us what he looks like naked, can't you Mary?" George's eyes danced with glee saying it in such a deadpan way as if it were just an off-hand comment about the weather. He watched Mary's temper rise, which only egged him on further.

"What is it like inside the king's bedchamber? You have seen it enough times." She turned red in the face, which only aided in his humour, as he nearly fell from his seat with laughter. He was so pleased with himself, proud of his apparent wit, and it was contagious.

At first I held my hand to my mouth in shock, not knowing how to react. It was not something that one should say, especially not at the dinner table, but then I started to giggle. I could not hold it in as I watched him, consumed by his own joke, rubbing Mary's arm in apology and secretly pleading with her to see the funny side. I could not help it. It was not even that George was as funny as he thought. It was more that I could not contain my joy at being in the same room as the two of them, I could physically feel my heart lift, the longer I was in their company. Mary and George felt it too, I could sense how happy each of us was at the proximity to the people we love.

It did not take long before Mary cracked a small smile. She could not help it when George looked at her with apologetic eyes. Shrugging his shoulders and shoveling food into his mouth as if to silence himself. I could already imagine her slapping him after dinner was over, and then we were all laughing again, much to the discomfort of Mother, Father, and Uncle who just wanted to get through the meal in peace and quiet.

"George shut up." Mary tried to complain, but her eyes were filled with tears as she laughed her way through it. "You're such a horrible little boy." as she had said endless times over the years. But she was not mad; she tried her hardest to sound displeased, but could not keep the humour out of her voice. It was almost impossible to stay mad at George. He never meant any harm, but he got such enjoyment out of teasing. He was the lightness in a gloomy world, always there to cheer up the dullest of moments. He liked to go past the limit, and he certainly did that with Mother and Mary. I knew better than to react to his taunting and enjoyed his jabs at me as much as his mockery of anyone else.

It pains me to write about this moment, even as I write "was"...I cannot help but feel my heart crack a little more. To say my brother "was" rather than "is," is to admit that he is gone. It is to surrender to the fact that he is no longer around to make my pain go away. I think of him with such joy, and feel my heart sink as the memory of yesterday takes over. It is so unfair that he suffered in such a way, and that all I have now are the memories of him. I will never see his happy face again, never hear his voice break as he told a rude joke, never have him hold me together, or feel his hand on my face, as he traced his thumb along my cheek, smiling down at me even in the hardest of times when my heart was heavy and life was too hard to bear.

I can still picture us in that room. Mother was so angry...

It was probably one of my last lighthearted nights. I look back on it with such fondness. George, Mary, and I sat around after dinner. They had crept into my room late that night after Mother and Father had gone to bed. We spoke long into the night. Catching up on the many years that we had missed. The bond I had with my brother and sister only grew from that moment onward. However, I had not returned to England so that I could sit in Hever and talk nonsense with my siblings. I had come back so that I could introduce myself to the world, to English society, and I was eagerly awaiting my first day at the court.

CHAPTER FOUR

On the 4th of March, 1522, I made my debut at the English court. I had been asked to take part in a pageant alongside my sister, the king and all of the other young men and women looking to make their mark in England. I loved to perform, and the idea of having everyone look at me filled me with excitement. I loved to be watched, to put on a show and have people applaud as I acted out my part. The whole court would be watching, and I could think of no better way to begin my life in England.

The theme of the pageant was to be unrequited love, and I would play the part of Perseverance. Perseverance was the essence of a strong quality, one who would continue through trials and tribulations to achieve the goal in her sights. She was strong and beautiful, her eyes set on what she wanted, taking her aim, and capturing the object of her desire. It is funny to think that my having been given this role should predict so much of my life to come.

The idea of the pageant was that each lady represented a quality of the perfect woman. There were eight roles to fill. Alongside the qualities that myself, my sister, and Mary Tudor filled there was also Honour, Constancy, who was played by Jane Parker, Bounty, Mercy, and Pity.

There were also eight male virtues; these men were led by King Henry himself, and he would march onto the scene followed by Amores, Nobleness, Youth, Attendance, Loyalty, Pleasure, Gentleness, and Liberty. Everyone looked stunning as we readied ourselves at York Place where the spectacle would take place. On that day, all of us ladies were dressed in the most beautiful white satin gowns, with Venetian gold headdresses and Milan bonnets. We each had our character on us picked out in yellow 24 times so that the audience would know which of us were which. The men wore cloth of gold coats with tinsel, caps and great mantle cloaks made of blue satin. Each of them looked dashing in their costumes. They were presented as the men that we are told of in stories. The ultimate incarnation of the perfect man. The ladies looked on as they tried to decipher who was behind the masks. Which one looked the most handsome? Where was the king hidden? Who would they be thinking about later tonight when they should be thinking of their husbands?

Not only did the characters look fabulous, but so did York Place itself. Cardinal Wolsey had spared no expense in the preparations for such an event, doing everything possible to transform the hall into something magical and wonderous. It was lit with candles everywhere, setting the scene, lighting up the hall so that it looked enticing and warm to welcome the audience. The walls were hung with beautiful tapestries draped all around the chamber. At the end of the room stood the most unbelievable château vert, built for the setting of our performance. It consisted of three towers. The battlements were covered in green leaf and each lady had her tower to stand in while she waited for the dashing men to come to her.

The tower that held me was made to look as if on fire, as I stood looking down on the battle below, waiting for my moment. As the audience was led in we could hear the gasps escape their mouths; we could see the look of shock on their faces. They each wanted to reach out and touch the decorations, to immerse themselves into the set that had been built. It was an escape from reality, a chance to forget about normal life for a while. The men of the court looked on appreciatively at the women who had been put up on show for their amusement, enjoying us as we stood beautiful, glowing in our towers. Everyone watched in awe as the whole spectacle took place, amazed at the show we had put on for them.

I had stood perfectly still in my tower, waiting for all of the excitement to begin. Waiting for the moment the perfect men would come to take us away. Joy and anticipation had begun to build in my belly as we got closer and closer to the final dance. At the moment where we would be able to show ourselves off for everyone, the dancing skills I had acquired over the years would take centre stage. The idea of being taken from my tower by one of the men was thrilling. It stirred something within me; the idea was so romantic, and my heart pounded in my chest while I waited for it to happen. I remember thinking that I was made for this, to be on show for people, to stand in front of them and perform. It was the thing I was best at. I loved having eyes on me, to be watched by many.

King Henry led the attack on the tower. He led the men in a bombardment of the chateau. They launched fruit at the tower to bring it down and as they did, the other qualities and I began to throw back sweetmeats and rose water to push them back. A row of choristers, whose job was to stop us from leaving our towers, tried to stop the virtues from getting to us, keeping the masked men back. Desire had tried and failed to lure us down, as we all refused to be captured by his charms.

This only urged the men on even more. They would stop at nothing to have us. We each looked beautiful and unattainable as we beat back the ones who tried to scale the walls, never giving in to their advances. We were the perfect chaste women, not allowing ourselves to be swayed by any of the appealing virtues before us. The choristers, who consisted of such things as Scorn and Jealousy, were not strong enough. No matter how hard they tried to fight on, Good was always going to win out. They thought long and hard, but the male virtues were just too strong, and eventually they overtook the choristers, pushing them back and climbing the walls of the towers to finally take hold of their reward.

King Henry captured his sister Beauty, Mary was captured by Loyalty, and I was taken by Pleasure. We resisted no longer and allowed the virtues to take us from our towers, led away by their unavoidable magnetism; we were each bewitched by the men who captured us, as we no longer fought them off. The audience watched in amazement as the romance played out in front of them, dazzled by the story of love conquering all. Love won out in the end, defeating Scorn and its evil accomplice, winning a great battle and finally being rewarded by a kind heart and one of the many virtues sought after in a woman.

Next, the men would lead us in a dance, sweeping us around the floor in one final show of love before they obtained us completely. Finally breaking down both the physical walls and the ones that we have ourselves built up inside. We ladies smiled as we floated around the hall. Our dresses swaying beautifully as we were lifted into the air and placed back down again. We had practiced this many times leading up to this point, and I had memorised the steps perfectly. As I followed each one, I felt on top of the world, my head spinning with the buzz of the day's festivities. We must have looked magnificent, each of us twinkling. Gracefully dancing with the partner who had chosen us. It was like being lost in another world altogether as if this was no longer a performance, but that we had been rescued by the handsome men. I wanted it to never end.

As I spun around, I could not help but feel eyes on me; they made my face hot with nerves. I could feel the gaze almost baring into my soul, and when I turned around I saw the deepest blue eyes staring into mine. They truly were a sea that I got lost in and I let the waves overtake me. I continued to dance never taking my eyes off of this man. Who was he? Why did he stare at me so much? As I looked on, his lips crept into a slow smile. It started small, but spread across his whole face revealing the most dazzling charm. He must have been the most handsome man there.

The music stopped, and I broke out of my fog. Now was the time for us to reveal ourselves to the audience. We took off our masks one by one, so that we were finally revealed as our true selves. I could not resist looking around as the last mask was removed. Those eyes I had stumbled into, the man I had been watching, was the king. It was King Henry. And I could not stop staring at him, watching as he turned to me—he was very handsome—while the audience clapped and cheered. He was staring back at me, too. We were locked in some sort of world of our own.

I realised at that moment that all the talk about him was completely true, he really was rather beautiful, and that was it, I thought no more on it. I acknowledged that he was indeed the most handsome man at court, and then I turned away as the audience continued to clap and cheer for us, forgetting all about the face I had just looked upon, and instead enjoying the applause we were receiving. He continued to stare at me. I could feel his eyes on my face even after I had stopped looking and then finally after a moment he turned and he was king once more.

After we had finished the performance the festivities continued with food, drink, and more dancing. I stayed close to my brother who introduced me to a man named Henry Percy. Henry was the son of the Earl of Northumberland, and if his title was not enough, he was also very good looking. He was shorter than me, but slim and lean. He had dark alluring eyes and a sweet smile. He was very nervous and when we first spoke. It took all of his efforts to keep the shake from his voice. I found myself drawn to him as he told me all about his father and the inheritance he would receive being the first son.

The Earl of Northumberland was a very prestigious title and would mean that he would be one of the most important men in England. I found myself thinking about all of the benefits his wife would receive. After all, Father had wanted me to find a match. We spoke for a long while.

I flicked my hair and giggled in all the right places, fluttering my eyes at him. I had liked Henry Percy; he seemed like a good man and I thought about getting to know him more.

This was the first time that I had seen Henry Tudor. However, it was not the start of our story. At this point we were just two people swept up in the excitement of a performance. It was not our time just yet.

CHAPTER FIVE

After the pageant, I returned home to Hever Castle for a
while, but not for very long. I received the news that I was
to become a lady to Queen Catherine. So again I set off
from Hever on another new adventure.

I arrived at court early in the morning, ready to meet
Catherine. When I first laid eyes on her, I realised just how
breathtaking she was up close. She was every bit as
wonderful and feminine as I had been told. She was small
and delicate, at the same time as being curvy and well
rounded, her features fair and light. Her face was so soft,
with rosy cheeks and round plump lips, but in her eyes you
could see the steely determination that sat within her. She
had that look of power about her. You could tell that she
was comfortable with herself, knowing that she could
command everyone in this room with just a flick of her
finger. Her hair was covered in a headdress, hiding away
her fabulous light, almost golden, hair.

I looked on her in amazement, standing in front of
someone so magnificent. It may come as a surprise that at
first I liked Catherine. I very much enjoyed being one of
her ladies and found her to be both interesting and good
company. Had things been different, I imagine we might
have been friends.

After first being awestruck by her beauty, I was then
taken aback by the way she spoke. Her voice was so
commanding. It was harsh and deep, still thick with her
heavy Spanish accent as she spoke to the ladies around her.
She was talking about her home in Spain, and the places
she grew up. She talked with such a fondness that you
could hear it in her every word. We bowed to her as we
entered the room, standing before her and waiting for her to
speak. She was sitting propped up in the centre of the room
with all her ladies seated around her. They looked like
children waiting for a story to be told. The love they bore

her was plain in each of their faces. She looked up and acknowledged our appearance in her room, smiling a small smile at me.

"Ah, Mary Boleyn has returned to us, ladies," she spoke, nodding her head towards Mary. "And she has brought someone else with her. Who do you present to me, Mary?"' she asked.

If she had held any malice towards Mary, at that moment you could not tell. She looked at her in the same way she had anyone else. Her voice changing not one note.

"I bring you my sister, Your Highness. Anne. She is to join us as one of your maids of honour." Mary's voice shook a little, nerves clear as she spoke to the wife of the man she was sleeping with.

"Oh? Another Boleyn amongst us. You Boleyns will be taking over the court if I do not keep a close eye," Catherine giggled, her ladies following suit. "What could you possibly add to my maids that I don't already have?" she looked at me quizzically.

"Anne, has..:" Mary began, talking for me.

"Does your sister have no voice of her own? I cannot very well have a mute for company," the queen snapped, for the first time showing a bit of her distaste at my sister.

"I do indeed have a voice Majesty. You must forgive my sister, being the elder she is very caring and likes to boast about me," I explained, trying to smooth over Mary's mistake. "I was first schooled in the court of Margaret of Austria and later in France at the court of Queen Claude."

"Very well. You can sing, dance, speak other languages?" She asked.

"Yes, Majesty." I bowed my head. "I am a keen art enthusiast. I love to explore poetry and learn. I grew up in the court of three different queens, and I am well versed in the way that a queen's court should work. If you allow me, I believe I will be a useful addition."

"We shall see about that. I look forward to getting to know you, Anne. Let us hope that, unlike your sister, you know your place." She eyed me, looking at me from top to bottom, trying to take a measure of me, as if to judge a story by the way it is presented. "My lady Margery will show you around." she waved me off.

With that a woman stood up, she was tall and dark, her hair nearly matching the blackness of mine. She was thin and tall like me, her face square, with small dark green eyes. She beamed at me before gesturing me to follow her.

To start with, some of the other ladies were a bit distant from me. I believe this was because of my sister. Unfortunately, I would be tarnished by the same stain for a little while. It was Margery who first gave me a chance; she was kind and sweet. Margery and I were friends immediately; we had the same sense of humour, the same opinions on the world. We bonded over our shared thoughts on religion and our taste in art. We found the same men appealing and disliked the same people. It was the start of a lifelong friendship.

Eventually Elizabeth Brown would join our little group, which would include Margery, Mary, Elizabeth, George and me. We would become inseparable. Once George was married we would allow his wife, Jane Parker, into our group, but she never quite fit. She would always be just on the outside, not understanding our jokes or wanting to share in our gossip. I believe that it was all those years ago that she started to hate me, as I became a natural leader of our small group and failed to make her feel welcome enough. We did enjoy laughing at her expense, which was unkind of us, but she was such a stick in the mud. She was hellbent on following the rules and never able to have fun and let loose like the rest of us. She was a complete bore, and even George found her hard to stomach.

Life as Catherine's lady was mainly practicing our religious devotions. Religion would be the most important part of our day. We would strictly follow the Liturgy of the Hours, with prayer in the morning — lauds, sext at midday, and vespers before bed. We would receive mass twice a day and most importantly Eucharist on a Sunday. We would often stop to pray at intervals during the day; it was important to Catherine and us ladies to give our thanks to God as often as possible.

We followed the idea that everything we do would be a prayer, that in each moment of our lives we were either continually thanking God for his blessings, or asking for his guidance. I enjoyed serving yet another woman who was so dedicated to her maker. Whether we had the same idea on religion or not, at least I was with like-minded people. If we were not praying we were usually sitting down to a meal with our queen, or passing the evenings with cards or court entertainments. Life as Catherine's lady was easy. I wish I appreciated it much more at the time.

CHAPTER SIX

In 1523 I would become acquainted with Henry Percy.
He was often at court with Cardinal Wolsey, as he was
working as his secretary at the time. His father had wanted
him to spend time at court, mingling with the important
people and making some good connections for himself.
Wolsey was the perfect man to be around, as he was always
in and out of the King's privy chambers. Henry would
come along to the queen's room's flirting with and
entertaining us ladies. He spent almost every day with us,
always joking and teasing, winning us over with his good
looks and sensitivity. It was obvious after a while that he
favoured me above the rest. He would bring flowers to me
and place them in my hair, and choose to dance only with
me. I would be the first person he strode over to when he
came in, and it would make the others mad with jealousy. I
loved to watch as their pretty faces fell.

I fell for him very quickly. He was very handsome, tall
and slender, his eyes green like beautiful gleaming
emeralds. He had a child-like air about him that only added
to his charm. He was ridiculous and silly in the best way,
overactive like a child who had been given too many sweet
treats and was now bouncing off of the walls. When he
would look at me it was as though I was the most exquisite
thing he had ever seen. As if he were lucky to have the
honour of looking upon me. He would brush my hand
gently in passing, or touch my hair, looking at me
whenever he could. He made sure that I knew that while he
was talking to another it was me who he thought about. His
eyes were permanently fixated on my own. He would make
any excuse to be next to me and was utterly besotted. He
said that he found everyone else to be lacking when
compared.

I would make it my goal to obtain him, desiring him for both his sweet demeanor, good looks, and standing in this world. I truly believe with Henry Percy I may have both had happiness and been well provided for. Both appealed to me in a strong way. Most women would have already resigned themselves to a loveless, unhappy marriage that was mutually beneficial, but if I could somehow be content with both my marriage and wealth, then why would I not strive for both.

Henry Percy was next in line to be the Earl of Northumberland. After his father, it would be passed down to him, which would make him one of the greatest men in the country. The wife of such a man would also be powerful and wealthy, giving her a little freedom in how she would spend her days. Not only that, but it offered security for any children we would have together, as they would inherit the Earldom of Northumberland after him. It was exactly the type of safety that I wanted for my life and family.

In time, I feel we both realised what we could have together. We were both so innocent, stealing small kisses when no one was looking or holding hands behind our backs. It was a sweet love with little passion, but we had an understanding of the other. We knew that together we could make a good life for ourselves.

It did not take very long for him to ask me to become his wife, and I was overjoyed. It was something that I wanted very much. I wanted him to claim me as his own, for our love to be made official in the eyes of God and the country. He came to find me while I was with the queen one day and had pulled me aside grinning from cheek to cheek like a young boy with a secret to share. It was all I could do not to laugh in his presence; his joy was always so infectious. When he asked, I practically jumped for joy. It was a good match, both in standing and in personality. Henry had wanted to wait to get permission from both the king and our families, but I wanted to marry him as soon as possible. It took a lot of convincing but I managed to convince him to leave with me two days later and marry in secret. I was sure that the king would have no issue with our match. We would tell everyone after the fact. If only we had been hastier in our nuptials. Perhaps then it would have been too late for anyone to meddle.

Our joy was to be very short-lived, indeed. Somehow Cardinal Wolsey had gotten wind of our plans to marry. I would find out years later that Elizabeth Brown had overheard Margery and me talking and she had sold me out to the cardinal for her own benefit, something she would not be shy about doing again. Wolsey had decided that he did not like the match and wanted to put a stop to our joy. At the time I was seething. Who did he think he was to destroy my happiness? While the cardinal was in Westminster he had sought out Henry and given him a very good telling off. Henry had come like a coward with his tail between his legs to break off our plans. When he found me he had gotten down on his knees begging me for my forgiveness.

"Darling Anne. I want you to know that I love you very much," he had started. hoping to soothe me so that I would not shout at him. He could not stand to be told off. He would hide away like a child scolded by their parent.

"What is it, Henry?" I could tell that something was wrong.

"I have been with the cardinal," Henry sighed. "He will not allow us to marry," Tears stung his eyes as he spoke. I remember waiting patiently for the rest of the story believing that Henry would have at least tried to fight back.

"Of course you told him that he should mind his own business?" I asked, already knowing that Henry had never spoken back a day in his life, especially not to a man like the cardinal.

"Anne…" he struggled as I glared at him. Daring him to prove me wrong. "Anne, I am sorry, but we cannot marry."

I drew in a deep breath, hoping to level myself. I did not want to lose my temper. I did not want him to see the pain that I felt in my stomach at the idea of losing what we had. I felt the coldness that was always just below the surface beginning to creep out—my protective layer to shield me from anything that would try to hurt me. I stared him down, a cold determination in my eyes.

"Will you do nothing about it, Henry?" I asked "Will you just stand at my feet and weep?"

At this the tears began to fall from his eyes which made him look every bit as weak as he was.

"He has sent for my father. He and the king are both offended. The cardinal said that they are amazed at my foolishness, to dally with a silly girl."

"And you said nothing in my defense when they called me a 'silly girl'? I am the woman you supposedly love, and you had nothing to say about this insult?" I demanded.

"No, Anne…I am sorry. I should have told him he was wrong about you. But…" his head fell ashamed at his lack of strength. "I agree with them. We were foolish."

I could not believe him. What a weak coward he was. Sniffling before me with tears in his eyes as he went back on his word. He had not one ounce of strength in him. Backing down without a fight. Although I was angry with Wolsey for his daring to tell us who we could and could not marry and calling me a silly girl, he was eager for power, and everyone knew it.

Even more than that, I was fuming with Henry. He was pathetic as his hand shook and lip quivered. He was not even brave enough to stand up to a woman, on his knees in front of me. He had hoped that I would let him crawl away without another word.

"Oh, are you not a man Henry?" I scolded. "You appear to be nothing more than a pathetic coward standing before me. Stand up and tell me that you do not love me. Or are you too weak and fragile?" I pushed him from his knees, feeling suffocated by his grasp on me.

He started to speak, but I was not finished with him. "How dare you pledge your life to me in one moment and in the next fail to defend me?"

"I love you..." He had tried to hold me as I backed away.

"That is not loving, Henry. If you loved me then you would fight for me." I continued.

"My love, can we not talk about this?" He tried again to step closer, but I was done. I wanted to get rid of him. "I would lose my inheritance."

"Do not touch me. I am no longer your love." I removed myself. I was sick of his face. He turned my stomach with his tears, and I wanted anything but to be out of his presence.

He straightened himself up, remembering for a moment that he was indeed supposed to be a man. He cleared his throat and wiped the tears from his face. Apparently deciding now to show a little courage. "I am to return home. My father is displeased, and I need to fix it."

"I am not stopping you." I arched my brow at him, crossing my arms over my chest. "I could not care less, Henry. Take your pathetic apologies and get out of my sight." I turned my back and left. Keeping calm until I was completely out of sight, I then ran straight to George's room.

I would not let a single tear drop from my eyes until I was safe behind a closed door. I went straight to George who was furious. He had threatened to kill both Wolsey and Percy had I given the word. But all I wanted from him was comfort, which he gave. He simply held me to him as I cried, and allowed me to release all of the hurt. He stayed

61

by my side as much as possible. If Percy even thought of coming near me, George would give him a look that could kill him in his tracks.

My father and uncle gave me a good telling off. It did not take long for the rumours to spread around the court and when they got wind of the incident they were most unhappy.

"How stupid must you be, a girl?" Father demanded. "What made you think that it was up to you who you should marry?"

"I loved Percy, Father..." I had tried to explain.

"Love? Foolish child! No one cares if you were in love," he continued. "You must learn your place, Anne."

"I have my own mind, Father, and I choose what I do and do not do with that mind and body."

Uncle looked as if he might strike me at this. If it were not for father standing in between us, I believe that he may have done. There was nothing to stop him hitting me. It was how he had dealt with anyone else disobeying him.

"You silly little girl. It is for a man to decide your fate and not you." Uncle was furious. "You are a woman and will listen to the command of your betters. Understood?"

"I understand none of your racket Uncle," I said remaining composed. "I will take your advice of course. But never think to control me." With that I left the room, leaving behind a couple of shocked and angry faces, I imagine.

I had decided then and there that I would make my fate. No longer would I bow to the will of people like Cardinal Wolsey, my father, and my uncle. I would marry who I pleased, with or without their permission. Not that it mattered of course. Fate was about to take control itself. Leaving Percy was nothing more than a memory. The thing I did not realise at the time was that George was right. I would love again, more than once, and the loves that came along next would make my feelings for Henry Percy look worthless. It was going to turn my whole world on its head.

* * * * *

The next man I would feel for would be Thomas Wyatt. Thomas was refreshing. He was young, and he held a beauty that was rare in men. He bared his soul for everyone around to see. His heart was always on his sleeve to be pulled apart. Which meant that it also got trampled on and disrespected. He was so open. So carefree. He loved without bars, leaving himself vulnerable to the cruelties of love. That was, until he met me and I ruined his ideas of the heart. Most men held their feelings inside, not wanting to appear vulnerable. Thomas had a way in his poems to show the whole world his glorious soul.

Anyone who would experience Thomas was honoured to know such a man. He was a rarity in a cold world. I enjoyed my time with him very much. He was and is to this day completely in love with me. I knew he was. And I believe that a part of me loved him. Not that I would ever admit to it. It was never enough. He was not the love that I was destined to find, and he was already married and completely out of my reach. My love would always be more platonic — that of a strong friendship. Perhaps if he were not married then it would have been different, but I knew from the start that it could never lead to much.

So I refused to let him in completely. If I had, then perhaps his love would have carried me away. Maybe it would have completely taken over my whole being. But I would not let it. I refused to let it, and clearly it was not strong enough to break down the walls that I had built.

Each new love brings with it a different quality than the last. And the old loves should not diminish the love that we finally allow to take hold of us. For the one that captures us encompasses all of the qualities from before, and more. It takes hold of your heart and gives you little choice. I did not realise that I was waiting for that love, but I was. Unfortunately for Thomas and Henry Percy; they were just stepping stones on my way to my greatest love.

CHAPTER SEVEN

Early in the year 1526 I had started to notice that the king would spend more and more time in the company of Catherine and her ladies. He was always lingering. Up until this point I had never really noticed him pay Catherine much attention. He left her to go about her own business. He was too busy running the country and chasing after other women to care much for his wife.

All Henry needed from Catherine now was an heir. Catherine had given him a princess, and although it was plain that Henry adored his daughter, it was never enough. She could not carry on the Tudor line. I think Catherine could feel him slipping away. She could sense as he moved further out of her reach. I believe that each time she realised she had not conceived she felt a part of him break away.

I know just how desperate she must have felt to become pregnant. She suffered that failure for twenty-four years. As time ticked forward she probably knew just as well as anyone else that the chances of her conceiving and carrying a healthy child, let alone a son, was becoming impossible.

She must have known that something would need to be done eventually, but I doubt she imagined just how far from grace she would fall. It was of great importance for the country to have an heir. If that did not happen, we would be thrown back into conflict. No one wanted that. Some people could still remember what it was like the last time there was a struggle for the throne, and to relive that was unacceptable. The only way to get an heir for England would be through legitimate conception between the king and queen.

And that was almost impossible when he refused her advances. Catherine really tried. Each night she would ask him to share her bed. She swallowed her pride every time he said no and asked again the next night. She must have felt unwanted to be refused by her husband, a man who was supposed to want to lay with her. It must have made her feel like there was something wrong with her. She probably questioned her allure. She was aging. It was clear to see that she hated that fact. She knew as her years slipped away, so did her beauty, and her husband's desire for her.

Henry only confirmed that when he pushed her away. Instead he spent time in the company of her and her ladies, leaving little time alone for the royal couple. He would be more interested in sitting and talking to us than he would in romancing his wife. Although it hurt her to be turned down, I could also see how happy it made Catherine have him close. She loved her husband. It was clear in the way she looked at him. She glowed whenever he was close. She smiled to herself while talking or thinking about him. She was just as in love as she was twenty years ago, and wanted as much time alone with him as possible. She lit up whenever he was in the room.

It always caught me off guard to see how much someone's features changed when in the company of someone they loved. Catherine seemed more youthful around Henry — a reflection of her past self. I was allowed to see a totally different side to her. The side of a loving wife. She was a wife who would do everything in her power to please her husband. She adored him, and you could tell that she would do anything he asked of her.

Henry's love for Catherine was also clear. His fondness was plain on his face. No matter what may have happened later on down the line, I cannot deny that they did love each other for a long time. It breaks my heart to write this. I wish I had met him first and he had no opportunity to have loved someone else so deeply. But that's just not the case. I owe it to Catherine to say that she did at least hold his heart before he found me.

From the moment he entered the room he would become a different person. It was the look of two young lovers in the grasp of first emotions. He doted on her, and would always ensure she had everything she needed. The first thing he would do was to kiss her on the hand and enquire after her health. He would refuse to make her stand and curtsey, admonishing her if she tried. He had such a gentle touch for her, becoming a loving husband rather than a king. He ensured she wanted for nothing.

It was very sweet. A long-time married couple caring for each other. He wanted to protect her; I could see it. She wanted to be safe in his arms. When I looked upon them I had thought that this is how it looks when one is in love. The blush in the cheeks. The gleam in the eye. The way the eyes would follow one's love wherever they moved. The reaction to every word they would say as if it were the most exciting sentence ever uttered. There was genuine interest in the smallest part of their day. It was something to watch. They reflected each other. Smiling when the other smiled or laughing as their partner did. A couple must feel almost inseparable after over 20 years together. I felt a strange pang of jealousy as I watched them.

Unfortunately, as much as Henry may have been a loving husband, he was also a man with many needs. Since my sister had been discarded by him, he needed to find someone new to fulfil those needs. He may not wish to share Catherine's bed, but that did not mean that he did not want anyone to share his.

Henry claimed that the reason he came to see Catherine so frequently now was that he wished to spend time with his love. He apparently wished to be close to her, but the truth of it was that he was not coming to see his wife. He quite clearly was in the market for a new mistress, and Catherine's ladies were the perfect group from whom to choose. Mary was away from court and was no longer of any interest to him. He was bored.

Poor Catherine must have known what he was doing but had chosen to ignore it. In those days, I really felt sad for her. She watched as all of her ladies fawned over him. They were all desperate to be the one that the king picked. He was very handsome, after all, and to be honest, they loved his title. Loved what being his mistress would do for them. Their families would have been given all of the power and wealth they could ever want. They would be given all of the best jewels and heaped with gifts.

For many women this was the way that they could advance their family and themselves. Once the king was done with them they could use their families' standing to find a good husband. The ones who were already married could provide wealth to their husbands and children. It was a unique opportunity for some, and they would fight tooth and nail to be noticed by Henry.

I wanted none of it. I would not hang around waiting for someone else's husband to look my way. The king was very handsome and if he were a duke or an earl, then perhaps I would have wished to know him. But at the time I wanted nothing to do with any of it. He was tall and muscular, with a stunning face and chiseled jaw. His eyes were spectacular. Small blue gemstones. He held his appeal for sure, but it would take more than good looks to turn my head.

I intended to find someone for myself. I am sure that the king would have gotten the idea by the distaste that was plain on my face whenever his eyes skimmed me. He probably thought I disliked him, but really I just did not want to be considered. I disliked watching the other ladies all behave like beggars after another's scraps. Marge and I compared them all to a pack of vultures diving for a piece of meat.

It was embarrassing how they all lost themselves in the presence of one man. I had seen a relationship like this before with Claude, and I hated the idea of another suffering in the same way. How could they all be so cold? Climbing over each other to get to him while his wife, their queen, looked on. Henry was loving and kind to Catherine. It was not like he mistreated her or beat her, but he showed her little respect when it came to matters of the heart. He ran around the palace with one or another of his mistresses.

She endured his relationship and child from Bessie Blount and then watched as he openly courted my sister, which told her and the kingdom that she was not good enough. Not that Catherine would allow anyone to see how it affected her. She was too strong for that. Not once in the whole time that I knew her did she let one tear fall from her eye. She had an unbreakable shell that surrounded her. It protected her heart from any visible wounds.

* * * * *

The king would put on great festivities, all of which involved delicious food and wine. We would drink and dance the night away, feasting until we were full to bursting and then quenching our thirst with the wine provided. We would return to our rooms, feet aching and heads weary. It was a chance for the people at court to let go of their day-to-day lives. The men could forget about the politics and the passing of laws for a time, and the women could have a respite from serving the queen.

We loved our evenings at court. It was a chance for our small group to get together. Margery, Tom, George, Elizabeth, and I would be found in our own space. Passing the night with dancing and merriment. Henry liked to see his court having fun. He liked to see the happy faces of his close friends. He was a generous king, and he liked to balance out the boring business side of his title with lavish parties and entertainments. Paying for the best chefs in the land to cook exquisite feasts. Each and every meat you could ever want. We had the best veal, magnificent cuts of beef, or roasted duck. The jellies were delicious, and there were enough sweet treats to feed the palace three times over.

He ordered in the best French wine and the most renowned musicians. He liked to watch his men enjoy the many ladies on display. He enjoyed watching the chase as much as he enjoyed taking part in it. He wanted romance at his court, and would sit upon his throne like an audience member, clapping his hands and giggling like a child as the events unfolded before him. He watched as the men tried and sometimes failed to seduce the women, most of whom were already married to others. He watched it as if it were a sport. The aim of the game was to collect as many hearts as you could.

Often he would come amongst us and join in the dancing. Sometimes it was hard to believe he was king. He acted like any of the other young gentlemen at court. Chasing women and causing mischief with his drunken behaviour. The king wanted everyone to believe that he was another of the young courtiers, young and attractive. He wanted to appear as much fun as he had been in his early years. He would order drink after drink into his cup, barking orders and taking his pick of whatever lady he fancied that night. He would look past the queen and over to the gathering of her ladies.

He was fabulous at the game he played; the best at court. He would make his way through each lady, spending a little time with everyone. It was as if he were weighing everyone up in his mind to see which of us he liked best. He enjoyed nothing more than flattering the pretty girls surrounding him. He was good at making them feel on top of the world as he led them in a dance. Paying court to them for one evening alone.

Margery and I seemed to be the only ones untouched by his charms, and we were both happy to not be chosen. He had glanced our way but had not at this point bothered to interact. I had thought that he would have avoided me due to his previous relationship with my sister. It would have been wrong for him even to consider me as an option. So luckily for me he was not interested in sparking up a conversation — for that moment anyway.

He paid less and less attention to Catherine as she sat on her throne, looking older by the day. The entertainments were clearly very tiring to her, but she refused to retire early. She would never leave her husband to his fun for one moment. She did not want to miss anything. Although it began to make her appear drained and worn out, she stayed into all hours of the night. She became a bit of an annoyance as she looked on grumpily, trying to convey with her eyes that it was time to go. Once or twice she had asked Henry if he would like to retire with her, but Henry was having too much fun. He was still young. Or so he acted at least.

He would drink late into the night with all of the men at court in their twenties. Never wanting to seem that the fact he was heading into his late thirties had affected his ability to drink and dance at all hours. He had a young spirit about him and never appeared even slightly weary as it slipped into the small hours of the night. He would always be the last one standing. The ladies and I would retire at a more decent hour. It was more seemly for women to go to bed early. This was something that annoyed me. I was never ready to leave. I enjoyed the dancing too much and would have continued into the next day had I been given half a chance. But more often than not, Margery dragged me away like a mother taking her child off to bed.

Henry and the chosen few would sit around singing songs and telling crude jokes all night. They were like a bunch of naughty children. It was as if they had never grown up. George and Thomas were always by his side, losing track of time and forgetting that they each had lives to lead the following morning. When I would see them the next day they could barely stand to be spoken to as their heads throbbed and throats dried up. These were honestly some of the best days at court. Everyone was still so young and fresh-faced as we danced until the sun came up. We slept the mornings away and returned to the same thing the following night. The king was happy. And if the king was happy, then the court was happy as well.

* * * * *

I do not know exactly when I had caught the king's eye, but something that I had done had grasped his attention, and he suddenly seemed to notice me. I had begun to notice how he would watch me from across the room. While the others danced and laughed around him he fixated on me and whatever I was doing. He seemed to want to listen to me talk. He would listen in close as I spoke to Margery, George, or Thomas.

Always appearing to be close by, I could feel his eyes on me as I spoke and my cheeks would grow red with blush. I could sense as he fixated on my lips, watching them move. He seemed to enjoy the things I had to say. He would nod along or mumble his approval as he passed, never joining a conversation but staying close by.

I had seen him more in those few weeks than I ever had. We happened to pass each other as I was leaving the queen. Or in the hall. It was as if he knew exactly where I was going to be and made sure that he was there to catch my eye. I would bow every time and say "Your Grace." as he smiled down at me like a predator with its eye on the prize.

I would leave no room for conversation, making myself scarce before anything could be said.

I disliked having him look at me. It made me uneasy having him so transfixed by me. I could not understand what I possibly could have done to attract his attention, but I didn't want it. He was the last person I wanted to watch me. It was strange how his eyes followed me while I danced. He seemed utterly taken by me before we had even spoken and the warning bells began to ring in my head. At first I had thought that he might have been curious to look at Mary's sister. Perhaps comparing the two of us or looking for a family resemblance. I ignored it and carried on, thinking myself overreacting or imagining things.

As time went on, I could see it was different altogether. It was not as if I were catching his eye as he scanned the room or took even the briefest of looks. It seemed that I captivated him. I had done nothing to encourage this, that I knew of. It was as if he were under a spell and his eyes were allowed to wander to no other place as he stared deep into my soul. It was as if he were trying to find something within me.

I had been careful not to attract his gaze. I faded into the background wherever possible. I did not want this. I did not want him to see or notice me. He was a dangerous man, and I wanted to hide from the possibility of his finding me attractive. I would avoid conversation where possible and steer clear of his immediate circle. It scared me, the idea that he wanted to look at me. I wanted to run from the room so that I would be safe from his quizzical eyes.

It started off small. It was a look. A stolen touch as he moved past me. It was in the way he stared as if sizing up a deer he was hunting. It was as if I could see the wheels turning in his mind as he planned the best way to pursue his intended conquest. It was not much to go on, but already I had begun to feel a slight fear. It was a small niggling in the back of my mind telling me to turn and run as fast as I could.

I did not like the way he looked at me and even less the fact that he had started to ask questions. He had approached both my father and George to ask after me. He wished to know everything about me. He had come right out and asked my father how I would feel if he had begun a pursuit of me. Father had come to me and expressed the king's feelings. He had told me that if I was clever I would put myself in the king's way. I should let him court me.

George had the opposite advice. He told me to get as far away as I could. He was worried that I would follow the same path as Mary and he could not watch another sister destroy herself. I had to agree with George. I would be mistress to no man. I cared little for what Father or my uncle thought. I was my own woman and I would not sell myself to the highest bidder for nothing more than the benefit of my own family. Especially not to a man as dangerous as the king. I had detested Mary for what she had done to Claude. How could I now do that to my queen? It was out of the question. Still the king watched. Still he asked questions. He was wherever I turned.

He had yet to approach me, but I knew that he was building up to it. I wanted to stop that from happening as much as I could. I would move if he joined a conversation. I looked cold as he turned his eyes on me. Even when he smiled, I replied with a curt nod before moving along. He would not find me as eager to jump into bed with him as the other ladies. They would sell themselves short for nothing more than a glance from the king. Scrambling to make themselves the lover of a man who could raise them high. It was embarrassing to watch and I wanted nothing of the sort.

I refused to allow myself to become used and abused as my sister had been. I wanted to become a respectable wife one day. There was no way that I intended to be a king's plaything. I thought more of myself. The idea that the king wanted me frightened me. I did not want to play a game that I knew I could never win. Certainly not for the benefit of others. One of the other ladies could have him. How could my family expect me to do that to Mary? I had thought that I could never betray her and the fact was she had been with this man. She had already claimed him. Would I really want her used goods?

The king could ask whatever he wanted and my family could order me to comply, but I would never give in to their demands. I removed myself from the entertainments. I avoided him wherever I could. I would serve the queen and then return to my own room. I had hoped to remain out of sight and out of mind. However this king was not as easy to dissuade as I had imagined.

* * * * *

I was leaving the queen's rooms one afternoon. I had intended to find my way to the gardens to get some air. I enjoyed being out of doors as much as possible. Something about being surrounded by nature made my soul lighten. I enjoyed the cooler days when the breeze would brush lightly against me, and the smell of spring danced in the air. It made me feel at peace. I had become cooped up lately. Either in a room with the queen or seated in my own room reading.

Catherine had given a few of her ladies and me the afternoon free to take some time for ourselves. She said that she was feeling unwell and that she would spend most of the day in bed and that she only needed one or two of us for company. I had not been away from her in such a long time that I relished the idea of being away from the palace walls.

It was not hard serving Catherine, but it was repetitive. Each and every day was the same as the last one. Waking in the morning and readying her for the day ahead, dressing her, going to prayer, eating, playing cards or sewing in the evening. It got a bit draining doing the same thing all of the time and I jumped at the chance to leave.

I had already made plans in my head to seek out Thomas Wyatt. I had spent little time with my friends of late. I was avoiding any social event I could, not wanting to see the king. I had missed their company and wanted so much to be outside in the sun with Thomas. Margery was staying with the queen and George would be busy with the king. I would try to see them later. I had thought that the king had probably forgotten about me at this point. I had not been to any of the entertainments in over a week and was sure that he had probably found someone else by now. I would join the rest of the court tonight. I had missed dancing, and imagined that the king would not even notice the fact that I had been gone or bat an eyelid at my return.

I had my head in the clouds as I left the queen's rooms that day. I was thinking about what Thomas and I would do. Where we would go, I had thought that it had been a while since I had been for a ride and maybe it would be nice to take a couple of horses out. Or we could have a picnic, and he could read to me. Being in his company always lightened my mood.
As I stepped out of the door I was not looking in front of me like I should have. I was too busy lost in my own thoughts, and I nearly ran straight into someone who had been heading inside.

"I am very sorry. I did not see you there," I said. As I got my bearings and looked to the person I had nearly knocked over I realised that I was looking straight at the king. I stood dazed for a moment while my brain caught up with the situation. Then I remembered myself and swept down into a curtsey

"Your majesty," I smiled "Forgive me. I was not looking where I was going." He offered me his hand, pulling me up from my low bow. He smiled at me, and it was that smile I will never be able to erase from my mind. It was the smile that he seemed to use just for me. The one that showed just how special I was. That look as if I were the only one in the room. The only one in the world even. He was amazing at making me feel on top of the world. Still, why was he here now? I had done so well in avoiding him. What dumb luck that he was just outside the door I was leaving. I had been so careful, and it seemed unfair that he would happen to be in that place at that time. I had to be wary. I would be polite, but there was no need for this to be any more than a brief exchange.

"Forgive me, mistress. I should have not been lurking outside of these doors." He looked into my eyes so intensely that I felt almost as if I was being interrogated, suddenly nervous under this great man's gaze. I did not often experience nerves. This was a new feeling for me. I had been around royalty all of my life and had never felt like this, so I had no idea why this was any different. It was something about the way he held my eye. Not letting off for one moment as he held me to the spot. It made me nervous for some reason, as if he could read my thoughts and would somehow know that I wanted to be as far away as I could.

"Can you forgive my clumsiness?" he asked.

"Nothing to forgive your Grace. I should have been paying attention." I dipped into a bow readying myself to leave. I did not want this conversation to continue, and he was clearly heading to see his wife. I would bustle off and find Thomas. There was no need for us to talk any longer. The king could see that I was in a hurry to escape and had held his hand up to stop me from going any further. This would not be as easy to avoid as I had thought.

"Why do you leave in such haste? Do you not want to talk awhile with your king?" he asked, chuckling. "I won't bite. I swear," he laughed.

His eyes danced with humour as he spoke. He was good at this. He knew that I would have to accommodate him. I could not very well admit that the last thing I wanted to do was talk to him. Instead I would try to put him off of wanting to talk to me. He would find me dull and uninteresting if I could help it.

"Why would your Grace wish to talk to someone like me? I am only a lady to your wife and could not possibly interest someone with such high intelligence as His Majesty," I responded. I tried to keep my voice as level as possible, not wishing for my nerves to escape into my words. I knew how to handle this. I just needed to have confidence in myself and everything would work out just fine. Or at least that is what I told myself over and over in my mind.

"You interest me very much," he said looking at me through thick lashes. He rubbed the back of his neck. He was trying to look as coy as possible. Here it was, I had thought. He was turning his charm on me. I imagine most women fell head over heels for this. I, however, would not react in the way most do. I would not instantly throw myself at him. He would not find Anne Boleyn an easy target. I gave a brief smile in reply, ever edging towards the moment that this would be over and I could remove myself.

The king was silent a moment, fixed on my eyes. I don't believe I could have moved if I wanted to. He had a confidence about him. A power that poured off of him in waves. Without even speaking he could command a nation. I must admit that there is something attractive about that kind of power. He had a presence that one could not ignore.

"What is your name, lady?" he asked. He already knew, of course. He probably knew every last detail about me and my life. He was getting most of his information from my own family. The thing that baffled me was that he knew I was Mary's sister. So what did he think could possibly come of this? He must have known that I would want nothing to do with him.

Or maybe he expected that I would give myself to him as easily as Mary had and he wanted to claim two Boleyns for his bedpost. I do not know what his initial motives were, but I imagine that he never for one moment expected that day to be the start of something wonderful and irrational. I know I did not. If I had done, perhaps I would have run away even faster. Perhaps I would have dropped formalities and run back to Hever. It would have incurred some royal wrath, but I would have avoided the advancement of this moment.

"Anne Boleyn, your highness. Daughter of Thomas Boleyn," I played along.

"Anne Boleyn." It was as though he was testing how the name sounded on his tongue. "Now I will be able to write that name across my heart." He held his hand across his chest looking at me with that smile again.

This was not good. My head pounded. My heart raced. He was declaring his interest in me, and this is exactly what I had been hoping to avoid by removing myself from his presence. I had to keep reminding myself to keep my breathing level. I could not allow one tiny bit of my panic to appear. I had to stay calm and on the ground no matter what he may throw at me. Someone like this needed to be told straight. I could not allow him to think that I was breakable.

"You may write it wherever you like your Grace. I am your servant." I surprised myself with how calmly it came out. It sounded so natural. I was proud of myself at this moment. I would bat away anything that came my way.

He smiled to himself. He found me amusing if nothing else. It was almost like he enjoyed how I made it hard for him. I suppose he was used to giving a woman the eyes one moment and seeing her in his bed the next. He thought for a moment and then to my surprise his hand was on my face. He tucked a stray lock of hair into my hood and let his fingers linger as they made their way down to my cheek.

I stood frozen at the moment not knowing how to react. I wanted to hit his hand away to tell him not to touch me, but I couldn't. He could do whatever he pleased and touch whoever he wanted to touch. This was one of his moves. I could tell: small touch here and there. A touch that lingered just a moment too long. A promise of what was to come if you should succumb to his advances. He was working his charms on me, and I refused to fall for them. He bit his lip before removing his hand from my face.

"Forgive me Lady Anne. I should not be so forward." This was all part of a carefully choreographed plan. He had done this before. Each step tried and tested on various women. I imagine he expected me to be as easy a conquest as his other women. He had thought that his formula would hit the exact spot. He had a lot to learn if he thought that I would fall for his tricks.

"No need to apologise Majesty," I nodded. Not letting the smile reach my eyes. I decided that this was my moment to leave and had started to walk around the king thinking that I had made a clear getaway. I had taken a few steps when the king turned to continue talking. I stopped in my tracks. Annoyed at my failed attempt.

"May I ask where you go?" He asked. What more could he possibly want? I had to answer him, and I was beginning to realise that my day had little chance of going in the direction I had wanted it to.

"I intended to find my friend Thomas. I was looking forward to a stroll in the gardens," I answered him, hoping that he would allow me to continue with my plan. Tom would get such a kick out of this story. I was desperate to find him and tell him of this exchange. I could already hear his laughter. He would have loved to hear how I squirmed to escape while the king laid it on thick.

The king thought on this for a moment before asking. "Well, as Thomas is not here then perhaps you will allow me to accompany you?"

My heart sank as I realised that I had no option but to agree. I could never say no to the king. It was impossible. If the king wanted something from someone, then it was given to him, and this would be no different. I smiled sweetly on the outside, while inside I was filled with dread. I knew at that moment that nothing good was going to come of this. If only I had trusted my gut instinct. I think now that my initial feeling on the situation was completely right. I should have never allowed my resolve to be broken.

"I would like that very much. If your Majesty has the time?" I said practically through gritted teeth.

"I always have time for a pretty face." The king winked at me before offering me his arm and leading the way out of the castle and into the gardens. He was ever the charming gentleman. I could see why women obsessed over him.

The day was stunning. The sky blue. The sun was out: a rare sight at this time of year. Summer was a distant dream. The gardens were all greens and browns as the leaves fell from their trees. The cold air danced around us, bringing with it the feel of a storm to come which sat just on the horizon waiting to darken London with its gloom. If only I had known that this in itself was a foreshadowing of what was to come.

We walked in silence for a long while. I had nothing to say, and I don't think that Henry knew what to say. I had not been as forthcoming as he was used to. If he had gone for Elizabeth or one of the other ladies he would probably already have them in his rooms. Pulling their dresses off and getting exactly what he wanted. He was not prepared to have much of a conversation, and I think this was new territory for him. After a while we stopped just by the rose bushes. Henry and I sat underneath as they created a beautiful shelter above us making almost an archway.

This would quickly become my favourite place. It was somewhere I would go when I needed to think things through. Whenever I needed to make a decision, it would be there that I would sit. Come rain or shine, I would sit below the white and red roses and meditate. It was so beautiful as the scent of the flowers surrounded me. I could not possibly imagine anything bad happening when I was here. It was like my little heaven on earth. It would be the place I would come when I wanted to think about Henry. To be close to him.

I would sit with Elizabeth when she was very small, and I wanted time alone with her without her servants bustling around me. I would bring her here for five minutes of just the two of us before she was sent away. It became my solace. Thomas and I shared moments here. George would comfort me here. If anyone should wish to feel me long after I am gone I suggest that they go to that spot. They will feel me as the wind blows. My presence will be in the blossoming flowers, in the petals that fall. The butterfly dancing in the breeze is my spirit. I like to think that one day maybe Elizabeth will sit here and think about me.

After we had sat, Henry turned to me. He took hold of my hands and looked deep into my eyes.

"I want to know about you Anne," Henry spoke breaking the peaceful silence. "You are someone of interest to me, and I find that I cannot help but want to know everything."

What was it about me that he had found so interesting? I had barely spoken to him and found it impossible to grasp just what I had done to make him seem so interested. If anything, I had appeared cold and unfriendly.

"What would you like to know, Your Majesty?" I asked, a brief smile crossing my lips.

"Well, for a start you may drop the formalities," he laughed. "Call me Henry."

This was becoming too familiar already. Only his closest friends and family called him Henry. Even George who had become close to the king while being a groom, had never been allowed to call him by his name. I had to play it cool and keep my calm. Even on the inside, my head spun and my stomach filled with butterflies. I had started to feel like there was nothing I could do to control this situation. He was not losing interest as quickly as I would have liked.

"Tell me something you like. What do you enjoy?" He was eager to know more. Like a child desperate to get as much information on something as he could. He was like an excited puppy as joy danced in his eyes. I seemed to affect him. He seemed to brighten in my company.

"I enjoy serving your wife. She is an outstanding woman," I said, knowing what I was doing by bringing Catherine into our conversation. I wanted to centre the conversation back around the fact that the reason I was even at court was to serve as a lady to Catherine. I wanted him to be aware that Catherine was in my mind at this moment. That I was thinking about her while sitting next to him.

Henry visibly rolled his eyes. "Just like your brother. You Boleyns seem to know exactly what to say," He chuckled, "What do you like doing for yourself? In your free time?" He sighed.

"Well I guess I like poetry a lot. I even like to write it myself sometimes." I gave Henry a small answer.

"In bed at morrow, sleeping as I lay,
Me thocht Aurora, with hir cristall ene,
In at the window lukit by the day

And halsit me, with visage paill and grene;
On quhois hand a lark sang fro the splene,
Awalk, luvaris, out of your slomering,
Se how the lusty morrow dois vo spring"

The king spoke poetry so beautifully. I had been
shocked by just how wonderful Dunbar sounded coming
from his lips. I was impressed. He had managed to quote
one of my favourite poems so effortlessly. Either he had
very good taste, or he had done his research excellently. It
sounded fabulous. He had a way of saying the words that
made each one come to life. I looked at him, seeing him for
the first time. I had been so focused on not being with him
that I had not bothered to look at him. His smile really did
light up his face, and with his words his eyes shone as his
love for poetry was clear in the way he spoke it. I was
surprised by my sudden need to hear him speak more. It
was the first conflicting feeling I had felt all day.

"You like William Dunbar?" I grinned, forgetting
myself for just a moment. The look I gave him then was of
genuine joy, happy for the first time to be in his company.

"He is my favourite poet," Henry beamed. "His words
speak to me. There is something about the images he
conjures. It takes me away from myself." The king smiled
shyly. "There is nothing more healing than poetry, Anne."

He was deeper than I had given him credit for. Clearly
there was more to him than just being king, but I had been
so consumed by avoiding him that I had not bothered to
look for anything else. He obviously had many hidden
qualities that are ignored when your position is to rule a
kingdom.

"I agree. It is the one thing I go to when I am in need of
comfort. Good poetry is always there for you like an old
friend." I smiled warmly mirroring the clear grin that sat on
his face.

"Reading too. I must admit that Chaucer is a favourite of mine." Henry said.

"Chaucer certainly has such a wonderful way of telling a story," I almost jumped in. I had never discussed these things with anyone before. Most people were too busy with their lives to get lost in a book. They had no idea of the joy they were missing out on.

"How strange that we should share love in the same things."

Henry gave me a coy smile. This, I decided, was his best smile. One that showed that even though he may be a strong king who bows to no man, there is still a shyness to him just below the surface.

We smiled at each other for a while, a comfortable silence taking over. I was surprised that, distracted by court life, it was strange to picture him leaning over his desk, book in hand. Obviously even a king needed to escape from time to time. He must have wanted something that was just for him and not the whole kingdom. I began to think that maybe he just wanted someone to talk to. Maybe I could relax in his company without worrying that he wanted something from me.

We got lost in conversation for a little while. We discussed all of our favourite poets and authors. We talked about art and music. He told me how he enjoyed composing when he had a moment to himself. I found him interesting and even intriguing. I allowed him to lure me into a false sense of security before he pulled the wool from my eyes. Of course he wanted something from me. He had only had one thing on his mind when he found me earlier in the day and I would not be at all surprised if in actuality he had been intending to find me in the first place.

"I want to continue this conversation Anne. but I need to go and get some work done," he said. "How about you come to my chambers later and we can talk some more?"

And there it was. The one thing that the king had wanted from me. He wanted me to go to his chambers tonight and give myself to him. He had been slowly edging towards this from the moment we had met this afternoon. He was waiting for the right moment and had apparently found it.

That was never going to happen. I had promised myself I would not fall into his trap, and I would not. He wanted me. I could sense that anyone who was asked to go to the king's rooms were comfortable in his bed one moment and then next cast out and he was back to worshipping Catherine. I could not go to his rooms. I would not allow myself to end up as Mary had, to be his mistress one minute and then cast out the next. To be propped up so high and then fallen from grace. Belly full with a baby and a husband who has lost interest. To be used as nothing more than a chess piece to advance our family.

I looked at the ground. Letting the smile drop from my face. Making sure to lower my eyes to my feet. "I would like very much to know your majesty but as you understand I cannot come to your rooms. I wish to keep my name intact. I am a maid to your wife and I love and respect Her Grace." I said. Making sure that I looked bashful as I spoke. The last thing I should do is upset the king. I had to tread carefully even as I turned him down.

"I only wish to talk..." he lied. Henry did not talk. He made advances. Some subtle and some more obvious, but his whole intention had been to coax me into his chambers.

"I am sorry, Majesty. I cannot do it to my reputation," I cut through. Which was silly. He could have lost his temper with me. It was disrespectful to interrupt the king, but I could let him go no further. I could not let him think that he had even a chance of changing my mind. Give a man like this even the slightest bit of hope and one has already lost. I could not afford to let him think there was any chance that he may win me over. I would have to be firm if I wanted a clean escape.

"I understand," He nodded briskly. He stood up to leave. He did not look back, clearly wounded by my refusal. He was gone before I had chance to say another word. I had guessed that I had just ended any ties with the king. I had managed to beat his advances back.

When he left he seemed to take the warmth of the day with him. I had to admit that having the attention of someone like Henry was a thrilling experience. Even if only for the briefest of moments.

* * * * *

Only that would not be the end of it. Henry would act wounded for the next three days, walking around with his tail between his legs. Whenever we would pass he would put his head down and ignore me. He was in a strop, just like a child who had been refused his favourite toy. This was a good thing. If he was upset with me, it meant that he no longer had an interest in me. I could deal with his mood until he found someone else to chase. Henry was finally done with me, and I was elated at my new-found freedom. I knew that eventually I would be able to start living my life again.

But my celebrations were too quick. Within a few days the gifts started to come. Jewels, gowns and a beautiful new headdress. Each morning I would receive a knock at my door and standing on the other side would be a young lad. His arms full with whatever gift Henry had decided to lavish on me that day. I would never once thank the king for the things he sent and honestly decided to ignore their existence completely. The boy stood shocked each time I refused to take them into my room. Who in their right mind would turn their nose up at a gift from the king? Who did I think I was? Each day I would open the door to his standing there. Take a look at his delivery and tell him to run along before shutting the door on his shocked expression.

I would however take the note from the top. Each time Henry would place a small note on top of the parcel. A few sweet words. He explained that he was not giving up and that he could not erase me from his mind. He knew not what to do with himself and had no clue as to why I haunted him so. He begged me to release him from his anguish and grace him with my presence. He was very good with his words and it did make me feel special to have him talk of me as if I was a gift from God. For some reason I kept his notes, locking them up in a box in my room. Safe from prying eyes.

With each day I grew more certain that soon enough he would grow bored of my refusal. There were only so many times a man can be told no before he gets the hint. Henry was just the same as any other man. Yes, he was persistent; but how much could he really allow before realising that he looked like a fool. It became a game. He sent me things and I ignored them. He would not win. I refused to let him have his way. It had become a nuisance.

The king was annoying me with his lack of respect for my answer. I had told him no repeatedly and he just would not listen. I was running out of ways to put him off. He was like a dog with a bone that he refused to drop. George told me that Henry had confided in him. Telling him that I was the reason he was losing sleep. He was awake all night thinking about me. His days were ruled by the image of my face. He had asked George for his advice. Surely there must be a way for him to win me over. George, ever being the loyal brother, had practically told the king to give up. He explained that I would never settle for being less than a wife. Still the king pushed on.

At first I was annoyed at his persistence, but as time went on I enjoyed refusing him. It was like our own little game. He threw all of his usual tricks at me and I batted them away. Each and every day I received a small note from him.

"Darling Anne. How you torment me so. I see you in my dreams and in my every waking moment. I am driven to madness at the thought of your beauty. Please end my torment and visit me tonight. Always in my thoughts. H. R"

Each had a small variation but every one led to the same point. He wanted me in his chambers. I must admit that there was some part of me that enjoyed beating him back. I liked to picture his wounded expression as he realised that I did not want his gifts or his attention. There was a part of me that enjoyed the power I held over him. I believe that at this point I could have asked anything of him and he would have happily granted it. No matter how hard I pushed away, Henry advanced forward. I would quite literally walk in another direction if I saw him coming and still he did not stop. I do not believe I could have been more obvious in my distaste.

But Henry would not take the hint. It would be a small touch as I passed. Lightly taking hold of my hand when no one was looking. Ensuring that as we passed our bodies would brush together. He would gaze at me from across the room. The way he would look at me was like he couldn't get enough. He took the whole of me in, as though if he looked away for one second he would forget and have to find me again.

He would be waiting outside of my room either early in the morning or late at night when I would return from seeing the queen. He'd stand outside of my door, always holding a white rose which he would present to me. He looked like an innocent young boy who was in the first blush of love. He would beg me to stay awhile and talk with him. Pleading with his eyes as I shook my head. I would make my excuses and continue on into my room. I was always too tired to talk or suffering with a sore head.

Only once did I actually humour him, and that was because I was fresh out of excuses. I took a heartbeat too long in coming up with something and Henry took that as his chance. He was particularly stressed on that day. He told me of all the pressures on his shoulders. How he sometimes wondered if he was offered the chance, then would he step down from the role that God had given him. He loved being king some days. Others, he just wanted to be a normal man. Free from the pressure of making decisions. He loved and hated that a whole country looked to him for wisdom. Some days he did not feel up to the task. Sometimes he wished his only duty was to look after a small household of people. With a wife and children. Happy in the countryside somewhere.

On this we agreed. If I could, I would hide away in the country. Surrounded by nature and having nothing more than what I needed. For someone considered ambitious, people are surprised to learn that I would have been happy tucked away in my own corner of the world. A loving husband. Children. Nothing to worry about apart from my own small family. I would cook for us while my husband was out hunting. Growing our own vegetables. Providing for ourselves. We would have as much as we needed and no more. We would be content with the life that God gave to us.

Henry wanted the same sometimes. Most of the time he loved the control that being king gave him. He loved to tell people what to do. He loved that no one could refuse him. He got pleasure from the fact that he held the fate of a nation in the palm of his hand. This was the egotistical side of Henry, the one that it would take longer to fall in love with. This was the side of him that I had to convince myself to get used to. Once I fell for that side as well, there would be no stopping us.

At other times he just wanted to be alone. He wanted space away from the eyes on him at court. He wanted to tell everyone to go away and leave him alone. Inside of him lay a sweet young man who was thrust into the title of king. A boy who believed he would always be the Duke of York. He had thought he would go into the church. He was supposed to have his own freedom. The role he was in now was someone else's, and I believe there was some part of him that still grieved for the life that was taken away from him. Sometimes he was saddened by the fact that the control was taken from him and that he had little choice other than to accept his role as king.

It was nice to see the side of him that was a man and not a king. The side that wanted the freedom of making his own choices. Choices that affected him and him alone. It was a sweet side that he hid from the everyday world. I remember thinking that if he were just a man then perhaps I would pursue this. Maybe I would let him court me. If he could offer me nothing more than to be the Duchess of York then maybe he would hold more appeal. Unfortunately, nothing could change the fact that he was king, so still I was unchanged.

However, there was another side of Henry. The side of a child who had lost his mother. A parentless young boy. A grieving son. I had found him one day. He was under the rose bushes. Apparently he also found solace tucked away from court. This place had become to him what it had become to me. We always knew that no matter how busy life got we could find each other here. He stood gazing up with his eyes full of tears. When he first realised that I had approached he had wiped the tears away and ordered me from his sight. No one should see the king like this and I had been unlucky enough to stumble on it. I had begun to leave when he called me back.

"I am sorry Anne," he sobbed. "I needed to escape."
What could I do when a man stood before me clearly
filled with a deep sadness. I let him cry onto my shoulder.
He gently wept as I held him. He missed his mother with
all of his heart, he told me, and some days it got the better
of him. He had never been able to get past her death and
that sunk him. It was like an anchor constantly dragging
him down into blackness, and it was all he could do to
keep from drowning in it. Some days he could barely lift
himself from grief. Weighed down by the hold it had on
his heart.

This young boy who lived inside of Henry had lost his
older brother and mother in the space of no time at all. He
had grieved one loss to be bowled over by another. As
king he was not granted the courtesy of grief. He had to
hold it all in. He put a false face on every day for the
court. It was like play-acting, looking one way to the
outside world and another in private.

Why he confided in me on that day, I do not know. He
could have ordered me to forget what I had seen. To move
along and never mention it to anyone. Instead he opened
up to me in a way I do not believe he had ever opened up
to anyone. I believe that Henry needed the guiding hand
of a woman. He looked for his mother in everyone, and no
one was ever enough.

I believe that part of the reason that Henry ended up
having little respect for women is that he did not have
Elizabeth around long enough to teach him. The only
influences he had as a parent was from his father and
grandmother, who both put England and her needs above
their family. Margaret Beaufort, his grandmother, wished
only to control him for her own benefit. She wished to
rule through him. She had thought to get the Tudors the
throne, and she would reap the reward.

Henry needed to be cared for. He needed a woman who would love him in the way he needed. He needed her whole heart. Someone who would walk through Hell to find him. Someone who loved him to a fault. As he opened up to me on that day, I could feel it as a small crack in my resolve began. It started small as Henry chiseled away. I believe my heart began to grow on that day. It began to feel for him. I would not admit it yet, but I believe that he took a gentle hold of me then and there. Gentle but unbreakable.

At another time, I was walking through the halls of Greenwich trailing behind with the other ladies and suddenly I felt pulled from our line and tucked into a corner. I found that Henry's face was mere inches away from mine. I could feel his breath on me as he stood close, holding me in place — his hands on my shoulders. My initial thought was that it felt good to have him hold me. I almost wanted to lean into him. To allow him to enclose me into his arms, but I could not. I could not allow myself to give in. I had shocked myself with my initial feeling of comfort.

"Anne," he breathed. "I have missed you."

Turning his dazzling smile on me, he smelled so sweet. He would talk so close to my face that I was sure that he would kiss me. But he never did, not once without my permission. He said that he held me in the highest regard and would never do anything that I was not comfortable with. It was torture for him to resist the urge, but for me, he would fight back his instincts.

"I'm ready for you the moment you are ready for me." He said, almost silently in my ear. "The day will come when you want me as I want you."

"That day will never come, my Lord." I made sure I was clear. Not breaking eye contact for a second. I had to appear strong. Henry would not break my resolve.

"Anne. You cannot still deny our feelings?" He sighed.
"Christ. I know you feel it too. Look me in the eyes and tell
me that you don't love me."

"Love you, Your Grace?" I had laughed. How could he
think for one moment that I loved him? This revelation
scared me. If he was talking about love then he was serious
about his feelings for me. Maybe this meant that he would
never be able to drop it. Perhaps it meant that I would have
to leave court altogether. I would have to start putting a
plan in place to return to Hever. At least if I were there then
I would be out of sight.

Henry's face fell. He truly believed that I had loved him
back at this point. I had given him nothing. He had no
reason to believe that I loved him. I was at a loss as to what
my next move should be. Whatever I did do, it would have
to break his heart. I felt sorry for him. He was smitten with
me, and I had no idea why. How could I tell this man that
his love was unrequited?

"I love you as my king and nothing more," I explained.
"I'm sorry Henry. It's never going to happen. I could never
love you."

He had not answered me. He looked too disheartened.
He turned and walked away, head in his hands. I had felt
guilty, but what was I to do? This had to be cut short. I
could never allow myself to feel for someone like Henry
Tudor.

Deep down in my soul I was not so scared that Henry
loved me. I was scared that Henry had no idea how close to
the truth he was. I certainly had begun to feel something for
him. All of his persistence had truly worn me.

My feelings for the king came to me like a sudden wave
that swept me off my feet. I had no control over the way I
felt. I had never wanted to feel like this. I had done so well
at avoiding his charms, but something had changed within
me. For some reason this day was different. Something
made me see him differently. I had not seen him for four

days, and I had missed him. I had found that I constantly thought about him, that he was in my mind at every hour in the day. As I tried to sleep I would see him. While I was at prayer his face would be at the front of my mind. I could not shake him, and it scared me.

Perhaps on this day my heart was ready to see him. Or perhaps it was because I could not get our last conversation out of my head. His words had stuck to me. As he confessed his love to me he awoke something inside. They did not let me get one moment of rest as they replayed over and over in my mind.

"Tell me you don't love me."

I was tormented by the thought of being drawn to someone like the king. It was never going to come to any good, and I spent the night admonishing myself for my own stupidity. I was following Catherine back to her chambers. We had just left morning mass. The king was crossing the hall with his usual followers beside him. Wolsey, looking ever smug, Nicholas Carew, with whom I had yet to be acquainted, and my father and brother. George always beamed at me as he walked past.

I will never forget the feeling that lifted me when I looked upon the king that day. I suddenly noticed Henry and not the king. He had a charisma that shone out from his every move, and it was hard not to watch him, but something was different on this day. Something made me want to look a little longer. I let my eyes linger over him, appreciating his manly stance. I took in his full figure. He was strong, tall and muscular.

He wore the most exquisite of fabrics. Golds, reds, and greens in the brightest shades. They fit his character perfectly, surrounding him in a beautiful aura of colours. A black feather cap covered most of his gorgeous red hair, the tiniest amount visible at the front. How I loved his hair. Crowning his perfect head in flames. I could run my fingers through that hair all day. I imagined how it would feel under my touch. How soft it must have been.

He was covered in jewels. Oh, the jewels. They were everywhere he could fit them. Every finger held a different ring. His clothes adorned with rubies and sparkling emeralds. His shoulders were so broad and man-like. I lingered on the idea of those wide shoulders enclosing me. How safe it would feel to rest my head on that broad shoulder of his. His arms would remove all of the world's problems as he held it together safe in his great hands.

If I could describe what the perfect godlike man would look like, I would describe Henry. His light eyes were piercing. His mouth turned up in a smile that filled his whole face. His cheeks were red with joy, and he seemed to blush as the whole room looked upon him. He must have been used to the attention, but there was still a part of him that grew a little nervous as people watched his every movement. There was a coyness about this that I found sweet and lovely. His face was so strong. His whole stance showed that he was in control of everything. He was every bit the king he was supposed to be.

As he gazed around the room he caught my eye straight away. Our eyes locked. Almost like the first time we had looked at each other. It was a shock to my core, coursing through me and rooting me to the spot. There was a sudden stillness as my mind went silent and I held my breath. My whole body seemed to respond to him. It is like my soul somehow recognised him. Like something inside of me suddenly clicked into place. It was almost as if I was drawn closer to him, as if we were familiar somehow. I almost wanted to go and throw my arms around him. If I had not remembered myself, I might have strolled over in that instant and taken hold of him.

Why did I feel drawn to this man all of a sudden? I had never had this reaction before, so what was so different today? Perhaps it was because I had never really looked at him before. I had been so focused on ignoring his advances that I hadn't bothered actually to see him. I had not allowed myself to see him. It is strange how you can look at a person one thousand times and never really see them.

Well, now I saw him, and I could not look away. I had looked through him, seeing only the title of king. I had never played close enough attention. But now It was the way he was smiling at me and only me. He looked past the other ladies and found my face. Holding me there with his almost unbearably stunning grin. Perfect teeth biting his lower lip. His eyes held mine as no one had before. He looked straight through Catherine at the head of the train to find my face in the crowd.

Today I wanted him to look at me. I wanted his eyes never to leave my face. I wanted him to know that I saw him. Today was the day, Henry, that I fell completely and passionately in love with you. Today my heart betrayed me. Our eyes stayed locked on each other for what seemed like a lifetime. I was totally lost in his dazzling blue eyes. A calm sea before a storm. It was as if I could look into them and see his soul laid bare. Like it was ready to unlock its secrets for me and only me. I began to feel a little lightheaded.

Then suddenly he was laughing away with such joy that I could have laughed along with him. His chums had said something funny, but the way his lips quirked up as he laughed and his eyes seemed to glow made something inside of me stir. I had never felt anything like it before. I remember thinking how odd it was to let myself be so affected. Had I finally let him win? Had all of his months of trying to obtain me finally worked? Either way, I felt like I needed to rest. To close my eyes and assemble my thoughts before I went crazy. I was hot all of a sudden, as if the room was too small and too full of people.

When he finished laughing he strolled toward us, and we all bowed low in respect as he addressed Catherine. "Good morning, my love." His eyes were not on Catherine. Even as he kissed her hand he looked directly at me. His eyes squinting in a smile once more. Even his voice seemed to make me shake and seemed to awaken something in me that I never knew existed. I longed for him to say something else. Anything. My name. If I could hear that voice say my name again I would be content. I longed to hear him tell me that he loved me. Perhaps I never would again. What if I had lost my chance? Could I live another day knowing that I had pushed him away? He turned and left the room. One last look at me that told me all I needed to know. Yes, he loved me. He knew now that I was ready for him.

We returned to Catherine's rooms, and I could not concentrate for the rest of the day. Trying and failing to justify my sudden feelings. I had worked so hard to avoid his attention. I had done everything I could to stay safe from his feelings. What was I thinking? Not only was he a married man, but he had not so long ago been sleeping with my elder sister.

It was impossible. He could offer me nothing more than a fling. A quick affair that would be over almost as quickly as it had started. I wanted more for myself. I cannot put into words exactly how much I blamed myself for my feelings. I was harder on myself than anyone else. For anyone who says I saw an opportunity with the king, they could not be more wrong. I fought myself every single step of the way.

* * * * *

That night I returned to the festivities. I joined in with the rest of the court again as everyone made merry with wine and dancing. That night I felt as if all of the weight had suddenly been lifted off of me. That night I could not take my eyes off of the king. I watched him from afar, appreciating every last inch of him. That night I allowed him to lead me in a dance. I allowed myself to float around the floor as it felt like he carried me through the room. For the first time I allowed myself to enjoy the feel of his arms around me. The feel of his chest as it lay so close to mine. I allowed myself to stand close to him both of our hearts beating fast within our chests. I got lost in the moment he had a hold of my hand, the feel of his hand on my waist. I allowed Henry to get closer than he ever had before, and he had no idea that whatever he was feeling I was now feeling, too.

CHAPTER EIGHT

Things changed from that day onwards. Henry had cast
a spell over me, and that spell was only to get stronger as
the days went on. That afternoon I received a note from
him. It was delivered into my hands by George. He pressed
it into the palm of my hand while at the same time giving
me a warning look. That look conveyed everything he felt
about the situation. He did not like the fact that the king
was paying me attention. He had told me just the day
before that I should watch my back. He was getting worried
about how much Henry spoke about me. He had warned me
that I was falling into the same trap as Mary. The king was
clearly besotted, and the best thing I could do would be to
remove myself from the situation altogether. He hoped that
I had not been encouraging him. I could have throttled
George. How stupid did he think I was. Of course I hadn't
been.

George should have known better than to accuse me of
such things. I was annoyed at his warning. I explained to
him that I was much more intelligent than our naive sister
and that I would not let myself get into a situation I could
not control. He had apologised. He told me that he was
only concerned because he knew how convincing the king
could be. I loved how protective George was, but this was
really none of his concern. Plus I had told him with great
confidence that I was handling it. He had agreed, promising
to speak no more on the matter.

However, after witnessing how the king and I had
looked at each other earlier in the day and now being
appointed to deliver this note, his fears were returning. The
look George gave me told me that he would wish to speak
to me later. I would have to brace myself for a trying
conversation. It also told me to be careful. The look I gave
him back told him to mind his own business. He rolled his
eyes and left. That is all it took for George and me to

communicate. One brief look from each other and we knew exactly what the other was thinking.

As soon as I was alone, I unfolded the note that George had given me. My heart leaped at the king's handwriting. Something that had previously had no effect on me now filled me with happiness as I read his words.

"Dearest heart. I have been able to think of nothing else since my seeing you earlier in the day. I humbly ask that you join me in the gardens tonight. As the hour strikes 8 I will be waiting not so patiently for you. I believe that you know the spot where I shall be. I do hope that I shall be blessed with your presence tonight sweet Anne. My heart can hardly bear to wait a moment longer.
All of my heart and soul
H. R"

My initial instinct was to run to him. To spare not one moment longer without him. So much time had already been wasted, and I wanted him. In that moment, I wanted nothing more than to be with him. It was only 5 o'clock. Hours yet until he would be waiting beneath the roses. Time ticked on so slowly as my head and heart waged war between the part of me that knew no good would come of my meeting him, and the part of me that wanted nothing more than to see him. I was conflicted, completely at sea.

On the one hand, I knew that the clever thing to do would be to avoid Henry wherever possible to let my feelings run their natural course so that I could cleanse my heart of the king. On the other, all of my impulses told me to run towards him rather than away. Something had taken hold of me, and my heart was winning out. It was like my legs were desperate to find him. My eyes searched everywhere for him. I made my own head ache as I argued with myself, knowing deep down that it was useless. I had been going through this all morning, battling between what was right and what I wanted. Something told me that what I felt for Henry could not possibly be wrong. Why would something that felt so right ever be considered wrong? Why would my heart betray me in that way?

Everything that I had ever been taught or learned should have been enough to convince me that I was wrong. I knew how kings worked. They had their loyal wives, and they had their mistresses. The mistress was always on the side. She never had a deeper connection with her king. She was used for her body and then she was traded up for a newer, better version. Mary kept on swimming into my thoughts. Had she felt like this? Had she felt for Henry the way I do? What would she think of me? As I considered starting something with the man she not so long ago shared a bed with.

This was ridiculous. I was stupid. Of course I would not meet him. That would not only be disloyal to my sister, but I would be betraying myself and the promise I had made always to guard myself. If only I could talk to Mary now. To ask her advice. It had been so long since I had last seen her. She had no idea of the things that had happened recently. She would be devastated to learn that the king pursued me. I had settled. I would not go. I had made up my mind to stay as far from Henry as I could. I would return to Hever.

So why was it that as the clock ticked nearer to 8:00 I was desperate to remove myself from the queen's rooms and go to the gardens? Why did I run through the many ways I could make my excuses to Catherine? I knew deep down in my soul that I would go. I was already making a plan in my head for how I wanted to look. I could picture my green dress that hung in my room. Already decided on the lapis accessories that I would adorn. I would wear my matching French hood tonight. It always annoyed me to have my hair fussed over. I was happiest when it was loose rather than braided up and stuffed in a hood, but I wanted to look perfect.

I had no idea what would happen, but my stomach grew tight with knots as the time moved faster and faster — slipping away now. Guilt built up inside of me as I realised that I would be lying to Catherine so that I could spend an evening with her husband. In one moment I was elated at the idea of being with Henry, and in the next the joy came crashing down as I thought about the many people I would be hurting just by doing this. Still I would go. My mind had been made up the moment George had pressed the note into my hand. I didn't know it. I had no clue what I was about to get myself into. All I knew was that if I did not go, then I would regret it forever.

* * * * *

That night I dined with the queen in her chambers, and then we ladies sat with her to play cards. I had stayed for a while. Up until the last minute still fighting with my inner emotions. As the time struck seven I had told the queen that I was not feeling too well and that if she did not mind excusing me I would like to go and lie down for a while in my own room. She was more than happy to let me go for the evening. "Of course, lovely Anne. Go and rest. Feel better." she smiled, making it harder for me to come to terms with the evening I had ahead. This poor woman who had been so kind to me had no idea that I was lying about my true intentions for the evening.

I felt the awful stab of guilt at that moment. I had just lied to her so that I could go and spend the evening with her husband. The man she loved more than anyone else in the world. The father of her child. I hated doing this. In the beginning I found it so hard to smile to her face while I opened my heart to her husband behind her back. It was not and still is not fair. She deserved better than the treatment she received at my hands. Still it was not enough to stop me.

I rushed back to my room eager to change out of my gown and into something more flattering. I also needed a moment to compose myself. There was little point forgetting myself. I still had to keep a cool head. I had no idea what to expect from this evening, but I would not do myself the disservice of acting like a silly fool in love. After I was changed and ready I took a steadying breath before leaving my room. I walked calmly from my room to the gardens. It was slightly chillier this evening, and I wrapped my arms around myself to protect from the cold.

The sky was dark and full of sparkling stars. The moon was full and created the most beautiful glow as it lit up the leaves that glistened with the drops from the earlier rain. I breathed deeply letting the air fill my lungs before I began my slow walk to where Henry would be. I felt a calmness wash over me, as my body sensed that this was right. The nerves washed away. It was as if I headed toward an old friend and my body became relaxed as I drew closer.

When I got to the rose bushes Henry was nowhere to be seen. I had left my room a little before eight expecting Henry to be already waiting, but there was no sign of him. I wondered briefly if I had come to the correct place. Henry had never specifically said for me to come here, but I had assumed that this was the place he meant. Nowhere else had immediately come to mind. I decided I would wait here. If he were somewhere else, then he eventually would come searching. In the meantime, I would appreciate my surroundings.

I took in the fantastic flowers that surrounded me. The thing that always amazed me with roses was how many variations there were. Each one is as beautiful as the last. I walked underneath the archway reaching out to touch the roses in front of me and pulling them closer to my nose so that I could take in their sent. I felt so at peace, completely at ease surrounded by one of the many things that God had blessed the world with. As I stood with my back to the garden I felt a great big pair of arms around me. Breath gently tingling down my neck. My name was just a whisper in my ear "Anne.."

I turned in the great arms that had a hold of me — already knowing who had crept up on me. My face was but inches away from his.

"Your Majesty." I blushed. I was so happy to see him. To feel him. This is exactly what I needed. I smiled at him. "I would curtsey. But as you can see, I am being held against my will," I teased.

The king released me and stepped back. He had no idea of my feelings at this point. As far as he knew I still wanted nothing to do with him.

"Well, my lady, if I am holding you captive then I had better let you go. I would not want to cage such a pretty little bird."

He stroked my cheek. I let his hand cup my face. Appreciating the feeling as it cradled me. They were so soft. For such great manly hands, they had no roughness to them. They were like silk on my cheek. I had wondered how it would feel to have his hands on me. To have him hold me in them and never let go.

"Birds do not like to be caged, your Majesty. They wish to be free. They long to spread their wings and fly off to other worlds," I began as his face fell. "But if I had to choose my cage, I feel yours would be my pick." I said, finally confessing my feelings.

Henry almost stumbled backwards. He had grown accustomed to my rejection. Within moments a smile crept on his face, and I do not believe I have ever seen anyone look so happy. It was like I had given him the greatest gift he could imagine. If I were not already falling, that look confirmed it. I truly believed him. He loved me. He really loved me.

"Anne...you mean it? You feel the same as I do?" He beamed as tears began to fill his eyes. "If you wish for me to hold you, then you need only ask."

My heart grew bigger with each passing moment finally allowing him all the way in. Of course I wanted him to hold me. I wanted nothing more in this world. I wanted to be as close to him as it were possible to be to another person.

"I mean it," I giggled. "I love you Henry."

This was the first time I had called him by his name, and he was overjoyed. He took me into his arms, lifting me off of the ground. It was so warm to be held by him. Nothing felt safer. It was as if he could hold all of my pieces together.

"Anne. I love you," he spoke through tears. "I wish to give you my heart. Can you promise me you will never hurt it?"

"I would never harm a hair on your head," I promised. Kissing his hands and pulling him closer to me again.

"Nor I, you, Anne. you will always be safe with me."

And then he was kissing me. It was the first time he had ever kissed me as he pulled me close and placed his lips onto mine. It was like the whole world had stilled for this one moment. Like nothing could ever be wrong again. In that one kiss I had felt all of the love that had ever existed in the world. I felt light as a feather floating softly through the sky. I lifted out of my own body and watched from above as my Henry smothered me with kisses. I could taste him. He was sweet. I wanted more — wanted to be closer. I wanted to connect with him. I responded, holding him to me so tightly that I do not know how we ever separated. If this is what it felt like to be loved, I never wanted it to end.

He pulled away, never for one moment breaking eye contact. He kissed me on the forehead showing that he cared for me. It was a sweet gesture that just meant that he loved me. It always meant that he loved me. I let my heart run away with me forgetting about the fact that a court of people surrounded us. Forgetting that he had a wife, a child and a crown. I could see only us.

Henry began to chuckle as we sat snuggled into each other.

"It is funny how in that one kiss everything makes sense again." He stroked my hand. "Anne, I was lost without you."

He turned to face me. He held my hand to his face as he kissed the palm, sending shivers all the way through me. "Do you agree, my love?"

I did. Kissing him was the last piece of the puzzle finally being placed into the correct spot. I could not remember why I had fought so hard against this in the first place. Henry soothed all of my worries with that kiss. He made everything seem that it was going to work out, because how can a connection like ours not make sense?

"Loving you makes sense," I answered.

"Then love me, Anne," Henry said. "Be my everything. Would you consider letting me love you?" he asked.

"There is nothing to consider."

Henry grinned. He was even more godlike when he was happy as the perfect painting on display in a palace. I could not believe how lucky I was. How had I managed to obtain the love of this man? What had I done to deserve him? It was unbelievable to me that I had somehow found my reason for being in this world.

"Then be my mistress?" Henry asked.

His words cut through my happiness, bringing life back into view. My face dropped, and I let go of his hand in an instant.

"Anne, say you will be my mistress and I will take no other lover."

How foolish I had been. I had forgotten for a moment that this was all he could offer me. Of course he wanted me to be his mistress. He could not possibly want anything else. I stiffened upstanding from my position. I no longer wanted him to touch me. How silly I had been to let myself kiss him. He was king.

I was so angry with myself. So disappointed that I had allowed myself to fall for his glamour. What did I truly believe was going to come from this. That he would run away with me? That we would somehow be together? No the truth was I hadn't been thinking at all. I had had my head in the clouds. I had not been facing reality, and for that I only had myself to blame.

"Your mistress, my lord?" I could barely keep the quiver from my voice. "I will be no man's mistress."

Henry looked confused. He had thought that he had won. That I had not only admitted to being in love with him but that I would also go to bed with him. He had probably thought that I would have followed him to his bed that night. He looked at a loss for words. Disappointed at my further refusal to give him what he wanted.

"Anne...what more could you possibly expect from me?" He sighed. "I have a wife."

I believe that my hatred for Catherine began that very moment. She was the only thing standing between me and what I wanted. I grew a coldness to her that day. Her only fault was that she loved the man I now wanted.

"I expect nothing from you." I grew bitter. "And I play second fiddle to no one."

"Anne, I love you..." Henry pleaded. "But Catherine is my wife."

"Then you should return to your wife, sire."

I turned and walked away. I could scarcely stand to be in his presence. I could hear as he called after me, but I had already resigned myself to leave. I could not allow my own heart to break any further. Yes, I loved him. I truly loved him, but I could not allow myself to be used. Although it almost killed me to walk away, I owed it to myself to leave.

What respect could I have for myself if I allowed myself to become a mistress?

It hurt so badly to turn from him. Where moments earlier I had been so happy. So content. Now I was filled with a loss. I felt like I had turned from his love. I had forsaken it. For that I felt terrible. I did not deserve his love. My heart ached as I climbed into bed, crying myself to sleep.

* * * * *

The next morning I was awakened by a tap on my door. Henry stood before me, filled with apologies. He understood why I had refused him and explained that it would be enough for him simply to be in my presence. He loved me so much that he was willing to push aside his needs and ensure that I was in his life one way or another.

I was not convinced, but I also hated the thought of not seeing him all the time. I loved him, and that was the truth of it. Nothing I could do would stop me from loving him. He would have to do some serious damage for me to turn my back on him. I knew that nothing had changed. He was still the king and I was still not his wife, but what harm were we doing by spending time together? We could be together without the need to become physical. How important could that part really be? I had never experienced it, so at this point it wasn't something I knew I needed. That is, I didn't know until I wanted to get closer to him. Then I realised that love could not survive without the touch of the one you adore.

Over the course of the next two weeks, Henry and I would meet almost every day in exactly the same spot. It was getting harder by the day to resist him. I would have to stop myself from leaning into him actively. I would sit across from him to stop from wanting to kiss him but as I watched his lips move it was all I could do not to take hold of his face and show him everything that words could not convey. Each time it would start off sweetly. We would sit together and talk about our lives. Henry would quickly become the closest person to me. I spent more time with him than I did with Margery or Thomas.

I shared everything with him. All of my hopes and dreams. All of my secrets. Henry knew all of my darkest thoughts and I knew all of his. We hid nothing from each other. He knew what I truly thought of the world, and I knew everything about him. He would flirt and try to woo me, but most of the time he would not overstep, always cautious to respect me and my decision.

He was always so gentle. We would joke and laugh. Finding our little happiness outside of the court. Then each night as it drew closer to its end, he would begin to pressure me again. The night would usually end with me walking off in anger. I was so frustrated by him. Why did he have to make it so difficult? He just had to put pressure on our situation. He would beg me, and at one point he actually got down on his knees, holding me around my waist.

"Anne, how can you refuse me? All I want to do is love you. Forget about Catherine. I only see you."

I pushed him off of me. "Henry, please. Show some dignity," I scolded. "I will not be your mistress. I wish to be a wife. And you cannot make me a wife, so I cannot dally with you any longer." I turned and made to storm away. It was true. I wanted and needed to marry. I could not get through this life as a mistress. Any children I may have as a mistress would have nothing to their name. It would not matter that Henry declared his love for me to the whole world, because no one would care. If I was not a wife, then I was worthless and had no standing. I would not do that to myself — to my family.

Henry grew angry for the first time. Up until now, we had both been frustrated, but he was beginning to boil over. He was sick with misery at not having me, and he lashed out. I know he did not mean it. But truly it was probably for the best that we should end things there. I hated being with him and never truly belonging to him.

"Fine. If you do not want me then I waste no more time on you lady," He sneered. "You are dismissed from your duties. I will return to the queen who will happily keep my bed warm."

He was so awful when he was angry. Always had a cruel tongue. "She is far fairer than you. I would rather look upon her face every day."

I continued to walk away. I would not spar with him. "Or perhaps your sister? The pretty Boleyn."

My eyes began to burn at this. Of course. How could I be so stupid? He was with my sister. Of course he would prefer Mary. She was undeniably beautiful, and I only had my brains to sell. Oh how I hated Mary in that moment. She just had to get there first. My heart shattered at the thought of how Henry must hate me for rejecting him repeatedly. I did not want to. I wanted to be with him. I wanted to marry him! I would give anything to be his wife.

This was wrong. I needed to be as far away from him as possible. The problem was I wanted him to love me in the way he loved life, to need me in the same way he needed air. I wanted to be the thing that made his heart beat, to be his every thought. Every word and every need, I wanted him to run mad with desire for me. To see me in his dreams. To feel me long after I had gone. I wanted to be his everything, and I couldn't be his everything. This country was his everything. Catherine was his everything. I was nothing more than some bit on the side that he wanted to get into bed.

The other problem was that he was all of those things to me. I was consumed by him. Totally and utterly tied to him. I felt I could not breathe unless he shared the same air. As if I would be lost in a great blackness should he remove his light. I saw him everywhere. He was everything to me. I loved him in a way that could only mean tragedy for me. I had to be free of him. I would suffocate if I stayed here.

* * * * *

I held my tears all the way back to my room. When I got there, my father and uncle were waiting for me. This night was about to become even worse, and all I wanted to do was shut the world out. My heart was in pieces. All I wanted was to say yes to Henry. To let him have the whole of me. It was cruel that fate had laid me in his way, only to make it impossible for us to join. The last thing I needed at that moment was to be in the company of these two.

Father held a small smile on his face. Uncle was full of beaming. He was unable to keep his excitement, and in an instant I knew exactly why they were here. They, of course, had heard about the relationship between Henry and me and wanted to weigh in with their opinion on the matter. I did not need any words from them about it, and I cared little for what they thought of me. Before they could start there was a small knock on my door and in came George. He had bumped into the king outside. Henry had had some choice words to say about me, and George was worried.

"Father, Uncle. I did not expect to see you here." George was as shocked as I to see them in my room at such a late hour. "Anne, is everything all right?" George took hold of my arm.

"Yes George. I'm fine." I smiled warmly at my caring little brother. "We shall talk later," I promised.

"We have come here to talk to Anne about the king," Father began, caring little for the sad expression I held on my face. "Anne. you know as well as we do that the king has taken a liking to you."

It was all I could do not to turn around and walk away. They were both so transparent.

"What business is that of yours, Father?" I asked.

I knew what they were getting at. I was not going to make it easy for them. Father hated the pressure. You could see where a small bead of sweat began to build on his forehead. He was bright red, hated any type of confrontation, and was terrible at telling anyone what to do.

"We believe that it would be beneficial to the family if you should choose to pursue the king's advances." Father stumbled over his words.

In other words, they wanted to use me, as they had Mary, by selling me off to the king so that they could reap the rewards. They had a great advantage with Mary, and it had helped to advance our family to a position of power. Yet they wanted more. They wanted to be back in the king's good graces, and I was a means to an end. It is an odd feeling to be used as a pawn. Especially for the benefit of one's family. It's as if you're worthless up until the point where they find a way to use you. I always wondered what it would feel like to receive real love from my family, to have parents who loved me for me and not because I may one day become an asset. I thank God they treated me as they did, because it taught me exactly how I did not want my daughter to be treated.

"Beneficial?" I laughed. "And why exactly should I care what benefits the two of you?"

Uncle now too turned red in the face. He was angry. I loved getting him riled up. Loved that he knew that he held no power over me. He could order me around as much as he wanted, but nothing would make me listen to him. He was a cruel man who enjoyed seeing the pain of others. He liked to think that he was in the superior position, and that we simply had to follow suit. But I had never been as easy to manipulate as he would have liked.

"Listen here, young lady. If your father tells you to do something you better do it." Uncle barked.

He stepped closer to me. Raising a hand above his head as if he may strike me. I was ready for the blow. Bracing myself. It was not the first time a man had hit me, and it would not be the last.

"I would calm down if I were you Uncle." George cut in. He took hold of my uncle's hand.

"If you lay one finger on Anne, I do believe you will have the king to answer to." George stood in between the two of us protecting me from the incoming blow.

"The king wouldn't care that I beat his whore." Uncle sniggered. "He'd simply find another."

George was angry. I could almost see his blood boil. He hated our uncle, especially after the way they had treated Mary. His biggest fear was the idea that they could do the same thing to me.

"You may be right. But Anne is no whore. The king loves her." George defended me.

My uncle dropped his arm. Speechless for the first time in his life, he rubbed his forehead as he tried to understand this new information.

"Loves her?" He asked.

His anger was once again swept away by a wave of happiness as he realised what this meant. If the king loved me, then the profit they could collect knew no bounds. He was silent for a while, concocting a new way forward. He now knew I did not only hold the king's eye but his heart as well.

"Is this true Anne? Does the king love you?" Father asked. His voice was a quiet whisper compared to the boom of my uncle.

I stayed silent for a long while. It was none of their business what went on between Henry and me. So what if he loved me. They would only use this as a way to get into the king's good graces, and I did not want to taint or use our love.

"Father, I really do not think that is any of your business," I said.

"And you love him?" Father asked.

I did not answer, but I believe it was written on my face. I could not hide the way I felt from anyone. The mere mention of his name was enough to make me blush.

"This is wonderful." Father clapped, joy filling his expression. "Well, then there is no reason for you to work against us."

I was close to tears at this point. I had just lost Henry, and now they wanted me to become his mistress simply because it suited them. I needed to get away from this room, from the palace, from London altogether. It only held heartache for me now, and I wanted to put as much space between myself and these people as possible.

"I am leaving court, and there is little you can say to change my plan," I told them of my intentions.

The look they gave me was as if I had just hit one of them. They were angry, to say the least, but I would do nothing to aid them in this.

"Anne, I really think it would be better if…" Father started, but Uncle had had enough, and he cut through him. It was all he could do not to shout.

"Oh stop dithering, Thomas!" He ordered.

Father shrunk inside of himself. What a weak little man he was.

"Anne, you WILL become the king's mistress. In fact, I order you to go and find him this instant and do whatever he bloody well asks of you." He was beside himself. As if he could not believe that such fools surrounded him.

"I will do no such thing, Uncle," I simply said.

"WE are your family. Better than that we are the men of this family. You do as we say. If we tell you to jump you better jump. If we tell you to whore yourself out then you better get used to the idea of sleeping with whoever we want you to sleep with. As a woman, you are no better than a slut anyway." Uncle spat at me.

George had had enough. In three small strides, he was swinging my door open and grabbing uncle by the collar. He held him up and dragged him to the door.

"Talk to my sister like that again, and I'll kill you."

He shoved him into the corridor. I thanked God that no one was around to see the commotion coming from my room.

"Father the same goes to you. Anne has said that she will not do as you say. You have your answer, now go before I am forced to lose my temper." George's eyes had turned dark with anger as he held the door for father to scurry from the room. He slammed the door and within an instant was holding me.

"Anne, are you all right?" He stroked my hair. "I'm sorry, sister. I will not have them using you like that."

"Thank you, George."

I buried into his shoulder. I was so grateful to have him. He always looked out for me. He had gone a step further in standing up to Father and Uncle. He may find himself in very hot water tomorrow, but he did not care as long as I was safe.

"George I am returning to Hever. I cannot stay here. It is too dangerous."

"Hush now. I understand. You never have to explain anything to me," George silenced me.

He helped me prepare for my return to Hever. He gave me a hand in packing my belongings and arranging transport. He promised to visit me the moment he had an opportunity. I could not wait to be at home. I wanted to leave all of this behind me and move forward.

CHAPTER NINE

I was so happy to return to Hever. Back at home, I suddenly felt lighter leaving Henry and the court behind me. There is something about being in the place where one grew up that feels like being wrapped in cotton wool. Its familiar walls surrounded me like a comforting blanket wrapped around my shoulders. The smell of the countryside as I stepped out of doors for my morning walk cleared my head of the buzz that London had left behind. I could hear the birds clearly again as the noise of London was replaced by the quiet of Kent. The streams trickling along replaced the hustle and bustle of a palace.

I felt calm and relaxed. It was as if I could think clearly for the first time in months. I was practically alone, barring the servants and Mother, who kept herself locked in her library. At court I was always surrounded by people. I hardly had any time for myself. Here, if I wished to be alone I needed only to walk outside or to my room. I went riding most days or walked in the surrounding greenery. I had plenty of time to read and to paint. It felt good to worry about no one but myself, to decide how I wanted to spend my days. It was good for healing my soul.

I had gotten myself into a complicated situation back in London, and I needed to separate myself from it before I was forced to endure more heartache. The problem was I could not remove the cause of that heartache from my mind.

I missed Henry badly. Even Hever could not erase him from my mind. I felt as if a piece of me had been cut off and discarded. I ached for him. It was always as the evening fell and the stars began to appear I would think of him. What was he doing? Who was he with? Had he found someone else yet? It tormented me, and I found that many of my nights were sleepless as I lay awake longing for him.

I believed that it would get easier, hoping that the longer I stayed in Hever, the less I would care for him. I thought that I would wake up one day and would have forgotten how much he meant to me. That my love was a fleeting fancy and one day I would laugh at my stupidity.

I had a few visitors, all of whom brightened up my day in their own special way. Margery came first, bringing news of Catherine and the court. She told me of Catherine's fading. She grew worse by the day apparently. It was clear that she grew tired of court life. She wanted to shrink back to her rooms more often than not. Margery made me laugh for the first time in what felt like a lifetime — telling stories of Tom and his drunken behaviour, of George and his pining for his dear sister.

Tom came as well. He sat with me for the day. We took the horses out and sat in the gardens with a small picnic. He was as comforting as ever. He made all of my problems seem so small and unimportant. Somehow he always helped to put things into perspective. I hadn't told him yet that I had feelings for the king. I did not want to hurt him. Instead he believed that I had returned to Hever so that I could avoid Henry's attention. It was wonderful to talk nonsense, to spend the day in pointless gossip and make-believe.

Thomas was a great storyteller, and he loved to try out his newest ideas on me. There was a relief in not talking about the issue at hand. I allowed myself to be totally lost in Tom and set my aching heart to the side for the day. Part of me wished that he could stay longer to permanently distract me from my thoughts. He promised to visit again soon, and I found myself excited for the next time.

Mary also visited. She brought with her my niece and baby nephew. He was utterly adorable, and I tried my hardest to ignore the slight sleek of red that went through his hair. He was a picture, and as I gazed on him I wondered if I too would be cradling my own child one day. It came so naturally to Mary. Would it be the same for me?

It was heartwarming to chase little Catherine through the gardens. She reminded me so much of Mary when she was that small. She had a head of beautiful blond curls, her eyes the same dark shade as Mary's. She had nothing of her father in her. She was all Mary, a chubby little thing. She was so sweet as she tottered around on her little legs. How it must feel to be that young and carefree again. I would love just one more moment of childhood when the world was nothing but a big and exciting dream.

Mary had heard all about the king's new fancy from her husband. William always returned from court with some sort of gossip for her and she loved that, in a way, it kept her connected. She had wanted to come and see me for a while now, but having a newborn child was a very trying feat. She had been unable to travel for a long while after the birth.

She was here now, and I was beside myself with joy to see my elder sister once more. Life was never quite the same without her. I missed having her comforting sisterly gaze around. I had missed her words of advice and her kind smile. When we came together it was always as if no time had passed and before I knew it, we were talking the day away. Laughing and joking. We could talk about anything and everything. Also the fact that Mary had been in a similar position meant that she was unusually qualified to offer me advice on Henry.

"Anne, darling, how are you coping?" Mary asked.

She was more of a mother now than she ever had been. Having children suited her as she cradled one close to her chest while the other bounced up and down on her knee. I had smiled to myself to see her so happy and content with her life. She deserved all the happiness in the world, and it brightened my day to see that she was truly happy with the life she had been given.

"I'm all right Mary. Honestly," I had smiled. I did not want to let on how I was feeling on the inside. "You have enough to worry about without being concerned for your little sister as well." I pinched Catherine's little cheeks.

"I do worry, Anne. I was Henry's mistress for a long while. I know how hard it is to escape his advances." She sighed as she stroked Henry's little head. "I am proud of you for escaping his clutches. You have done better than me." She smiled warmly.

This was too much for me. Suddenly the heartache of the past few months came flooding towards the surface. I had held back so much emotion for so long that it needed a way to escape. Mary's proud expression had been the breaking point for me. The tears began to fall from my eyes. I struggled to wipe them away. I did not want Mary to know how hurt I was. I did not want to disappoint her when she found out my true feelings.

"Anne. Love, what is it?" Mary grew concerned. She gave little Henry and Catherine to their wet nurse and put her arms around me. "I understand how hard it is. But you should be proud. You have removed yourself from a difficult situation and stood up to our father and uncle. You are a stronger woman than I."

This only made me cry even harder. I hated the idea that Mary was proud of me when I did not deserve it. She thought so highly of me, and all I had done was get myself into a big mess.

"It's not that, Mary." I began. "It's Henry. I..."

I had no idea where to start. How could I tell her that I had grown to love a man who was once hers? But somehow Mary understood. I did not need to explain because she had worked it out for herself. Her face softened even more as it dawned on her.

"Oh sweet girl. You love him, don't you?"

All I could do was nod my head. I did not have the strength to explain myself. I looked at Mary expecting her to grow angry at any moment, but I did not have enough faith in my sister. She was always a much more understanding person than I was.

"And you think that I did not love him at one point?" Mary sighed again. "I was besotted, Anne, which means it hurt even more when it ended," Mary confessed.

I always believed that she hated their arrangement. The night she had told me about it she had not indicate her feelings for him. I instantly felt even more guilty than before. It was bad enough that I had fallen for a man she used to sleep with, but it turned out that it was more than that. Still it was not the same. Mary had grown to love him. Henry had loved her body. They did not have a joining of minds as Henry and I did. She didn't say they were in love, just that she loved him.

"This is different Mary. I have not been with him. I have refused. He loves me for me." I explained justifying it to myself as much as I was trying to justify it to her. Mary looked down saddened in one moment for my disregard for how she may have felt and worried for me because I had clearly fallen for Henry's tricks.

Mary sighed. "Anne. I thought what I had with the king was real. I thought that he would keep me as his one and only mistress, but he didn't. He cast me aside and went straight back to Catherine. How could he have ever loved me? If he did, he would never pursue you. Surely the fact that he dares to aim for my sister shows what little respect he had for me and the feelings I had for him."

Mary was angry. It was not directed at me. She held hatred for Henry now.

"He is a philanderer, and I do not believe he knows what true love is."

Perhaps Mary was right. Maybe it was part of his game, to lead me to believe I was head over heels so that I would give him exactly what he wanted; and then he would tire of me. Or maybe Mary was wrong, and the king did love me. We were just unlucky in the fact that we were unavailable to each other. Perhaps it was different with me, and Mary just could not understand that.

"Did he ever tell you that he loved you, Mary? Honestly during the whole time that you together did he confess any feelings other than lust?" I asked.

Mary's face dropped. She had not expected me to interrogate her. She had come here thinking that I wanted nothing to do with Henry.

"I do not ask this to wound you, sister. I ask for my peace of mind."

Mary thought for a moment. Mentally looking back through all of her time with the king. After a moment she sighed.

"No, I do not believe he did," she answered honestly keeping any emotion from her face. This is what I had expected to hear. It meant to me that he did not say it as a way to win me over. He said it to me because he truly believed he loved me.

"He tells me he loves me daily, Mary. He loves me. I truly believe that he loves me." I wiped the tears from my face. I was silly. My tears would get me nowhere. I would stay strong. I had promised myself long ago that I would never let a man get the better of me, and today would not be the day that broke me.

"The reason I left was that it was too hard to refuse him. I wanted to be with him, Mary. but I will never settle for second best."

Mary was speechless. She had no idea what to say to me. Concern was clear on her face as she looked at her younger sister, who was on the same path that she had once trod. She kissed me on the forehead before taking her seat across from me again. She took hold of my hand.

"Well. Even still, you have done what's best, sweet girl. Keep your distance." She stroked my cheek. "Even if he loves you, that does not make you safe. This is a game that you can never win, sister. You are a clever girl, and as much as this hurts now, one day you will be thankful that you stayed away. Keep a clear head and move forward with your life."

I knew she was right. I had done the best thing for myself and Henry. Even still, I wish it did not hurt as much.

"I know Mary. Which is why I am here and not at court." I reassured her.

"I am so proud of you, Anne. You truly are a much stronger woman than I ever was."

Mary stayed for a couple of days. It was refreshing to be in her company again. She was different in the sense that she had two small people to care for now and not just herself. She had lost her selfish ways, and instead everything she did now was for the benefit of her own children. She was nothing like our mother. She cared deeply for her children. She sang them to sleep at night. She hugged them throughout the day. She played games with them. I loved watching her with them. It was like she had finally found the thing she was supposed to do with her life.

I was sad to see her go, but I knew that this time we would not leave it so long before seeing each other again. I promised her that her children would know me and that one day when I had my own they would know their wonderful Aunt Mary. We hugged, and she made her way to her carriage with one last warning to stay as far from Henry as possible.

* * * * *

After a couple of weeks of being away from London, Henry began to write to me. He would write the most beautiful love letters. He wrote of how he missed me. Of how he felt incomplete without me. He begged me to return. He could not cope without me in his sights. He asked again that I become his mistress, promising that he would never take another. I would be his one mistress, and he would place no one above me. I would know in my heart that although Catherine was queen, I was the one he truly loved. Which all sounded wonderful apart from the fact that a mistress was owed nothing. Henry could promise me everything I ever wanted, and still his word could amount to nothing.

So far I had replied that I would not be his mistress. I could not do that to myself. The only way I would give myself to a man was if he were my husband. Becoming a wife was important to me, and I would not settle for any less than that. Being his mistress would ruin me, and I would not allow myself to become used goods tossed to the side and discarded when no longer required. Any children I would have by him would be bastards, and although he promised to care for them as if they were legitimate, I did not want to run the risk. If he wanted me he would have to marry me, and we both knew that he could not do that.

His replies were always so heartfelt. So understanding but also so saddened by my absence. They were sweet and loving. They showed me exactly how he felt, and it pained me to refuse him, knowing that he felt so deeply for me. The idea of hurting him made me despair. I never wanted to cause him one moment of pain. If I could give him everything, I would. He had such a kind soul that was reserved only for his closest of friends, and I was lucky enough to be able to see the man behind the king.

Henry made me feel like anything was possible. He made me second guess myself time and time again. So many times I nearly wrote to him that I conceded and would become to him whatever he wanted of me. He made me foolish. Stopped my head from thinking straight. I fought hard to keep a grasp on my will power. I must admit that I felt even more deeply for him while we were apart. First I fell in love with Henry, and then I fell in love with his words.

Surely it was impossible that he had ever spoken to another in the same way as he had me. I believed that I had his whole heart and that he truly wanted to be with me. That's one thing I never doubted. He loved me. But I do not believe that he had any idea how to love me.

I have one of his letters in the tower with me. The one that knocked me off my feet, bowled over by his unmistakable love for me. I have kept it close to my heart since the day he sent it to me. It is tucked away safely, so that whenever times had begun to get tough I may read it and know that what we had was the most real thing in the whole world. I will probably have it on the scaffold with me tucked at my breast. Henry will be with me when I pass, in one way or another.

"In turning over in my mind the contents of your last letters, I have put myself into great agony, not knowing how to interpret them, whether to my disadvantage, as you show in some places, or to my advantage, as I understand them in some others, beseeching you earnestly to let me know your whole mind expressly as to the love between us two. It is absolutely necessary for me to obtain this answer, having been for above a whole year stricken with the dart of love, and not yet sure whether I shall fail of finding a place in your heart and affection, which last point has prevented me for some time past from calling you, my mistress; because, if you only love me with an ordinary love, that name is not suitable for you, because it denotes a singular love, which is far from common. But if you please to do the office of a true loyal mistress and friend, and to give up yourself body and heart to me, who will be, and have been, your most loyal servant, (if your rigour does not forbid me) I promise you that not only the name shall be given you, but also that I will take you for my only mistress, casting off all others besides you out of my thoughts and affections, and serve you only. I beseech you to give an entire answer to this my rude letter, that I may know on what and how far I may depend. And if it does not please you to answer me in writing, appoint someplace where I may have it by word of mouth, and I will go thither with all my heart. No more, for fear of tiring you.

Written by the hand of him who
would willingly remain yours,
H. R"

This was the first letter he sent me, and after that they came every few days. Some of the things he said to me at that time I will have etched on my soul for eternity. I conjure them up in my darkest of moments seeking a small amount of comfort from knowing what truly lies within his heart — knowing that even when things are at their hardest he truly did love me. He truly loves me still.

"My heart and I surrender ourselves into your hands, beseeching you to hold us commended to your favour, and that by absence your affection to us may not be lessened."
"The longer the days are, the more distant is the sun and nevertheless hotter; so is it with our love, for by absence we are kept a distance from one another, and yet it retains its fervour, at least on my side."

It was hard not to answer him with love and hope for our future when he spoke in the way he did. He was so gentle and sweet with my love. He never forced the way he felt on me but instead worried that I had lost the feelings that were so deeply ingrained now on my heart and soul. How could I ever lose the way I felt when he spoke in such a way? If anything, by the moment my love grew until it was almost too much to bear. With each of his letters I could feel as my heart got bigger to accommodate the new emotions.

I allowed myself to bask in his words and then allowed myself to cry for a love that would never belong to me. With every part of my heart that grew, a worry grew deeper within me. A fear that the more Henry loved me, the less chance I had of making it out of this without an immeasurable amount of pain. How could so much love also bring with it so much anguish? For every smile I had for Henry there were the same number of tears for our situation. Why could I not fall in love with a man I was allowed to have, for once?

This was so quick. I had gone from distaste to love within the briefest of moments. I had to allow myself to think seriously. I needed to decide for sure what all of this meant. Was this true love, or was this something that would pass should I let it sit long enough? Did people really fall in love so quickly? In an instant? Was I swept up in Henry's love for me and nothing more? Perhaps I had allowed Henry's feelings to reflect on myself. This had all happened so quickly. I had gone from seeing him as someone to escape from to someone I wanted to run to within a number of days.

Henry was a very persuasive man. Was it possible that he had simply won me over? Even as I tried to justify my emotions, I knew in my soul that I was wrong. This was not something that would pass. This was something that would torment me for the rest of my life. But what could be done about that?

If I allowed myself to be Henry's mistress, then perhaps I would have been happy. Maybe I would have had my moment with such a man and then allow myself to move on. If I gave him what he wanted, then surely it would be an acceptable situation for both of us. Oh, but how my friends would look down at me, how Margery would judge me for allowing myself to be conquered. How disappointed George would be that I followed the same path as our sister. I believe Tom would have scarcely been able to look at me in the same way. To know that I had sold my body to the king. The one thing that I said I would never do.

Was it worth all of the judgement if it meant that I could be happy? Could I face them down with my obvious joy at being with the man I loved? I had no idea, and I was getting nowhere. Being at Hever was not helping me to make a decision, and I knew deep down there was only one answer. No matter how much I loved him I had to put myself and my life first.

I had sent him one last letter. In it I had wished to tell him that of course I loved him and I wanted to be with him as much as he wanted to be with me, but fate had made that impossible. This would be the last letter I would send to Henry, and with a heavy heart, I sent it to Greenwich. I would make no more replies to anything he sent to me from that moment onwards. I could not keep playing at this game where my heart was on the line. It was too painful to continue our words of love and knowing that they would never amount to anything.

"My dearest sovereign lord.

I write to you in thanks for the words that have up until this point made my heart leap for joy at the love that you have heaped upon me. I wish to in some way convey the deep affection that I myself have for Your Majesty, and have chosen to write you this letter in reply to tell you that I do indeed love you with all my heart. I am not so good with words as His Majesty but wish for you to know that you are forever in my heart.

I long to be with you as you long to be with me, but unfortunately many obstacles seek to stand in our way. As I have told you before no matter the content of my heart I cannot consent to be with you. There is too much against us. I hope you know that if things were at all different then I would find myself married and happy with you in an instant. Unfortunately it cannot be, and this will be the last correspondence you receive on the matter. It has become too painful for me, and I need time to heal.

> Always in my heart and in my
> thoughts.
> Anne Boleyn"

With a heavy heart and a pain in my chest I sent this letter on to Greenwich. I hated ending things with Henry, but I had to face the fact that it was never going to work.

* * * * *

I had been back at Hever a little while when George and Margery had come together to visit me. I had missed them both so much. It was almost unbearable being away from George and I had been a little annoyed that it had taken him so long to come and see me. He was too busy at court trying to stay in favour and advance his own position. Something told me that this had been a little easier since the king's affection for me had begun.

It was lovely — the perfect day. We walked in the sun and drank wine. We spoke of court and George's annoying wife, who still bothered him to no end. Margery told me that she had been bored at court without me and that there were absolutely no new suitors for her to ogle. They told me that Henry's temper had only grown worse since I had left and it was beginning to put a bit of strain on the court. There had been a lot of chatter about my reason for leaving court so suddenly. Most people had heard that the king was attempting to court me and had expected me to become his mistress sooner rather than later and they were confused as to why I had not jumped at his offer.

Now everybody could sense the king's unhappiness and have wondered what effect I must have had on him for him to pine for me in such away. They dug up old closed wounds by recirculating my failed attempt to marry Percy, laughing at me for my obvious naivety in matters of marriage. They also spoke of my relationship with Thomas and some had expressed that they felt I was more likely to become his mistress than the king's. They had seen us together and seen how he romanced me. They spoke of how I was his muse and how he wrote poems confessing his admiring of myself and my beauty.

They knew little about the complex relationships that one has with certain people. If they had looked closer they would see that although Tom may feel for me, we were great friends. We were able to get beyond the ridiculous notion that you cannot be around the opposite sex without wanting to tear each other's clothes off. I turned my nose up. They were all at their happiest when they had someone or something to gossip about and thankfully I was away from court and would not have to face their questioning eyes.

Unlike Mary I was able to avoid the whispers as I passed. I did not have to look on as they spoke closely to each other's ears. Covering their mouths, as if that meant I had no idea that they were talking about me. I now understood how Mary felt back in France. Something was thrilling about being the name on everyone's lips. I wish that they were saying better things, but it felt good to know that my life and what I was doing consumed them daily.

George and Margery had thus far been excellent at defending me, and I was sure that they would never let any untruths be told. Margery would root out the gossipers in the queen's chambers and hush them. She would laugh at them. Explaining that they had no clue as to what was going on. George took charge of the male gossipers. He had told them that I was away at Hever to rest and that they should know better than to gossip like a bunch of women with nothing better to do.

George was not here simply to visit his favourite sister. Margery had come to be a friend. She was here and ready to support me the moment George confessed his news. I had wondered at first why they had come together. The king had asked George to visit me and, in typical fashion, George was awful at hiding a thing. He was always very transparent, at least to me he was, and it was obvious that he had had something to say from the very moment he had entered the castle.

By the afternoon I could take no more of his timidity. It was tiring as he bit his lip, again and again, trying to hold back from giving the game away too soon. Even Margery seemed to try and prompt him from time to time. I imagine he would have been very mad if she had spoken up, but she was getting restless. He held that twinkle in his eye. The one that told me whatever he had to say, he was very happy about. He was such a child at times, and I found myself bored with his humour on that day.

"Come along, Brother. What is the real reason for your visit?" I had asked. Eyebrows raised and arms crossed in front of me. I wanted an answer now. We had done enough of avoiding the real reason he was here.

"I wished to see my sister." George lied. It was so obvious that he was lying as his eyes lit up, and his mouth turned up in a grin.

"I can see right through you, George. You never were a good liar." I said. "Is it about Henry?"

George made no move to speak. It took all of his might to keep from spilling the beans. I grew tired very quickly and wished for him to get it over with. My temper was shorter these days especially as I relied on other people to know what was happening while I was away from court. After a while, Hever had become a little isolated with only my mother for conversation.

"Oh for heaven's sake, George. Tell the woman!" Margery admonished him. She too had grown impatient waiting for him to spit it out.

George laughed and then sighed before beginning his story. "You have driven him mad Anne. He does nothing but speak of you. He curses you for leaving. Then he won't shut up about your beauty. It is really rather sickening."

Even though I already knew how the king felt about me it was always nice to hear of the effect I had on him. To know that the thought of me took up so much of his time. That while he was busy running a country he was consumed by the idea of me. It made my stomach flip at the thought of his mind constantly being on me.

"Yes, and what about it George? I already know how the king feels." I spoke barely able to keep the smile from my face.

"He has sent me to bring you back to court," George said. He was smiling as well, now grinning like a child who has just been overloaded with sugar.

"That is impossible, George." I waved him off. "I am staying at Hever."

The king had apparently given up on writing now and was delivering the same message but this time hoping that my brother was able to convince me.

"Just listen to what George has to say, Anne." Margery took my hand.

"Anne, there is something you should know..." George began. "The king no longer talks of making you his mistress."

"Oh?" I had asked.

I should have felt instant relief, but instead I felt fear. If the king no longer wanted me as his mistress did that mean that he had finally grown tired of my refusal? I know that I would have never become his mistress, but I did not want to lose his love, either. I could not stand the thought of losing his love. To be without him was to live in constant darkness. To know that he no longer wanted me was to become unwanted and unattractive. Even if our love was at a distance, at least it existed. It felt like it was the one thing that made the world turn, and without it my world would turn no longer.

George was silent for a long while, which only added to my anxiety. But for some reason, he was smiling at me. He looked like someone who held the answers to everything in his hand, as if he could wipe away the world's problems with the secret he knew. I understood that George never wanted me to become involved with Henry, but I had thought he'd be more supportive at a time like this.

"Anne, the king no longer wishes you to be his mistress..." George repeated. He took a deep breath. Steadying himself before revealing the next part. "He wishes you to be his wife."

Time stopped. My breath caught in my throat. I blinked slowly thinking that perhaps this was some strange dream and at any moment I would awaken in my bed at Hever, laughing at the ridiculousness of the fantasy. I did not move to answer George. I stared at him wide-eyed, mouth hanging open. My hands started to shake as the panic set into my body gently.

How could Henry possibly want to marry me? I know that I had told him that that was the only way I would ever be with him, but it was ridiculous. He couldn't marry me.

He has a wife of over 20 years. He has a child and a country. He could not just choose to marry another. I wanted to know exactly what George meant, but at the same time I could not form a sentence. Instead I stood and made my way to the garden. I sat on the edge of the estate, staring off into the blue sky wondering how I had ever gotten to this moment.

In an instant, Margery was behind me. She knelt in front of where I sat and took my hands. George followed closely behind. He was confused at my reaction. I believe that he had expected me to jump for joy as the truth was revealed. Instead my instant reaction was a mixture. On the one hand this was everything I had ever wanted and more, but on the other it was not nearly as simple as it sounded.

"Anne. how do you feel?" Margery asked, worry clear on her face.

I took a breath allowing my mind to become clear. I had to know the details. I had to make sense of this before giving any sort of answer. There was only one answer, and I had already begun to feel it forming on my lips. Ready for the moment I could use it and finally seal the love between Henry and me.

"I feel confused," I answered honestly. "George can you explain it to me? From the start?"

I turned to my brother who stood a little way off looking into the surrounding trees.
He walked nearer, and Margery left us alone for a moment allowing George to relay to me everything that had happened since I left for Hever.

"The king believes that his marriage to Catherine is false," George started.

I began to speak, but George hushed me.

"Hear me out first," he said before continuing. "The king believes that as Catherine was his brother's widow when they married, they went against God in their union. He believes that Catherine and Arthur's marriage was indeed a true one and that is the reason he has been unable to sire a son. The king has come across a passage from Leviticus that says if a man takes his brother's wife they will be childless. He is utterly convinced that he is being punished for their union."

"But George, the Pope gave a dispensation. Catherine and Arthur never consummated." I said as my head swam with all of the new information laid upon me.

"You're right. But the king believes that the Pope was misinformed and that the marriage was consummated all of those years ago. He believes that Catherine has been lying throughout their marriage and can see no other reason why all of their male children have never lived."

I had to take a breath. This was a lot of information to understand. If Catherine had consummated her marriage to Arthur, then she should have never been allowed to marry Henry in the first place, which would mean that their whole marriage had been illegitimate. Did this mean that the king wanted to put Catherine aside and marry a true wife. so that he could have male heirs through a legitimate line? It is sad to admit that a part of me began to grow hopeful. That as Catherine's honesty was denied, I began to feel a hope inside of me. I still needed more than this. This was all well and good, but until the marriage was proven to be false, it meant that Henry was not free to marry.

"So what does this mean for me, George?" I asked. This was a lot of information, and I had begun to feel a headache creeping in.

"Henry wishes to marry you, Anne, plain and simple. He believes that this will be a quick matter and the second that his marriage is pronounced false he will take you as his wife."

I smiled as tears began to fill my eyes. I had never imagined it possible. I had thought that Henry and I were destined to love each other from afar. But he had found a way. He had been looking for a way to make me his wife.

He wanted our love to be seen in the eyes of the whole country, and he would remove a queen from her throne to do it. This was yet another dangerous game. The difference this time was that the reward was worth the risk. I would have Henry at the end of it, and for him I would be willing to fight this battle by his side.

"If you accept, sister, you will be Queen of England." George wiped my tears away with his thumb.

I had never dreamed to be queen. It was never anything that had even crossed my mind. I had forgotten for a moment that Henry was king and should I have chosen to be with him, then I would not just be marrying a man but a country. Surprisingly this was not something I instantly leaped at. If anything, I had seen how a queen had been treated. How hard their lives could be, and I did not know if I was up to the task.

It would be a great responsibility to become someone that a whole country of people looked to. I would be on show for everyone to see and I would be openly taking Catherine's place. If Henry could happily displace Catherine for me after such a long marriage then what did that say for his love? Was my love for Henry worth all of the heartache it would cause? I knew it was. It was different with me. He loved me more than he had Catherine. Which, although it is a sad fact, it is indeed the truth and I knew that.

I knew that I had been offered a life-changing question and that all I had to do to get the man I so desperately wanted was to say yes. I know I should have been more level headed. I should have taken time to weigh my choices, but I had already spent so much time running from Henry that all I wanted to do was run to him. It was not something I had to consider. Call that naïve or foolish. Call me a silly girl who lost her mind for the love of a man. You would be right. Still if I could rewrite the past and change my answer I would still say yes again.

If I wanted Henry, I would have to take the whole package, and if this were true and he was willing to turn everything we knew upside down to have me, then I could take the responsibility of becoming queen. I loved him, and that is all I needed to know. I did not need convincing of one way or the other because the answer was always obvious. I always knew that if given the opportunity I would be with him in an instant. I was reminded that God had a plan for us and clearly God wished me to be with Henry. I would follow His lead above anyone else's.

George looked at me expectantly. He was waiting for me to answer him one way or the other. I believe he already knew what I was going to say. He could see inside my heart when no one else could. He looked at me now, pride obvious on his face. He had such a big heart, especially for me. We turned as we could hear footsteps coming towards us. Walking from the house was my mother and Margery. She had assumed that we had been left long enough for George to have explained the situation.

"Anne, George. Is it true?" Mother asked.

She was smiling, which meant that Margery had filled in the gaps. She was doing all that she could not to giggle with joy. She was a pathetic leech who had heard my news and instantly realised what it would mean to her.

"Will I be the Queen's Mother?"

I took a moment. George simply shook his head at a loss for words at our greedy mother. She was lucky that I did not cut her off then and there, but it is funny just how much one will tolerate in the name of family. She may have been a heartless witch, but I loved her. I could not help it as much as I despised her wickedness and her lack of any feeling whatsoever. She was my mother, and I could not help but hold her in my heart.

"Slow down, Mother." George chuckled. "Anne is yet to decide."

My mother looked so disappointed. As if she could not understand how her children let her down so easily. The answer was obvious, and she could not grasp the reason for my hesitation.

I needed to know more before I admitted the truth. That no matter the details, I was in. They could tell me now that I would have to lose an arm and I would agree.

"George. You need to explain how this would work?" I asked.

"Anne, are you seriously considering this?" Margery asked, shock clear on her face. "I had thought you were loyal to Catherine."

I noticed Margery properly for the first time. I had not even considered her opinion. The truth was that yes, I was loyal to Catherine, but I was more loyal to myself and my needs.

"I was Marge," I answered. "But I love him." I looked into her eyes hoping to make myself clear. I hoped that she could see the longing in my eyes.

"And it's enough to turn against everything you know? To steal someone's husband and ruin a woman?" Margery asked, judgement clear in her voice.

She made me feel a stab of guilt for my answer but even as I knew what it meant, and I did feel sorry for Catherine, that did not change it. I was so used to bowing to everybody else's will that I had never done a singular thing that was completely for me. It was time I started to put myself first.

"Yes," I answered looking down.

I expected her to admonish me. To tell me that I was selfish and that she wanted no part of this. I thought she would turn from me. Unable to stand by me as I agreed to help remove our queen from her throne.

"Then, I am with you." She smiled. "I support whatever decision you make."

I breathed a sigh of relief. I hadn't wanted to do this without her. I would have still gone ahead, but it would have been a rough journey if I did not have Marge by my side. We turned to George so that he could tell us what we needed to know.

"If you agree to be his wife, then I am to bring you back to London with me."

I did not answer straight away. This would be the most life-changing decision I had ever made, and I needed to be sure before I answered. I smiled to myself thinking of what it would be like to be with Henry every single day. How happy it would make me be able to sleep in his bed or dine in his room without feeling guilty because I would be his wife, instead of Catherine. We would not be committing any sin against her because she would no longer be married to him. We would be joined forever in the eyes of God, and I could think of not a single thing that I wanted more than that.

"Take me to him George," I said simply.

And with that, I had just made the decision that would prove to be the making and breaking of me. I felt lighter somehow. Like things finally made sense to me. Like I had decided on something that would make everything all right. What could possibly be wrong with two people who loved each other as much as we did being together? This was the right thing to do. I had not a single doubt in my mind. I was going to marry the man I loved, and that made me the happiest woman in the world.

I decided that I would send Henry a small gift in answer. I had bought him something a little while ago and was saving it for when the time was right. It was a small beautiful ship. It contained within it a diamond and on end hung a small damsel who was tossed about as the boat sailed on the rough seas. I knew that Henry would understand this as my acceptance. I was showing him that I was willing to take a risk for our love and that I was laying my heart and life in his hands knowing that he would protect me from any harm that may come my way. I was showing him that I trusted him and was leaving our fate to his capable hands. I knew that I had made the right decision and I wanted Henry to know that too. As I sent him the gift my heart felt lighter, knowing that I had chosen to follow a path of happiness.

Henry replied within days of receiving the gift with a letter. He not only thanked me for my gift but also made his apologies for asking that I be his mistress as he held me in higher regard than that. He also had taken the meaning of my present in the exact way that I had meant it. He truly understood me. This was the final piece slotting into place. He truly loved me for me.

"FOR a present so beautiful that nothing could be more so (considering the whole of it), I thank you most cordially, not only on account of the fine diamond and the ship in which the solitary damsel is tossed about, but chiefly for the fine interpretation and the too humble submission which your goodness hath used towards me in this case; for I think it would be very difficult for me to find an occasion to deserve it, if I were not assisted by your great humanity and favour, which I have always sought to seek, and will seek to preserve by all the kindness in my power, in which my hope has placed its unchangeable intention, which says, Aut illic, aut nullibi*. The demonstrations of your affection are such, the beautiful mottoes of the letter so cordially expressed, that they oblige me forever to honour, love, and serve you sincerely, beseeching you to continue in the same firm and constant purpose, assuring you that, on my part, I will surpass it rather than make it reciprocal, if loyalty of heart and a desire to please you can accomplish this. I beg, also, if at any time before this I have in any way offended you, that you would give me the same absolution that you ask, assuring you, that henceforward my heart shall be dedicated to you alone. I wish my person were so too. God can do it, if He pleases, to whom I pray every day for that end, hoping that at length my prayers will be heard. I wish the time may be short, but I shall think it long till we see one another. Written by the hand of that secretary, who in heart, body, and will, is,

Your loyal and most assured
Servant
H. R"

*"Either there or nowhere"

Once I had received his letter and seen with my own eyes his intentions, I could not wait to make my way to court. I was beyond eager to begin my new life beside the man I loved.

CHAPTER TEN

It was the spring of 1527 when I finally made my return to court. I had been unable to wait for my return to Greenwich and had yet to hear from Henry. I looked forward to having him explain to me exactly how he planned to make me his wife. To hear it directly from his lips. There was still a small part of me that could not believe what was happening and until I heard it from Henry I do not think I could completely believe it. Whatever we did from this moment onwards would go down in history. This event was monumental, and I knew that I was a part of something wonderful.

Everyone at court knew that something was happening but had no idea what it was. There was a buzz as a new idea came into play, and whispers had begun to try and decipher what that was. Catherine had heard that Henry was convinced that their marriage was void and he was looking for a way to remove her. Of course in typical Catherine style she had begun to dig in her heels. She claimed that this would pass. She knew that I was part of his reason for wanting to separate and had said that I was nothing more than another of his playthings and his infatuation would pass. How wrong she was. She did not worry in the early days because she believed it would blow over like it had done previously when Henry had had a mistress. She was wrong. I was no mistress, and Henry wanted me for more than my body. I think Catherine wildly underestimated us in the beginning. Which is why for a long while she did not bother putting up much of a fight. She continued as queen with no worry for the safety of her station. She would realise soon enough that life was about to change for her drastically. It was about to change for everyone in more ways than one.

* * * * *

When I arrived in Greenwich, my future husband waited to greet me. He was a sight for sore eyes as I took all of him in. If it was at all possible he was even more handsome than the last time I had seen him. He stood so tall and broad. His eyes gleamed, and he smiled with such joy that my heart left my chest altogether and floated towards him. He walked over to my horse and lifted me down. Kissing me as he did. He held me with no words. He just kept his arms around me, and I buried my head in his chest breathing in the sweet scent of him and somehow feeling safer than I ever had. It was as if I were whole again as he held me in his arms.

Tears filled my eyes as our time apart suddenly felt so long. We did not need to speak. Words were useless between us. We conveyed all that we needed to by holding each other. How I had missed being in his arms. I realised in this moment exactly how much I had hated his absence. It was terrible being without him, and it was now that I was with him again that I realised just how terrible it truly was. In a way he was always with me in letters and my thoughts, but nothing compared to actually standing before him. Now that we were together again, I realised just how much I needed him.

I also knew in that instant that I had made the right decision. Of course I wanted to marry him. He was everything to me, and I would fight with everything I had to make sure that we would be together. It was more than desire or simple fancy. It was a deep-seated need to be with him, and now that we were together he soothed away the part of me that ever had any doubts.

I suddenly hated that there were others around; it felt as if too many faces watched our every move. Silently he took my hand and led me inside. Through his privy chambers and into his office. There were men gathering and waiting for a moment with the king, but Henry wanted none of it.

"For heaven's sake will you all get out." Henry boomed. The command in his voice thrilled me. There was something about the way he took control, and everyone instantly stopped what they were doing and listened. It made my need for him even stronger. He was such a strong man. So sure of himself. So confident. There was an attractiveness to a man in complete control.

Henry slammed the doors behind him and pulled me over to his desk lifting me on top of it and kissing me with such passion. like with his kiss he wanted to make up for all the time we had been apart. It felt wonderful, all of the hunger we had held back for the past year finally coming into the light. I realised now what I had been missing. To be kissed by him was the most exquisite thing in the world. In his movements he told me all that i needed to know about how much he loved me. He held my head gently into him and gave me feather light kisses all over my body. His hands searched the whole of me touching places no man had even touched before.

"God, how I've missed you, Anne." he breathed in my ear.

It was alluring. His voice quiet in my ear. His breath all over me. I could have cried for how happy I was at this moment. The despair of the past year melted away as I realised that all of our waiting, all of my heartbreak had been for this moment, when he was mine. I could not answer. I was pinned to this moment. Struck breathless and wanting him so badly it hurt. We stayed like this for a while. Kissing and pulling each other close. It was like no matter how much I pulled him to me I could not get him close enough. Like there was constantly too much space between us and I wanted all of him to be touching all of me.

I allowed myself to be lost in a moment of pleasure to forget myself and allow us to continue in a whirling mess of kissing and touching. Henry made to undo his hose, and

I was suddenly sent hurtling back towards reality. "Henry we cannot." I breathed "Not until we are married." I backed away. As much as I wanted to allow him to take the whole of me I could not. If I were to get pregnant before we were married then my child would be a bastard. It was no good creating an heir if he was to be illegitimate.

He looked saddened. Annoyed even. I understood. I wanted him as much as he wanted me. I finally understood what it meant to need someone physically. To yearn for that connection. I now knew that being able to touch him and have the whole of him was as important as any of the emotional stuff. However, I had come this far, and I would not give myself up. Not now. Not when everything I wanted hung in the balance. I would fight through this, and if Henry truly wanted me he would do the same. Silence filled the room for a moment as I worried that Henry would not understand. But I did not have enough faith in him. After a moment Henry breathed a sigh, then raised his hands above his head in defeat.

"You are right my love. Of course you are." he touched my cheek. "I am sorry, I got carried away."

As he spoke, his annoyance of himself was clear on his face. He knew as much as I did how important it was to wait until the right time. He wanted a legitimate child as much as I did. He knew he would never get that from Catherine, so I was his only hope now. He too did not want to ruin the chances of creating an heir.

"Soon enough we shall be married my love, and then we can be with each other as much as we want." I ran my hand through his hair feeling its softness with my fingers. I marvelled at just how wonderful he was. How lucky I was to have this man. So understanding. So loving. He was perfect in every way.

"I love you, Harry," I said simply, for the first time using his preferred name.

"I like how that sounds." He chuckled. "And I love you, Anne." he pulled me off of the table taking my hand in his. Before I knew it, he was leading me from the room again.

"Come, let's eat. There is a lot to discuss."

Henry and I dined in his room. We were alone in our private place, happy on our own without prying eyes watching us. We sat for a long time just looking at each other. It was almost as if we believed that if we looked away for too long the other would completely disappear again. We had spent too much time apart, and we would make the most of every moment from now onward. I drank him in. I do not believe that I could have looked away if I wanted too. He was so pleasing to me. He was everything I had ever wanted or needed in the shape of a man. I did not want to move my eyes.

The more I looked at him, the more it confirmed that I had made the best decision. That I had somehow unlocked my future happiness and that fate had set me in the right direction. He looked back so lovingly. Not in the way he had looked at other ladies, the ones he wanted to sleep with. He looked at me like I was everything to him. He seemed to worship me with his eyes, and it felt good. The best thing that I can say is that it felt right — more right and real than anything else in this world.

"I suppose you would like to know how I intend to marry you, my love," Henry asked after a while. "Were you shocked when I sent George to you?"

"It was a surprise, I will admit."

I blushed under his gaze. He made me nervous somehow. The good kind of nervous that filled my stomach with butterflies and made my pulse quicken.

"A happy one?" he asked, beaming from ear to ear.

"The happiest," I chuckled as I took his hand in mine and kissed it. He truly made my heart sing. Every moment with him was a blessing.

"Good," he laughed. Then he began to explain everything to me.

"Very soon an ecclesiastical court shall meet, and they will decide on the validity of my current marriage."

He had already started making arrangements to divorce Catherine. He really was very serious about his intentions.

"I hope that they find a cause for divorce."

"And is that something you truly believe should happen, Harry?" I asked.

I hated the fact that I still held some doubt in my mind, but this was a big step. It was not something to be considered lightly, and I needed to ensure that he was happy with his choices.

Henry looked down at the table. Tears began to form in his eyes.

"It is important to me my love. I am pained by the idea that I have lived against God for all of these years."

The emotion was plain to see. It was obvious that this was something he had thought about a lot. He clearly believed every word of what he said, and this was in no way an excuse to remove Catherine and replace her with me. It hurt him to believe that he had gone against God.

"I should have never married her, Anne. What if I have damned my soul?" he cried.

He was very emotional about the situation. His relationship with God was the most important thing to him. The idea that God would have turned from him scared him. Clearly he was truly worried about the effect his marriage would have on his soul.

I was by his side in an instant. I held his head against my chest, wishing to protect him from the pain he was inflicting on himself. I hated to see him so down. If I could soothe away all of his pain, then I would. He was such a kind soul. He did not deserve one ounce of pain.

"Hush now, my love. You are putting it right, now, and that is all that matters." I stroked his hair. "God, forgives. He will forgive you. I promise." I kissed his head, and Henry pulled me onto his lap kissing me gently as he did.

"What did I do to deserve you?" he asked.

He looked at me with so much love that I was hot under his gaze. The lust in his eyes made me feel as if I was on fire. I burned at his touch. Feeling like the slightest lingering and I would burst into flames. My blood seemed to heat as he looked into my eyes, and I felt like I could not move even if I wanted to. He kept me there with just a look.

"Ahh, I know," he continued. "God has sent you to me. Like an Angel to set me on the right path."

I kissed him, for the first time realising that now I could do this as much as I wanted. I could hold him and kiss him and touch him whenever I wanted to. He was mine, and I was his.

That night I stayed in Henry's bed. I slept soundly for the first time in months as I lay my head on top of his chest. Listening to his gentle breath as he slept soundly. I have never felt more content than that night lying in his arms. If I had died at that very moment I would have been happy. Carried off gently into the next world as my love lay beneath me. This was the first time I had been in his bed. Having for so long refused his advances, but this felt right. He never once tried to convince me to lay with him. He held me in his arms and kissed my worries away.

CHAPTER ELEVEN

I cannot say that we got off to the easiest start. Henry and I were perfectly happy. Happier than either of us had ever been. We spent every moment we could with each other. I joined him on hunts or royal visits. He would show me off to all of the important men in England introducing me as the love of his life. They were all respectful. No matter their opinion on Catherine's situation, they were loyal to their king and trusted that he would make the right decision.

We would picnic together in the sunshine or take long walks in the beautiful gardens. Often we would meet for a little bit of time alone in our special spot.

Sometimes I would be seated in my room and would hear his gentle song outside of my window. I would lean out, and he would be waiting for me. Grin on his face, and a rose in hand. I would run down to him, eager to be alone.

When we dined, we dined together. Either in his privy chamber or side by side with the rest of the court. Catherine still took her position of queen sitting at Henry's side, but I would be on the other side. I would not yet have a throne and I was lower than the two of them but I had to focus on the fact that one day the seat where Catherine sat so comfortably would become mine and she would not look so proud when that happened.

She would do whatever she could to annoy me. Or at least it seemed that way as she would lean over and hold Henry's hand or lightly touch his arm or cheek. She would kiss his hand and run her fingers through his hair. All the while I looked on, enviously wishing that it was I who sat beside him. I wished that it was my fingers running through his hair or my lips that touched his fingers so lightly. Henry would tell me to ignore her. She was doing all of these things while she still could and I was the one he was longing to touch. He told me that whenever he was with her, he was busy imagining the day he could wed me and be rid of her. Let her get her fill for now knowing that soon enough she would be out of sight.

Catherine had begun to annoy me during this time. She would do her best to spend as much time with Henry as possible. She'd turn up in his chambers requesting to spend time with her husband making a point of calling him "my love," or "my dear husband," staring me down all the while. Apart from the odd distasteful look she was almost too kind to me, and her sweetness turned my stomach. She would ask after me and comment on my beauty. She liked to talk of how well "mistress Boleyn" looked.

Everyone had to see that she was rising above it and being the better person. All the while she got pleasure out of watching me bow. She loved the fact that she was still above me and that I had little choice but to pay her the respect deserved. She ensured I knew my place and would always ask me about the health of "her" husband. It was all I could do to tell her that he no longer belonged to her. He was mine now, and she should give up now. It was a pathetic play for control on her part, but it annoyed me no end. She had had her time with him and lost him. It was my time now.

Henry begged her to make it easy for him. He explained his reasoning to her in as many ways as were possible. He told her that it was best for both of their souls to move on. He even offered to let her retire to a nunnery knowing how important her relationship with God was and hoping to appeal to her Catholic side. She would not budge, and if it were not for her stubbornness, I do not believe it would have taken nearly as long for us to achieve our goal. She kept on chattering about how "she and Henry were married in the eyes of God." and she was his "one true and loyal wife." I kept thinking that if she were so loyal then she would step aside. If she truly loved him then she should let him go and be happy. She would have made it easier on herself as well as on Henry and me.

I could never understand why she put herself through so much heartache, especially when she lost in the end. Old and alone. Kept away from court and the husband she fought so hard to keep. She was left without kindness in this world, all because she did not know when to surrender. Her problem was her sense of entitlement. She believed that she was chosen to be queen and she would fight with all of her might to stop anyone from diverting God's plan. In the end it was all for nothing. She fought so bitterly and achieved nothing at all. Small victories that were useless when it came down to it. To me at this point Catherine was just another obstacle to deal with.

* * * * *

The ecclesiastical court was all but useless. After many discussions back and forth, they decided that they were not qualified to make such a monumental decision. We did have one ally, and that was Cardinal Wolsey. Or so he appeared to be. He fought for Henry's case. I believe that he wanted this dealt with efficiently and easily. If he could be the one to bring about the King's wishes then he would forever be safe as the king's advisor. He would do anything to stay in the king's good graces, and Henry had tasked him with bringing about what he wanted.

I did not like the man much myself, but if he could accomplish what both of us wanted, then I would not stand in his way. He was a small man in height but round in size. As he walked it was his large stomach that you saw first. He often cradled it as if he was a woman full with child rather than a man who had gorged on too much food and wine over the years. He had beady little eyes that appeared always to be concocting some sort of plot as they followed the king wherever he moved. His hair was a grey colour to

152

show his years, and his face was like that of a dog. It was scrunched up and wrinkled. He was the type of man that never looked happy.

If his size and appearance were not enough to make him recognisable, then one would know it was he by his cardinal's vestment. He was always clad in red to show off his position within the church. I always believed that he had furthered himself in the church for power and wealth rather than religious belief. It always seemed that God would guide him in whichever direction served him best at the time. Wolsey only cared for one man, and that was himself. Still, if he was going to fight in our corner then I was happy to have him for now.

Catherine was not short of her backers. Being as pious as she was meant she had made many friends within the Catholic church. Not only that but she held the respect of many, due to her position as queen. One does not manage to stay queen for twenty years without picking up a lot of loyalty. The people truly loved her and wanted to see her restored to her proper position. Catherine's main advocate was a man named Bishop John Fisher. This man would truly prove to be a thorn in my side as he fought tooth and nail for Catherine's cause. He would never back down, and he fought Henry all the way to prove that their marriage was a good and true one. Many times Henry threatened in private to do away with him. To find some way to be rid of him even if that meant trumping up charges and having him executed. Fisher was so sure of himself. He never doubted for one moment that he was following God's plan.

He must have worked day and night preparing his counter arguments, and a few times I believe he caught Henry off guard. He was such a frail man. Thin and old. He was the opposite of Wolsey. Where Wolsey overindulged, Fisher appeared to have never had any enjoyment in his life. He was so devoted to serving God that it had left him little time for anything else. He was not a young man and

clearly was very weary, but still he did not let anything
knock him down. He was so loyal to the queen that he
would fight her cause to the death.

Fisher and his chums had begun to refer to me as "the
king's whore." a name which unfortunately would become
one that stayed with me for the rest of my life. The label
that they put on me would be a permanent one, and years
later there would still be people who believed that I was
nothing better than a whore. It hurt me at first, but in these
situations one must develop a thicker skin. They would
blame me for Henry's head-turning saying that I had lured
him into my bed and away from his true wife. If only they
knew just how wrong they were.

They argued that Henry did not truly believe that his
marriage was void. He wanted to put Catherine to the side
so that he could fulfil his lustful desires. They argued that
he was bewitched by me and had lost all sense, and that he
was following my lead blindly. So our matter would not be
made as easily as we had hoped. Due to a lack of decision
the case would be sent to Rome so that it could be decided
there. Now all Henry and I had to do was wait. He was
sure that the Pope would find in our favour once his case
had been put to him.

* * * * *

It would be hard going for a long while. All anybody
could talk about was "the king's great matter." It was on
the tip of everyone's tongues as whispers circulated the
court. At first, everyone stood on tenterhooks waiting for it
to blow over. I do not think that anyone believed that Henry
would actually go through with it. People believed that
after the ecclesiastical court had failed Henry would grow
bored and move on with his life. They were all waiting for
me to be thrown away just like my sister had been. I knew
they were wrong. Henry worshipped me. It was clear in the

154

way he behaved. He treated me so well in the beginning. Tending to my every need and ensuring that I wanted for absolutely nothing. I believed him when he said that he would see this through to its completion. He did not care how long it took. He would marry me one day, even if he had to execute the whole of his court to do it.

* * * * *

The relationship between Catherine, Henry and me became strained very quickly. I felt like the third person in a marriage as they continued with their royal duties. Henry had to appear to the outside world like he was really trying to make an effort at his relationship with her. But it did not feel good to watch him fall all over her in public and treat her in almost exactly the same way as he had before all of this began. For a long while I felt like I was still second best. Like I was the bit on the side. Only I was not. Henry and I did indeed share a bed from time to time, but we both still knew that our relationship could go no further until we were married. We could not prove that to anyone, but our closest friends knew that we had yet to consummate our relationship.

Every now and then he would even share Catherine's bed and although he explained that it was for appearance sake only, I was just about ready to burst with rage. How could he love me so much and still lay with another? Even the thought of another man was dreadful to me. I saw only him and could never imagine another. I had hoped that he would pay me the same respect and lay with no one else. Catherine knew that I hated the idea of the two of them together and she took every night she spent with him as a victory.

I was walking through the halls one morning after leaving mass, and Catherine just so happened to be coming in the opposite direction. Of course I bowed to her and made sure that I was as cordial as possible. After all, this was not her fault, or that is what I had to keep telling myself. She had decided that today she would speak to me. I was in no mood for it. The months were dragging, and Henry and I were still no closer to our desired end. Plus Catherine was looking extra smug on that day, and I could barely stand to look at her.

"Ahh Mistress Boleyn," Catherine spoke her voice level as always betraying none of the hate she must have held.

"Your Highness," I said through gritted teeth.

"How lovely to see you this morning. You look wonderful dear," she began a small smile creeping onto her face. "I am exhausted." she feigned a yawn.

"I could never tell, ma'am." I made a small curtsey. If she was to play nice with me, then I could return the favour.

"Well, you see, I did not get much sleep last night." she laughed.

"I am sorry to hear that Your Majesty," I said.

"Oh, it was for a good reason." she smiled. "Henry paid me a visit late last night."

I had had enough at this point. She was playing a game, and she knew exactly how to get to me. Although the idea of Henry sharing a bed with her sickened me to my core I would never allow Catherine to get the better of me. It was a battle of wills, and I would never allow myself to be beaten.

"Well I suppose you had better make the most of it while it lasts." I smiled too sweetly. "Soon enough, he will no longer be obligated to visit you." Then I bowed again and made my way around her followed by Marge and Elizabeth who could barely contain their humour.

I was fuming. His sleeping with Catherine would have to be put to a stop. It was bad enough that I was kept on the outside unable to be fully with the man I loved but to have to watch him romance another as well? I would not stand for it. I hoped that Catherine enjoyed her night with Henry because it would be the last time she shared her bed with him. I told Marge and Liz to leave me, and I made my way to Henry's privy chambers. He was in a private meeting with Wolsey and Brandon, but I couldn't care less at this point. I was his betrothed, and he would have to spare a moment for me. I walked in barely giving Henry's groom chance to announce me. When Henry saw me his face lit up in a smile.

Henry stood as I entered and strode over to me, taking both of my hands in his. "My love." he kissed my cheek. "We were just discussing our matter."

Henry must have realised that I was less than happy when he noticed the emotionless look that was spread on my face. "Charles. Thomas. We will continue this later." He ushered them out of the room. He gestured me to a seat, but I was too on edge to sit down. He began to look worried as it dawned on him that my obvious anger was directed at him.

"What upsets you, darling?" He asked.

"Did you share Catherine's bed last night?" I asked already knowing the answer.

He was intelligent enough to look ashamed before answering as realisation dawned on him.

"I did my love, but it was only to sleep." He explained. "I must look as if I am trying to make it work."

He could not understand that even just sleeping in her bed was an insult to me. It should be I alone who he slept with. Sharing someone's bed meant something even if you only slept side by side. It showed that they were connected enough to sleep soundly in each other's company.

"I cannot take it anymore, Harry." I cried out. "She mocks me."

He was at my side soothing me in an instant. He attempted to hold me, but I stood still. I was too angry to be comforted.

"Love, it means nothing," He explained.

"How do you think it feels to know that you sleep in her bed?" I asked, looking him in the eye. "It turns my stomach. Put yourself in my shoes. If it were the other way round you would be driven mad with envy."

"It makes me sick to do it. I am driven mad by the idea that I am living in sin." Henry answered.

"Then, do not do it," I said. Henry made to speak, but I was not finished. "Think about it. If you stop sharing her bed it will become clear that you are too concerned for your soul to continue your intimacy with her."

Henry thought for a moment. He was clearly weighing up the options in his mind. Surely if the church was able to see that he steered clear of his sinful marriage, then it would only add to the case. Henry hated the idea of living in sin so there was no good reason that he should continue doing it.

"Maybe you're right darling. It does pain me to be with her." Henry released me so that he could turn my face to look at him.

"If you do not do it for your soul Henry, then please do it for me." I said, holding his hand.

With my eyes I was pleading for him to hear me. I touched my hand across his heart. "It breaks my heart in two at the idea of you being with her. You swore that you would never break my heart." I said genuinely as tears began to prickle my eyes.

It truly hurt that I was not his one and only. That is what he had promised me, and that is what I wanted. I did not want to share him with another person, and Catherine was making that impossible.

He held my chin and looked me in the eye. "You are the only one I want, Anne." He smiled. It was contagious. Soon enough, I was smiling back.

"I will tell Catherine that we may no longer behave as man and wife. Does that make you happy my love?"
"Thank you, Harry," I sighed as relief filled me. "I truly love you."

Henry kissed me then, and I felt so much better knowing that Catherine would be put in her place. She would not be able to mock me any longer. A part of me wished that I could watch her face fall as Henry delivered the news. This would devastate her. I hoped that it would at least convince her of the seriousness of her situation. Maybe now she would finally see that Henry was mine and not hers.

CHAPTER TWELVE

At the beginning of 1528 Henry and I were growing impatient, to say the least. Still we were nowhere near closure, and it was getting harder by the day to resist each other. We had refrained from sleeping in the same room so that neither of us would become tempted to break our vow. Henry no longer shared a bed with Catherine or paid her any attention at all. He refused to speak to her until she gave us what we wanted.

He was sure that soon enough she would grow tired of the life she now led. She was kept away from her husband. She was shunned as Henry chose to sit with me or as I escorted him into court events. I was surprised that somehow she still had not taken the hint. Surely she would give up soon enough. It cannot have been comfortable being a wife only in name and not in deed. I had now begun to make a point of snubbing her in public. I refused to bow to her any longer. She was no queen to me. I laughed at her as she passed and was petty. It is something I regret now. There was no need to make Catherine feel so small but it made me feel better about my situation. And her proud look was unbearable.

In January Henry ordered Wolsey to write to Rome. He asked that a papal legate come to England so that he could investigate the matter. They agreed to send a man named Cardinal Campeggio. He would come to England and hopefully make a decision on The King's Great Matter. Henry and I were sure that this would be the answer we needed. Once Campeggio was in England Henry would set out his case.

* * * * *

1528 was to bring its devastation. Many lives would be taken by the sweating sickness. It had swept through

England previously in 1485 and had killed thousands of people in its wake. Now it was back, and the whole country was afraid that it would come for them too. It was an excruciating illness that caused the affected at first to become very nervous and on edge. Then they would break out in cold shivers and become consumed by pain in their limbs and neck. One would be suddenly set upon by an extreme headache and once the cold sweats subsides, a great heat then overtook the whole body. There was no stopping the sweat that overcame them. The heat would be unbearable and brought with it a quickening pulse and confusion. It made the affected feel as if their heart was to give in as the pain spread through their chest and then eventually the bearer would be suddenly desperate to rest. Their body exhausted with the effort of continued sweating. Finally it would overtake them, and the terrible disease would kill them.

By June it had already begun to claim many lives, and unfortunately many had begun to fall around London. On the 16th June, one of my ladies had become ill. It did not take very long to overcome her, and I knew that if I wished to be kept safe I would have to get as far away from the palace as possible. Henry had heard what had happened and sent me a note. He explained that he and Catherine were getting away from London to avoid the sweat and that I should do the same. He told me to return to Hever where I would be more isolated, and I would be less likely to come into contact with anyone affected by the illness.

I was saddened, to say the least, by his instant need to take Catherine with him and leave me to fend for myself. He still clearly valued her life above mine. I saw no reason why I could not go with him. I had not contracted it myself so why would he not want me with him. Again, when it came down to Catherine or me, Henry chose wrong. I was jealous. That was the very basis of it. I hated that while I would sit alone in Hever, Catherine would be by Henry's side and I hated that this would make her believe that she was back in his heart again as the both of them made a quick dash out of London leaving me behind to face my fate. But even through betrayal I followed Henry's order. I made my way back to Hever with my father. George stayed with the court and kept me up to date with their progress. When I reached Hever it became very obvious very quickly that I was not feeling myself. On the journey I had started to feel a little faint but had put it down to general weariness. However, before long I began to feel weak to the point that even stepping out of my carriage was hard work. My headache came on all of a sudden, and I could not concentrate on a thing. Father spoke to me, but his voice just pounded away in my head. The brightness of the day stung my eyes, and all of the noises of the outside world pierced through me. I began to worry obsessively.

I was going to die. I just knew it. I fretted over my life and the frailness of it all. This was the sweat, I was certain. It had come to claim me next. I had no escape. I was the next on a long list of victims claimed by the disease. I went on to Father about what he should tell Henry and George. They needed to know that I loved them. He needed to tell Henry that I was sorry. I didn't want to leave him. I was anxious about anything and everything. I could barely sit still from jumping at the slightest of movements. I scratched at my hands from nerves as my whole body began to itch with anxiety. I sat like a woman driven mad in the corner of my room, every noise making me uncomfortable. Every time someone spoke to me I worried after their motive.

Father was the first to notice that something wasn't right and he ordered me to bed. As he stood before me, my vision blurred and I allowed him to lead me up to my room. I was thankful to lie down on my bed and rest for a while. Soon after the anxiety subsided the headache became worse. My head began to pound uncontrollably. It was all I

162

could do not to scream from the pain that seized my skull. I could not concentrate or think straight. I was cold. I was freezing, even. No matter how many layers were draped over me I did not seem to warm up. I was desperate to sit by a fire to warm my bones. The shivers made my teeth chatter. Made me feel as if I would fit from the effort. The fear came on quick as it dawned on me the severity of my situation. I was dying. I knew it. People rarely survived the sweat, and I would be the next to succumb to it.

Twenty-four hours. That's how long people would survive if they were lucky. Within twenty-four hours I would be dead. The cold lasted a long while, and during that time I was beside myself with the fear that I would never see Henry again, that I would die far away from him and never able to touch him or hold him again. He would stay with Catherine while I was laid in the cold ground. Even more than my worry of dying was my worry about our separation. The idea that I would be without him pained me more than anything else. I cried for the life about to be cut short. I cried at the idea of leaving Henry behind. I was scared. I was just to be a number included on the long list of people who had been killed by the disease this year. I did not want to die. Alone and isolated at Hever. Not one friend around to say goodbye. I was distraught at having contracted the disease.

I truly believed that it would take me. It had killed almost everyone it had ever affected. I tossed and turned in my bed, shaking with the strain of not giving in. I begged my father to write to Henry. To tell him that I loved him and that I would soon be dead. Father agreed that he needed to know, so he sent a letter off to find the king. He told him that I was seriously unwell and that he did not know if I was strong enough to survive this. Henry was beside himself. Within no time at all he had sent me his second-best doctor, the first being unavailable at that moment.

Dr. Butts arrived at Hever ready to give me any medical attention that I may need. He held in his hand a letter from Henry. I was unable to read it, but my father had decided that it would do me good to hear from him. He hoped that his words would give me what I needed to fight — that the thought of my future with Henry would be what I needed to push through.

"There came to me suddenly in the night the most afflicting news that could have arrived. The first, to hear of the sickness of my mistress, whom I esteem more than all the world, and whose health I desire as I do my own so that I would gladly bear half your illness to make you well. The second, from the fear that I have of being still longer harassed by my enemy, Absence, much longer, who has hitherto given me all possible uneasiness, and as far as I can judge is determined to spite me more because I pray God to rid me of this troublesome tormentor. The third, because the physician in whom I have most confidence is absent at the very time when he might do me the greatest pleasure. For I should hope, by him and his means, to obtain one of my chief joys on earth — that is the care of my mistress — yet for want of him I send you my second, and hope that he will soon make you well. I shall then love him more than ever. I beseech you to be guided by his advice in your illness. In so doing I hope soon to see you again, which will be to me a greater comfort than all the precious jewels in the world.

> Written by that secretary, who is,
> and forever will be, your loyal and
> most assured Servant."

Father read the letter aloud to me. "See the king wills you to survive, Anne. You can fight this so that you may be with him again. He loves you still. Even while you are separated he still pines after you. Let your heart be glad of this." My heart was warmed by the fact that I was in Henry's thoughts and It had succeeded in making me want to fight. I would will this illness away if I could. I had to see Henry again. Dr Butts updated him on my condition when he could. At this point the sweat had begun and instead of trying to warm up, I was doing everything to keep cool. All of the windows in the castle had been opened up to allow some air in. I was burning. It felt like my body had been placed on top of a fire and the flames were inescapable. The sweat soaked through my shift and my sheets. My face dripping. The panic took over, and I felt as if I could not breathe. This was it, I had thought. This was the final stage. God I was tired. I would have done anything for just one moment of rest. To be allowed to shut my eyes even for a minute.

But Dr Butts ordered me to stay awake for as long as I could. I fought to keep my eyes open, but I just wanted it over with. I had been suffering for days and even with the efforts of Butts and my mother, I had only gotten worse.

This was a crucial time and had I let the tiredness overcome me, then the disease would have won out. My chest ached, and my whole body was on fire. I felt for sure that the disease would consume me. Dr Butts felt the same and had told my father that he did not believe I would make it another night. Unless the fever broke, I would not make it until the morning. I was dying, and unless God stepped in to save me then there was nothing I could do to save myself.

I prayed when I could — begging God to allow me to survive this. I was too young to be taken. I had so much to give to the world and the idea that these were my last days tormented me. My mother sat beside me and prayed for God to save me. I believe that she was actually saddened at the thought of losing me. She must have held some love in her heart for me as she sat with me day and night. She held my hand and patted my head with a damp cloth. Even with the threat of catching the disease from me she stayed. She would not allow me to die alone. Father paced back and forth scared that the child he had treated so emotionlessly was going to die — that his dreams would die with me. He caught it soon after I had and was taken off to his own bed. Mother spent her time split between the two of us. Father's condition did not progress very fast, and there was hope that he would be spared.

The household prepared for the very real chance that soon enough they would have to bury me. My ladies wept around me, believing that they would have to say goodbye to the woman they loved, sooner rather than later. My mother despaired at losing another child and father lay in his bed unable to do anything other than fight for his own life. I look back on that time in my life now and think that if I had allowed the illness to beat me then I would have been saved from the amount of pain and suffering that was to come. My life would have ended there before it had chance to take such a disastrous turn. I would have died at home in my bed and not on the cold scaffold.

However, I thank God that I was spared. Because of God's mercy I was able to go on and have my Lizzie. I was allowed eight more years with the man I loved. He was the reason that I finally broke through the affliction. I truly believe that it was because of Henry that I pulled through. As his words rang in my head I found the ability to push on.

"I hope soon to see you again, which will be to me, a greater comfort than all the precious jewels in the world."

That night I broke the fever. As my temperature began to lower and the sweat began to dry up. I felt like I could breathe again as my body began to become a normal temperature. Where I had been soaked before now only beads of sweat laid on my face now. My anxiety eased and the room came back into focus. The doctor smiled over me. These were good signs. He had feared that he might disappoint his master had he failed to save me. The headache continued to rage on, but my pulse returned to a slower rhythm. The pain that had gripped my chest began to subside, and I was able to sit up in my bed for the first time in days.

I felt better. Much better. The illness seemed to pass as quickly as it had come on. I was exhausted. Still I fought the urge to sleep, but the Doctor informed me that at this stage it was perfectly safe and would actually do me a world of good. So I slept for what felt like days — falling into an exhausted sleep that completely took me over. The moment I closed my eyes I was taken off into a heavy sleep. My body finally happy to give in to rest. I did not dream or fret. I slept in a deep sleep for a whole day and night — my body doing its best to recover from the trauma of the sweat.

I woke the next day to see that father had made a full recovery and was sitting in a chair beside my bed. Mother stood at the foot, her hands clasped over her mouth. The doctor stood in the corner. They had all been watching me sleep holding their breath for the moment I would wake. They could only be sure of my having beaten the disease if I awoke with no signs of it. I sat up in my bed still feeling a little weary as my arms shook under the weight of me. The headache had seemed to start receding, allowing me to think clearly for the first time.

As everyone came into view I smiled with happiness at my family sitting around my bed in a silent vigil waiting for my recovery. It felt good to know that they cared enough to stay close by, even whilst running the risk of catching the sickness themselves. After a moment Dr Butts came over to me and ran his hand on my forehead. He breathed a sigh of relief. "She has survived it." He announced.

My mother cried and made her way to the bed and for the first time, threw her arms around me. She had never done this before and for a moment let her joy overtake her usual coldness. I let her hold me as the Doctor's words sunk in. I had beaten it. It hadn't claimed me. Somehow I was one of the lucky few to be able to survive the sweat. I thanked God with all of my might for sparing me. Dr. Butts explained that I would still need to rest. I was on bed rest for the foreseeable future until he was sure that none of the sicknesses lingered in me.

He wrote to Henry immediately expressing his joy at his accomplishment of saving me. Henry, of course, would be unbelievably grateful, and Dr. Butts would be awarded greatly over the years. He became a close ally of mine from that moment onwards, and he would no longer be the second-best doctor only. He was now the most trusted doctor in the whole of England.

I had survived the sickness, but many had not, including my sister's husband. William Carey had succumbed to the sickness on the very day that I was taken sick — leaving my poor sister a widow and her sweet children fatherless. I promised that the second I was back at court I would invite Mary to come and stay with me for a while as she grieved the loss of her husband. It was sad news indeed. She was so young to be a widow, and she loved her husband dearly. It was a tragedy for her small family, and I would write my condolences to her the second I was able, offering my help with anything she may need to make this time a little easier on her.

I was desperate to hear some good news from Henry. So far there was nothing to suggest that he or anyone surrounding him had been affected, but I would not be happy until I could hold his letter in my hands. His letter would arrive soon enough and bring with it his joy at my beating back the awful sickness.

"The uneasiness my doubts about your health gave me, disturbed and alarmed me exceedingly, and I should not have had any quiet without hearing certain tidings. But now, since you have as yet felt nothing, I hope and I'm assured that it will spare you, as I hope it is doing with us. For when we were at Walton, two ushers, two valets de chambres and your brother, master-treasurer, fell ill, but are now quite well. And since we have returned to our house at Hunsdon, we have been perfectly well, and have not, at present, one sick person. God be praised. And I think if you retired from Surrey, as we did, you would escape all danger. There is another thing that may comfort you, which is, in truth and distemper, few or no women have been taken ill, and what is more, no person of our court, and few elsewhere, have died of it. For which reason I beg you my entirely beloved, not to frighten yourself nor be too uneasy at our absence; for wherever I am, I am yours, and yet we must sometimes submit to our misfortunes. For whoever will struggle against fate is generally but so much the farther from gaining his end: wherefore comfort yourself, and take courage and avoid the pestilence as much as you can, for I hope shortly to make you sing, "la renvoyé." No more at present, from lack of time, but that I wish you in my arms, that I might a little dispel your unreasonable thoughts.

> Written by the hand of him who is
> and always will be yours.
> H. R"

To hear from Henry truly made me feel better. I rejoiced at the fact that he was so grateful for my recovery. His love had not stirred at my absence, and that eased my heart so much to know that he was faithful all of the time I was unwell. I was sad to hear that George had been ill. Mother and father had known but refused to tell me should it make me worse for fear of losing him. I was pleased to hear of his complete recovery and thanked God for the blessings he had put on all of the Boleyns to survive such a terrible time.

We had all fully recovered; we truly were the lucky ones. Many had lost their lives. I was thankful also that Henry had avoided becoming infected. I had been sick with fear of his becoming unwell, and now his words did the job of completing my recovery. His words pulled me from the depression that had been left in the wake of the sickness. When he wrote "For wherever I am, I am yours." my heart came back to life. It meant that even as he hid from the illness with Catherine at his side he was still completely mine. Neither time nor distance would come between us, and I had nothing to fear.

* * * * *

Within a month the sweat seemed to disappear completely, and I had been secluded long enough to return to court. It was all I could do to run from Hever to London where Henry now waited for me. When I returned I didn't think he would ever let me breathe from kissing me. He held me so tight promising to never let me out of his sight again. He regretted ever letting us be separated. He blamed himself for my suffering alone. I told him that he did the right thing for I could not bear if he were to become ill because of me.

I was just happy to be with him again now. I told him that I had thought that I would never see him again and that this was the thing that scared me the most. If I had not had him I would have succumbed within hours of contracting it. But it was because I had him in mind I was able to pull through so that we could be together again. He told me that the fact that God had chosen to save me when so many others had failed proved to him even more that we had found each other for a reason.

CHAPTER THIRTEEN

29th September 1528 Cardinal Campeggio arrived. His job was to come to England and hear both arguments on Henry's matter, and then pass a judgement. At least that is what Wolsey had told us. It seemed, however, he had a different idea of what he was here to do. He seemed to think that rather than pass judgement he would try and convince Henry to drop the matter and return to Catherine.

Before he even heard any of the details he went straight to Henry hoping that he could remedy the matter with a reconciliation. This would be easier on everyone he explained. He told Henry that I was not worth all of the efforts he was going to. He should not threaten to put aside an anointed queen in order to marry a whore. This made Henry mad with rage. How dare this man be welcomed in to his country to tell the king then that he was acting foolish. And to call me a whore? The women he loved. This was a matter that affected Henry's conscience. Not simply a reason to marry me. Henry could have killed him in his anger. But Campeggio was our only hope. We needed him on our side so that he could make the correct decision. Henry would keep him sweet for now, giving him the nicest of rooms in the palace and ensuring that his every need was catered to.

After seeing Henry and realising that it was no use to try and convince him to change his mind, Campeggio turned to Catherine. He clearly did not want to deal with any of this and was looking for an easy way out. He spoke to Catherine hoping to persuade her to retire into a nunnery. He told her that if she did so then Henry could remarry and she would keep her pride intact. He pleaded with her to end this civilly before it went too far. Catherine would hear none of it. She was so stubborn that it made my blood boil.

Why could she not listen to everyone around her? The people who wished to give her an easy way out. She was making life harder for everyone. No one wanted to be dragged through a hearing and court proceedings, and I could not see why she was so determined to fight us all the way. The thing I should have understood is that she was in love. That she wanted to be with Henry as much as I did, and the idea of losing him was heartbreaking to her. She did not want to lose her crown, that was for certain. But more than that, she did not want to lose her husband.

Because Henry could not take his frustration out on Campeggio instead, it was Catherine who took the brunt of our anger. Catherine had annoyed the both of us to no end with her constant refusal to see sense, and I was just about ready to lose my temper with her. I had told Henry that I could not take much more of her defiance, and wished that she would just go away altogether. I was also beginning to be annoyed just by sensing her presence. I was tortured by her smug look. She thought for so long that she was winning and my competitive side wanted nothing more than to knock her down a peg or two. She was doing all that she could to stop our happiness, and I was fed up.

"Does it not annoy you, Harry?" I asked as Henry sat in my room. Cards in hand. It was a cold evening, and I had sent Marge and the others away so that Henry and I could be alone for a while.

"What's that, darling?" he asked absentmindedly.

"Catherine. How she still digs in her heels? Even though it is clear that you no longer want her," I vented.

Henry sighed. He looked over at me as I scowled. He placed his cards down in front of him and chuckled, which only added to my annoyance.

"I don't know why you let her bother you so much," he said, rolling his eyes.

I believe he quickly read that by the narrowing of my eyes I was less than happy with his response. He held his hands up. "Love, do not let her bother you. She will be gone soon enough."

"When?" I snapped. "Have I not waited long enough, Henry?"

I only ever used his given name when I was angry, which did not happen very often. Most of the time I was completely contented with him and our lives. Even though we were still not wed, I still thanked God for every moment we were together.

Henry looked annoyed. He had me in his ear for months now and was coming to the end of his wits with my complaining about Catherine. I could not help it. I just loved him so much and was driven crazier by our lack of marriage. He always tried his best to stay level with me, but the stress was getting to him as much as it was with me.

"And what would you like me to do about it, Anne?" He shouted at me for the first time as his temper rose.

"Make her understand Henry," I spat, "It does not help when you play happy families with her and Mary. How do you think I feel to know that the two of you share a child while I am childless and husbandless?" I said with spite.

I hated when they visited their daughter together. It only made it clearer to me that I could not have a family with him yet. It made it all the more obvious that Catherine had had the whole of him while I was still just on the outside.

"What do you think I am trying to do?" He raged. "Mary is my daughter. Would you like me to remove her too?" he asked. His face burned with anger.

"No, Henry. Of course not," I said. "My problem is with Catherine."

I honestly had no issue with Mary other than the fact that she was Catherine's daughter, which meant that she had something with Henry that I did not.

"I am doing my best, Anne," he ran his hands across his face. "I am doing everything in my power to give you the world. What more could you want from me?"

The tears began to well in my eyes. I did not want to argue with him. It had been such a hard few months. My illness had taken it out of me, and now I felt like I had to fight every day to keep Catherine at a distance. It was hard work, and I was tired. We were both tired, and I should have been more understanding.

Henry was at my side, holding me. "Do not cry, love. Hush now," he soothed me. "I am sorry, Anne. I should not have lost my temper." He wiped my eyes.

"No, Henry. I am sorry." I said, kissing him on the cheek. "I just hate her for being so stubborn. It's hard to see that the two of you share a child. I am unable to conceive a son for us, and Mary brings Catherine such joy."

Henry thought for a moment as he held me close. His face had softened, and I believe he felt genuinely guilty for shouting at me. The last thing that we wanted to do was argue with each other.

"You're right sweetheart. I am going to make sure that Catherine knows we are not playing her silly games." He kissed me on the head.

"Thank you. Harry." I said.

We kissed and made up. Henry was true to his words. Perhaps he was more cruel then I would have chosen to be, but he kept his promise. Catherine was told later that day that until she chose to see reason she would be banned from seeing her daughter. Henry had thought that this would be enough to convince her. She loved Mary so dearly that it would break her heart to be kept apart.

Still she did not budge. She did not move an inch. If anything, I think it only made her hold on even tighter. She was determined to make things right again. I did not defend her. Not once did I ever say a word on her behalf. I would not have chosen to keep Mary from her. This was too cruel a fate. But neither did I tell Henry that what he was doing was wrong. I allowed him to continue with the torment. It's wrong for anyone to be separated from their child and now that I have been subjected to the same fate I realise that I am only getting what is deserved. If I had said a word in their defence then maybe fate would not have turned on me.

* * * * *

The court would be led by Campeggio. He was in no rush to get it done however, and we were waiting until the 31st May, 1529 before proceedings began. Henry was confident that we would come out winning. He could think of no real reason that he would be denied. He did what was best for both his and Catherine's conscience. If anything he believed that Catherine should be thankful to him for his efforts to save her soul.

His confidence made me feel secure. He was so convinced that we were right that it was hard to even consider that we may fail yet again. The night before the court he came to my rooms and spent the evening by my side. He promised that very soon I could begin to consider myself queen. It was well within my reach now. We just needed to push on a little further. I could do that. I was sure that I could wait a few more days. No matter how trying things had gotten, Henry and I never once doubted that we were doing the right thing. Our love never failed for one moment. I just had to put my faith in him and know that God had a plan for us.

* * * * *

I would not be granted admittance to Blackfriars and instead I relied on others to fill in the gaps. It was not hard to find out how things were going. It was all that anybody could talk about and the court was alive with the gossip surrounding our matter once again. Henry would send for me every night and he would give me a detailed report on the goings on.

Catherine only bothered turning up for one court session. She believed it to be nothing more than a pathetic joke that should not be taken seriously. She made a spectacle of herself. Strolling up to Henry and protesting that she had always been a good and loyal wife. Begging him to reconsider his actions. She had the hearts of the court with her. She knew exactly what she was doing. Looking like a poor and pitiful abused wife. She made her speech and then she turned her back on the king and left. She would not acknowledge the authority of the men in that room. She refused to acknowledge the proceedings at all. I hated her. She would use whatever she could to manipulate the people into loving her. She had hoped to manipulate Henry but thankfully he could see right through her.

It did not matter. The legatine court would be of no use. It went on for almost a month, and at the end it all came to nothing. The whole thing was more or less a distraction technique. Henry and I knew soon after that Campeggio's only goal was to stall us. He had never planned to pass a judgement. His instructions from Rome was to keep us all running around long enough for Catherine to find a way out.

After many tiring days of arguments and examples on Henry's part, Campeggio decided that he would end the proceedings. He said that the court would reconvene in October when a decision would be made. However, that would never happen. The Pope would decide in Catherine's favour before long, rendering the legatine court useless. It was clear that Henry and I had to start to think of other ways that we may achieve our goal.

* * * * *

177

Henry was furious at the result of the court, and he needed someone to take it out on. As Wolsey was the main man in charge of obtaining an end to his marriage, he was also the one to receive the worst of Henry's rage.

Wolsey appeared to be useless when it came to getting the result we desired and Henry had grown weary of the constant back and forth. By this time it was obvious to both myself and George that Wolsey's interests lay with Rome and not with his own king. We had said as much to Henry. I truly only hoped to remove Wolsey from my sight. To have him sent from court so that I would not have to bear his presence any longer. There was a part of me that still hated Wolsey for the part he had played in the breakdown of my betrothal to Henry Percy. It was an old grudge and perhaps I was silly to allow it to affect me so many years later but I knew exactly what I was doing when I complained endlessly to Henry about Wolsey's failure.

When I had George tell Henry that Wolsey put Rome above the wishes of his own king. I knew that Wolsey would suffer because of this. That spiteful side of me. The one that I am more than aware of had to get involved. I had to seek my revenge from all those years ago. It worked. I knew it would.

I knew that the king put me and mine above any other and as such would listen to whatever we had to say. Henry banished Wolsey from court and then he had him arrested. Wolsey had committed treason by thinking of Rome first and England second. I did not think Henry would arrest him. I had thought that he would leave court and stay away quietly in the country somewhere. I definitely had no idea that Wolsey would die soon after. He was so saddened by his fall from grace. Heartbroken by the titles and land that was removed from him. His life ended in misery because of me. Another person who fell for the sake of Henry and me.

.

* * * * *

I would soon give Henry a book. "The Obedience of a Christian Man." by William Tyndal. This book explained that the king should be the highest authority in the land and that a king should answer to no higher authority, including the pope. This was the thing that lit the spark that would make Henry realise if he wanted to remove Catherine, then he could do it himself. With or without the permission of the pope. The seed had been planted. Now it just needed a bit of attention, and it would grow into something beautiful soon enough.

CHAPTER FOURTEEN

It would be four more years before Henry and I got what we wanted. Four long years of fighting to obtain the one thing we wanted most in the world. We realised rather quickly that the pope was never going to give up. He had stalled for a long time, refusing to make any sort of decision on the matter. Then finally he had sided with Catherine. He said that she was indeed Henry's true wife. The fact that Arthur had passed away meant that she was free to marry whomever she pleased. It was only considered a sin if you married a living brothers wife. Henry despaired at the news. He was lost on where to move next. One thing he was sure of was that it would not matter. He was going to have me one way or the other, and he would continue to fight for our love. I was glad to hear it. I had become concerned that there was a possibility that he may give up. Admit defeat and return to Catherine without a second look in my direction. But still, he loved me. He was still willing to go to the ends of the earth to obtain me. I allowed him to reassure me that we would find a way, and although my confidence had been shaken I trusted him completely. Putting all of my faith into his hands.

Thankfully, a saviour came to us in the shape of a man. Thomas Cranmer. Thomas Cranmer had his own idea about how we should approach the matter and it had caught our attention. He believed that we should put our argument to theologians rather than church men. They would be able to make an informed decision based on their understanding of the Bible. He offered the idea that we put it to a vote to the universities around the world. Henry who was quite taken by the idea allowed Thomas and a man named Edward Foxe to travel around the globe to each university willing to weigh in and put it to a vote.

Fortunately, they sided with us. It was not by many votes, but in the end there were more theologians with us than against us. After years of struggle Henry and I finally had a victory. Finally our argument had support.

Next Henry had to put himself in a position to order his annulment. I had already set the wheels in motion when I had given Henry my copy of "The Obedience of a Christian man." A book which helped him to see that he should be the highest power in England. It made him realise the absurdity of his having to answer to the pope. He was king and chosen by God himself for the position. Why should he bow to another power? Cranmer also helped in this. He was of the belief that Rome was corrupted. Much like myself, he wished to see a lessening of the power held by men of the Catholic Church.

It was all of these pieces that fit together to convince Henry that he should break from Rome. He had decided to make himself head of the church in his own country, and rightly so. He had not only done that but he had also managed to get his parliament to agree with it. I remember thinking that there was nothing this man could not do.

Henry was now declared as Head of the Church in England, and although the clergy would initially kick up a bit of a stink, in 1532 they would sign a document that expressed their acceptance of the new law. They would no longer be able to make a new law without first consulting the king. The rules that already existed would be looked into by someone appointed by the king and they would no longer be able to meet without Henry's permission. They had voted with him, and it gave him power over the Pope.

Not only that but Henry was happy to live with me openly as a couple now. He had said that his marriage was void so he could court whoever he wanted. We were so happy together at Greenwich and Henry was desperate to do something that would prove to everyone exactly how much he loved me.

Henry would name me as Marquess of Pembroke. It was an honour. I was the first woman to ever be given the title. Yet again, Henry and I were making history. It also made me the most prestigious woman in the whole of England. On 1st September 1532, Henry yet again proved his love for me as he laid on a lavish ceremony and officially gave me the title. No one could argue at how much he loved me. He was stating it to the whole world. As the whole court looked on I was finally placed above all others, and soon I would be above Catherine too. Her time as queen was coming to a swift end.

* * * * *

The thing to keep in mind is that it had been seven long years of waiting. Henry and I had fought hard, and we were drained. We were sick of Catherine. We were sick of waiting. We hated that for seven years we had been a couple that could not share the same bed. We were so close to our goal that it seemed silly to wait much longer. I wanted him so badly that I was sure I would combust if I were unable to touch him any longer. We kissed, and we held hands. We were together in any other way, but it was not enough. I wanted desperately to be able to climb into his bed at night and give him the whole of me. I wanted to feel that connection with him. To let him hold me through the long nights. I wanted to show him how he made me feel, not with my words but with my body.

Both of us had worked so hard to ensure that we were respectful of the other. And although we had nearly succumbed to our desire many times we had managed to restrain ourselves. I could wait no longer. Henry could wait no longer. I decided I would give myself to him. While we were in France on a visit I decided that this would be the time. Henry was not expecting it when I climbed into the bed next to him. I kissed him more passionately than I had before. I felt his whole body with my hands exploring the man that I loved. He kissed me back not knowing what I had planned and when I pulled him on top of me he all but begged me to stop.

"Anne. I won't be able to control myself," he practically growled against my mouth.

I pulled him closer. Kissing him deeply. "Then don't," I breathed.

He pulled away from me. Confusion crossed his face as he gazed down at me. For so long, I had been determined to avoid this moment. I had pushed his advances away again and again. Even though all I wanted to do was allow him to take advantage of me. I wanted him to do what he wanted with my body. I lusted after him as the night fell and I lay alone in my bed. Still I refused. But tonight. Tonight was different. As he had said earlier in the day, our marriage was only a matter of time now. Catherine was out of sight and out of mind. We were together for life, and I saw no reason to torment ourselves longer.

"Love, are you sure?" Henry asked. "You know it is better that we wait."

I placed my finger over his lips to quiet him. He wanted this. Wanted me. I could tell in the way he looked at me. He had a hunger in his eyes, and that only made me want him more.

"We have waited long enough Harry," I said kissing him again.

I needed to make no more argument. Henry did not need a lot of convincing.

We lay together that night for the first time. At first it was uncomfortable. It was not what I expected at all. But after a while it was really quite wonderful. The last piece finally slipping into place. There was no better feeling in the world than being fully with the man you loved. I relished every second that we were together as small explosions went off inside of my mind. Henry was so gentle. So soft. He did not let his hunger get the better of him. Instead he ensured that I was okay. He made sure that at no point was I uncomfortable. I have never felt more whole in my life. I will never forget that night. That night was magical for many reasons but most of all because it was the night that I finally conceived the heir that Henry and I so desperately wanted.

* * * * *

We realised quickly that I was pregnant. Henry was a matter of weeks away from his annulment, and we knew that we would have to marry soon to ensure that the baby I now carried would be legitimate. Henry officially asked me to become his wife, and we made plans for a quiet wedding.

CHAPTER FIFTEEN

On 25th January 1533, Henry and I wed. Finally, after seven long years of waiting, we would become husband and wife. I woke in the morning, my heart as full of love as it was all those years ago. I looked around my rooms thinking that this would be the last time that I was simply "Anne Boleyn." From now on I would be a wife to the man I loved and a queen to the country that I called my home. I barely touched my food that morning, my stomach so full of butterflies. I was not nervous; I knew in my heart that this was what I was born for, to love this man and be with him. I was anxious to get to the chapel and make it official. To finally be able to live together as a couple, to know that now we were one in the eyes of God and no one could ever question that.

Henry was still technically married to Catherine. However, soon enough their marriage would be annulled, and it would be like it had never happened. Twenty four years of being together would amount to nothing. I felt for Catherine in this sense, that day she finally lost the man she had stayed by through everything. She finally lost her great battle. We could not wait any longer, for I was starting to grow big with child, we could not have any question of our son's legitimacy. It was better if we were legally married, and he would grow to be heir to the Tudor throne. I had everything I wanted at last. I grew our precious son within me, and I would forever be joined with Henry in matrimony.

The ceremony took place in Henry's personal chapel in Westminster. Attended by only my closest family and a few privy council members. Among them were Henry Norris and Lady Barkeley.

I was dressed by my ladies, including Margery, in a gown of exquisite gold. The bodice made of intricate white lace details made to look like Tudor roses, I wore red and white Tudor roses in my ears and pearls around my neck, set off with my B necklace, which I would wear as a sort of talisman for good fortune. I had decided to wear my hair down, something which was unheard of, I cherished my hair and was proud to let it be shown in all of its raven black beauty. Margery brushed it out for me and let it loose, it reached all of the way down my back. The shoes I also wore were magnificently golden, small, and delicate. George, who had come to wish me luck, had told me that I "shone with the beauty of the sun on a perfect summer's day."

Father and Mother also wished to see me before the day began.

"Anne, today you do this family a great service. We are very proud of you." father told me.

Mother was more affectionate. "Sweet girl, how marvelous you look. I wish you all of the fortunes in the world with this happy day." She patted my cheek and they made their way ahead of me to the chapel.

Mary, of course, was not interested in attending. I believed her to be still bitter, in the fact that I had done one better than her and married the man, rather than being cast off. Looking back now, I realise that she may have foreshadowed my downfall. She had somehow seen what would come of my marriage. I believe this because of a letter I had received two days after.

"Darling sister Anne, I was sorry to have missed your wedding. I have heard that you looked exceptionally beautiful, which is not hard to believe. I am so proud of you in every way, and I would like you to know that I do not hold any ill will towards you. Your only sin against me was to fall in love with a man just out of my reach. You were willing to reach further than I ever would. I wish you great happiness, and I do so look forward to meeting the wonderful children you bear.

However, sister, I do not send this as congratulations. I send this as a message of warning. Please guard your heart, watch carefully the people around you, who strive for nothing but power and always watch every move you make, for we are all always one step away from crossing some invisible line. The court is a place of savagery and power play. I do not wish for you to be caught up in the games that these men play with such expertise. I am always thinking of you, always holding you close to my heart and wishing for the best for you. I do believe that Henry loves you very much, I just hope enough always to be your protector. However, if he is not, Anne, you need to protect yourself and trust no one. Please always look after yourself before anyone else. Care for your interests, not everyone else. I do send you all of my love, Anne.

Forever your loving sister.
Mary."

At the time, I dashed the letter into the fire. How dare she? She was just trying to ruin my happiness. She was not looking out for me; she was trying to sabotage me. She wanted to create paranoia in me. I would not let her have that over me. She was surely just bitter that I had won Henry's heart and she was away from court out of his mind. Now, of course, I wish that I had listened to Mary, she was truly only looking out for me. I should never have shut her out of my life; she cared for me even after I had betrayed her. She was a true loyal sister always. I have missed out on years of sisterly companionship because I believed her to have an ulterior motive. When actually she just wanted to protect me. Poor Mary, shunned from my life, kept away from her family, she has lost her brother and now she will watch her sister breath her last. It is not the life she deserves.

* * * * *

At three in the afternoon, I was dressed and ready to
become Henry's wife. I had bathed and dressed, soaked in
roses so that I would smell and look like the summer's day
that would reflect our love. For when we were with each
other, the sun always shone brightly on us. Promising a
future that was never written in the stars.

I made my way through the halls of Westminster. I
could barely contain my feelings. My heart wished to burst
from my chest. My legs wanted to run to him. My eyes
craved his wonderful face. I could not bear being away
from him even for a moment. I could feel my pulse rushing
through my body. My mind buzzed with excitement.

When I first arrived at the chapel, I could see how
wonderful it was. Draped in candles, and flowers hanging
on every pew. I saw my mother, father and brother, stood
waiting patiently. And then I looked ahead, and there he
was, standing like a god in human form, waiting for me at
the front of the chapel. He looked at me with such intensity.
I felt sure that I would burst into flames at his touch. He
smiled. That smile that could melt me at any moment. I no
longer walked through the chapel. I was being pulled closer
to him. It was like we were two souls destined to fit
together, and when we were apart the universe would do
whatever it could to draw us nearer. I floated along, closer
and closer, until finally I could wait no longer and I reached
out for him, anchored to him. He would hold me down on
the ground. Keeping me still in this moment. His eyes filled
with tears as he sucked in a deep breath at the sight before
him. He touched my hair crying now with joy.

"Anne, is there anything else in this world so beautiful?"
he whispered. "My love, the look of you has made my heart
fall all over again. I am about to be the happiest man in this
kingdom. Nay, the world."

Whenever Henry spoke, I fell in love all over again. His love for me shone through so deeply. The love he bore me was written so obviously across his face. We may as well have been the only two people there that day. No one else mattered. We centred each other. He was my link to this world, and I was his. When he smiled, I smiled. When he cried, so did I. He comforted me in my darkest moments; he made me a better person by loving me. If love were the thing to keep you alive in this world I felt like I could live forever in his arms.

"I love you, Henry." I cradled my ever-growing stomach. "I have everything I will ever need in this world right here in this chapel."

We were married. After years of wanting nothing more than to be together, we were finally married. We had gotten what we had wanted, and we could not be happier. All those years ago when I had refused to be the king's mistress I never for a second thought that I would be his wife. But now I was his wife. I am his wife. From a romance that should have never happened. To an uphill battle that had resulted in two people being happier than I thought possible.

After the wedding, we celebrated together. The people who had attended the wedding were also invited to join us for a meal. Henry spared no expense. He had ordered John Bricket, his chef, to put on the best meal that could be made. We had the most succulent beef, the juiciest venison, deer that had been hunted only that morning. After, we were presented with jellies, creamed almonds, and custard tarts. It was everything a woman in my condition could dream of. Henry knew that at this particular moment my pregnancy craved custard tarts all day every day. He had ordered the chef make them daily.

Everyone laughed and made merry. The wine flowing through the evening. My father looking happier than I had seen in years. Pleased as punch with "his" achievement. He made a toast to the king and me.

"Your Majesty," he bowed. "Anne," nodding in my direction. "From our family, we wish you both the greatest of happiness. We thank you for letting us join in the celebration of our two families joining together today." He raised his cup and sat back down. I was just glad that it was short and sweet.

George came over to us after the food had been removed.

"Your Majesty." he bowed low. Henry gestured for George to take a seat. "I have just come to wish you both well," he said. "Your Majesty, I ask that you please look after and cherish my sister, for she is a rare diamond indeed. And I hold her very dear to me." George beamed at me.

Henry nodded. "She is very dear to me as well. You have my word that I shall put her first in everything I do." He held my hand tightly.

"Thank you, Highness." George bowed his head. "Now that I have done my brotherly duty, I will leave you both to your happiness." George stood and kissed me on the head. "Sister." He kissed the king's ring. "Majesty." He returned to my mother's side and picked up a conversation with Henry Norris. George was ever the courtier. He always knew how to behave when around the king, but he was also a protective younger brother who loved his sisters with his whole heart. He would protect them against anyone.

Next Henry would stand up and say a few words. He took command of the whole room, everyone hanging on his every word.

"First of all, I would like to thank you all for attending today. Everyone in this room has supported from the start the love Anne and I share." He held his cup to the room.

"Now, I would like to address my love." He took my hand in his and kissed it. "My sweet, sweet Anne. How can I possibly begin to tell you how I feel about you. You are the calm behind the storm. The sun rising in the morning. You are the bird that sings to wake me gently. The air that sustains me. You are my heart, my soul and my very being. I was never a complete person before I met you. I was in a sinful marriage, only half a man. You have brought me out of my dark days and completed me.

"I vow that I will never harm one hair on your beautiful head. You will never shed one tear because of me. I will forever put your happiness above my own and share in each of your joys. Anne, you will soon give me a son. Our family will be complete. Soon you will be my queen; you will be the queen that not only I need, but this country needs. You are perfection in the shape of a woman." he pulled me from my seat. "I give to you all, your new queen."

He gestured to the room. "And now I believe my wife and I will take our leave of you and head to our marital bed." Henry laughed and swept me off of my feet; he carried me all the way to his rooms, my arm draped around his neck. When we were alone he kissed me hard and set me on my feet.

"Have I made you happy, my love?" he asked.

"There is no woman ever been so happy." I kissed him. "Thank you for your beautiful words, Harry. You are not just king of England. You are the king of my heart. Now and forever."

He stroked my hair smiling down at me. He looked young and in love like a boy first discovering the allure of a woman. I stroked his hair and kissed his hands.

"And you, Anne, are the queen of my heart. Know that I will look after you and never turn my back on you."

We laid together that night, our first time as a married couple. Cementing the vows we had taken that day.

That night, as I lay in bed next to Henry, I had the most vivid nightmares. I dreamt that Henry and I were arguing, I am not sure what we were arguing about, but he was so angry, he stood up and lunged at me. Pinning me to the ground, and strangling me to death. I woke to clutch at my throat, gasping for air. I awoke sobbing gently, not quite realising that the dream had released me from its grip. Henry stirred next to me.

"Darling, what makes you despair at this hour?" He stroked my hair.

"I dreamt that you hurt me, Harry. You wanted to kill me." I sobbed, "you held your hands around my throat and tried to choke the life from me."

"Anne, sweet, sweet Anne." He pulled me in and cradled me against him. "I would never wish to hurt you so. It was a nightmare and nothing more, my love." He wiped the tears from my face. "Come now, love. Lie right here and go back to sleep, safe in my arms."

He laid down and pulled me onto his chest. Contented now, I tried to dispel the dream from my mind. I convinced myself that it was the stress of my pregnancy that was making me dream so. I slept soundly for the rest of the night, in Henry's arms. Right where I knew I was supposed to be.

The next morning, I woke, still in Henry's arms. The early morning sun shining brightly through the window, waking us gently from our deep sleep. We laid in each other's arms for the remainder of the morning. We only moved to go and finally have something to eat. I had never been happier than at that moment.

We sat and ate our meal together, smiling and laughing like a pair of happy newlyweds. We were two people without a care in the world. Henry reached over from time to time to touch my belly where our child grew peacefully. He was so loved already, before he even had a name. Before we had ever laid eyes on him, we loved him. We were sure that he was to be born into a happy home, with parents who loved him to the ends of the earth.

"We must talk about your coronation, Anne." Henry had said as we finished our meal, and it was taken away. "Now that you are my wife, I long to make you queen." He kissed my hand.

"Oh, Harry, I look forward to becoming your queen." I held his hand that rested on my stomach. "I am so content with just being your wife that I forgot all about the other part of my duty."

"You will make a wonderful queen, my love." Henry touched my nose so gently. "We have discussed a date, Cromwell, and I. How would you feel about the first of June? That way we will have plenty of time to prepare. I want you to have the best coronation that money can buy. I want the whole world to see my new queen in all of her glory."

"The first of June sounds perfect. Thank you, Harry," I smiled. "You will help me to prepare? And be with me every step of the way?"

"I will teach you all that I know do not worry. You are in safe hands." Henry told me. "However, my sweetheart. I cannot be with you. The king may not attend your coronation. But I will be hidden away watching, so as not to outshine you."

I nodded at this. It would be all right. It was nothing more than performing at a masque, I thought. I loved to have people watch me perform, and this would be no different. I would be fine with knowing that Henry would be close by watching silently. I could not wait to see the pride on his face.

The next few months were wonderful. Henry and I were so very happy. I cannot say that I didn't enjoy it very much that people would bow low every time I walked into a room. The power that surged through me was like nothing I had ever felt before — knowing that I could command these people around me with just the one word. I was in complete control here. I could decide on the fates of everyone in this palace. With one sentence I could make or destroy anyone I wanted.

Margery stayed by my side constantly through the next few months. She was a steadying presence when I found my new title to be a touch overwhelming. George and I would meet and play cards in the evenings when the king was busy. We would talk into the small hours, and he would keep me company on the days that pregnancy made me weak. Thomas Wyatt was also back at court; he knew not how to act around me now that I was queen. Before, we would flirt and enjoy teasing each other, now we could not do this anymore. He would have to love me from afar as I had once told him.

Some days I would not move from my bed, I was growing bigger by the day, and the baby often made me feel nauseated and bloated. Henry, the gentleman that he was, would come into my rooms and lie with me — often bringing custard tarts along with him. Such a sweet man, caring for my every need. He would cradle and kiss my stomach. Talking to the son that grew inside.

"You are making your mother sick, little prince. Let her have some peace for there will be none once you are here. I will keep her very busy indeed."

Henry and I were almost inseparable. We spent as much time with each other as his kingship allowed. Sometimes we'd just lie there and stare at each other. Just drinking in the sight of the other, both basking in how fortunate we were to have each other. He would make sure that he checked in with me at least once a day — whether he crept into my rooms for a quick kiss and then left again or we would spend the day together, in the gardens or playing chess or sitting under the roses. After a long walk, if I were especially tired, Henry would scoop me up into his arms and carry me back to the palace, barely breaking a sweat as he lugged around his hugely pregnant wife.

Then he would lay me in my chair by the fire, kiss my lips and say "Rest, love. Let our son grow strong and sweet, like his mother."

We were so happy at the start. So in love. Every moment we spent apart from each other was agony. We slept in the same bed every night for the first year, which was unheard of. My rooms were practically unused as we would always sleep together in Henry's bed. We would dine together, spend the evenings by the fire and then fall asleep holding each other. We were so excited to make our little family complete. We did not have much time to ourselves now, as before we knew it, I would be crowned. Things were harder once life hit a normal rhythm. Henry had to put being king first, and I had to look to the future. There was a lot to prepare, and I had no idea if I was ready to become queen.

CHAPTER SIXTEEN

On the 29th May 1533 my coronation celebrations would start. It would include four days of festivities that would end in me being crowned in a lavish ceremony at Westminster Abbey. We had planned this for many months, and not a detail was skipped in preparation. I was the happiest I have ever been. Henry and I had wed after seven long years of waiting. I grew our precious child in my stomach, and now I would become queen of our country. I truly was the luckiest person in the world. I am surprised my heart didn't burst for all of the love it held. Henry was giving me his whole world and more.

The love I felt for him and our child was unbelievable. I cradled my belly in wonder at the love you could have for someone you had yet to meet. The child I grew within me was the product of the love shared between Henry and me, and that made him the most precious thing in the world.

I could not wait to become queen. It felt like the crowning moment to all of our achievements. To me it was the final piece coming together. I deserved this moment. After all of the strain that had come with getting to this point, I felt like it was part of the reward. This was Henry showing me off to the world and giving me the highest honour in the country. Everyone would know that I was the queen of both his heart and his country.

* * * * *

When the day came, I was to be received as queen by all of the lords of England. They would accept me as their queen in the traditional way. I would travel by water from Greenwich to the Tower of London where the mayor of London and other lords would await me. The Tower of London would be my home for the day as I awaited my coronation.

I grew nervous with the thought of staying away from Henry. I had become accustomed to always being close to him, and I felt uneasy about the separation. He had stayed with me the night before. He held me for the whole night. He disliked the idea of my staying away as much as I did, but we would not break formality. So on that day, I made my way to the Tower ready to start the beginning of my life as queen. My stomach full of butterflies and legs uneasy, I entered the great building with my head held high and a smile on my face. I could do this for Henry. He had given me so much. I could at the very least hold my nerves for a few days.

When I arrived at the Tower, Henry formally received me. There were a thousand guns fired to welcome me as each of the lords received me, ready to be their queen. I was so overwhelmed by it all. Thank God that Margery had come with me to help me prepare for the days ahead. This was only the beginning — the easy part. For the next few days I would be on show to the whole of England. I would stay here tonight before continuing with the rest of the festivities.

All of the lords were kind and courteous. Each one welcomed me warmly and offered me words of luck for the next few days. I would make a beautiful queen, they said. They were all overjoyed at being included in a day that would go down in history, and were glad to welcome me kindly into the walls of the Tower. I wonder now if any of them had the slightest inkling that things would end up coming full circle, as they smiled at me on that day. They probably had not the least clue of the magnitude of it. They had thought they were welcoming a new queen — someone who would rule for the rest of her years. I doubt very much that they suspected that the rest of my years would only equal three.

I sit now in the same rooms that I slept in while waiting for my coronation and I almost giggle to myself at the irony of it all. Three years ago I sat here aglow with excitement ready to be crowned queen, and now I sit and prepare to die. My uneasiness at staying here at the time now makes sense. Some part of me must have known that this place held a dark future for me. Somewhere inside I believe I already knew the fragility of it all, that my position was not necessarily a permanent one.

I remember thinking it a strange place at the time to hold so much death within its walls. That day, I felt a chill as I walked into the place, almost as if I could sense the spirits of the people who had been there before: anger at how they would meet their end. They, as I, had stayed in these walls before they were executed for their crimes. Some of them guilty. Some were innocent but swept up in someone else's story. The place held each and every one of those stories. Within its walls it held the tale of tragedy and hatred. Murder and blood stained the floor. Sadness filled the air as mothers said goodbye to sons here, as lovers held each other for the last time. There were young men and women waiting for the executioner to strike. My story will be added to these walls, and it will not be the last story of woe.

* * * * *

The day after, on 30th May, I was introduced to the people of London. My new subjects. In the morning, I was dressed in a delightful white gown with an ermine mantle. Margery and Elizabeth helped to ready me, and I was yet again thankful for the continued presence of my dear friends. George was unable to be here. I would have loved to have him reassure me. But it just was not done. Margery was as close to me as family, and I was glad that she was here with some comfort from George's words of pride.

198

I again let my long dark hair flow loose setting off my look perfectly. I was proud of my long locks, and I was happy to show them off to the world. Jewels were placed on me. Pearls and diamonds as I sparkled like a beautiful gemstone. I wore my B necklace. It had always felt lucky to me, and I wanted to show off who I was with pride. Today my name would be on the lips of everyone in London, and my stomach grew with excitement at the prospect. I longed for everyone to look at me in wonder. I wanted them to marvel at their new queen. Needed them to love me. To think I was beautiful. I wanted their approval today, and I was certain that I was going to get it. I believed that being queen meant that people automatically loved you. I could not wait to feel the love of hundreds of people, to feel like I finally found my place in the world and that I was adored. I was excited to be shown off to the Londoners.

After I was prepared and ready, I left the Tower of London and rode from the place through the streets of London. I was in a divine chariot which was covered in cloth of silver, with a canopy of cloth of silver that hung beautifully over my head. The chariot was carried by the four lords of ports who were dressed in gowns of scarlet. As they carried me along, I looked out upon my new people and at the country that was now my own. My heart filled with pride as I took in the wonderful home that I now ruled. There was a part of me that still could not believe that all of this was for me. It was as if I had been dreaming for the last year. Things had only gotten better and better since I fell in love with Henry.

Riding with me I had a number of lords, gentlemen, and knights, as was tradition as part of the coronation ceremony. Behind me were four chariots of ladies and more ladies and gentlewoman on horseback. They were all wearing the most fabulous crimson velvet gowns. Each and every one of us in the procession looked like the stuff of dreams. We were all dressed in the richest of fabrics and adorned with the brightest of jewellery.

London itself had been made to look amazing. They had hung out many banners and decorations to see me along the way. There was almost too much to take in as scaffolds had been erected to display pageants and the fountains provided wine for anyone who would come along to see. Hanging above us was a huge white falcon displayed for all of London as the badge of their new queen.

Everyone should have been in an excellent mood as they were treated to a fabulous spectacle. They should have made merry as the wine flowed freely, and should have been overjoyed at such a treat from their beloved king. As I progressed through the streets I waited to be accepted into London with open arms. I waited for everyone to accept me with open hearts and for them to react with glee at the sight of me travelling through their city.

However, that never happened. They did not cheer for me or wave at me as I greeted them. They stood and looked on. Uninterested with the spectacle before them. I had thought that there would be hundreds of people lining the streets to get a glimpse of all that was going on, but people seemed bored and uninterested. Henry had spared no expense, and the people seemed as if they did not want to be here at all. As if they had only come to get out of their homes for the day. It was as if they had better things to be doing with their day and this was an unneeded distraction.

The only people who seemed animated were the ones who booed me away. Shouting for the "imposter" to be removed. "We want the real queen," they screamed at me. Others joining in. "Where is Queen Catherine?" they sneered. "We love Catherine. Not this whore." They snickered at me as the procession moved along. The guards made many arrests that day as the people got out of hand They hated me. Before they even knew me, they already hated me.

I was distraught. I had thought that being queen came with automatic respect, but they detested me. I was a joke in their eyes. Henry loved me; why could they not? I felt unwanted and stupid. I had been sure that this was my moment and yet I was a laughing stock. I kept thinking that I just wanted to be with Henry. I wanted to be away from all of this now. I was tired, and the people did not want me. What was the point? They shouted and jeered.

At one point in the procession they simply chanted "Catherine" together as if they had all planned to come along and taunt me together. Of course they loved her. She would have to win today. Even in what should have been my happiest moments, Catherine was here. She would not allow herself to be forgotten. Not just when everything was going my way. She would be laughing to herself at my misery. For I may have won Henry, but clearly I would never win the love of her people, and she knew that.

The procession ended at Westminster, where I would be left for the evening. I thanked God that it was finally over. I do not think I could have taken another moment. It had been a horrible day and it could not be over quickly enough. What was I thinking? That England would just be satisfied with the fact that a woman they had loved for twenty-four years had been kicked off of the throne to make way for me? I was a nobody, and I had expected them to sing my praise. This was my own fault for wishing to be loved instantly. I just wanted to lie in Henry's arms now. I wanted his love to consume me so that I could forget about the day I had been forced to bear. The day was not to finish on a high note, however.

After all of the spectacle had finished, Henry rushed into my rooms and pulled me into a hug. It felt amazing as I allowed him to hold me. The tears falling freely now from my eyes.

"Anne, I am so sorry." He held me. "The people are stubborn. Give them time, my love," he soothed as I cried into his chest.

"They hate me, Harry." I breathed. "They want Catherine. Everyone prefers Catherine," I said with spite in my voice. I felt bitter. I hated all of them for the way they made me feel. They and Catherine had ruined something that should have been special.

"They just do not know you. In time, they will love you as I do. I promise." Henry spoke softly.

I pushed him off of me. "You should have stayed with Catherine, Henry. Your life would be easier. Why did you marry a whore?" I raged.

I doubted in that moment everything I had fought for. I suddenly felt stupid for thinking that the people would love me in the same way as they had Catherine. I was just a usurper who stole the crown. Why should they like me?

"Oh? I should have stayed with Catherine?" Henry asked, anger filling him. "If that is how you feel, then perhaps I should have saved myself some heartache," he shouted back at me. "If you were a whore, Anne, I never would've married you. I would have slept with you and left as I intended to do in the first place." Henry shouted, for the first time admitting his initial plan for us. I had always thought as much, but it still stung. I hated when he raised his voice. It made me feel like an insecure little child, and it was the last thing I needed that night.

"Get out, Henry. I want to be alone," I screamed. It was not his fault, but he was bringing little comfort to me tonight. I was angry, and my anger had to go somewhere.

"Is this the thanks I get? I have given you everything. I have turned my world on its head for you. And you repay me with hate?" He spat. He was furious. Why wouldn't he be? I was throwing it all back in his face.

"You did not have to turn the world on its head Henry. You could have continued sleeping with my sister and left me to marry Percy," I said the words with instant regret. I have no idea what possessed me to turn on him, and I knew all the while that I was behaving like a petulant child.

"Is that what you want? You wish you had married Percy," he fumed. He grabbed me by the shoulders and shook me. "Perhaps this was all a mistake then. Perhaps I should have stayed with Catherine. I would be much happier than I am now." He threw me to the ground and made to storm off as I laid shaking on the floor. My hands automatically going to where our baby lay inside of me. This was the first time he had ever physically hurt me, and I was in shock. He had never been so harsh with me before. I must have really angered him for him to take hold of me so, and it felt terrible. It was like our relationship changed in that moment to one where he now resulted in being physical, should I anger him so much. It was the first time, and it would not be the last.

He turned back. "You should thank me, woman. I have changed the whole of England for you. You should be worshipping at my feet for raising you so high," He bellowed.

I felt all of the guilt in that moment. How wretched I was to speak to him in the way I did. Instead of reacting in the way I should have by telling him he could not lay a hand on me, I instead begged for him to forgive me. I was foolish. He had no right to throw me to the ground, especially not while I carried his child in me. He disrespected his child and me when he reacted in that way. But I was so blind to abuses. I allowed him to use me in any way he wished and then pleaded with him to forgive me.

"Henry…I am sorry." I took hold of his hand pulling myself up a little. "I just want them to love me." I cried. I did not want him to be angry with me. I wanted him to love me always. Why did I have to be so ungrateful? I did this. I blamed him for the cruelty of others,

"You were nothing but a common little slut. But I chose to love you anyway, against all of my advisors."

I sobbed into my hands, not moving from where I fell. How could he say this to the woman he loved. I wanted him just to go back to the way he was before. I wish I had never said anything to anger him in the first place. I sobbed as I sat still on the ground. The strength to move having left me altogether.

"Henry, I am sorry. Do not leave me like this. I love you. I am sorry." I pleaded. Wishing that he would take me in his arms and this could all be forgotten.

He pulled me up from the floor. "Do not apologise to me now. I will not hear it." he practically spat in my face. "Now to bed with you before you damage my son." He practically threw me at the bed.

"Our son...Henry." I reminded him through my sobs.

But he was already gone. I let myself slide down the wall and spent the evening curled up in a ball on the floor. He was so awful sometimes. His rage was so much stronger than his love would ever be. But if I loved him, I had to take that side of him. I had to let him shout and scream at me from time to time; the good times were so worth it. For every one bad day there were a hundred good days, and I was willing to accept the bad if it meant that I could live in the good. The guilt was undeniable. Why did I have to rile him up?

Of course he loved me and not Catherine. He has done nothing but show his love, and I just spat it back in his face. I was thankful for everything Henry had given me, but I found it hard living in Catherine's shadow. Even the people loved her more than me. They had not even given me a chance. They turned from me before they even knew me. I would stay like this now for the rest of the night wallowing in my own sadness. I was pathetic, but I had no energy to move. I would lay sleepless for the night, full of regret from our conversation.

* * * * *

On Sunday, the 1st of June, I was finally crowned as Queen of England. After months of planning and preparation the day had finally come along. I had been living and acting as queen for some time now, but this would make it official. No one would be able to question my authority after this day. God had put me in place to be a queen, and I would now be anointed as such in a holy ceremony in front of the whole country. The people would just have to come to terms with the fact that there was now a new queen and whether they liked it or not, they had to accept me. After this day they could no longer question my authority. I held power over all of them and did not require their love or permission to become their queen.

The day started like any other. I was very tired. The pain of my argument with Henry had kept me awake all night long I could not wait to be queen in every single way But I wish my coronation celebrations had gotten off to a better start. Henry came to me in the morning, bringing me some beautiful red roses he had taken from the garden. I feel that this was in a way his way of apologising. Of course, I would forgive him without a second thought. It was not his fault he got so angry; I had pushed him to it by not being grateful.

To think that I was so weak when it came to his anger makes me sick now. I wish I had had more of a backbone. Especially now that I know how it will end. I had decided to let yesterday's woes float away. Today was a new day. He was so proud of me he told me. The look he had on his face when he walked in to see me in my bedclothes was indescribable. The evil man that had been in his place yesterday was but a distant memory. He looked like a man so very in love as his eyes shone with tears as he looked upon me. I was sat picking at my breakfast not having much of an appetite that morning. Both the baby and the stress were doing no good for my stomach.

He smiled so gently that I allowed myself to fall in love all over again, forgetting about the stupid argument. When he walked in he put the flowers down beside me and cupped my face with both hands. The disagreement from the night before was not brought up, and I was glad for it to be forgotten.

"Darling, you look positively glowing today," he said. "How much I love you. Today more than I did yesterday. It grows more by the day. And the look of you this morning is enough to fill my heart to the brim." He kissed my forehead.

"Oh, Harry. I love you too." the tears pricked my eyes. As I was flooded with relief that I had not pushed him away.

"Why do you cry, my love? Are you not happy?" he asked.

I giggled as I held his face. "I cry because I am happy. I could not be happier. I am the happiest." I said wiping my eyes.

Henry seemed to think for a moment. As if concocting some sort of plan.

"The most happy?" he asked. "That should be your motto, my love. How does that suit you?"

It sounded perfect. It summed up everything that I was feeling and hoping for the future.
"Oh, Harry. It is perfect! The perfect motto to start my reign." I took his hand. The sadness that had filled me only moments ago had been completely forgotten. I now felt as happy as I had been on our wedding day. So full of hope for our future together.

"The baby started to kick last night." I grinned. "here feel." I said, holding his hand firmly to my stomach. We both felt a thud as the baby kicked at his hand.

"I felt it!" he exclaimed. "I felt our little prince kick me. Now we are both the most happy," Henry chuckled, happiness filling his whole demeanor.

"I think he is excited for today. He has not stopped all night," I giggled. "We are so fortunate, are we not?" I took his hand and kissed it gently. "I do not love you more everyday Harry. I love you more by the minute." I told him. It was true. My heart grew so big that it might soon overtake me.

"We are the most fortunate people in the whole world." he pulled us both up and kissed me almost as fiercely as the first time. "My queen. You will be wonderful today, I know it."

He held me to him tightly. "Good luck, beautiful Anne. I will be watching, just out of the way. You will do this country, and me, proud." He beamed at me. With a quick kiss on the lips, he was gone again.

* * * * *

I was dressed in purple and velvet ermine, the colour of royals. I was led out of Westminster and walked under a canopy to St Peter's abbey. The monks of Westminster leading me in gorgeous robes of gold. There were also thirteen abbots with me, and behind us, the kings chapel, with two archbishops and four bishops. I was led by Charles Brandon, the duke of Suffolk, who carried the crown along with two more bishops who carried my sceptres. The old duchess of Norfolk carried my train as it reached over two meters behind me. Ladies dressed in scarlet with golden coronets on their heads were behind, along with my ladies, including my dear Margery, in gowns of scarlet edged with white Baltic fur.

I was in awe the whole way there. I looked around me at the country that I now was responsible for. I was about to become the second most powerful person in all of England. This was it. Today was the day where everything I had worked for would finally be given to me. Today we celebrated me and the new life that had been presented to me. It felt like everything from the past few years had built up to today, and I found that I wanted the crown almost as much as I wanted Henry. This was another wedding day for me. But this time I was being married to a country rather than to a man.

When I got to the chapel, I was led to the front of the place and seated in my high royal seat above everyone else. I was anointed by the archbishop of Canterbury and the archbishop of York. I looked straight ahead of me, keeping my composure for the whole ceremony, I was handed the sceptres, and had the holy oil placed onto my forehead. I sat as still as a pretty little statue while the ceremony took place around me. I breathed deeply as I took in everything, step by step.

The moment was nearing closer as the whole of the abbey looked on. Everyone was waiting to see me crowned. I had pictured this moment in my head for the past few months, and now Cranmer was readying to give me the crown and make it official. My heart seemed to stop as I saw him pick it up off of its great pillow and draw close to me. This was the moment, I thought. This was the start of my life. I was thrilled to become queen. All of the nerves and worries washed away at that moment. This felt almost as right as marrying Henry had. It was as it was meant to be, and this was me fulfilling my destiny. Cranmer finally placed the crown of St Edward on top of my head and announced me as Queen of England.

I took a breath, ready to stand for my people. I was finally queen. I had arrived here. I was now Queen Anne Boleyn of England, and it felt so right. This was what fate had in store for me. And as I looked out at the sea of the people watching I could have cried with joy. The first time in my life my father looked genuinely proud as I caught his face in the crowd. George stood beaming at me as his sister became a queen. The feeling that overtook me was indescribable. It was a sense of great achievement mixed with a great sense of pride for myself and for my country.

My love for Henry met no bounds this day; he had given me not only a loving husband and child, but a whole country. No woman before me had been so fortunate. I looked out on all of the people in the chapel as they cheered for me. Each of them bowing low to their new queen, and I realised that today my new life had begun. Today I signed my name in the history books and my legacy would take hold. I stood, head held high, and made my way back through the chapel, as they all fell to their knees before me.

After the ceremony, my first queenly duty was to preside over the coronation feast. I walked into the grand feast, laid out for me. Still covered in my canopy of state, I made my way to the high table, where I sat in the centre, ready to look out at my new loyal subjects. I had my aunt Anne Howard on one side of me and Elizabeth Brown on the other, it was nice to lean over and see a comforting face. They were there to ensure that I looked presentable at all times.

Thomas Cranmer was also seated at my table, and I was glad of this. He had been a dear friend since his help in ending the marriage of Henry and Catherine, and now he had made me queen. There would be two gentlemen sat at my feet for the entirety of the celebration. I could not help but feel sorry for them. It must have been rather uncomfortable knelt down at my feet while I enjoyed a grand feast.

After I had sat down, in rode the Deputy Earl Marshal, the Lord High Steward and the Sewer. Behind them came the newly knighted men of the Bath bringing in my first course. This first course consisted of thirty-two dishes. As I ate the food that was placed in front of me, including cranes, fabulous cuts of beef and wonderful lobster, trumpets sounded all around us. I was served first. Then the archbishop and then the rest of the guests were given their food. There were over seventy different dishes throughout the three courses, and by the end I felt weary, I looked forward to sleeping in my own bed that night. The past few days had exhausted me no end. Becoming queen was tiresome enough without carrying a growing baby inside of you.

While this went on, I could sense Henry's presence. He was not to be part of this feast because I had to be the highest person presiding to mark my place as queen. He and a few of his ambassadors sat in a room just to the side. Watching everything that was happening. I could not see him, but I was aware the whole time of his eyes on me, and it felt good to know that he was close, looking on in pride as I fulfilled my first act as his queen.

Once I had finished my meal I stood, and the whole room stood in a sign of respect. I moved to the centre of the hall, where the lord mayor stood with a golden cup, offering me wafers and hippocras. I received these things gratefully and then I gave him the cup as I had been told to. This was to thank him and his men for their efforts over the last few days. Then I walked from the hall finally ending the festivities. Every one bowed as I left. The past few days had been carefully choreographed step by step. I had been preparing for months on end and practicing each part until I knew exactly how to behave. Even down to the point of handing the lord mayor the golden cup. I had rehearsed that more times than I care to admit. I was exhausted. Happy and overjoyed, but so very tired.

Just outside of the hall, George came to my side; he practically had to hold me up. I would have slept in that very spot had he not come to my side.

"Your highness, you must rest," George said.

"Do not call me that, George. Always call me Anne. I am your sister still" I stroked his cheek. I would never change towards him.

"I am the proudest brother alive today, Anne." he smiled. "You did a wonderful job today, Sister." He looked at me, prouder than he had ever been, and this was the perfect ending to a perfect day.

"Oh, George. You really think I did well? I tried so hard." I said. Tears threatened as the tiredness took over. "The people did not like me much." I laughed.

George smiled down at me all the time guiding me to my room. "You were perfect in every way." He answered. "They will grow to love you. And if they do not, well, who cares? They have no say in the matter. Henry loves you, and you will be by his side for the rest of your lives."

George opened my door to let me into my room where I could finally rest for the first time in days. I had never been so happy to return home. Waiting just inside was Henry. He stood by the door ready to welcome me. George delivered me into his open arms and left with a quick bow. I fell into his arms so happy to see him. He led us both over to the bed where we lay in silence for a while.

"I am so proud of you." Henry broke the silence eventually. "Queen Anne," he said it with such passion; it sounded so good on his lips. "It suits you, does it not?"

I kissed him. I wanted to convey in that kiss just how grateful I was. Just how much I loved him. I had no words to show the joy I felt inside of me, but I needed him to know just how happy I was. After another long while I simply said "The most happy, Harry." Then we just lay there and eventually I fell asleep.

CHAPTER SEVENTEEN

Three months later, I was a month away from the date
the baby was to come. I went into confinement in
preparation. I would spend confinement at Greenwich
where Henry himself had been born. The chamber where I
would give birth was richly carpeted and hung with
tapestries of gold all of the light and windows were blocked
out, bar one, should I wish to enjoy a moment or two of the
sun. I was told that this should be avoided as it was not safe
for the baby or myself, but Henry wanted me to have as
much comfort as I could and if that meant me being
allowed a little sunlight he would not deny me.

I and my ladies, who included Margery, ever by my
side, were led in a mass beforehand. We prayed for a son.
Then we drank wine and made merry celebrating the near
arrival of a prince. After we had enjoyed our last moments
in the outside world the chamberlain blessed me and said a
prayer for the safe delivery of our son. Then I was locked
away in a room with just my ladies.

No men were to be anywhere near me for the next
month, and I had been filled with dread at the thought of
not seeing Henry for a whole month. We had spent the
whole summer locked away together at Windsor, away
from the prying eyes of the country. We were wrapped up
in our own loving privacy, and did not want to be
disturbed. Of course the court continued as always, but we
had chosen not to go on progress this year. Henry wanted to
be by my side and progress would have proven too stressful
on my heavily pregnant state.

He came to me the night before my confinement, and we
spent the night in my bed. He wanted to wish me and the
little one luck. He told me that he could not wait to meet
him. We were so sure of our little prince. I could not wait
to present him to his father. I was anxious for the birth
itself but overcome by excitement at finally being able to

meet the little boy that I had grown in my stomach for nine months. The pain that I was about to go through would be worth it once we had our reward. I knew that a lot of the time women severely struggled in childbirth, but I had great Doctors around me including my most trusted Dr Butts.

* * * * *

It turned out that I was only to be in confinement for two weeks. The precious little bundle that I had delivered did not want to wait any longer. The 7th of September 1533 at three in the afternoon, I gave birth. I gave birth to the most beautiful little red-haired girl I had ever seen. A wonderful little package of pure joy and as she was placed on my chest and confirmed as being female the worry of having a boy melted away. How could I be disappointed with such a beauty? I had never felt true love until that moment. The second that she was finally pulled from me I forgot all about the question of an heir and all I could see was that delicate little flower placed into my arms.

She filled the whole room with her strong piercing cries, and I knew from that very moment that she would truly be her father's daughter. My heart was so full to the brim, no one else in the room mattered, no one in the world mattered, only my daughter and I. I instantly felt the protectiveness flow from me, and knew that from this moment on, I would do everything in my power to keep her safe. I would die for this little girl. No harm would ever come to her, so long as I was around.

Her eyes were so blue already, just like her father's. She came out with a head full of hair, as bright as any Tudor ever lived before. She held nothing of me yet, and that was just as it should be. She was so sweet, so gentle; I did not know it possible for something so perfect to come from me. I was shocked by just how much she meant to me. The doctor cleaned her up, and I looked on astounded at her.

She was the product of Henry and me, and I was amazed at the instant love I felt for this small thing that scrunched her face up with tears.

The birth had been agony. I had never felt pain like it. It felt as if I was being ripped apart. I cried and I begged for the pain to stop. I wanted so desperately for it to be over. But the second my daughter was placed on my chest, the pain melted away and was replaced by the most astonishing love that I had ever felt. I would relive every ounce of agony again if it meant that I could feel that love coarse through my body once more.

After I had time to marvel over her a little while, I realised that her father was probably being told right now that I had failed him — the one thing he needed from me, I had been unable to do. He had given me the whole world on a plate, and I could not even bear a son. If we were a normal couple, if we were not royalty, then a girl could bring us all the joy in the world, but Henry needed a son to carry on his line. We were so sure that she would be a little prince. I had not doubted it for a moment. God had smiled on our match I was convinced of it, so surely he would want me to give Henry a brood of boys to follow him?

I decided that I would not allow it to ruin the joy I now felt. I did not care, I would take Henry's wrath, in whatever way it may come. I was happy to have her now; I was happy that she was a daughter, for I could not have imagined anything more adorable in the whole wide world. I think, maybe, we were supposed to have a girl. I just knew that one day she would be important and people will look back and be glad that we did not have a son straight away. She was born to do great things; she would be important. I did not doubt that.

Not long after she had greeted the world, it was time to greet her father. Henry came bursting into the room, he ran to my side and enclosed me in his arms, before noticing the child I now cradled close to me. He looked down on her, his eyes gleaming with barely concealed tears. I thought he had been crying from anger and frustration at failing yet again to have a male child. I braced myself for the blow that I was sure would come from him. I had promised a son. A daughter was not even a possibility. I could not be more wrong. They were tears of joy; he looked so content and happy. He kissed me on the forehead and stroked my hair.

"Oh Anne, you magnificent women," he smiled at me as he sat on the edge of my bed. "Can I hold her?" he asked.

"Of course you can, Harry." I said shock clear on my face as I handed him the little one so carefully not wanting to disturb her from the quiet sleep she was in." This is your new daughter," I said as a great pride filled my chest. I already loved being a mother. It was the most wonderful feeling in the world.

"And how beautiful she is, just like her brilliant mother." He kissed me on the head as the tears and tiredness finally gripped me.

I was more content than I had ever been. I was sitting in my bed with my husband, who cradled our beautiful little daughter. We were complete finally as I lay my head on his shoulder.

I waited — waited for him to suddenly grow angry and rage at me. I had thought I was in for a peek of the king's famous rage. I had thought he would hate me now. I had prepared to grovel. To make my excuses and apologies for the clear failure. When he simply sat on the edge of my bed and stared down at our child in wonder I could take it no longer.

"I am sorry Harry, I was sure she would be a boy for you. These things happen, and I promise…." but he cut me off. He never let me get to the end of my sentence.

"Hush now, Anne. You need to rest." He moved my pillows so that I could lay back down again. "We have our whole lives to have sons. Our next one is sure to be a boy. This just means we will have to keep trying." He chuckled softly so as not to wake the sleeping angel.

"Harry, you really do not mind?" I asked confused.

He nodded, smiling his beautiful smile at me. "And we will have boys I promise. Lots and lots of boys," I wept.

"Why would I mind when you have given me such a lovely daughter?" he chuckled gently, as he cooed over her. "You have given England a new princess. The people will love her."

"As I love her." I stroked her hair.

"As we love her." he kissed her forehead and gave her into Jane Parker's hands. I hated the idea that I could not hold on to her forever, but I was too exhausted to protest.

"Now. our little princess needs a name? Perhaps Jane or Margaret?" He suggested looking thoughtful

"I would like to call her Elizabeth? After your mother, Harry." I had thought long and hard on this, Henry had loved his mother with his whole heart. He was still so broken after her death, and this way he could remember her. This was how we could honour her memory. He beamed from ear to ear. I had never seen his look more awed. Tears reformed in his eyes as he thought on my suggestion.

"Oh, Anne. It is perfect. Then she shall be Princess Elizabeth Tudor. After my mother. Thank you, sweet wife. You do both my mother and me a great honour. I am so lucky." he kissed me. "Now rest darling. Sleep well and grow strong. We have work to do if we want to make our little princess a brother."

As I watched Elizabeth grow, I grew prouder and more in love by the second. She was a little treasure. I wanted so much to nurse her myself and after many arguments with Henry over the correct order of things I managed to convince him. He knew that it was important to me and that I would never back down on the matter. I would not let a stranger feed my child when I was perfectly capable of doing it. It was a mother's duty to provide for her children, and I would have it no other way. I spent every spare moment in the nursery just staring at her. I could look upon her for hours on end without needing to move. She was so peaceful, so innocent. I wondered at how we could make something so delicate and perfect.

She had no idea of the world she had been born into, or the cruelty that she would surely face one day and I knew that I wanted to keep her from experiencing any of it. She slept soundly, loved more than she would ever know. I spent more time holding my baby than I did with my husband. I would keep her with me as often as possible. Even during state events she would be by my side and as she grew I would place my daughter on a cushion next to me while I sat on the throne and presided over the court. I would shower her with affection and all of the gifts that money could buy, whether it was new dresses or jewellery for when she grew or little toys to keep her entertained.

Henry grew to hate this. He raged at me one night that I must love our daughter more than I love him. Of course I did. I remembered thinking, she was a part of me. She came from me and with her holding a piece in her heart. I could not possibly put anyone above her. I did not tell him this for it would have been an argument that I did not need, and I did not want to upset him, so I told him. "Henry, there is nothing in this world that I love more than you." Knowing all the while that I would always place her needs above his.

* * * * *

When Elizabeth was only three months old Henry decided that as a royal princess, she should have her own household. I was outraged. He wanted to separate me from my child; he wanted to hide her away from the court to be taken care of by strangers. I begged Henry to let her stay with us. I cried and I cried, telling him that it would not be good for us to be apart. She needed her mother in order to grow strong, and I would be at a loss in her absence. At one point I refused to speak to him. Why would I want to talk to someone who was trying to steal my daughter? My mother came to see me one night. I was staying in my own apartments, refusing to be anywhere near Henry. She was charged with convincing me that this is the way things should be. She said of how much it had hurt her when I departed for Austria, something that I had never known.

I had thought that she was more than happy to be free of me. How she had cried every night at the start, but she understood that it was in my best interests to be sent away and it would be in the royal family's best interest to send Elizabeth away so that she could learn her royal duties. I dug my heels in refusing to listen to anyone. The thing is that I could scream and shout as much as I wanted, but Henry was king, and I would have never won this argument no matter how I pleaded or cried. It was Thomas Wyatt who finally convinced me. He had been back at court for some time, but we had not seen much of each other. Our lives had taken such different paths. I was clearing my mind in the open night air walking with Elizabeth when I bumped into him seemingly doing the same thing.

"Your Highness." he bowed low to me.

"Thomas, how lovely to see you," I said as he straightened. "I hope that you are well?" I was happy to see such a dear friend. He had been away from court working on something for Henry, and I had missed him.

Lady Elizabeth stepped away. Ever lurking, not too far off. I wish I had realised her true motive all those years ago, but she had disguised herself as a friend so that she could listen in on my conversations.

"I am well, your grace. I hope you are well also?" He asked with formality. To which I could have laughed.

"Oh Thomas, are we not friends?" I asked. He nodded at this. "Then call me Anne. None of this silly protocol when it is just the two of us." I did not want anything to change between my friends and me. I may be queen, but to the loved ones I was still just Anne.

He smiled, and we found a spot in the gardens, where we sat and talked the evening away. I told him of my problems, and he told me of what was bothering him. He was finding it hard to adjust to his new life at court, so I told him that if he ever needed a friendly face then he only need to look for me, which would happen on many occasions during the course of my reign.

We picked our friendship up where it had left off. He had suggested to me that if I were to agree to send Lizzie off, then I should at least be in control of who was to care for her. I took this to Henry. He agreed without hesitation. I think he had grown as weary by the argument as I had and was glad to be done with it.

So Lizzie went to have her own household in Hatfield. My heart broke to send her away. I had not spent a single day away from her before this, and it was unbearable to lose her now, but at least I had chosen some of the ladies to go with her including Margaret Bryan who I held in the highest esteem. She would visit us, and we would visit her. Henry had promised that we would receive regular updates and although I was still frosty with him I nodded my agreement. I took myself away to my own chambers and wept for my little Lizzie. Promising myself that I would see her again soon.

* * * * *

Henry and I went back to being happy very quickly. I forgave him for sending her away. He was only doing what was expected of a royal. The same thing had happened when Catherine had had Lady Mary. He liked it as little as I did, but he told me that now we could focus on making an heir. And soon enough that would become a reality.

In January, I was with child again. It was something I had suspected for a while now, but the doctor confirmed it. Our perfect little family was about to get even bigger. I could not wait to tell Henry that I was finally carrying a little prince. I found him with his privy council. I did not care that they were in a meeting; my news could not wait.

I walked through the doors and everyone scrambled to their feet to address me. "Your highness." they all mumbled.

"Anne. we are in an important meeting." Henry said looking slightly annoyed at my disruption.

"My love, I have some news for you" I spoke only to Henry now. "I am sorry to interrupt, but this is something you would like to know straight away."

"Come then." Henry said and gestured me into his personal office. "What is this news that could not wait, Anne?" He looked tired. He had been in many conversations with these men lately, and sometimes being king really got the better of him.

I took his hand and placed it on my stomach. "I am with child again." I giggled. "We are going to have another child, Harry."

His face lit up as he heard my words. He suddenly looked joyful again. The tiredness sweeping away as he cracked the most fabulous smile.

"You are pregnant?" He picked me up and spun me around, kissing me hard. "Oh Anne. you make me more happy than I thought possible."

We had only just been married a year, and already we were looking forward to our second child. We were overjoyed. Life was treating us well, and the more happy I made Henry, the more the people of England would have to accept me. I knew that this time I would have a prince and make all of our efforts come to fruition.

* * * * *

I seemed to grow big with the child rather quickly the second time around and as such lost all interest in my wifely duties, much to Henry's dismay. I was just so uncomfortable all of the time. This little one seemed to cause me no end of trouble. I found myself having to rest frequently throughout the day. Sometimes not being capable of leaving my bed altogether.

Henry strayed from me during this time. He took a mistress. He thought that I did not know, but I always knew what was going on when my back was turned. How stupid he thought me, to assume that I did not have eyes and ears all over the palace. What my brother George failed to report to me, Thomas would tell me. I was beside myself. How could he truly love me if he was to share his bed, our bed, with some whore who was not his wife? While I prepared to birth our child he ran around with some stupid girl. How low he must hold me now, to put someone else in my place.

I barged into his rooms one evening when I knew he would not be alone. I truly wish that I could have captured the look on their faces; the silly little girl was petrified. I told him that I would never be second best to anyone. He had me and me alone or he had no one.

"Anne…what are you doing here?" Henry shouted. Looking shocked at my sudden arrival. Unannounced and catching him completely off guard.

"What am I doing here? What is this whore doing here?" I demanded, walking towards them.

I grabbed her by the wrist and pulled her naked from the bed. "Leave before I have my guards drag you from this place," I commanded. She was worse than scum, and I would have her dirtying up my marriage bed no longer.

"Ye…yes…Your Highness." She made to get dressed. She was shaking from head to toe — silly little witch. Henry just looked on in shock. He had no idea how to deal with this situation. Most wives allowed their husbands to do whatever they wanted.

"Did I tell you to dress? Or did I command you to leave?" I spat at her as she tried to get into her shift.

She held her gown over her as she glanced at Henry. He was going to be of no help to her. He listened to me.

"You heard your queen. Go." he waved her out.

Once she was gone, he rounded on me. "Anne, what do you think you are doing?"

I was furious. Honestly, I could have hit him in that moment as he lay with some vile little whore.

"How dare you sleep with another while your child grows big in my belly," I screamed at him.

"How dare I? I have needs Anne." he fumed. "How dare you cast me from your bed." He dared to look angry.

"It is not safe for the baby. And you know this." Crying now, I leaned against the bedposts, my legs weakening under me. I was exhausted. This was the most I had done in weeks, thanks to the pregnancy.

"It is only right for a king to have a mistress. What makes you different than any other queen? Why should you be treated differently? Better queens than you have had adulterous husbands." Henry spoke to me as if he were explaining the rules of our love.

"Maybe when I am no longer with child I shall take a lover then. How would you feel about that?" I spat. "To imagine me in the arms of another?"

It ws stupid. I should have never said it. It was one of the silliest things I have ever said. I did not mean it. I would never lie with another, but I wanted to hurt him, and I knew that would do the trick. He needed to be in my shoes.

Henry came for me pinning me down on the bed. "Oh, you are going to take a lover? Who? Thomas Wyatt?" he growled in my face. Fear coursed through my body as I was motionless against the bed. Would he strike me again? Why not. He could do as he pleased with me. I was his property.

"That is, if you have not already slept with him? Maybe the child you now carry is his and no Tudor at all." Henry accused me. This was new territory. Why would he jump straight to Wyatt? And to say that I was unfaithful. I never would.

"Harry, I would never...Thomas is a friend." My fear turned to panic now.

"You walk on a dangerous ground woman. I could have you sent away." he gripped my chin as breathed in my face. "Maybe I will. Maybe I shall cast you off."

"Henry...I am sorry, I would nev..." He cut through my words.

"Hold your tongue in my presence from now on, or these accusations could suddenly become a lot more real than you realise." he let me up finally. "You will shut your eyes as your betters have done."

CHAPTER EIGHTEEN

On the 24th of April 1534, I had taken myself off to bed. I was not feeling quite myself that evening. I had a slight stomach ache and had imagined it was the baby giving me a bit of trouble. He had not started to move yet and being four or perhaps five months in now I had been waiting for it to start. This was the part of pregnancy I most looked forward to. When a woman feels her child kick inside of her, it makes the whole thing seem a bit more real. Henry and I had enjoyed it so much the last time. I was sharing in our joy at the first steps of being parents. I wanted to experience all of the same joy this time around.

I had been in the middle of a meal with Henry and some of the other members of the court when a headache started to throb at my temples, and I began to feel very tired. Henry was in the middle of a conversation with Charles Brandon when I had leaned over.

"Henry, I am feeling a little weary." I had said to him hoping that he would offer some sort of comfort.

"Go to bed then, Anne. You are not needed here." he had brushed me off, waving me away with a hand. It was not the reaction I had hoped for. I had thought he would at least ask me what the matter was, but sometimes he was so obtuse. Especially when in the company of his friends.

"Goodnight, my love." I kissed him on the cheek before getting up to go. As I stood, my legs felt a little weak. Almost as if they could scarcely bear the weight of me. I had to hold myself up for a moment before I found the strength to take a step. Henry did not notice. He carried on with his conversation without even giving me a second glance.

"Yes, goodnight." he was too engaged in whatever Charles had to say to care much what I did.

"Goodnight, Your Majesty." Charles kissed my hand.

"Goodnight Brandon." I nodded before catching Margery's attention and making my way out.

As I left, the whole room stood and watched me leave, bowing as I went. My ladies followed me in quick succession. Margery running to my side to find out what was wrong. I had told her how I was feeling and sent the rest of my ladies back to their own rooms for the night. I just wanted her with me tonight. All of the fuss from my other ladies would have bothered me too much. I wanted a bit of peace and quiet.

I got back to my apartments and sat in my chair by the fire for a while, trying to distract myself from the pain. It worked for a little while, but when the pain got so intense that I could no longer concentrate she read a little bit to me. The pain spread all across my back and around the front of my stomach now. Sitting was no longer possible as my back ached from top to bottom and no matter how I sat or wriggled about. It was impossible to get comfortable.

I was annoyed that the baby was causing me so much grief, but the truth was my pregnancy with Elizabeth was also an uncomfortable one at this stage, and I knew that I simply had to let it pass on its own. At least I was not suffering greatly with sickness as I had with Lizzie. Margery helped me out of my chair and led me to the bed. The tears streamed down my face. Pain and worry taking over my whole being. I shook with each jolt. My chest felt as if it would burst into flames at any given moment as it burned and ached. As the pain got more intense, so did my worry.

Now this I had not felt with Lizzie until I was ready to birth her. What if I was further along than expected? Was the baby ready to come out at this moment? I had not felt him move yet and it was unnerving, the more I thought about it. I had not felt pain like this since my last labour. Perhaps I had done my calculations wrong, and the baby was already full term. As Margery laid me into bed I could keep my worries to myself no longer. My head was flickering from thought to thought as I worried about different scenarios. I was not ready to have him yet. The dark thought kept crossing my mind that perhaps something completely different was wrong.

"Margery. Do you think he will come now?" I asked as pain seeped through until my voice was nothing more than a harsh whisper. "I am not ready just now. Should we call for the doctor?" I said panicked as another sharp pain had me in its grip. I had to double over from it. A small sweat broke out on my forehead as the effort of continued pain exhausted me.

"No, the baby is not coming just yet Majesty…" Margery tried to calm me. I broke through her words with my cries. She dabbed my sweat-soaked forehead with a cloth. "Hush now. You need to rest. Sometimes the baby gives you a little trouble before they are ready to come out. I have seen this before. He is just making himself known. Try not to worry, get some sleep." She moved the pillow so that my head may rest comfortably.

"Can you tell the king?" I reached for her hand. "I need Harry. He needs to be with me." I suddenly wanted Henry by my side. I needed his hand in mine. Needed him to smile and reassure me. No one else would do.

"I'll ask the guard to go to His Majesty." She walked out of the room and spoke to one of the men standing at my door. I laid with my eyes closed and a damp cloth on my head for what seemed like forever waiting for my husband to come and lie next to me. I wanted him to make everything better and kiss the worries away. I wanted him to hold me until I slept soundly. To lull me into feeling secure.

* * * * *

Around ten minutes later, there was a light tap on my door. Margery went to open it and spoke quietly to the person on the other side. She then came over and sat on the edge of the bed smoothing my hair away from my face as I dripped with sweat while the pain crippled me. Her face was sad as she took hold of my hand. The worry reflected in her eyes only aided in making my panic rise.

"The king has said that he is busy. He does not want to be disturbed tonight," she repeated the message, pain on her face as she did. She had always secretly imagined that in one way or another Henry would let me down. He had proven her right when he refused to leave his men and see his fragile wife.

I was livid. How could he refuse to come to my side when I was so much in need of him. I was bed-bound as the pain ripped through me, crying in agony while he laughed and played games with his friends. He was supposed to be by my side through everything, and he had failed me.

"Did the guard tell the king of my state?" I asked hoping that the blame lay with someone other than my sweet Henry. Surely the guard had not spoken of the severity of my situation. He must have played it down in some way because if Henry knew of my state he would have been with me. Henry would hate to see me in such pain. He could not bear to be away from me if I needed him so desperately.

"He did, my queen." Margery looked down. She was trying not to cry. She knew that her worry would have only fed mine. Instead, she looked anywhere but directly at me fiddling with her hands in her lap.

"Then, the king does not care," I cried as I began to feel abandoned by Henry. As my husband, he should have rushed to my side.

"Rest now, Your Majesty. The king will be along in the morning. He loves you with his whole heart. It is plain to see," Margery soothed. "It is just that he knows everything will be all right and he does not want to worry you," she tried to reassure me.

I cried myself to sleep. The pain subsiding for long enough that I managed to drift into a fitful slumber. I dreamt of my boy running around in the gardens at Hever. I just knew that it was Edward. He looked just like me. He was skinny and tall for his age, just like I was. Where Lizzie looked the picture of her father, Edward was all me. I would have known him anywhere.

Lizzie was there beside him as she took her younger brother's hand. A lot like George and me when we were that age. She was a beautiful little thing. Her hair fell softly in tight ginger curls and her blue eyes big and beautiful. I sat in the gardens watching peacefully while they ran around chasing each other and giggling. Lizzie must have been around 6, and our little Edward was about 5. He was gorgeous; how I wanted to take him and scoop him up. I wanted to cuddle and kiss my little boy.

I stood and tried to walk closer to them and hold them in my arms, but it seemed that with every step I took they got further away. I started to run, but no matter how fast my legs went I could never catch up to them. The boy smiled and shouted for me. "Come on, Mother,   ` come and play." He chuckled while waving me over. He was like a little cherub with chubby cheeks and dark eyes just like mine.

I desperately wanted to be with them. I ran faster and faster trying to reach where they played. Tears streamed down my face as I was held back by some invisible force. It was as if someone had tied weights to my legs and I was unable to move them. I realised with a start that they were not in Hever at all. As my vision cleared, the true picture presented itself. They were quite some distance away. At first they had seemed to be within reaching distance, and now they seemed to be far off. Away from the earth and in the clouds up above me. All around them shone a golden light. Every colour was the brightest I could ever imagine. The reddest roses that I had ever seen. The light purple lilacs that I could almost smell from my place on earth. The sky around them as blue as the ocean on a beautiful day. It was the type of day where you lay outside and have to squint because the sun is so bright that it hurts your eyes. The children were dressed like little angels — all in white with halos circling their precious heads.

The boy looked at me with hopeful eyes. He was waiting for me to find a way to them. I wanted more than anything to pick him up and hold on to him forever. He was my baby and the love I felt for him was stronger than anything in this world. He was everything I had ever imagined and more. To see him stood with my little Lizzie made my heart skip a beat. They were adorable as they stood hand in hand looking down on me.

"How do I get to you?" I asked. "Where are you?" I wonder, confused. If they were not down on the earth with me then where were they? How did they get into the sky? They looked like they were having so much fun, and I wanted to join them.

"We are in heaven, Mother," the boy answered me, as if I should have already known.
My stomach dropped. What did he mean he was in heaven? The last I knew he slept soundly in my belly. He would soon meet the world. Heaven was no place for such a sweet little child. Heaven was not the place for a living child. It was a place for the old. For people who had passed away from disease or old age.

"In heaven? But why are you in heaven?" I asked panicked. "Heaven is for the dead, Son. Lizzie is alive and well. And you are sleeping soundly in my belly." My hand reached down to touch my stomach where my bump was only moments ago. I now felt a flat stomach under my dress.

I looked up in shock, scared now as I realised that I no longer carried the baby inside of me. I had been able to cradle him not so long ago as he lay inside and now he had disappeared. I felt empty. As if a piece of me had been stolen away. I began to weep as I realised that I had lost the child inside of me and had no idea where he had gone. Edward smiled at me and took hold of his sister's hand. Looking down on me like a little guardian. He seemed happy as he looked down on me. His eyes seemed calm as he smiled gently at me. He was contented, while I looked terrified. I did not know what was happening and I just wanted to hold my children.

"I will see you in heaven one day, Mother," the little boy waved to me as the clouds began to close around him. "Sooner than you know," he told me. "Goodbye. Lady Mother. I love you very much," he said, his voice sweet and childlike.

The clouds now filled in the space where my children had been. They were gone. In a blink of an eye they had disappeared from my view. I searched all around me. I hoped that they had come down, but they had disappeared completely. Had God taken them? Why would God want them for himself when they are so young? They should be with their mother. I could protect them. Love them and keep them safe from harm. God surely would not be selfish enough to steal two young children away.

"Come back. Where did you go?" I screamed, terror filled me. "Edward? Lizzie?" I asked looking all around me. "Do not leave me," I pleaded. "Come to your mother," I begged, holding my arms out as if they may run into them.

When they did not come I began to look frantically around me. I realised that the flowers which looked so beautiful and full of life only moments ago now began to wilt and die. Their heads bent over and the bright colours now fading to decay. The sky grew dark, and the heavens opened up. Rain poured down on me in my despair as the picture changed to suit the new feeling of the dream. Lightning struck, and thunder boomed as I fell to my knees, soaked to my core.

I was desperate to have them back. I wanted the sun to shine on me again. For my children to run into my arms. I felt lost and alone as I lay on the cold ground while the rain fell around me. I shivered as the cold took over and wrapped my arms around myself.

"Come back…" I begged. "Please, I am not ready to lose you." But my voice failed me…

I looked up, and Henry now towered over me. He had an evil look about him as he looked down on me in disgust. He was disappointed with me, but I had no idea why. He did not look like a man in love. He looked as if I was no one to him. He did not speak or move to comfort me. Instead he turned his back and walked away from me. No matter how much I called after him, it was as if he could not hear me. He walked out of my sight.

I woke in the greatest agony I had ever felt, clutching at my stomach and shouting for Margery. My face was damp as the tears that had filled my dream now filled reality. I knew something was not right. The dream was a warning.

"Margery. something's wrong." I shouted as dread took over. "The baby. He's dead." I screamed into my pillow. She ran to my side and took hold of my hand. She looked at me like I was crazy.

"Majesty, the baby is fi…" she began, but as she looked down at the bed she knew that she was wrong. He was not fine.

As she looked upon me the blood had begun to spread through my shift and onto my bed covers. I was soaked. Her silence had brought my fears crashing down on me as she stared in shock at the blood-stained covers. The baby had already started to come.

"Margery…" I asked. No answer, "Margery. what is it?" I begged. But I already knew.

I looked down at my soaked body, which was red with the blood that was still flowing from me.

"No, no, no, no...Please no," I screamed. "Please not my baby," wailing now as the sobs broke from my chest. I felt the urge to push as labour took over my body.

"Anne…" Margery started. "Anne, is he coming now?"

I held my stomach so tight as if I could somehow save him even now. Banging my fists against the bed, my hands now covered in my own blood.

"No...why?" bunching my fists up and hitting my head. "Margery, why is my baby dying? Can we not save him. Can he not be a little early, the doctor can save him? Call on Doctor Butts. He will know what to do" Margery looked on in complete shock.

"Margery, you need to bring the doctor." Still she did not answer me. I grew more panicked at her silence. "Margery. Answer me." I demanded.

But Marge looked on in shock as the baby came from me as she had a hold of my hand. He did not cry. He laid still on my bed. His eyes closed and his body stiff. He was so tiny that I barely felt him. She looked at me. Her face was a blank canvas as all of the colour appeared to drain from her complexion. Her terror filled me as it dawned on both of us that he was too small to fight.

"It is too late, my lady." She wrapped her arms around me. Then slowly pulled the sheets away from where they covered my lower body. "He is lost," she spoke in such a monotone as she stood gobsmacked. The shock had frozen her. There, in between my bloody legs laid the tiniest most fragile little baby. He was so small. He lay all balled up like a little egg curled around his whole body. He did not move. He did not cry. He just lay lifeless. Still and beautiful. He had tiny little hands and feet. His features barely formed.

I picked the fragile thing up in both of my hands and held his little body to my face cradling him as if he had lived. Holding him as if I was experiencing the joy of holding my new baby boy for the very first time. And he was a boy. Of course he was a boy. I rocked gently back and forth holding him in my hands as tears streamed down my face. I curled myself up into a ball and lay on my bed.

I cannot possibly put into words the feeling of realising that the child that I had held in my body for the past months was now dead; that he had been taken from this world without even a fighting chance. He had never known the love his parents bore him. He would never play. Never run around and cause mischief. He would not be made the Prince of Wales, and he would never take over his father's throne.

I loved this fragile creation already. I had held him within me and loved him with every breath in my body. I was ready for him. I had already begun to imagine holding him in my arms and soothing him gently to sleep. I was already worried over him. Began preparing for the day he left me, as Lizzie had. I had pictured him in my mind a thousand times as he grew and I would never see that. Never get to watch him grow from babe to child. From childhood to adulthood. I would never nurse him. Never hold him when he cried. Never laugh when he learned a new word or feel proud as he became a charming little prince.

I felt sick to my stomach. I vomited into a vase that was to the side of my bed. How long had he been gone? Did he die because he was too small to survive? Or had he died whilst within me? Had I carried my little angel like this for days without knowing? Perhaps he had never moved because he never had a chance. He had not made it. I was shaking from head to toe as Margery covered me with a blanket and wrapped her arms around us both. All I could think was how unfair this was.

How could such an innocent little dot never have a chance in this world? He had done nothing yet but lived inside me. He deserved a chance. I had thought that we would be together for another few months, but now I had him with me. Only he was in heaven and not here to greet me. Just like in my dream. Was that his way of telling me not to worry? He would not be christened. So perhaps he wanted me to know that God would accept him anyway. He was born a prince. No matter how early, he was a prince of England. My little prince.

I wept, and I screamed out. Desperate for him to somehow take a breath. I wanted to see him move. For his small fingers to curl around mine just like Lizzie who had gripped my hand from the moment she lay on my chest. I rose from my bed to pacing backward and forward and all the time clinging on to my small Edward. Margery took him from me and wrapped him up so delicately in a cloth. He laid on my pillow. Almost as if he was sleeping soundly. While his mother worried over him, he looked to have not a care in the world. His face was so peaceful. He looked as if he had never felt a moment of pain. While I stood in despair, he looked worry-free. He was, never having felt the pain of death.

My mind was all over the place. What did this mean? Was there something wrong with me? Had I somehow done this? Maybe I had not given him enough care. Maybe I could not carry a son. All I knew was that I wanted him to wail. I had never wanted to hear the cries of a baby more. I couldn't help but think of my Harry as I realised he would be as devastated as I was. He had been waiting patiently for the day we would meet him. Already he had started to plan celebrations for the day he would arrive.

It was as if I could see all of a sudden the years we would miss. The Christmases we would not share. The joys of parenthood that would now not come. I would not see him walk or talk. His first laugh had been stolen. The first time he learned to read and write. He would never know my love or his father's love. We were as lost to him as he was to us. I wanted so much to reverse time. Perhaps with hindsight I could go back and save Edward. I sat on my bed. I had no idea what to do with myself.

Margery held me tight, but the truth was she had no clue either. She had never experienced this, and she did not know how to help me. I shrugged her off. I did not want to be touched. I wanted to be out of this room as the air stifled me. I wanted to be outside in the cold early morning air. I wanted to open my eyes and realise that this was still part of the dream I had been in. it was my mind playing tricks on me. I wanted to hold my baby and hear him cry. I wanted to feed him from my breast and bring life to him, but he lay still on my pillow. I could scarcely stand to look at him any longer. Seeing him there made it all real.

I held my stomach automatically as if to bring him some comfort and realised that, much like in the dream, it was now empty. The dream had foreshadowed this moment. I wanted to take this whole night back. To go back to yesterday when I had carried my baby inside of me and had laughed and joked with Henry.

Today brought despair. A despair that would never leave me. To lose a child is the singular most devastating thing I have ever felt in my whole life. It was as if I had been torn open. As if someone had taken something precious from me. It was lost to me now, and I could never get it back. He was gone, and I had never experienced pain like it. Even now it has not gone away. I still feel the agony as I had on that day. As I watched the small body of my baby lie still by my side. It is something I will never be able to remove from my sight. It is still there as clear as the day it had happened. I can see the whole thing play out in my head and if I think about it, it's just like I am there again. Experiencing the pain all over again. At that moment once more as Margery and I sat exhausted and afraid. I love my little Edward as much as I love Lizzie and I had never had the chance to know him. His loss will be with me forever.

* * * * *

After an hour or so Margery told me that we should inform Henry. I did not want to do this. It would break his heart to see me like this. I wanted to protect him from the pain I had felt at losing our son. Wanted to shield him from the agony that was about to come but I could only keep it quiet for so long. I agreed to let her send for him. She settled me back into bed. We had not had my sheets changed yet. If we had, everyone would already know something was wrong. So I had to lie in the same sheets that I had lost my son in. I had to be wrapped in the sheets still bloody from the tragedy so recent, but she settled a blanket around my shoulders as I sat shivering and cold. I moved to the other side trying to put some distance between myself and the horror that was next to me. I picked the little bundle that lay on my pillow up and laid him under my sheets; I did not want him to be out in the open on view for all of the spectators. Even in death all I wanted to do was protect him.

My door burst open and in came Henry. Hatred across his face where sorrow should have been. He had not one fleck of sympathy in his features. He came over to me in three short strides and ripped the sheets from me. He cared little for the wife that lay shivering underneath them. He looked down on my blood-stained sheets. Disgust filled him as he looked at the scene that lay before him. His eyes glanced over the baby. Tears welled up for the slightest moment. I moved to take his hand. We would share in the loss together I had thought. I would comfort him.

"Well. What happened?" He demanded of me. His voice harsh. He could barely look at me. He stared down at our little baby as I picked him up and held him close.

"The baby came early Harry. He was too little to survive," I explained through sobs.

He looked angrier by the moment, and I suddenly felt ashamed as I laid in my blood-soaked shift. I no longer wanted his eyes on me. I felt disgusting as he continued to look at me as if I was a monster.

"So you are useless then?" he said after a moment. "What is the point of you, if you cannot even carry a son?" he asked.

His words caught me off guard. I had expected sympathy or shared sadness, not scrutiny. I cried into my hands. I could not understand why he was treating me in this way. As if I were to blame. I had just lost my child, and now the one person I relied on to make me feel better was doing his best to make me feel miserable. What had I done to deserve such treatment? This was a tragedy, not an act of malice.

"I am sorry my love." I sobbed." It was painful. He.." I began to explain as I tripped over my words. The pain was easier now as I no longer felt the baby push down on me, but the pain of the birth still made me exhausted. "I was terrified."

"I care nothing for your pain. I married you so that you could give me a son." Henry shouted. "You seem unable to complete such a simple task."

He was cruel. He looked like he had in that dream. Evil and like someone I did not know. Nothing like the sweet soul I had fallen in love with. I was in shock. This happened to many women over the world every day. It was the world we lived in. It was something that happened. Tragic, but through no fault of my own. Carrying a child to full term was a hard feat. They were so delicate, and birth carried with itself so many problems. One would be hard-pressed to find many women who had never experienced this. I was in despair, I had lost my baby, and now my husband blamed me. I felt vile. Used and battered when I did not fulfill my duty.

"This is your fault. You must have done something to upset the baby." Henry continued. "Why else would he die?" Henry cared little for the tears that flowed from me or the anguish plain on my face.

"He was a boy Harry. He just was too little too live." I tried to explain. I could carry boys is what I was saying. This was just an accident.

"Well if you can have one boy, then you can have another," he spat. "Now clean yourself up. You're a queen and look at the sight of you." He practically spat at me.

This was not the man I had married. This was some twisted, crazed person with not one bit of kindness in him. This was like a monster who had taken over my loving husband. I did not know this man.

"I will take today to rest," I told him. I would have one day. He would not force me to stand in front of the court and answer for this atrocity.

"Why do you need to rest?" He demanded. "Your sadness is not needed. You have not lost as much as I have. We will have another boy."

Henry made for walking out of the room. He opened the door and spoke to the doctor who was preparing to enter the disastrous scene that played out in my room. He had stood trying to gather his courage before coming inside. I imagine he had listened in for a while and decided that entering would not be in his best interests. "Oh and get rid of that thing." Henry barked gesturing at our son.

That "thing" was his child. How could he care so little for the son we had just lost? How could he care so little for me, the woman he supposedly had loved and cherished above all? After the trauma that I had just lived through, he had not one word of comfort. As if I had chosen this. As if I had killed our baby. There was nothing to be done; the doctor told me. Sometimes they just don't have what it takes to survive, and I should not blame myself. I should move on from this. I was still a healthy young woman and could make many more children to replace this one. I was saddened and shocked by the treatment of a young woman who had just lost a baby.

The coldness of everyone around me shocked me. It was like my grief did not matter. I was simply the object that had not fulfilled the job in the way expected. I should not feel sadness over a child that barely existed. One who was born without life. I should rejoice that I survived the ordeal and could continue with my queenly duty of making children. I should forget him and focus on my husband's needs. I felt weary to my very core, as if all of the air was removed from my body. My heart may as well be in bed next to me. It had exited me as the child did. When Butts made a move to pick the bundle up and take it away with him, I rushed to grab him — wanting to protect this little boy and wanting to shield him from anyone wishing harm.

"Majesty, with all due respect. The creature must be examined and buried." He explained. I hated how he referred to my child. I hated the idea of my baby cold in the earth. It was not right for him to be buried alone without the warmth of his mother.

"I will bury him myself. He deserves respect as a prince. You will not lay one finger on him." I tried to sound in control, but my voice cracked on every word.

"My queen, that is not how things are…"

"No." I snapped. "That is not how things were done…I am queen now, and I command you to leave well enough alone." He looked unmoved by my command. He made to take him again. "Would you like me to have your head?" I desperately threatened. I regretted it as soon as it was said.

I would never do such a thing. "Leave, and the king need not hear of this."

"Of course. Highness." He bowed and scurried out of the door. Head bent low as he submitted to my authority.

I had my chaplain come to my rooms. There I commanded that he help me bury my child. He did as he was told and we crept out while it was still dark. I buried him in the grounds of the chapel. Bundled up in a cloth, wrapped up tight, to keep the chill away. I cannot explain why I worried about this, but I did. I kissed his little face and placed him into a small wooden box. Then I placed my son into the ground. No mother should ever have to bury their children. It was not the right order of things but I knew it happened more often than not.

Many women before me had lost their children, in one way or another. I felt each and every one's pain at this moment, I felt sorrow for all the women in the world who also had to endure this heartbreaking task. I said a few words as Margery held me in her arms. She comforted me in the place of my husband who should have been by my side.

"My little prince. I have loved you from the very moment you began, and I will love you for as long as I shall live and beyond." I wept into Margery's shoulder. "I bury my heart in the earth next to you and ask that you do hold it until we meet again."

After the deed was done and the tears had been wept, we made our way inside, and I dressed for the day, plastered a smile on my face, and faced the court like the darkness of the night before was a long-forgotten nightmare. But I would not forget; I was a changed woman, and everyone was about to see it.

CHAPTER NINETEEN

To say my love for Henry went away would be a lie. It never went away; it was buried under a thick layer of hatred and distrust. My heart had taken one too many knocks, and I refused to let it be my guiding force any longer. I don't believe that I could ever truly lose the love that I felt for him, but I could hate him as much as I loved him. He had never seen me when I was not out of my mind with desire for him, and he was about to learn a harsh truth. Do not betray a mother. Her natural urge to put her children above all else will win out.

Henry had looked at our child as if he was naught but something gone wrong. He had looked at me like a failure, and not a woman in despair. I could not allow him to continue on as if that were acceptable. It had been a month and a half since my baby was stolen. A painful month of pretending that every day I was fine, acting as if Edward did not matter, that this was just an inconvenience in Henry's and my attempt at having a son. I hated every smile I gave. I loathed every nod. And happy conversation was unbearable.

I relished the moments when I was alone in my room, when I could cry myself to sleep without prying eyes, away from the gossip and rumour in the centre of each and every day. People wondered "did she miscarry?" or "Was she ever really with child?" They accused me of making up the pregnancy to please Henry.

Henry decided that we would not announce his death.

Instead, we would move on and wait for everyone to forget. The people who said such vicious things were, of course, all the people who had witnessed my growing stomach. They had seen me getting bigger month by month, and yet they questioned my pregnancy altogether. I even caught my ladies whispering behind my back. Margery sent them away with a scolding. I had done nothing but favour them and place them within good positions, but they showed not one ounce of respect. I told Henry they were to be dismissed. I was in no mood for second chances. I needed a court around me that I could trust.

* * * * *

I had not shared a bed with Henry since before the baby. The idea of his touch repulsed me, where it had once set me aflame. I did not want my body invaded. I did not want another child. I needed time to heal. Henry would have to wait for his precious heir, and accept it. He was enraged, of course. He demanded that I come to his chambers at once. That I do as promised and fulfill my wifely duty. I refused. I made my excuses and stayed in my own rooms. I would spend as little time with him as possible. In my eyes he was the man who had no kind words for the woman he had held above all others. He shed not one tear for the baby we lost. He had been cruel and spiteful, and now he demanded that I make him another son. I would not be used as he pleased. I had no interest in being near him.

After two months he could bear it no longer. He had come to my rooms and demanded to know why I had been avoiding my wifely duties.

"Anne, why do you torment me so?" he had asked. He actually sounded at a loss.

"Oh, I assure you, Henry, I am the tormented one." I raised my voice. I was angry at the fact that he still could only think about himself.

"It has been long enough. I had thought it long forgotten." He looked on innocently. He truly had no idea just how much he had hurt me.

At his words, I lost my senses. "Long forgotten? Have you ever carried life within you and then saw that child dead in your lap?" I spat. "You know nothing of the hell I live in. Each and every day driven to madness by the thoughts of what might have been." I refused to cry. My driving force would be anger. If I were furious with Henry then he would never see how broken I was.

"Then we will make another son. And what might have been, will be."

He truly was ignorant to my plight. To him, it was not a life. It was a project that did not work out. He had no idea what it felt like to hold another person inside of me. To be full of promise for the day I would get to meet the life I had sustained, and then to find out that he had died while he laid in my room.

"Henry," I said as exhaustion swept over me. I had no fight left. "Please leave. If you stay, I am afraid I may no longer love you tomorrow." I said, exhausted. I was weak with the effort of getting through every day. I could not bear to speak with him a moment longer.

He made to speak, but I just raised my hand and opened the door. He left without another word. He could tell that I was not going to argue. I did not want to argue, but I did not want to make peace either. I just wanted him out of my sight.

* * * * *

Yes, I went back to Henry, eventually. I fulfilled my wifely duties, and I intended to continue to do so but in me there grew a coldness. One that would not easily be warmed. Where Henry once occupied the whole of my heart he now held only the smallest piece. I loved him still. I could never imagine a world where I would not love him, but the wounds he had created within me would not be bandaged over with words of regret or apologies. He had taken a knife to my heart and wounded me so deeply that I felt it would never heal. I played my role. I behaved as I

always had. I kissed him, held him and told him how I
could not live without him.

I never once revealed my feelings. I would lay with him
every night, even when it pained me to do so, even when
the thought of another child made me sick to my stomach.

No matter how well I held my composure, even he could
see the hatred behind my eyes. He could sense where I held
back. He knew that I did not give him all of me. He played
along for a time, accepting that this was his punishment for
neglecting me. He noticed that now my touch was not as
soft, not as lingering. I did not wish to laugh with him in
our own private little heaven. I went to bed with him and
then I slept. I no longer wished to talk tonight away
together. I dined on my own when I could, relishing the
space that I could have to myself.

He let me have my time, hoping that one day I would
crumble and return fully to him. He sent me gifts and
bought me many jewels and trinkets to show his love, but I
would not be moved so easily.

Even in my cold hatred, my heart called to him. My
resolve hurt me as much as it had hurt him. I hated holding
back my soul from him, but I needed to protect myself. I
wanted to run into his open arms and let him soothe all of
my anger. I wanted him and no one else. I wanted to love
him fully again, but I had sworn to guard myself against
him. And I would.

One evening I went to his rooms as usual, after I had
eaten. He was waiting for me. As I walked into the room,
he enclosed me into his arms and tried to kiss my lips. I had
turned my face so that it would land instead on my cheek.
Then I shrugged him off and started to ready myself for
bed, keeping my gaze away from him as his face dropped.
He sank into a chair weeping gently and holding his head in
his hands. He had expected me to run to him and comfort
him but I would not. I continued to undress.

"Anne, why do you turn from me?" he broke through the silence. The pain was clear on his face. He hated not being able to hold the woman he loved, and it was clear that my avoidance was hurting him.

"Whatever do you mean Henry? I am here, am I not?" I asked him. "I am here to be your wife, as I had promised." I was doing nothing wrong. I had promised to be here, and I was. He could have my body and nothing more.

"You do not even call me Harry anymore?" he cried. "Do you not love me still?" He looked pathetic.

"Oh, do not be ridiculous," I ordered. "Of course I love you, Henry," I spoke. It was true. I did, but I had no idea when I would be ready to show him that love again.

"There it is again. 'Henry.' You hate me now, don't you, my love?" He walked over to where I was standing and tried to place a kiss onto my lips. I moved out of the way. "You hate me because our child did not live. You blame me."

The tears streamed down his cheeks, but I felt not one bit of sympathy. He did not care while I cried for our child.

I sat down on the bed taking a deep breath as I did so. "How could I blame you for what happened? That was never the issue, Henry," I explained.

"Call me Harry, Anne!" he suddenly shouted. Sadness was turning to anger and frustration. "Tell me. Why do you no longer love me? I must fix it. I cannot be without you." He kneeled before me.

"I do love you, Henry." I took his face in my hand. "But I no longer trust you. You turned from me when I needed you most. You cast me into the shadows when all I needed was your love." I stood.

He was silent in shock at my reply. He was used to the side of me that was only trying to please him. Before now I would have forgiven him for his outbursts. I would have taken his coldness and moved on.

"You have lost a piece of me, Henry. That night. You cut it out yourself. Carved it out with your cruel words." I walked away from him. "I will always love you. With my dying breath I will love you, but I love you a little less than I did before." I admitted the cruel truth of the situation.

He followed me, gripping my hands and crying as he tried to pull me close. "Do not say that, please do not say that to me," he cried. "Anne. I am sorry. I am so sorry."

"Oh Henry, get up. You look weak." I pushed him off of me. It was I who held the power, and he would feel as low as I had done. "It is too late. I will never leave you. That much I swear. But you will only have half of me from this moment onwards. We will have more children, and we will appear happy to all who look on, but it will not be the same. You have made sure of that."

"How can I fix this?" he begged.

"You can't," I said and walked out of the room.

I would thaw eventually; a love as strong as ours could never be completely destroyed. But at that moment, I truly believed that I would never feel the same as I had before.

* * * * *

Three months later, Henry and I were all but living completely separate lives. I would visit him weekly, and we would try to create a new life without any success. He would really try to bring me back to him, and I would do my duty and then leave, returning to my room to sleep.

During this time, a musician at court had caught my eye. Mark Smeaton. He was so very talented, and I had decided that I would like to get to know him. He and George seemed to be close companions, always found drinking and laughing in the corner together. I had asked him to introduce me to Mark. To say we had an instant friendship would not do it justice. He was so kind and funny, we had a connection from the very first meeting. He would become a

247

dear companion to me when life proved hard. I found that I could talk to him in my lowest of moments. He always had an ear for me. He was always happy to comfort me and reassure me with kind words. He gave me almost everything my husband did not.

Of course I did not love Mark in the way that I loved my husband. Mark was no more than a friend. He was a confidant. I trusted him deeply to keep my secrets and tell me when I was behaving foolishly. I stayed true to Henry for ten years, no matter what anyone says, but if I am honest, I may have betrayed him where my emotions were concerned. He gave me none of the support I needed regarding my feelings, so I was bound to look elsewhere. But I would never betray him in act. He was my one true husband, and I could not bear the thought of being with anyone but him, no matter how much he had hurt me.

Mark was a nice distraction, and I would employ him as my musician. I had decided that if Henry were happy to entertain himself with his own festivities, then I would too. If he enjoyed entertaining his friends in his own private court, then I would entertain my friends in my own apartments. There would be music, and dancing, food, and wine that would flow all night. If he wished to lead separate lives when it suited him, then I would do the same thing. He enjoyed the company of other women; then I could enjoy the company of other men. I would never commit adultery as he did, time and time again. But a few harmless flirtations surely would not hurt.

He protested his love for me in one breath, and in the next he would whisper sweet nothings into some stupid young girl's ear. No wonder it would take me so long to forgive him. While he drank the night away with Henry Norris, William Brereton, and some of the whores of court, then I would entertain my friends. My brother, Thomas Wyatt, Margery, and my other ladies would come along to celebrate with me. We would dance long into the night. This carried on for a long while.

Henry knew it was best not to attempt to tell me what to do. If he wanted me to go anywhere near him, he would need to keep me sweet. Henry had not seemed concerned at first. He let me carry on as I wished. He did his own things and I did mine. He got curious eventually, and one night decided to invite himself. He and a few men from his own gathering had adorned masks and made to sneak into my room. I was presiding over the proceedings at the time, Thomas and Madge Shelton were dancing, George and Mark played a game of cards in the corner, and Margery sat by my side refilling my glass as needed. I had drunk an awful lot of wine on that particular night as I had been feeling particularly low.

Out of nowhere my doors flew open and in came five men. All in masks, each one pushing aside the men in the room and capturing a woman that lay within. It was much like the pageant that had begun my days at court. I recognised my captor the moment he had crept up behind me and wrapped his arms around me. The kiss he planted onto my cheek. The way his hands lingered on my chest. He placed a hand over my eyes and whispered breathlessly into my ear. His sweet breath on me. A wave of desire swept through me, unwanted, but ever-present. It felt like we were young again. When we first fell in love, and he would do his best to woo and charm me. When his only desire was to capture me. Still I could not break. I could not give him the chance to hurt me again.

"Do you know who has come to rescue you, fair maiden?" He smiled at me, looking every bit as handsome as he had at the beginning.

"Henry…" I breathed. I hated the way I responded to him. Even though I was angry, my body automatically wanted him.

He stepped in front of me and lifted me from my chair, kissing me so deeply on the lips. He presented me with a small parcel. "This is for you to keep," he told me.

I unwrapped it and within lay a small heart made from red velvet. It had been sewn together by his own hand. I could not believe that he had hand-made me a gift. Usually, he threw his money around by trying to keep me with expensive jewels and gowns.

"I give to you my heart again, and ask you to trade it with your own?" he pleaded. He looked bashful and innocent as he said so.

"Harry...it is not that easy." I shook my head. I wanted to lean into him. I had missed loving him. Had missed his arms around me. Being cold was not something I enjoyed, but I had to put myself first. I could not be hurt again.

"You called me Harry..." He grinned. "Anne, please let me spend every day making it up to you?" He waited for my reply. All I did was shake my head but my heart screamed at me to allow him in. "Please my love, just say yes..."

I had to admit that this did make my heart flutter in a way that it had not for such a long time, but I still could not give in. If I risked my heart again, what would I have left of me? I had to hold back from him.

"Henry. I'm sorry..." I began; I felt the sting of tears in my eyes. But he would not see me cry. I would not let myself become that vulnerable again.

"I understand." He nodded to me and pulled away. "Come, gentleman, let's leave the queen to her own entertainments." They all bowed to me and swept out of the room.

It was agonizing watching Henry leave. It was like my soul cried for him when I did not.

Over the next few days, Henry would suddenly become the man I fell in love with again. It was like he had become the young man desperate for my attention. The one who would do anything he could to catch me and keep me. He would come into my rooms every morning with some roses he had picked fresh from the garden himself. He would walk in and kiss me on the cheek telling me how beautiful I looked on that day. He would ask me what I had planned for that day and tell me of all the things he would be doing. Then he would leave, but return to me whenever he had a moment to himself. He told me that he just wanted to check in on me and see that I was doing all right. I had had a hard few months, he told me, and I needed to rest and get myself back to full health.

He would come to me in an evening and sit beside me like we used to. He would talk to me of all his feelings and thoughts, and I would nod or give him one-word answers, to begin with. As we sat by the fire I could physically feel the ice melting away from my heart, and as the days went on I would find that I enjoyed talking to him once again. We would tell each other how our days had been, how we were feeling. He would tell me of his fears for the kingdom, and I would tell him how I feared to have another child.

To my surprise, he really understood, and he explained that we were both so young, it could wait. There was no rush to have a son because we would have plenty of time. He planned to reign for a lot longer, he laughed. He just wanted me to be happy and healthy. We could worry about duty when I was stronger. This warmed me, I must say. I knew just how important having a son was to Henry, but if he was willing to wait, he must truly love me.

I was reading with Thomas on an especially lovely day. He was showing me his newest poetry. It was beautiful. I cannot say for sure who it was about, but whichever woman had taken his interest was a very lucky lady. He was an exquisite poet. Cromwell was looking for me and had found me perched in a window seat, tucked out of view with Thomas, head resting on his shoulder as he read to me. Cromwell cleared his throat.

"Excuse me, Majesty."

I jumped up from my sate, broken from my reverie. I had not seen him come in, and he had startled me a little.

"Thomas...you scared me," I said voice pitched slightly higher due to my rushing heart.

"I apologise, Majesty. The king has sent me to look for you." He bowed low.

"Henry? Well, what does he want?" I asked, still slightly flustered.

"He has given me this note." he handed me a folded bit of parchment. "No other instructions I am afraid."

"Thank you, Thomas." He bowed and left.

He always made me feel uneasy. He seemed to lurk around corners, always watching the goings-on at court, always trying to further himself with the king. This would prove troublesome for me, of course, especially when situations were twisted in his little head.

Thomas left me with my own thoughts, telling me that he would be around should I need him. I opened up the note that had been given me and out fell rose petals. They had been tucked inside. The note was short and contained instructions.

"My dear heart, the day is so lovely; it makes me think of you. If I could find the words to describe you, I would simply explain today, with the suns warmth, the birds singing and the smell of the summer flowers that fill me with such joy, that I cannot contain. Would you do me the honour of meeting me in the spot where we first fell in love? I will be stood waiting for you. You will know the exact spot to look without a word from me. I wait with little patience to see you, darling.

Yours forever.
H. R"

My heart skipped a beat at his words; I felt like a young woman again, the first bubble of love building in my stomach. I ran to my rooms to check myself over in the looking glass. I had a flush in my cheeks that gave me a slight glow. My waist was drawn in with my green corset. The green offset the colours in my eyes along with the emerald around my neck. I took my French hood off letting my hair flow loose and made my way to the spot where Henry had wooed me so sweetly all of those years ago.

There he stood right next to the rose bushes, exactly where I had expected to find him. He had his back to me. I walked over and placed a gentle hand on his shoulder. As he turned a smile crept across his lips. He held a single rose in his hands. How changed he was from the man I had fallen in love with all that time ago. He had grown in stature, his shoulders wider. He had less muscle definition now, and a slightly rounder waste replaced it. His hair had flecks of grey now, in the place of some of the red. But his eyes, oh his eyes they were still the same as that very first day I had seen him. I could fall into those eyes, and drown in their beauty. When I looked into them I had seen the young man who had stood there before.

How changed I must look as well, I remember wondering. The years must have started to show in my face. I was twenty-five years old when he first pursued me, and by then I was thirty-three. I was no longer the young woman who had caught his attention at court. Did he still look upon me and enjoy what he found in my place, or did he miss the Anne he had known then? If he did, it did not show in his face. He looked at me like a man struck with the dart of love all over again. He took my face in his hands and placed a gentle kiss onto my lips. Stroking my hair and holding me tightly to him.

253

"Anne, you came," he said. "You look delightful. This day holds no beauty when you are here. It looks bleak compared to the sun that shines from you."

"Of course I came, Harry." I kissed his cheek. "I am so pleased to be with you." It was true. The last bit of ice was finally thawing, and I loved each and every moment with him.

"I know that this year has not been kind to you, Anne." He took my hand and led me to a seat in the garden. "I have a surprise for you."

We sat, and I leant into him welcoming the feel of his arms around me once more. There had been a time I thought it impossible to want to be this close again, but he had won me over. Slowly but surely, bit by bit, he had broken my walls down.

"It has been harsh Harry…" I looked down at my lap as the memories of losing my child came back to me; it was still so hard to bear. Even now, after all this time, when I sit in this dark and dingy place, having lost everything, I still feel the trauma of that first loss so keenly. I always will.

"But I want us to move on now," I told him. I truly was ready to carry on with my life, I remember thinking at the time that I could no longer live in the darkness. I had to come back into the light, or my life would be full of sorrow.

"So I am forgiven then, Anne?" He leaned to rest his chin on my head and took hold of my hand. "I treated you so awfully; I can never forgive myself. But if you forgive me then I will finally be able to feel joy again. I am truly so very sorry and…" I stopped him, placing a finger on his lips.

"Harry. It is all in the past. Yes, you pushed me away, and I was hurt. But you have paid your penance," I reassured him. "Can we continue to be happy now? Please? These months have not been easy."

"I would like nothing more of you, my love. As long as you can fully forgive me this time?" he asked.

"Harry. You need to forgive yourself now."

Henry kissed me, and that night I returned to his bed properly for the first time and allowed him to have me fully. I gave everything to him once again, and it felt wonderful not to hold back any longer. I allowed him in once more, and we would be happy again for a long time to come.

CHAPTER TWENTY

Soon enough, I truly enjoyed every second in Henry's company again. He was really so kind and so caring. He did not push me to have another heir at first. He would always ask me how I was feeling and if I was coping well. He listened to all of my worries and all of the things that I would fret about.

We had had many arguments before about the line of succession, and Henry had previously created a new law that put Elizabeth and any children we would have above Caroline's daughter, Mary. I had pushed him to it. I could not have Mary above my daughter in anyway. She was illegitimate now, and it was Elizabeth who stood as heir at the moment. We needed a way to make sure that my children would come into their own one day, long after we had gone. Henry had eventually agreed with me and decided that it was a matter we wanted to push through Parliament.

We both worried that the act of succession had not quite had the effect we had been hoping for. While most of the country had signed and recognised me as the rightful queen, there were still a few who had not. Henry had ordered everyone to sign a document recognising him as the supreme head of the church, and a few of his closest friends refused to do it. Of course, this included Thomas More and John Fisher.

Thomas More had stood by Henry who, although reluctant, decided that had no choice but to arrest them, for he had declared anyone against the act as treasonous and could not allow himself to look weak in the eyes of the country. He was king and what he said was as good as the word of God. He could not look to be lenient towards anyone, even if they were friends.

Along with More and Fisher, Henry had John Houter arrested. John was the prior of charterhouse and he had refused to swear the oath, along with all of his monks. Henry and his privy council worried that the common people would start to defy him again, as they had when he had passed laws to remove the pope's authority. Devout Catholics may take this as another blow and if they could have seen that we were allowing certain people to get away with disagreeing with us then they might have risen up.

Along with John, ten of his monks were also imprisoned. They were given one last chance to sign the oath, and when they refused they were tried and executed. Each of them suffered a traitors death; it was horrific. I begged Henry to let them live, keep them imprisoned, but let them keep their lives. He told me that if I wanted to be a ruler, then I would have to grow a backbone; no one had ever ruled without spilling a drop of blood, and I would have to strengthen my stomach.

They were hanged, but not enough to kill them; then were cut down and ripped into four pieces while the ones waiting to face the same death watched. last of all they had their hearts cut out and burned. Eleven people died in that way. Henry had told me that it was proof of what he would do for me and Lizzie, how far he would go and he would go further still, his resolve scared me. He was determined to have our way, no matter who he would have to cut down.

I never believed for a moment that Henry would order the execution of Thomas More. Henry loved him; he was one of his closest and most trusted friends. He had even disagreed with him before, but that was allowed because he was as family and could speak freely.

Henry was mad with rage at both Thomas and Fisher. He had thought that seeing Houter and his monks die would scare them into obedience, but it had done nothing of the sort. Thomas, even with the pleading of his family, stood strong and refused to "damn his soul" in the eyes of God. Henry was beside himself with anger, and could not understand why More would not just save himself. He cared little for Fisher, but the idea of losing Thomas scared him. Thomas had been there since Henry was a young boy. What would it do to him to kill someone considered blood? I hoped and hoped that Thomas would sign. I did not want Henry to have that choice in his hand, and I knew what must be done if he continued to disobey.

Thomas was given much more space than anyone else who refused to sign was allowed. I found that it angered me to know that he could go against Elizabeth and me without any consequence. Henry seemed to let the matter drop for some time. Yes, he left them to rot in the tower, but he did not force the issue for the moment. And I would not rest until everyone had accepted our rule. I refused to let the matter drop. I had succeeded in convincing him to create the action, and now I would convince him to make More and Fisher sign.

"Is it not embarrassing to you that some of your subjects ignore your rule?" I asked as we lay in bed. "I had thought you were the type of king who could command all of his subjects." I chuckled to myself.

"Whatever do you mean?" He was taken aback. "My subjects do as I say."

"I mean when you have people like More and Fisher doing as they please it makes it appear as if you have no command. Others have died for less, yet they sit comfortably in the tower," I pointed out.

"Anne. Not this again." Clearly he was as sick of this argument as I was, but I could not put an end to it until I was secure. "What would you like me to do? Kill them?"

"No Henry, I want you to force them to sign."

"And if they will not?" he asked.

"Make them. For the sake of your daughter."

More did not budge, there was nothing, he said, that would make him sign and condemn his soul. Henry ordered his and Fisher's execution. With a scribble of his quill, the warrant was signed. And I remember thinking how simple it was for Henry to order a loved one's death. With a flick of his wrist and the stamp of his seal, it was done. I wondered if he could do it to More, who else could he do it to? How far would we both go to get what we wanted?

The night before the More execution, Henry came to me. He had been crying, the tears barely dry on his face. He held me to him, sobbing into my gown.

"Anne, sweet Anne. How can I let him die?" he sobbed. "He is my true friend. How can I justify this?"

"No true friend would defy you in the way that he has," I said although my heart was heavy with the gruesome task, I could not afford to be weak in this. " Henry, you have given him chance after chance."

"Tell me not to do it. If you tell me that I am wrong, then I will order the execution stopped." Henry looked for a way out.

"Henry, you are king, I cannot tell you what to do."

"I do this for you. I told you I would do anything for us. I will kill my friend if that is what needs to be done." He looked me in the eyes. " But if you tell me that I do not have to, then I will spare them." he pleaded.

"Harry." Tears welled up in my own eyes now. "I just want to feel safe. I want Lizzie to be safe. I do not want More to die, but we need to make a stand and appear united."

"Give the order, and it will be done, or spare me and let these men live."

"Henry, you are the king," I said. "You give the orders, not I. I do not want them to die. I do not want anyone to die, but something must be done."

"I understand." was all that he said.

He spent the night weeping in my arms. I could have said the word at any moment and save two men from the jaws of death, but I stayed silent, and for that reason, I am as responsible for their death as any other. I had the power in my hands to save a life, and I did not. Their names will be scarred on my soul for all of eternity.

Thomas More was beheaded as a traitor on 6th July 1535. Fisher, who had been made a cardinal by the Catholic Church, had also been executed. I hate myself for the part that I played. Henry gave the order, but I did not stop it. Henry never looked at me the same way again.

CHAPTER TWENTY-ONE

In December of 1535, I was finally with child again. Henry and I had been trying for a long while with no luck. I was overjoyed at the idea of having another baby. I had my concerns after the last one, but I was ready to put that behind me and try again. My relationship with Henry had been strained of late.

He was having problems with his duty in the bedroom, for whatever reason; it was not working as we would have liked it to. He blamed me, told me that if I were not so ugly then perhaps he would be able to perform better. If I were beautiful like some of the other ladies at court, then he would have no problem at all. I did not satisfy him in the way I once had. He had told me that all it took was a look from Jane Seymour or one of my other maids and he was ready to pounce into bed, but I no longer stirred such excitement in him.

I was heartbroken. I had given my all to Henry, I had loved him, regardless of his many misgivings, and he repaid me by treating me with such a bitter tongue. At the time I worried that perhaps he was right. Maybe it was because I was not as pretty or as graceful as some of the other women around me. Now I realise that the problem lay with him, but at the time I just wanted to please him. I just wanted him to love me as he once had.

I wanted him to go crazy with desire for me again, but now all I received was a drunken fumble from time to time. He would have too much to drink and he would stumble into my rooms late at night when I was soundly sleeping. He would breathe his foul breath in my face and rouse me, telling me that he was drunk enough now to do the deed, and we would try, we would really try. I would lower myself to trying unladylike techniques in order to get him in the right mood. When they failed, he would get angry and leave, sulking for two days before the whole thing would repeat itself. Most nights it would not work. One night every so often it would. It was never very enjoyable. It was a means to an end and nothing more. Henry would get what he wanted out of our intimacy and leave me wanting. I could feel him slipping away; I could sense that he did not love me as strongly as he once had. This was only confirmed when he came to me one night, sticking of ale and swaying from side to side.

He came into my room and kissed my cheek, gently waking me from my sleep.

"Anne." He rocked me gently. "Anne, your husband has come to see you."

My eyes fluttered open, taking in the sight of him leaning over me as I lay in bed, clearly unsteady on his feet.

"Henry, it is late," I told him. "I wish to sleep."

"But wife, I have come to seduce you," he slurred.

I sat bolt upright in bed; I had had enough of this now, every night coming to me out of his mind on wine or ale. Waking me from my sleep and insisting that I lay with him.

"Henry, you smell like a barrel of ale," I scolded. "I will not lay with you in this state."

He took hold of my wrists and moved his face so that it was only inches away from mine, anger crossing his features. He laughed.

"I need to be in this state in order to sleep with such a mare," he sniggered. "Why did I marry such an unattractive woman?"

"If you feel that way Harry, then you can leave." His words had cut me, but he would never see this. I refused to ever let him see how he hurt me. I would not give him that power.

"But we must make a son. I will get some use out of you yet." He rocked back on his heels, eyes rolling as he did.

"And what of our daughter Henry…is she no use to you?"

"What would I want with a daughter? Sometimes I wonder if she is even mine…"

How dare he even question this. Elizabeth looked the image of him. She had the hair and heart of a Tudor. He was just being cruel; he was trying to get a rise out of me. He wanted me to get angry and fight with him.

"Henry. Never say that. She is every bit of your child." I was angry now, he had succeeded in that at least, he was pushing me over the edge.

"I wish you were not her mother." His words cut through me like the edge of a sword.

I stood and slapped him hard on his face. "Yes, well I am. Now get out." I walked to my door and opened it for him. He had gone red with rage. He scared me when he looked like this. I did not know what he would do. Would he strike me again? Pin me to the bed as he had many times? Or worse? I always worried that he would go a step further; he clearly had no respect for me or my body. How far would he take it in order to get what he wanted? Would he force himself on me? He did not like being told no. He believed himself to have the authority to take whatever he pleased.

He marched to the door and slammed it shut again. He caught hold of my hair, dragging me over to the bed where he dropped me.

"Why did I ever marry you, Anne?" he shouted. "Why did I put us both through this?" He let go of me all of a sudden. Letting me drop to the edge of the bed. He was crying now. "Oh God. What has become of me? Of us?" he asked "I am sorry." He was shaking.

I stood and held him, sitting us both on the edge of my bed.

"Shh, shh, Harry. It is all right." I rocked him as he cried into my lap. "The happiest couples argue." It was to convince myself as much as it was to convince him. I couldn't bear to see him despair like this.

"But we are not happy." He shook his head.

"We can be...I still love you," I chuckled. "And you still love me?" I asked.

"I do not love you like I did." His words crashed into me as a wave of sickness crept through me. "It is hard to love someone so damaged."

With that he lay back and fell to sleep in my bed. I sat on the end, in shock at his words, unable to move from my spot, solidified in this place, hand held to my mouth as his words sank in. He had just told me that he did not love me as much as he had; how was I supposed to feel? I still loved him with every fiber of my soul. I needed to heal myself. I needed to become the person I was when we met.

I could change this; I could make him love me again. I just had to get pregnant. If I could have another baby then he would love me again. I would put on a brave face and pretend that the last eight years of my life had not worn me down completely. Why did I have to be so stubborn? If I had just forgiven him more quickly or been a happier wife for the past few years then he would not tire of me. Even now, when he came to lay with me, if I had not turned him away he would have been happy. We would have never argued and things would have carried on the way they had been for the last few months.

Thankfully, the happy news of my pregnancy stopped the late-night visits and the arguments for a while. I had told him as soon as I had found out for sure and he announced it to the court, telling everyone that he was proud of his wife and lucky to be blessed by God, who must want him to have a son. I found my brother and Mark together, where I told them the happy news. They were overjoyed for me. I had confided in them a lot lately, especially with Mark, telling him of the strain on the king and me to have a child. My brother hugged me deeply and Mark took hold of my hand and squeezed it, behind us,

Cromwell swept into the room and offered me his congratulations.

The whole court was abuzz with the news of a new prince; the kingdom desperately wanted Henry and me to have a son. It was important for the country to have a solid heir so that the transition would be smooth. No one wanted another war for the throne, and without a male heir, it would be left vulnerable. I was treated like a precious flower; everyone was treating me like I was delicate and fragile, wanting to give me no stress so that the baby would be healthy.

This baby would not only provide an heir for the kingdom, it would amend the broken relationship between Henry and me. It would make us a stronger family, and once I had a boy my place as queen would be solidified. No one could touch me as the mother of the next Tudor in line to the throne; I would be untouchable and not a word would ever be said against me again. I was beside myself with delight at the idea of having a little prince. We deserved this, we had a lot of obstacles over the course of our relationship, and we deserved a little light in our lives. This boy would bring it and heal all of the wounds we had caused each other.

Henry became a shadow of the husband he once was. He would never go back to being the man I had married, but he treated me like I was precious cargo now. He was kind and courteous to me, not wanting to cause any unneeded anxiety. But he would never give me the whole of him again. That had been lost. I cannot pinpoint when it had happened, but it had, and what is broken would never be whole again. I pretended not to see this, I pretended that nothing had ever changed. I smiled like I was not in a million pieces, day by day. In almost the same way as he had fallen in love with me, he now lost his love for me. Just as our love had grown minute by minute, it now shrank by the hour.

Henry was so happy with my pregnancy, he would go around and tell everyone twice, no one on the outside world would ever believe there to be the slightest of problems. I had thought that the fact I was with child again would bring him back to me. I thought the child would piece us back together. It did not. Henry treated me like a glass bowl to be carried around gently, to be placed on show, away from anything that could cause it damage. He would not touch me; he could not even bear being in the same room with me for too long.

The last time I was pregnant, he would constantly enquire on my state. Instead now he would ask others if I was in good health, receiving a report from Dr Butts on the health of the babe that grew inside of me. If we were presiding over the court together he would appear perfectly chivalrous. Holding my hand as we sat, leaning over to ask if I was enjoying the food, pulling my chair out for me, or kissing me tenderly on the cheek. He would ensure that everyone thought we were as happy as the day we married.

He had explained to me that my role would be to play the happy wife, I must appear to be content with our life, I had to seem jubilant with my life as queen, even as my heart crumbled inside of me. The coldness I had once shown him, he now returned threefold, and each time I tried to get close he would push me away. I would take myself to his rooms and wish to be held, to feel some comfort in his arms, to feel his body close to mine, to have him talk me to sleep, and he would either bar my entrance in the first place or turn me away when I made it inside. I would return to my room's and cry myself to sleep, holding on to his shirt, trying to pull some comfort from it.

It was as if I could feel the crown slipping from my head, I could feel the grip I had on Henry loosening, could hear the mocking of the court, whispering behind my back as they could see his love fade, their chatter as he took another mistress, as he sent gifts to the whore Jane Seymour. I kept telling myself that I had one thing the rest of them did not have. Not only had I been anointed as queen in the eyes of God and the people, but I was mother to the princess and now the son that grew within me. Once I had our son, Henry would never be able to rid himself of me, I would be forever propped on a pedestal as the woman who had given him an heir to the Tudor throne, a Tudor prince to carry on the line, I would be untouchable and Henry would have to love me again. That spark that I knew still laid somewhere inside of him would have to be reignited, he could never turn me away again.

On 24th January Henry had decided that we should put on a joust, for we had much to be happy about. He said that we would celebrate the conception of this new prince and that I was to attend and support my husband as the attentive wife I was. He wished to silence the court's whisperings about us and put on a united front. He had decided to take part in the joust himself.

I was not happy about this as it was too much of a risk. Jousting was a dangerous sport, and without an heir he should look after himself. Of course Henry did not listen to me; my opinions no longer mattered to him. He would take part in the joust, and he would win. He was still a young, healthy king and he would show everyone that he was as much in command and untouchable as he was twenty years ago. I went to him on the day of the event before he mounted his horse, to wish him luck and to ask him one last time to sit and watch with me instead. I made my way into one of the tents that had been erected for this event. I found Henry being strapped into his armour; he was glowing with excitement.

"Harry, you look positively dashing." I reached for his face, smiling.

"Anne, what are you doing here? You should be in your seat." he pulled away.

"I have come to wish you luck, Harry," I told him. "And to ask that you reconsider. I have a bad feeling about your taking part."

He shook his head and took my hand in a rare tender gesture.

"Love, I will be fine. I know what I am doing." He had not called me "Love" for a long while. My heart brightened at this small display of the love buried deep within him, I had known that it still lay somewhere inside of him.

"Oh Harry, how lovely it is to hear you speak so." I grinned at him. "But please heed my warning, do not take part."

"Go and take your seat, darling," he brushed me off.

"But…"

"Do not push your luck, Lady," Henry cut me off. He kissed me briefly on the lips and nodded to Francis Weston to lead me to my seat.

On our way there, Francis stopped me. "Your Majesty, I do not wish to overstep." he stopped to make sure I would allow him to continue when I smiled he spoke again. "I have noticed that the king has treated you unfairly of late." Francis should watch what he said and where he said it.

"I think it best you do not comment on the king's behaviour, Weston," I replied. "You never know who may be listening," I warned.

"I only wish to say that he loves you very deeply. He is overstressed with affairs of the state at the moment, but he truly cares for you very much."

"The king is always kind and gracious." I would not be heard complaining about the king.

"I know, your highness. Just so you know that he expresses his love for you often." he smiled before offering me his arm again. "When we are all together drinking, you are all he can talk about. His love has never failed."

"Thank you," I whispered, a solitary tear falling from my eye.

I was pleased to hear that he spoke about his love for me with the closest people around him. If this were true, then perhaps things were not as bad as they seemed. Francis offered me a handkerchief to wipe away the tears, and when I was composed again he led me to my throne to overlook the event.

The joust was a long event; it was such a bloody sport to watch, blows being taken from every angle, men being thrown from their horses, lances being taken to the face, to the chest or the stomach, leaving patches of blood behind. All the gore made my stomach churn with anticipation. The crowd loved it; the scrappier, the better. That day even commoners attended, they were able to buy their way into the event and jumped at the chance to see their king and queen on full display. I waved as the children gaped at me, sat in my rich purple gown, crown on my head, looking every bit the queen their parents had told them about. I smiled as they clambered to get a closer look. The only thing I kept thinking was that Henry would be up soon and I couldn't explain why I was so worried. I just had a feeling, I guess, as if the pit of my stomach was telling me that something was going to go terribly wrong.

When Henry rode up to the tilt, I could not help but think about how handsome he was. He looked every bit the knightly king; the people loved him. They chanted his name as he galloped around on his horse, waving his hand, giving them the show they wanted. Children would shriek as he rode past. "It's the king. It's the king." Henry grinned from ear to ear. Kingship suited him so much. He stopped at the end of the tilt, readying himself to face his opponent. His helmet was placed onto his head, and off he went — two horses travelling full speed towards each other. Their lances were poised to strike, the confidence radiating off of the king. He would win.

We were all so sure that he was unbeatable. Until he was not. Everybody jumped from their seat as it happened, George and Norris, who sat with me, raised their hands to their faces as they gasped at the scene unfolding, they jumped over the stools and down to the tiltyard. I stood frozen in my place. Henry had just been thrown from his horse, crashing to the ground, his head connecting with the hard surface, I watched as a pool of blood swam from his ear. Men surrounding him, trying to wake him from his now unconscious state. I screamed as reality crashed into me — as I realised that he might be dead.

Thomas was at my side; he took my arm. "Anne," he shouted.

I ignored him, running down to where Henry's lifeless body lay. "Henry," I screamed as I reached him. He was just laid there, eyes closed, not moving, barely breathing.

Charles Brandon was on his other side, shock and sadness etched across his face.

"Someone get Doctor Butts," I commanded. "Charles. Is he dead?" I cried He ignored me, looking down at the king and shaking his head back and forth. "Charles, answer me!"

"I do not know," he shouted at me.

"Brandon, Thomas, lift him and get him into the tent," I ordered. "Where is the doctor?"

With that, the men lifted the king into the tent where he had not long ago prepared for his joust. Doctor Butts finally marched into the room, ordering everyone out of the way. I stayed and held onto Henry's hand. I would not leave his side. Butts examined him and explained that the king had received a severe blow to the head; the only thing that we could do was pray that he woke up before it was too late. If Henry did not regain consciousness soon, he would never wake again.

The doctor stepped away, head in his hands; he had no idea what to do. It was completely in the hands of fate now. I stood next to Henry for a while, stroking his hair and begging him not to leave me. I kissed his forehead and told him that I needed him to come back for his children, for our daughter and the son not yet born. I still needed him; I could not live without him; I was not ready to lose him, the thought crushed me from the inside out. I wept and I wept. Barking at everyone that attempted to come too close to him, they were all to go and leave me to be alone with my husband. I was the next person in charge without Henry, for now.

Thomas and George came to my side. Wyatt placed a hand over mine and George a brotherly arm around my shoulder, kissing my forehead. "Sister, you should rest," George said. "This is not good for you or the baby."

"We will come and find you the moment the king wakes," Thomas added.

"I will stay by his side." I would never for a moment, leave him in this state. If I could wake him up by will alone then I would at least try.

"At least let us get you a chair." Thomas offered.

I nodded. I would sit by the king until he came around, I would be the first face that he would see, I would soothe him and make sure that he knows he is safe and cared for. After they had brought a chair so that I could sit by Henry's side, they both made to leave. I wanted people I could trust by my side. "Can you both stay with me?" I asked. "Until Harry wakes?"

"Of course we will." George smiled. And there we sat for a long while, in silence, praying over the king's body, hoping that by some miracle he would soon awaken. After around an hour, Doctor Butts gave Henry another check-up. He then asked to speak to me privately. I told him that he could speak freely. He told us that the chances of Henry regaining consciousness were getting less and less; the longer he stayed sleeping. His state had not changed for an hour now, and he worried that we would have to start thinking about the possibility that the king may not make it.

"It is treason to imagine the king's death!!" I screamed at him, I knew I was unreasonable, and I did not care. "If you cannot save him, fetch me someone who will." He bowed and left the room, knowing that it was not worth facing my scorn.

Ten minutes after Butts had left, Cromwell came in his place. He crept into the room. "Madam, I see you have good company while the king lay injured." His words sounded like a judgement. I have no idea why he would judge me for wanting the comfort of a friend and my brother while my husband was so weak. However Cromwell was a strange man, and he never liked anything I chose to do.

"You will address me properly, Master Cromwell, or not at all." I really despised this man.

"Excuse me. Majesty. The good doctor has sent me to explain the situation again to you." He made a quick bow in my direction.

"I do not need you to explain to me. My husband will wake, and you should turn around and leave while you still have the chance." I snapped, unable to hold my feelings in.

Cromwell opened his mouth to speak, but by the look on my face thought better of it. He bowed again, turned and left mumbling to himself. That was a problem for another time.

The feelings suddenly overwhelmed me, the fact that I was so close to losing my husband finally found their way into my head. A voice in the back of my mind telling me he would never wake. I was so angry. If he had listened to me we would be enjoying the festivities together.

"Harry, wake up." I punched at his chest. "You need to wake up." I laid my head on him, weeping into his shirt. "I cannot lose you. Please wake up." I begged.

Thomas pulled me from the king and held onto me so tight as I fell to the floor. I was in turmoil; I was too young to lose my husband. He was too young to die. I thought about never seeing him again, I screamed with the thought of never touching him again. Balling my hands up into fists, I thought that I would never hear his voice again, he would never call my name again, or even admonish me again. I could not lose him; the country could not lose him. A scream broke loose from my lips, and it seemed to convey all of my feelings. I could not contain it as it burst from my chest.

I wrenched with the fear that had taken over me. This was Butts' fault; he was not doing all that he could do to save him. No. It was Henry's fault. Why did he have to prove a point? The country still loved him, jousting or not. What would have happened if the king had died? Would Lizzie be queen, I would have to fight for her place after her father. I had dreamed once that Lizzie would be queen. But not like this, not because my poor husband lost his life in a stupid jousting accident. Or would I rule as regent until the son that I carried became of age? I remembered suddenly the babe I carried. Would I now have to sit and be watched until we discover if I do have a prince only to have him ripped from my arms when he is born? Pronounced the new king?

I wanted Henry to wake; I needed him to wake up. We were not safe without him. I prayed to God to save him, I offered God anything in return — my own life, even — if it would save Henry. He needed to see his son be born, needed to see his family completed. He looked so peaceful, sleeping like an angel, he had not one single line of worry on his face, he just laid still, chest moving up and down slowly, sustaining him even in his sleepy state. As the time ticked up to two hours, Butts returned yet again. He again gave the same assessment, but this time, he suggested we start to make preparations. I ordered him to keep his mouth shut and if he told anyone he would be locked in the tower for treason. He was a fearful man and very easy to manipulate.

As I held onto Henry's cold hand, I noticed the smallest of movement. A slight wiggle of his finger to start, then his hand curled around mine. I stood, leaning over him, watching as his face began to become animated again, his eyes fluttered open, revealing to me a glorious blue. He looked confused at first, not quite registering who stood next to him or where he was. "Doctor!" Thomas shouted. "Someone get the doctor. The king is awake."
Butts was in the room without a moment's hesitation. He came to the king's side at once, relief plain on his face.

"Anne?" Henry spoke, raising his hand to stroke my face where a tear fell. "Anne, do not cry."

"Oh, Harry. I was so frightened," I wept. "I thought I had lost you."

"The queen never left your side for a moment." Doctor Butts told Henry. "You have a very loyal wife, indeed."

Henry smiled "I have the most magnificent wife."

"Your majesty. You must not speak. You need your energy," Butts told the king.

We each told Henry about the events of the past few hours, and after getting him into his own bed, Doctor Butts told us that he believed Henry would make a full recovery in due course. He was a lucky man and God must be smiling down on him, to pull him through such an ordeal. When he left, he told Henry that he would need to rest for the next few days and that he would be back to check on him twice a day. I sat in a chair in the corner of the room while they spoke and after he left I got up to follow.

"Thank god you are okay, Harry. I will leave you to rest now." I made my way to the door.

"Anne," he spoke, voice raspy from the events of the last day. "Why would you leave me now?"

"You wish me to stay?" I asked. I could not help the smile that spread across my face.

"You are the reason I am alive. You sat by my side, willing me to wake up." He patted the bed next to him. "Come stay with me tonight. You are my wife and queen, after all."

I rushed over to him, laying my head onto his chest. I was so glad to be able to hold him again.

"I had thought for a moment that we would not be able to do this again." The tears filled my eyes now, as the day caught up with me.

"I will never leave you. As long as it is in my power, we will forever be together." He kissed my head.

"You would never choose another over me, then?" I asked.

"No one can replace you. You are my queen, and you will always be my queen," he reassured me. "Now, stay by my side, and I will be able to sleep soundly."

"I love you Harry," I said before closing my eyes.

"And I love you, Anne." This was the first time he had said it since we visited Lizzie at Hatfield. I slept, a smile on my face.

* * * * *

At first, I am embarrassed to admit that I thought that the accident might have been a godsend, and it had brought Henry and me back together. I had not left his side since it had happened, sleeping in his bed for the next four nights. However, fate had been cheated out of one death, and it needed to balance it with another. It seemed when I had prayed for Henry to recover I had bargained with another

275

life dear to me. When I had offered anything for his health, I had not realised the price I would pay. The tragedy was not done with us yet, and it would strike again five days later. And with it, it would bring my whole world crashing down.

This was when my darkness began, this was when fate had decided that my life would now be over, and with a cruel stab of the knife it would begin the end of me. A cloud would hang over my head and follow me wherever I may go. I had signed my deal with death on the day that I had agreed to be Henry's queen, the day that I usurped an anointed queen from the throne; the world had decided that I owe a great price, and I would pay with two lives.

It was now 29th January, 1536, the day Catherine was buried. Finally she had died. Cold and alone as she laid in seclusion. I feel terrible to say it, but I felt instant relief. She had always been in the background. But she could no longer get in my way. On the day that her funeral took place, the day that Mary said goodbye to her mother, I would face a loss as well. I believe now that it was a punishment, for the part I had played in Catherine's death. The part I played in ripping a child from their mother's arms, I had helped to keep Mary and Catherine apart all of these years, and now I would have my child torn from me.

I had told Henry that I had wanted to sleep in my bed that night, feeling worn out and exhausted from his accident. He had understood and sent me off with a kiss. Madge and Margery had both offered to stay with me, but I said that I just wanted some time on my own.
George had come by to see me earlier in the night to see how I was doing and to say goodnight. I had told him that I was fine and just wanted to rest, he left me promising to come and see me tomorrow, he left, and I fell asleep...and then, the pain started.

At around one o'clock in the morning, I awoke from my sleep. Pain gripping my stomach, I wrapped my hand around myself trying to hold off the agony that was now filling my body. I knew what was happening straight away, I did not want to admit it to myself, but the dread had already started to fill my soul. I was three and a half months pregnant, what else could this pain be if it was not the baby? I climbed out of bed and realised that it was nearly impossible to stand, gripping hold of my chair as I made my way to the door.

"Send for Margery," I ordered through the door. "And my brother."

I heard a breath "Majesty," and then footsteps as the guard ran down the corridor to find them. I fell to my knees and practically crawled my way to the chair. There was no blood yet; this was a good sign. Maybe this just meant that I was going to have a difficult pregnancy.

I knew in my heart that I was wrong, but I could not lose this baby. Henry may be happy with me now, but if I lost this child then there was no hope at all for me. He would cast me off again. I tried to pull myself up into my chair, but the pain was too great, so I laid on the floor, cradling the small bump that had begun to grow.

My door swung open, and George rushed to my side, taking my arm and lifting me into the chair. His wife, Jane Parker had come along with him to see what was going on. He turned to her. "Leave, Jane. This is a family matter." She made to answer, but he shut the door in her face.

"Anne?" George's face was white with shock. "Sister. What is wrong?"

Before I had a chance to answer, Margery was coming through the door. "Majesty, what is it?"

"It is happening again, Marge," I cried sinking into the cushions. "My baby is dying."

Everything seemed to stop as the words sank in, the whole world around me seemed to hold still for a moment. Margery sank to her knees in front of me, George just stood, hand over his mouth, speechless for the very first time. I screamed as the pain shot through me again. This woke George from his reverie.

"Sister. What can I do?" He came to my side, and I took his hand.

"Just hold my hand, Brother," I said between cries.

The pain was not like last time, in the sense that it did not last as long. With a final crushing pain, the blood that carried my child broke free from me. It happened so fast that I barely had time to realise what had just happened. Why was this happening to me again? Why did God torment me so? Another child that I had carried within me, now lay dead at my feet.

In the mass of blood, I could see the tiny figure, lying there, wrapped around itself. It was so small, so precious. How could god kill such an innocent creature? This was too much for me. I could not do this again; I had already suffered one loss; I could not lose another child. This could not be right; I had done everything the doctor had ordered of me. What could I have done to kill my child? Why did he have to die?

I wanted so badly to erase the last hour, to wake from my bed as if from a terrible dream. I would get up, and I would deal with this. I was a strong woman. But I could not cope with this loss; I could not bear to lose another child. I just stared, I just gazed down at the crimson puddle on the floor, unblinking and unmoving. I just looked on; not a tear fell from my eye, not a thought crossed my mind. I just felt empty. I felt like my soul had been ripped from my body and I knelt on the floor an empty shell.

I could hear Margery gently weeping in the corner, George, traumatised by what he had just witnessed cried into his own hands, but I did not cry. Instead, I was taken back to the dream I had a long time ago, when I lost my boy, the dream of my son in heaven, and I thought that this one would be waiting for me as well. This baby was no bigger than a grape. He looked so peaceful, maybe he was peaceful, to be out of this world and in the clouds with his brother. George came behind me and wrapped his arms around my neck.

"Anne...Anne...I am so sorry."

I did not answer; I would not speak a word; I did not trust my voice. They probably thought me run mad, looking down at a puddle, my hand resting where he lay, wide-eyed with not a cry in my body. Margery spoke next. "Majesty, we should send for the doctor."

"No," I screamed, the most agonising noise I had ever heard breaking free from my body. "No," I repeated. "I want time with my son before they take him away."

"Anne, you need to be seen to," George joined.

"I want to hold my baby. I want to be with him before he goes." I knew that when Butts arrived he would take my child and examine him, I do not know now what I was thinking, I know that I wanted time alone with him, I wanted him to know that I loved him before they snatched his little body away from me.

"Anne...the baby is already gone." George took my hand. "You need the doctor to look at you."

I was filled with sudden rage, I stood, and pulled first George and then Margery up off of the floor. "Get out," I shouted in George's face. "If you cannot support me, then I do not want you here."

"My lady..." Margery started. I took her hand and pulled her to the door, ready to open it.

"And if you are no friend to me, then you can leave as well."

"Anne! Stop!" George ordered.

"How dare you speak to your queen..."

279

"Sister. If you open that door, then your secret will be known." George cut me off mid-sentence.

"What do you mean?" I asked, the anger starting to subside.

Margery took hold of my gown to show me how the blood had stained it. "Anne, you are covered in blood." I looked down at my gown, where the blood had soaked through, making its white now a dark red. "Oh, my sweet queen. Please sit down." Margery took hold of my arm.

It hit me then with a crushing feeling that weighed down on my chest and knocked me over. I slid down the door, holding my dress up and sobbing into it. It was as if seeing the blood soak through had brought my tragedy to the light; it had opened my eyes to what was happening. The shock finally wearing off and the reality hitting me like a tidal wave of despair.

"No, no, no, no," I shrieked. "Not again...this cannot happen again." I looked to Marge and then to George. Hoping one of them could offer me some comfort. They just stared on, unsure of what to say, grief for me evident on both of their faces.

"I need a son," I wailed. "Henry needs me to have a son."

George was at my side now. "The king loves you, Henry will not blame you." he rubbed my arm.

"No, George. You do not know him as I do. He will hate me for this." I grabbed him by the shoulders. "We cannot tell him. Let's hide the body," I raved.

"Anne, you cannot lie to the king," Margery scolded me.

"What do I do? He will never love me again now."

I felt light-headed and dizzy; it felt as if the world spun all around me. I stood to make my way over to the bed, running a hand through my sweat-soaked hair. As I stood I lost my balance, falling to the floor, where George dove to catch me before I hurt myself. Everything started to turn black, as small spots took over my eyesight. I suddenly felt unbelievably tired, and the next thing I remember was Margery and George helping me to bed.

"Rest now, sister. We will send for the doctor."

"No…" I managed to mumble, but I was too weak to put up much of a fight. "No, don't tell Harry…"

"Anne, you have lost a lot of blood. You need to be seen too. I will not leave your side, and George will speak to the king." Margery's voice was in my ear.

George kissed my head and was gone. The last thing I recall was George leaving the room, and I fell into a fitful sleep. I was too drained to worry about what I would wake up to.

I dreamed that I was a girl again, running around wild and free at Hever. George chased me around the trees; Mary sat looking pretty perched on her windowsill, laughing at the silliness of George and me. I was young, a girl, before I knew the ways of this world. I had no idea of the tragedies that existed. My only goal was to beat George in a race; I never gave a second thought to Henry Tudor, or the court. I was free, I was as light as a feather, and I had the whole world laid out in front of me. It was a beautiful lie, and when I woke I would return with a crash to the real world.

I woke to the sound of a man's voice filling the room; he was angry and ordering someone to leave. At first, I had no sense of where I was or who surrounded me. I was still in Hever in my mind. I realised with a shock that it was Henry's voice I could hear. At first I was glad, I had missed him, I wanted him to hold me, but then the memories began, and I remembered the events of the last few hours. I kept my eyes closed for a moment so that I could gauge what I was waking up into. Henry was angrier than I had ever heard him. I could not tell who he was shouting at until I heard the second voice. It was Margery.

"Your Majesty, with all due respect, the queen needs rest." Margery tried to sound commanding.

"I said to wake the woman up so you will wake her up and then you will leave," he bellowed.

"I promised not to leave her side..." Margery sounded defeated.

"She has her husband here now...I will wake her. Now go."

Margery knew better than to argue with the king. She touched my hand lightly and then the door opened, and she left. I was scared all of a sudden, left alone in a room with Henry on my own. I was too weak to defend myself, he would try to wake me any moment, and I would have to face the rage that waited for me.

The door opened again, right before I prepared to open my eyes and I heard Doctor Butts. "The queen needs rest, majesty," he suggested. "May I have a word in private?" he asked Henry. Butts was a sniveling little man; he had not one ounce of bravery in him, even his voice shook as he addressed the king.

"The queen is resting. You can talk freely here. She sleeps." Henry said, calmer now than before.

Butts took an audible breath before he began to speak again. "It is the child...the b-b-baby that the queen mis...miscarried..." he stuttered.

"Spit it out, Butts. I have no energy for your shattered nerves." Henry barked.

"The thing that your wife delivered...well it...it was...deformed." he barely got out.

"Deformed!?" Henry roared. "What do you mean?"

"The babe was more creature than babe.." Butts lowered his voice. "It is quite a rare thing to see."

"And what was this baby?" Henry asked he sounded sad now, despair filling his words.

"A boy, sire."

Silence filled the room now, not a word was spoken for what seemed like forever.

Then Butts started to speak again when his little confidence had returned. "The queen...will need a lot of attention. She lost a lot of blood."

"Do what you will." Henry spat. "For I am done with her."

There was some movement in the room, and then I heard the door slam with a great thud. I opened my eyes for the first time and found that I was totally alone, the king had left, and so had the Doctor. I was alone in my grief, he had sent Margery away, and I had no idea where George was. He probably took a beating from Henry with the sad news he was tasked to deliver. I openly began to weep now that I was alone.

What did Henry mean that he was done with me? Was he done with me that day? Or he was done with me altogether? Did he just cast me off completely? What was I to do? I had lost my child, and now my husband had had his fill of me.

What was wrong with the child? Deformed? How could that be? Was he too young to of had any features? Was he missing a crucial body part? I could not remember him looking any different than a normal babe, he was just so small, but there was nothing abnormal about him. Not that I had noticed. Why would this send Henry from the room? It was no one's fault that he was born wrong. It happened sometimes. He just wasn't made for this world. Henry and the doctor could not blame me, but of course, they would.

I was alone in the world, not one friendly face to welcome me back after the horrors I had experienced. For a day I sat on my own, no friend to comfort me. Margery returned to sit by my side, apologising for leaving, she explained that Henry had ordered that I be left alone in my sorry state. Why he wished such isolation on me, I did not know. I understood Margery's part, how could I hate her for following the orders of her king. George came to see me later that day, with Mark and Thomas. They all sat around my bed and tried to cheer my mood. Mark played for me the violin, and Thomas read to me. George joked and tried to make me laugh.

Henry never came. For three days, I waited to see him, and for three days he stayed away. There was no note, no apology for his absence. George told me that he was simply grieving and he would come to see me when he was feeling better. What about how I felt? I had asked. Did the king not care that I was unwell? Did he not wish to see his wife who was so wretched in her own grief? George just shook his head and apologised.

On the fourth day of not seeing Henry, I had almost lost my mind with worry. I decided to take it into my own hands and went to demand that he see me. I made my way from my bed, where I had spent the last few days, to see him. His guards refused to let me through at first, but after a bit of threatening and offering to relieve them of their duty, they backed down. They opened up the doors and announced me. Henry stood at the window. He held a cup of wine in his hand, lost in thought, he did not turn as I entered. I walked to stand by him and put my hand on his shoulder. He made no move. He did not smile. He was a blank canvas.

"Henry. Where have you been?" I demanded.

He did not answer me; he continued staring out of the window. Watching as the trees blew gently in the wind, paying close attention to the leaves that fell slowly to rest on the ground.

"Henry…." still nothing. "Henry! Answer me! Where have you been while I lay sick in my bed?" I raised my voice now.

He turned to face me looking me square in the face. As his eyes met mine, I realised that they were filled with such sadness. He looked like a broken man wrestling with his own feelings. I realised at that moment that my tragedy was actually our tragedy. Perhaps I had been selfish to wallow in my sadness and care little for his.

He breathed a slow, steadying breath. He was trying to control the feelings that lay so close to the surface. "You have really done it now." was all he said. Confusion crossed my face; I could not understand what he meant.

"Harry, what do you mean?" I asked.

"You have finally succeeded in ridding me of every ounce of love that I had for you." He was so calm. His voice contained no touch of emotion.

"Harry...I do not understand? We are both sad to lose a son...but we must get through it together." I tried to take his hand, but he moved away from me.

"Anne, the only thing I want from you now is to leave me alone." He looked me dead in the eye. "And please. Do not call me Harry anymore. That is reserved for the people I trust." He knew how this would hurt me, but still he made no sign of any emotion on his face.

"Henry, I have just lost a child, and yet you treat me as if I was some evil woman, intent on ruining you." I lost my composure. "Have you ever thought that you are as much to blame as I?" I shouted in my own rage. Turning to walk and just as I opened the door I shouted for everyone close enough to hear.

"Maybe if you could perform in the bedroom, I would be pregnant more often," I cackled. His face turned a bright shade of red; he was ready to burst. I simply walked through the door and closed it. The words he shouted as the door closed bear not repeating.

CHAPTER TWENTY-TWO

For the next few weeks, I kept my space from Henry as much as possible. I would entertain in my rooms and leave him to do whatever he pleased. I had heard rumours that he was now openly courting Jane Seymour, and I hated it. I now knew how Catherine must have felt while he courted both Mary and me. Jane was my lady in waiting as we had been to Catherine; it was such a betrayal. It felt as if my heart was being ripped out. He sent her gifts and spoke to her as a lover. Just like he had when he was chasing me.

I know that kings are expected to take mistresses, but I never liked it. The whole time we were together I wanted Henry to only have eyes for me, I wanted to be everything to him. Jane was different. People would talk about how he looked at her. How he paraded her before the court as if she were a prized trophy. He spoke of how sweet and innocent she was. Well, she could not have been that innocent if she was whoring herself out to another woman's husband.

I detested seeing her in my court. I would always send her away whenever I held festivities of my own. The sight of her turned my stomach. She looked like a pretty little flower. She was untouched by any man and blind to the world's darkness, but if she were to get into bed with my Harry then she would have her eyes opened in the harshest of ways. One evening she was playing cards with Marge and Madge Shelton. I was sick of her already. Her bubbly little giggle sounding off every now and then, her charming little smile and squeaky little voice.

"Jane, come sit with me awhile," I called across the room. She looked around her, hoping that I meant someone else. She nodded and walked over, Marge and Madge followed, eager to overhear the conversation.

"What can I do for Your Majesty?" her pathetic little voice shook.

"I want to get to know you," I said.

"What would Your Majesty like to know?" she was nervous.

"Well, we will start with something easy," I said, feeling spiteful. "Do you enjoy sleeping with my husband?" I stared her down.

"Majesty, I do not know…" she started.

"Oh come, Jane, don't be shy. Everyone here knows how desperate you are to fill my shoes." I laughed.

Jane looked around her, hoping maybe that someone would jump to her aid. The other ladies who were enjoying this too much avoided her gaze.

"Well come on then, does he fulfill all of your deepest desires?" I laughed. "I doubt it very much."

"Majesty, I do not like this conversation. If I could be dismissed." she squirmed.

"Oh, you will be dismissed when Queen Anne dismisses you." Margery joined the conversation.

"I cannot imagine the king enjoys you very much." I chuckled. "He prefers his women beautiful...and feisty. You are gifted with neither of those things...clearly." I said I waved my finger over her.

"You have nothing on the queen...she outshines you in every way," Margery was chiming in.

"I know I do not…" she squeaked.

"Ah, so you know you are worthless?" I smiled at her, my cruel words cutting deep. She looked ready to burst into tears. "If you are going to cry then do not do it in my presence. You will get no pity here." She looked down at her hands, playing with a strand of hair. "Is the king kind to you? Does he tell you he loves you and you are the only woman for him?"

"The king is very kind...He treats me very well and is upset with how you shun him," she said, being brave for the first time.

I stood and walked slowly towards her. She stood as I approached.

"Oh, really? I shun him, do I? That is funny as he is the one spending time in the company of whores like you." a bead of sweat broke on her forehead.

"You are dismissed." She moved so quickly, desperate to get away from this interrogation. She turned and went to leave.

"You are forgetting something..." Marge called. "Bow to your Queen, Jane. you would not want to fall from favour."

She hurried back towards me bowing and muttering words of apology. She was visibly shaking. I laughed at her weakness. If she wished to catch and keep Henry then she would need to grow a backbone. She turned and went to the door, but I had one more thing to say to her.

"Oh, and Jane? Just remember, the king may enjoy you now, or at least what is between your legs. But he will always come back to me. He will always be my Harry."

She left to the sound of my ladies and me giggling. I would enjoy tormenting her over the next few months, Henry had told me that I was not allowed to dismiss her, so I would at least have my fun with her. I enjoyed seeing her squirm.

I had realised that Henry no longer visited me with the intent of conceiving a child. He could not have given up hope because it was so important. I would have thought that no matter how mad he got with me, he would still put the need to create an heir above anything else. Instead, I spent my time in the company of other men who were not my husband. As I have said before and I will keep saying until the day I die, nothing happened. We would play games, or make music, I would never turn from Henry, no matter what he may or may not believe now, but my days would be very long and boring if I simply spent them hanging around and waiting for him to miss me. Now, I wish I had done that. Perhaps he would have come around eventually, but I will never know.

Henry Norris and Francis Weston had spent a lot of time in my company of late. They would join us in a game of cards, or sit and talk with my ladies. Weston had become a trusted friend ever since the day of the joust, where he had comforted me. I had wanted him around me as he had proven himself to be loyal and kind, and in this world you had to hold on to anyone that you could count on. Henry Norris spent a lot of time in particular with Madge Shelton, my cousin. I believed he had started to feel for her. He would always find an excuse to be sitting next to her, talking to her or touching her. Eventually, he had come to ask my permission to marry her, of course I agreed.

I was so very happy for Madge, she seemed to really enjoy his company, and I believed that they would make a lovely match. However, Norris did not ask straight away, two weeks after giving my permission he still had not gone to Madge with the happy news. I had begun to consider that his intentions may not be as genuine as he wanted them to appear.

He had come to me one day, in search of Madge and had found that I'd sent my ladies away for the day, wanting to be alone. I was feeling especially low on this day. Henry had still not spoken a word to me, and I had seen him in the halls, leaning into Jane as she giggled. He had kissed her on the hand and told her that he looked forward to seeing her later on that day.

I ran back to my apartments, slamming the door behind me and screaming at all of my ladies to get out. They bowed and left, some lingering behind to check that I was well, but I wanted no one in my sight, I needed time to think. Henry Norris came to see me not long after. At first he enquired after Madge, but when he did not leave to go and find her, it appeared clear to me that it was not Madge that he wanted.

"Why have you not married the lady Madge yet, Henry?" I asked. "You make a lovely couple."

Norris chuckled "I look to tarry a time, Majesty."

I snickered. "You look for dead man's shoes. For if ought come to the king but good, you'd look to have me." I batted my eyelids in mock flirtation.

Norris took offence to this; his cheeks reddened "I would rather my head was off." He bowed and left the room, anger plain on his face.

After he left, I realised that we were not completely alone. Elizabeth Brown was in the corner looking through some of my books. When I confronted her she said that she'd stayed behind to take a book back to her own room to read and had got caught up when Norris had entered. I thought no more on it, Elizabeth had always been a good friend to me. I would never suspect that she may have an ulterior motive.

Later that day Cromwell came to see me. He was sent on the king's bidding. Henry wanted me to dine with him that evening, just the two of us. So he sent Cromwell as his messenger; he was too busy to take a moment from his day and come to his wife's room, but at least he could spare his trained pet.

"Majesty." Cromwell bowed. "I have come to ask that you join His Majesty tonight for supper." His tone was so blunt; he hated every moment of being in my presence. I looked him up and down before answering. What an awful little man he was. Doing anything he could to further himself in the world.

"Of course. I would love to join Harry for supper." I answered curtly. Smiling sweetly at him.

"I will inform the king." He bowed. I was not done with him; however, I wanted to get him on edge, I enjoyed playing games with the people who looked to unseat me.

"Cromwell...how does it feel having to bow to me?" I mused aloud. "You hate me. Do you not?"

"I could never hate my queen, my lady." He was good with words. "I do however wish that everyone else felt the same," he chuckled, mostly to himself.

"What do you mean everyone else?" I snapped.

"Oh the rumours. The ones that question your loyalty." He spoke as if I should know what he was talking about, but I had no idea about any rumours.

"My loyalty is unwavering. What is being said?" I asked, shock and anger plain on my face. He was getting pleasure out of this; it was plain in the gleam that lay in his eyes.

"I, of course, do not pay any attention to the whisperings at court, Majesty." he smiled.

"Oh, say it, Cromwell. I know very well that you want to." I demanded.

"Well...they are saying that Your Gracious Majesty...they say that you have lovers." he looked elated at the revelation. He loved to see me under pressure.

"How ridiculous! I would never betray Henry." My head swam as the allegations sunk in. "Who says such things?"

"I would not know where they started your majesty.."

"I believe I look at the source as we speak."

"I would never," fake shock on his face now. He chuckled and raised his hands. "Do not attack the messenger."

"I will not, but perhaps instead I will remove his head," I laughed.

"You can try…" He bowed and left not giving me chance to reply.

He left me with all of the new developments to sink in. Someone had been spreading gossip that I lay with someone other than my husband. Who would be so cruel? Everyone close to me knew just how much I adored Henry. Even during the days where he pretended I did not exist, I still wanted him above any other. If any of us had turned from our marriage it was never me. I could not bear the thought of another man's touch. I just wanted Henry; I still want Henry. No one would ever be able to take his place. He could drop me and pick me up as he pleased and I would still give him my whole heart.

I did not know what these rumours could mean for me, but surely Henry would give them no weight. He knew just how much I cared for him; he would never believe me disloyal, of that I was certain. I had given him everything. I had spent seven years of my life fighting to marry him, to displace Catherine and be with the man I loved. We had fought through many battles, but we had been happy. The moments of joy outweighed the sadness a million to one. I would take all of the bad days again, just for one more good day with Henry. He had raised me to be his queen, and we were so in love.

I believe we were still madly in love even then, we just needed time to find each other again, and now he wanted to have supper with me tonight. Surely that was a sign that he missed me. Surely he wanted us to go back to the way we were before. I put on a brave face, but every moment we were not together was like a dagger to my heart. Every day I went without his touch I was driven further into madness, it was he who I craved, it would be only he who could awaken my soul again.

I would find the source of these rumours and I would erase them from my life, from this court. They would be forgotten. Was the court that boring these days that they had to make up stories, had to try to smudge my good name? It did not matter. Henry would not believe them, may not even hear them. Cromwell may have made them up on the spot for all I knew. He had a good way with stories perhaps he wanted to scare me. Well it would not work. I would not let him get into my head. I pushed it away and went about my day.

In the evening I readied myself to go to dine with Henry. I was very excited and nervous, it felt like the beginning of our courtship when he would invite me into his chamber. It had been too long since the last time we were alone, and at that time we had left with such angry words. Now was the chance to put it right again. Madge and Jane Parker Helped me to prepare. I had decided that I wanted to look perfect. I want Henry to realise why he had fallen in love with me again, to remind him of the day we married. I wore a dark purple dress; I knew this colour helped to set off my features and suited my complexion best, I had my hair brushed out and let it flow loose down my back, just as on the day we had married and the day I was crowned. In my ears I wore the Tudor roses that Henry had gifted me on our wedding day, and around my neck I wore my lucky charm. The B necklace that father had given to me all of those years ago when I was a young girl.

I gazed at myself in the looking glass and was happy with what I saw. I looked younger somehow. I imagined myself as that young girl again, trying to escape the king's advances, desperate to put as much distance between Henry and me as possible, at this moment all I wanted was to be closer to him. I was certain that tonight we would forgive each other for the past months of sorrow and continue with our happy marriage. We would work through our issues and look to creating a new son, and we would forget about the woes of the last year. This would be our fresh start. God knows we needed it. As I prepared to leave, Elizabeth pinched my cheeks, bring a blush to the surface. "You look beautiful, Majesty…" she said, tears in her eyes. At the time this meant nothing to me. I would find out later that she had been giving false evidence against me.

Henry was waiting for me when I arrived. I bowed as I walked in and he held my chair out for me, this was a good sign. We ate the first course in silence. The room full of

293

tension as words were left unspoken. He looked just as he had the last time we spoke. His face emotionless and unreadable. I could not understand his reasoning for inviting me tonight; it was not the reunion that I had thought.

After the servants had taken away our dishes, Henry rested his elbows on the table and looked at me. "How are you, Anne?" he asked.

"I am well, Harry. How are you?" I asked. "I have missed you," I honestly said as I looked in his eyes.

"I would be better if I had a wife that I could trust." He said it so calmly as if the words had no effect on him. "I have missed you too, but Anne, what am I to do when these rumours fly around my court?"

"You don't believe them? Harry, I would never even look at another man the way I look at you?"

"I know," he said, I breathed a sigh of relief. "But it is hard when you are seen with Wyatt or Weston all of the time."

"They are my friends Henry." I could not believe that he would use them against me. They had been my friends for a long while without a word of displeasure from him.

"You need to be more careful Anne. You never know who is out to get you," he warned.

"I don't care about anyone else. I only care what you believe." I took his hand. He did not flinch away for once. "And if you truly know that I would never turn from you, then can we go back to the way we were? Can we be happy again?"

He sighed, leaning back in his chair and running his hands through his hair. "Anne, I do believe you, and you must know that I do love you." he thought for a moment. "But the damage we have done to each other is too much. Are you not tired of this? The constant circle of love and hate, pleasure and pain?" I realised that he had been wrestling with this for a while. He looked as if he had not slept in days. I stood and wrapped my arms around him, trying to convey some level of comfort.

"Henry you are right, we do hurt each other deeply, but we also love each other deeply. A love like ours is worth the pain for me," I told him. "I would take a thousand stabs to heart to be in the same room as you. There is no level of pain that you could lay on me that would turn me from you. A love like ours does not come around every day. We must fight through all of the trials to get the beauty that lays at the end."

He stood from his chair taking both of my hands, and he kissed me. I had missed this so much. One kiss from him and I forgot all about the troubles in the world, I could only see him and myself, nothing else mattered, no one else could compare.

"Our love burns like a fire ready to consume anyone in sight, Anne. It is not pure love; it is a dark love that grows from the despair of others." He broke free. "I will never stop loving you, but I also will never stop blaming you. If I did not love you, men would still be alive. Thomas More would still be here, and Fisher; it is because I love you that I have been blind."

"You cannot possibly blame me for Thomas..." I was in shock. Henry had ordered his execution and not I. How could I be to blame when it was he who signed the order.

"Hush Anne, I blame the both of us. I believe now that God does not smile on this match any more than he did Catherine."

"Henry. How can you say this." I cried. He still held me in place, not letting me get away as I tried to pull free.

"Anne, I am saying I love you. Oh God, I love you. You are everything. It hurts me to be separated from you." he stroked back my hair, tears falling from his eyes. "But if I had to do it all again, I would not pursue you."

"Henry. Let go of me." I broke free from him. "If that is true then maybe I should have stayed in Hever or France, as far from you as possible."

"I am sorry." he bowed his head. "What have I put us through?"

"You did this Henry. If you had never wanted me, I would have married Percy." I fumed at him, but I was not angry, I was at sea, in total despair. "You wanted me so badly that you could never let me be. I would have moved on, but you would not allow me to leave. I would never have loved you if you did not push me."

"Anne, I...forgive me, please. It pains me to see what I have created." He looked so convinced of his own words. His stupidity began to bother me. Our love was beautiful, or so I believed.

"So what do you want Henry? Do you want to marry another? Jane Seymour, maybe?" Confusion crossed his face. He came to me again, taking hold of my shoulders and pulling me into his arms, I let him.

"No, Anne. God no, don't be silly," he sobbed. "I married you and promised to be forever yours." he kissed my head. "I told you I would be yours forever; you have left such a scar on my heart that I could never truly belong to anyone else."

"Then what is the point of this, Henry? Why are we talking of pain, if you do not want rid of me."

"I believe we need to live separately. We will put on a good face for the country, but we will have no private life together. All your face does is serve as a reminder of all I have...all that we have lost." He explained, his words crushing me.

"And what of an heir?" I asked, the obvious question hanging in the air.

"We will have an heir, but that is all I want from you now." he kissed me again. "Anne, I am sorry."

"Do not give me your pity Henry," I spat. "You have done this and you alone. Your cruel ways have twisted me into the woman I am now. Playing your games caused the death of those men, not me. You were the one who sought to push Catherine from the throne and turn your back on Mary. You are the reason I miscarried our son, and you are the reason that I spend my time in the company of other men. You can blame me, and you can paint me as the cruel woman who usurped a queen and forced you to execute friends, but deep down you will always know that it was you who wanted the divorce, and it was you who signed the papers..."

"Anne, watch what you say," Henry warned, tears drying from his face and anger, replacing his look of sorrow.

"I am not finished, Henry." I continued. "We may live separate lives now, I will hide in the shadows and watch you swan around with the whore, but always know that I am there. I will always be over your shoulder to remind you of the cruelty you bear me to remind you of the friends lost, and the enemies gained, the daughter you cast off, of the queen you abandoned. You will see my face, and you will never be able to forget the evil that lies in your heart. You will never truly be rid of me, no matter what you do."

I felt cruel now. His words had stung me, and I wanted him to know that he was not able to pin everything on me. All of this had been caused because he loved me and would do anything for me. Not because I had asked him to.

"And what if I choose to believe these rumours?" He was threatening me now. He hated hearing the truth, and I had given him a big dose of it.

"Believe what you will, Henry. For you and I both know it is not true."

This would turn out to be the last real conversation I ever had with Henry. After this we would only see each other by chance or if there was a reason for us to be on show.

After I left Henry I went in search of my brother, but instead I happened upon Thomas Wyatt, who was waiting at George's door, also apparently looking for my brother. We decided that as neither of us could find the man we were looking for we would keep each other company instead. I relayed to him the events of the last hour telling him how much Henry had truly hurt me this time. I cried for the first time letting the tears flow freely from me.

"I've lost him, Thomas...I mean for real this time" I wept. "He despises me now."

"How could anyone despise you Anne?" Thomas held me. "The king will come around, and if he does not, then it is his loss."

"No Thomas...it is too late. I have lost him." It was almost a wail. "I have lost Henry, and if I do not play my cards right, I will lose my crown too..."

"Henry would not do that. He would have to prove your marriage void. He has no ground to stand on," Thomas chuckled.

"He did it to Catherine..." I let my words hang there, the reality sinking in for the both of us.

Thomas had no words in the answer, he simply shook his head, but he knew that what I said made sense. "He will do to me what he did to Catherine, and I will get what I deserve."

"Anne...You cannot blame yourself; you were young and in love with a king. Yes you made mistakes, and yes people got hurt, but it is the world we live in; no one is completely innocent."

"If you ask Henry, Jane Seymour is." I sounded like a brat who was not their father's favourite child anymore.

"Jane Seymour will disappear and be forgotten about before you know it." Thomas tried to soothe me. It would not work. I had a feeling in the pit of my stomach that something was brewing and it would blow my whole world apart. "You are such a wonderful queen, Anne. You are kind, and you care about the people who live in this country. You do more for charity than Catherine ever did." Thomas tried his hardest to calm me down as I paced in front of him.

"It all means nothing without his love...less than nothing, it was he who I wanted, not the crown. Yes, I love being queen, I love the power, I love that I can command a country, but I love those things because I am by Henry's side. Even when he makes me angry, a passion burns inside me for him; even when he makes me cry, he is the one who I want to comfort me to tell me everything will be okay." I cried. I wished for Thomas to know that I never wanted the crown. I knew what people thought of me. They believed that I was power-hungry. That I had used the king for my gain. But this was not true. I wanted my Harry and nothing else.

"For God's sake. What does he have over you? He treats you like dirt. You have a hundred men worshipping at your feet, and you still want him? Would it be so bad if you were free of him? Free to live your life without him?" Thomas was suddenly angry.

I was not mad at him, I was worried for him. If anyone were to overhear, he could end up in the Tower. "Thomas, watch what you say..." but he did not let me finish.

"No, I am sorry, but if you were mine I would pull the stars from the sky if you asked me. I would climb every mountain that was put in front of me. You would never cry because of my words, never be in pain from my hand." Thomas took my hand now. "Anne, you know how I feel about you. How I always have felt.." He finally confessed the feelings that he had sat on for the last few years.

"Thomas...then your wife is a lucky woman." I was eager to end this conversation. It was far too dangerous. "We must leave what is in the past, in the past." he stood silent, looking down at the ground. "Thomas...do not hate me."

After a long while he finally spoke. "No, I am sorry. I spoke out of turn. Come, let's forget about it? Will you have a drink with me? It will mend my wounded heart." He held his hand to his chest in mock pain.

I chuckled, feeling at ease for the first time in weeks. We spoke for hours. I cried and let out all of the feelings I had held within me. We plotted Jane's demise together, and we laughed.

I think that must be the last time I laughed, and it felt so good, so carefree. It was all too short, but it is the memory of Thomas that I will hold close to me. It is the last time I sat and spoke with him before arrests were made. We let the real world fade away. Before long George had found us, along with his wife Jane, Margery, some of my other ladies. Henry Norris and Francis Weston found their way to us as well. I like to think of it as our goodbye to each other, for many of us in that room would not live another month.

CHAPTER TWENTY-THREE

The next few weeks passed without much to note. The rumours of my alleged love affairs continued to circulate along with the rumours of Jane's relationship with my husband.

Lizzie had come to court for a while. It was nearing the end of April, and she was supposed to be with us from then until the end of summer. It warmed my heart to see her again. She was going to be three this year. How big she had grown, tottering around the place and wanting to touch and play with everything she should not.

She is my pride and joy. Although I may not live on at least I know she will survive this. She will live on. Although she may remember little of me, she will have the chance to have a life of her own. It scares me to think that she may never know how much I love her. Will anyone tell her just how much she meant to me? I imagine Henry will pretend that I never existed. He will not talk to Elizabeth of me, I am sure. I am unsure if he will talk to her at all.

Perhaps he will do the same to her as he did Mary. Maybe that is my punishment for my part in the treatment of Mary, for the same thing to now happen to the daughter that I share with Henry. Is that what I deserve? It may well be, but that does not mean that Lizzie does. She is innocent in all of my wrongdoings.

If I could choose who I would like to spend my last days with I couldn't have picked better company than my daughter. She looked more like her father as the days went on. She was so very beautiful; you could see almost nothing of me in her features. I spent my days in her nursery, playing games with her or chasing her in the gardens. Whenever we dined, Henry would carry her into the hall and place her on a little throne by the side of us.

He loved her so much; it was plain to see for the whole court. If anyone looked upon us we must have looked like the perfect little family, Henry and I laughing as Lizzie sung to us or performed for the court; she got that from me. He would coo at her and squeeze her little cheeks; I forgot all of my worries when I was with the two of them. Every now and then he would look up and smile at me, sharing in the love of our child and for a second I believe both Henry and I would forget the strains on our relationship.

* * * * *

I will tell you now of May 1536. Mayday. It was not much of a day, and at the time it felt of little consequence, but it was the last day that I would be free. If I had known it to be my last day, I would have spent longer looking at the sky. I would have enjoyed every last moment of the sun shining on my face — the breeze in my hair. I would have studied my Lizzie's face a little longer. Touched her hair and kissed her a thousand times more. I would have told her that I loved her. I would tell Henry that I loved him one more time. It would not have changed a lot, but at least I would have told him. I would hug my brother and never let go. I would kiss his head and say goodbye. If I could only have said goodbye. I wish I could have him hold me one more time. For George to tell me things will be all right. I love him more than life itself, and I could offer him no comfort at his last moments.

There are no warnings for these things and the day seemed like any other. Henry and I were attending the May Day celebrations together. The day was beautiful. The sun was shining bright. There was not a cloud in the sky. We sat amongst the entertainments and enjoyed the performances that were put on. We ate, and we drank. Henry laughed and did not show for a second that anything was wrong.

"You seem in good spirits today Harry," I commented as he chuckled along.

"Yes. It is a good day." He smiled. Then everything changed when Norris approached him and whispered in his ear. Henry stood looking at me, and he simply said, "Good day madam," and then he left. It turns out he took half of the court with him and left Greenwich altogether. I would never see Henry again.

That evening I went back to the queen's apartments just like I always had. My ladies dressed and readied me for bed, brushing my hair and reading with me awhile. The only strange thing that I noticed was the lack of some of my friends at court. Margery and Elizabeth were nowhere to be seen, George never came to say goodnight and Thomas did not come to find me either. At the time I had thought that they were probably with the king and I never thought for a second that anything was wrong.

I went to kiss Lizzie goodnight as I always did. I held her for a while as she slept and then I placed her in her bed and gazed down at her, marvelling at how perfect she was. How lucky Henry and I were. She slept like a little angel. Peaceful and content. I will savour that image of my child for the remainder of my life. She was so sweet. So innocent. She had yet to be touched by the blows that life would deal her. I stayed longer than normal that evening watching her little chest rise and fall as she dreamed happily. She sucked her little thumb and scrunched up her nose as I lightly brushed her hair. I was thinking how soft her skin was. How delicate her little curls were. How impossible it was that something so pure had come of Henry and me.

After sitting there for a long while, I returned to my own room, content with my child sleeping peacefully down the hall. The bitterness of her father was far from my mind. I slept soundly in my bed unaware of all that the next day would bring.

* * * * *

First thing in the morning I received a note. This note summoned me to go in front of the council. I grew a tight knot in my stomach as my nerves took over. I could think of no reason why the council would wish to see me. Fear grew within me as flashbacks of how Henry had handled Catherine filled me with dread. He was sick of me, I knew that much. But was he sick enough to remove me? I could not believe the audacity of the ones summoning me. They had no reason to think that they could command a queen to go anywhere, but with Henry being displeased with me already, I did not want to give him any more reason to dislike me.

I arrived in the great hall at Greenwich palace where a council had gathered. Leading this council was my own uncle, Thomas Howard, Duke of Norfolk. I noticed that he did not meet my eye as I walked in. He stared down into his own hands knowing that what he was about to do would scar his soul for eternity. He told me that he and the men that sit on the council with him had been commissioned with the power to try and judge me.

"And what exactly am I accused of?" I asked. Trying my hardest to keep the shaking from my voice. I had no reason to know anything was wrong before this point. I had no idea that I was to be accused of anything.

"You are accused of committing adultery with three different men," Norfolk spoke. This took me off guard. I had no idea that it would ever be taken seriously. This was unbelievable; I would never commit adultery.

"Where have you heard such treasonous lies?" I almost laughed with the ridiculousness of it all, but Thomas Howard was serious. His face was grave. He looked me dead in the eye as he said "The men accused have all admitted to knowing the queen carnally." His voice never broke for a moment. The air seemed to leave my lungs in one great wave. The floor felt as if it had disappeared from beneath my feet...who would tell such lies? Who would put themselves in such danger in order to frame me? "May I know the name of these liars?" I asked.

"You will hear their names when you stand on trial with them." He spoke to me with harshness in his voice.

"Am I unable to defend myself then? Surely as my uncle you cannot believe this?" He had been there as I grew up. He had helped Henry and me attain our marriage. He had been there when my daughter was christened. Surely he should know that I was a loyal woman.

"You will have a chance to defend yourself when you are on trial, madam." Norfolk quieted me. I always knew that he was an evil man, but I did not know the extent of his bitterness.

"And as for our family connection, I do not consider traitors as my kin." He dealt the blow as if I should care. I had hated him for many years, still I would never do this to him.

"You have dealt with me rudely and disrespectfully. When this is put right all of you in this room will pay the price." I spoke with confidence at that moment, believing that this was all some great joke.

Along with my uncle there sat Sir William Paulet, who spoke up now. "Your Majesty, we mean you no disrespect. And I for one hope this to be proven false." He bowed gently. He was always such a kind and loyal man.

"Thank you, William. I will remember that." I smiled at him before rounding on my disloyal uncle again. "May I leave now? Or do you have any more pathetic accusations?" I asked.

"We here on this council do order you, Queen Anne Boleyn, arrested and attained in the Tower of London, where you will be tried for treason and adultery." My uncle gave the order.

"Treason?" I seethed. " What treason am I accused of?" I asked as the reality of his words cut me. Treason was serious. I had thought this nothing more than one of Henry's games but if treason was on the table then what I was really dealing with was a disaster in the making.

"All will be revealed at the time of your trial."

I opened my mouth to speak, but Norfolk raised a hand, the disrespectful waste of air. What made him think he could command a queen, I will never know. "You will now be taken back to your own apartment until it is safe for the Thames to carry you to the tower."

I was given no more opportunity to speak. The men stood and began to leave the room. I was taken with a man on each arm to my room where I would wait to be taken to the tower. I was shocked to my core. Henry. The man I loved so fiercely was having me locked away. On false accusations. I could not think. My head was full to the brim with the words that had been uttered from my uncle's lips.

Treason? I would never do anything to harm a hair on Henry's head. I loved him, for goodness's sake. I wanted to protect him, not injure him. How could he do this to me? And what of these men? The ones who had said they had slept with me. Where did they come from? And who were they? Maybe they were being bought, offered financial security in order to lie. I had no idea how awful the truth really was. A chill began to take over as the reality of the situation began to creep over me.

* * * * *

At two o'clock in the afternoon on the 2nd of May, my barge was ready, and I was taken to the Tower of London.

306

As the water carried me across the Thames I did not know that this would be the last time I would see the world outside of the Tower's walls. Master Kingston waited at the gate. He greeted me as queen, bowing low and paying me the respect that my station still commanded. "Your Highness." He led me inside. "You will be held in the royal apartments, my lady. I do hope that they will be comfortable enough for you," he smiled. I stepped inside the room where I had once slept on the eve of my coronation. It surely could not be so bad. Not if the king had ensured my comfort. I felt the familiar coldness that seemed to fill me whenever I entered these walls. I would not let it get the better of me though. I would be just fine. This was temporary. I was certain that Henry would see sense.

I was told that my trial was to be held on the 15th of May. I had not yet known the full reasoning for my arrest, but I had heard from Margery — who had joined me in the Tower — that six men had been arrested, including my brother and Thomas Wyatt. What possible cause they would have for arresting George, I did not know. I could almost understand Wyatt, at least the king had become jealous of him before. He had suspected that Wyatt loved me more than that of a subject. But George? He was my baby brother. What could he have possibly done?

Margery told me that Mark Smeaton, who had also been arrested, looked terrible. She had no opportunity to talk to him, but she had seen him brought into the tower and he looked as if he had been beaten to within an inch of his life. She also told me that she had managed to find out that he was one of the men to confess. It seemed a bit too much of a coincidence that he had turned up black and blue after confessing to a false crime. Cromwell was behind the torture. Margery told me herself that he was the one leading the investigation. Henry Norris, Francis Weston, and William Brereton had also been arrested. I had not been told what they were all supposedly guilty of, but at the very least they had all been friends of mine in one way or another.

I had Margery in the Tower with me along with a few other ladies who had become good friends over the years. I had asked that Elizabeth Browne come to me as well but had been told that she had no longer wanted to be involved with me. I was astounded that she would believe the false accusations. We had been friends for a number of years and not once had she left my side or abandoned me, but this was too much, she would not support me in my greatest battle, and for that reason I was glad not to have her in my sight.

The days passed slowly in the Tower. It is strange to be completely cut off from the outside world. I missed Henry madly in the first few days. I would sit and imagine him coming through the door at any moment, kissing me and welcoming me back into his arms. I ached for Lizzie. I wanted to see my daughter. I even requested it but had been told by Kingston that I would not be allowed to see her until my judgement had been passed. I did not realise quite the dire situation I was in.

I sat and waited for it to blow over, thinking that this was all a big test. That Henry had wanted to scare me into obedience. I thought that he would have his fun with me, and then I would be set free again. Not for one moment did I believe that these accusations would be taken seriously. I behaved as normal. My ladies would dress me every morning and then we would pass the days as usual playing cards, reading or sewing.

Margery would update me on the outside world when she had the chance to leave the Tower. She told me that the king was running around with Jane Seymour, but I should not worry because he would tire of her sooner or later. She was lying to me. I could see the fear in her eyes. She believed that this would be my ruin.

"Majesty, the king will come around I am sure," she said to me one night, trying to comfort me as I lay restless in my bed.

"But you do not believe that do you, Margery?" I had asked, patting the seat next to my bed.

"I worry my lady. The king is truly very angry," she said, tears starting to well in her eyes. "You have been nothing but true and loyal, yet he allows the slandering of your name."

"All will be well." I smiled at her. "Oh, my dear friend, how lucky I am to have you." I held her tightly to me. "I have never thanked you, but you have been my one true friend in this world. The days have been cruel and have taken much, but you have held my hand through all of my woes." I wished for her to know that no matter what happened, I would always love her.

"I could not serve a kinder or more gracious queen. You supported me through my own troubles; you put the needs of your ladies above your own. The king has run mad to try to remove you." She dabbed at her eyes with a handkerchief.

"The king will not remove me. It is all a game." I hushed her. "He wants me to feel trapped and alone, but he would never discard me. A love like ours does not simply fade. It is like a star in the night sky. Sometimes it shines brighter than anything else in this world, and at others it is dull. Our love will shine bright again. We simply have to wait for the day to pass and the night to come. Our love is dark like the night sky. It is cruel and unkind. Unfair and painful, but it is worth all of that, for within it holds the smallest glimmer of hope — a beam of light so bright that it blocks out all of the dark and it is the only thing worth looking at." I would take all of the agony that it has brought thousand times over. I would lay my life on the line for a glimpse of the shine that comes with Henry's love.

"Henry told me that our love had caused men to die, had destroyed lives and ruined families, and I would do it all again. I would take a knife to their hearts myself if it meant that we would be together. I would cut down anyone who stood in our way, and I know he would, too. For he loves me with as much passion as I love him. He would not hurt me like he does if he did not love me. You will see, Margery. We will laugh about this one day."

As I think about it now, I hate how I must have sounded. Selfish and uncaring for anyone in the world but Henry and me. I honestly believed it as well. How naïve I was. How evil I must have sounded putting myself and my life above others. I was not this person, I was not nasty and vindictive, I was what Henry had made me, a woman always walking a razor's edge, always having to hurt people to gain more for myself, and never truly feeling safe.

"You honestly do not feel one crumb of guilt for the people that were destroyed by the two of you? Catherine? Mary? What about Thomas More and his family?" she asked, judgement filling her voice. How could I blame her? Many have died because of our selfish behaviour. She had stood by me through it all. Whether she agreed or not she had never judged us.

"Of course I do...and if there was a way to save all the hurt we had caused them, of course, I would have taken it...but it had to happen."

"Did it? And if Henry removes you so that he could marry Jane Seymour, would you feel the same then?" she said, feeling disappointment in her queen for the first time. She wanted me to see how and why I ended up here.

I was speechless. Margery had never called me up on all of my wrongdoings before. She had always supported me, no matter if I was wrong or right. I had to realise that I was now in Catherine's position. A wife on the outside of her marriage while her husband swans about with another woman. I was now the one who stood to lose it all. To grieve over the daughter who was kept out of reach. What I had done to Catherine was now being done to me, but I would not lose this battle like she had. I would win him back. He loved me and that was something that Catherine had completely lost, or that is what I would tell myself. I began to weep. "I am sorry. I hate what I have done. I deserve all of this." I let the guilt finally come to the surface. I had spent so long convincing myself that we were right that I had forgotten about all of the hurt we had caused.

"You are a victim as well, Anne. You are blinded by the king, but you also have to see that you did play a part. I do not hate you for it. You were in love and could see nothing else. You have made up for your mistakes every day since then. The king is the evil here. I do not say these things to hurt you, I say them because I want you to realise who you are dealing with...the king talks of putting you in a nunnery Anne. He wants to marry Jane." She was softer now.

"He would have a fight on his hands.." I laughed. "The only way that he could get rid of me is by killing me." I giggled, but Margery did not, her face held no trace of humour. I felt scared for the first time since entering the Tower.

"Anne. I do not think you understand the severity of your situation," she sighed. "The king wants to get rid of you."

"Well then let him try. I am guilt-free, and as such will be found guilt-free."

"I hope you are right...I really do."

* * * * *

Three days ago, on the 15th of May 1536, my trial took place. I was taken from my rooms in the Tower early in the morning and led to the great hall where the men of the council waited to judge me. Henry Percy was one of those men. He looked as pathetic as the day he broke off our wedding. He visibly shook in his seat. Such a weak man he was. He was not brave enough to judge me. Why he was selected, I do not know. He had no words in him. All he did was nod his agreement.

I stood in front of my own uncle as he read the charges against me. I felt weak as he told me of the disgusting acts that I stood accused of. Whoever had come up with such rotten filth was truly wicked indeed. The room gasped as each thing was listed. Henry had not even bothered to show up. He probably hid in some corner not wanting everyone here to realise that he was a liar and a coward. Norfolk called the council to order and they bowed as I came in. I was still queen and they had no choice but to respect me.

"Queen Anne Boleyn, you have been put on trial today to answer for your crimes against our sovereign Lord and King Henry the 8th of his name. You stand accused of treason and adultery," he spoke directly to me. "You also must answer today to the charges of incest."

Incest. That dirty word, one of the most heinous crimes you can commit, and one that I was not guilty of. I was charged with incest, they had the audacity to accuse me of laying with a member of my own family. It hit me at that moment George had been arrested. George was to be tried after me. They believed that I had committed incest with my own dear brother. The boy I had watched grow. The baby who had come to complete our family.

I loved my brother with every ounce of love in my veins, the thought of anything but brotherly and sisterly affection sickened me to my core. I had cradled him when he was a child. He had been my rock over the past few years. He had been there for me in some of my darkest moments. He was a supportive brother, and that was that. They could not truly believe this. It was twisted and sickening.

"Incest, my lord?" I asked a hint of laughter in my voice. "That is the most ridiculous thing I have ever heard. You must know that this is a lie."

"I'm sorry is there something funny about this?" Norfolk asked. "We have had reports from a trusted source that you have on many occasions lured your brother George into putting his tongue in your mouth, and you have put your tongue in his. Is this not incestuous?"

Who would have said such vile things I have no idea. I would never do something to ruin the relationship that I had with my brother. I wanted to shield him from the world, not use him. It hurt to even think about the idea that someone saw our relationship as more than that of close siblings. He was the closest person in the world to me. I loved him with the greatest of sisterly affection.

"Well yes it is...but" I made to say that it did not happen, but my uncle had other ideas. I realised quickly that I would hardly be able to defend myself.

"We also have had a confession from the musician Mark Smeaton." Norfolk would not allow me to say too much. "He has admitted to two occasions where he had 'known the queen carnally.' He told us that on both the 13th and 19th of May in the year 1534, the queen invited him to her chambers and they proceeded to commit the act of adultery."

I had been with Henry on both of those dates. It now became very clear why Mark had looked so beaten. They must have tortured these lies out of him, for they were untrue and he was my friend. He would never lie to hurt me.

"A conversation took place between you and one Henry Norris. Henry was in your room alone and you were overheard telling him that: 'If the king come to ought but good he would look to have you.' You were overheard by one of your ladies, who has also told us that you would often entertain both Norris and his friend Weston in your rooms," Norfolk continued.

So that is why Elizabeth had left my service. She had repeated what Henry and I had said. She had listened in on that day and reported back. She had betrayed me.

"That was a misunderstanding uncle and nothing else," I spoke.

"But you cannot deny that you said those words?"

"I said those words in jest..."

"Well, there we have it. The queen has just admitted to treason." he addressed the other lords.

"Not treason...I spoke out of turn; I meant no harm." I refused to let this weasel win.

"Is it not treason to imagine the king's death?" Norfolk asked the room. The lords nodded. "And is what her majesty said not imagining the king's death? It sounds to me like it was." They nodded again.

"You have diabolically seduced these men in order to fulfill your own carnal appetites. Each one of them you have lured into your bed, and together you have committed treason against your king and husband. Henry Norris has violated you and known you in a way that is reserved for your husband." I tried to speak, but Norfolk only continued on. "You have despised your marriage and held malice towards your husband. You have by kissing, touching, and illicit means enticed men into your chamber. We have the dates of each of these crimes. We have the men held in the Tower and ready to be tried. The confessions if not already spoken will be and we have the statements of each of your ladies. There really is no other way to see this." My very own uncle pointed the finger at me. "How do you answer these charges against you?" He finally allowed me to speak.

My throat dry, my heart in my mouth, how could I answer? They had already made up their minds, already decided I was guilty. What could I possibly say to defend myself? What did they want from me? I would never confess to these lies that were for sure. I had my chance to speak and knew not what to say. I did not even know how to feel other than numb. The thought that Henry may now believe these things was more shocking to me than the fact that these worthless men believed it. What was I facing now? Would Henry really send me to a nunnery? If the whole country believed me to commit treason then there was no way he could let me off lightly. I had to speak. I had to say anything in my defence.

"My lords, these charges are not only completely false and untrue, but they are treasonous within themselves for you to sit here today and accuse your anointed queen of such atrocities. I have always been a true and loyal wife to my husband, the king. I would never dream of knowing another man in the way that I know him. I ask you to think about this; you all know me well. Do you truly believe that I could do such things?" I looked to them, holding my gaze steady on Norfolk.

"You all know too well just how much I love the king. Norfolk was present on the day we married, and he could see for himself just how much love we bear each other. Do you really think that I would do anything to jeopardize that love? I ask that you all please look within you and search your heart for the answer. These charges are clearly a concoction of fictitious evidence. Their only goal is to bring about my downfall. Now that I have said my piece, I leave it to you to use your consciences wisely."

Not one of them would meet my eye while I spoke. They knew their decision before I spoke; before my trial even began. My death warrant had been signed before we entered this hall. This was just the process we had to follow to look as if justice had taken the proper course. The men spoke for a few moments, not long enough for a real discussion. They were each of them playing their own part in this story, and they had rehearsed well. I knew that I was to be found guilty before my uncle spoke. What I did not know was my punishment.

Norfolk took command again. He loved the power was had. He loved being able to take charge of the queen.

"Anne Boleyn." He stared, but I interrupted.

"It is Your Majesty. Uncle." He would use my title. Whether I was on trial or not, I was still queen and the highest rank in this room.

"Your majesty. We on this council find you guilty of all the crimes you have been accused of." He delivered the verdict with a crushing blow. I did not weep or break my gaze. This I knew already. I would have been found guilty no matter what I had said. It was the next part that shook me to my core...

"Because thou hast offended our sovereign the King's grace in committing treason against his person and here attainted of the same, the law of the realm is this, thou hast deserved death, and thy judgement is this: that thou shalt be burned here within the Tower of London on the Green, else to have thy head smitten off, as the King's pleasure shall be further known of the same."

Deserved death.....

Those words condemned me to the fate I face now. A council of my peers condemned me to die. I would be burned at the stake, or I would lose my head, but either way, I had been sentenced to death. I never expected it. I never thought for a moment that Henry would go as far as killing me. Those words ring in my ears now...

"Do you understand Your Majesty? You have been sentenced to die." Norfolk spoke as I stared blankly. "Your Majesty..."

I did not answer...all I could see was my body, limp on the floor, lifeless, eyes shut and gone from the world. All I could think about was my daughter. I would never see her again. She would lose her mother. At under three years old, she would lose me.

If I were condemned to death then what of George? Would he face the same fate? Or worse? What if he was to be drawn and quartered? My poor little brother to die a traitor's death. It was not right. He was as innocent as I was. And the others, they were all to die too? Henry must be mad. for he is choosing to kill his wife. The mother of his child. The queen. No one was supposed to be able to touch a queen. I was supposed to be untouchable. It had never been done before. I just kept thinking the same sentence in my head, over and over "I am too young to die...I am too young to die."

My heart was and is broken. How can a man I gave my everything to suddenly turn on me in such a way. Was my love not enough? Had I not given him enough? All of my years of dedication and loyalty were worthless to him. The child I had given him was clearly worthless to him. I loved Henry and I still to this day believe that he loves me. He is just an arrogant fool who refused to ever back down until he got exactly what he wanted. I just could not understand it. Why now? Why had he sought to ruin me?

The king could not have possibly meant to kill me. He would straighten this all out; I would not die; of course I would not. George could not die. They had not mentioned Wyatt. Was Wyatt of the same fate? They deserved so much more. If I had not said anything to Norris then he may have been safe. If I was not friends with them they would be safe. I heard a gasp and as I turned saw Percy lain out on the floor. He had collapsed as my verdict was spoken, not having the stomach for murder. He was picked up and taken from the room. The verdict was unanimous. He did not fight for me so why should he faint at my judgement. He knew what was coming so why act like a pathetic little worm now? Why not defend me in my hour of need. If he had once loved me, or loved me still, then he could have said one word to my character, but he was too scared to speak out against his betters even if it would have saved his queen.

"Your Majesty...do you have anything to say?" Norfolk broke through my daze.

I had to speak again, but my head was full of noise. It was as if all I could hear was a ringing. My mind had gone off to a different place altogether. I could think of no words. But I also could not let them have the last say. I straightened up and looked each of them dead in the eye — one after the other.

"First of all, I would like to say that I deny all of these charges. You have judged me to die, and I deem that unacceptable, owing to my complete innocence." My voice shook, but I was still queen, and I would behave as such. "I do not say that I have always borne towards the King the humility which I owed him, considering his kindness and the great honour he showed me and the great respect he always paid me; I admit too, that often I have taken it into my head to be jealous of him...But might God be my witness if I have done him any other wrong." I left it there as the exhaustion of the morning won out. I would save my energy for the next few days.

Norfolk spoke up. "It is with great sadness that we condemn our queen to die, but her crimes were too great to ignore." Liar! He was not sad; he was only worried about how it would affect his position as he would no longer be the queen's uncle. "You are dismissed from the stand, Your Majesty, and required to see the testimony of the men accused with you."

I was led away from the stand and watched as each of them pleaded their innocence, and as each of them were condemned. They all looked to me as they spoke, each one conveying with their eyes either anger at being dragged into my mess or sorrow at sharing our downfall. Norris was angry. He was guilty of nothing more than words. Words that he had not even spoken. He blamed me for talking to him as I did. You could see the hate in his eyes.

Mark pleaded with his eyes, as he admitted to the accusations his eyes seemed to apologise, seemed to search for something in me that he could call to. It was obvious that he had been tortured. He had to be dragged to the stand. He could barely stay on his own feet. His eye looked as if it had been popped from its socket. His hands clearly broken, but of course no one saw that.

Weston did not look at me at all. He stared at the ground as he shook his head at each accusation.

Brereton argued. He spat and name called, doing himself not one favour. He was disgusted pointing at me at one moment and saying "you think I would lay with that? I have eyes." His words cut, but I knew them to be his defence. It did not matter what they said. Each one of them in their turn was sentenced to die. The day before my execution was set each of them would face their fate.

Then it was my brother's turn. George took to the stand as tears freshly dried on my face. He had seen his sister condemned, a sister he loved with all of his heart. Again he was read the sick accusations against us. He visibly heaved as they repeated the charge of our kissing. He stared in my eyes, fear visible behind them as he knew what was about to come.

He shook from head to toe, devastated by the whole mess. He was sick with grief. Of course he denied all of the charges as much as I had, but it was useless. If I was to die, then he was to die. He knew that. This was the last time I saw my brother alive. All I could see was the little child running around Hever and causing trouble. The chubby little baby that would keep us awake with his tears. The man who held me as I lost my own child. He should not have been allowed to die. He had so much to give to this world. He was so talented and intelligent. He was given a note while he was on trial and they told him to read it but not out loud. Of course he read it out loud. Condemning himself even further.

"Anne had conveyed to me that the king neither has the vigour nor ability to create a child." I now know why the king was not here. Henry would have been totally shamed. He was scared that the country would realise how much of a pathetic excuse for a man he was.

"That is ludicrous!" George shouted. "Anne would never say a word against the king."
George was also asked whether he believed Elizabeth to truly be the king's daughter. Apparently he had told friends that Elizabeth was the child of one of my affairs.
"I would never say that. Christ, look at the princess; she is every bit her father." But his pleading and excuses were useless. He had no chance, and the verdict was passed again.

"You will be returned to the tower, and from there you will go to Tyburn and then be hanged by the neck, cut down, and your body will be quartered into pieces. A death fitting your vile crimes. George Boleyn you are sentenced to die a traitor's death, your head will then be displayed with the other traitor's for all the country to see…"

"No!!" I shouted, standing from my seat and running to my brother, who I held onto with all of my might. "No, please not George. You already have me. He is innocent." I was on my knees begging.

"Sister, It is all right." George sobbed. "We will meet again. God will accept us."

"George, I am sorry. Please, George, forgive me." he lifted me to my feet.

"There is nothing to forgive." Both of us were crying now. "Sister, you did nothing wrong. I do not blame you." George smiled his very last smile at me. He was so handsome. So wasted. Why did Henry feel the need to take him from me. He could do what he liked to me but I could never forgive him for taking my George. I hated him. I still hate him for taking George. I looked upon my brother for the last time. I could have screamed for the agony splitting through my chest. I would rather have my death repeated one hundred times over than to have him die even once. They practically ripped him from me. Even allowing us our last precious moments together was too much to ask. I just wanted to hold him. Why could they have not let me hold him close one last time.

"Your Majesty, please return to your place." Sir William spoke as a guard tugged on my arm.

"Go, Anne." George kissed me on the head and delivered me weeping into the arms of Margery. "I will wait for you," he promised. I knew exactly what he meant. If I was to go to heaven he would be behind those gates. I almost wish my own death sooner just so I can see him again.

"I love you, George. More than anything," I sobbed as Margery held me tight.

George stroked my cheek with his thumb. "And I love you, Sister. With my whole heart." He said before allowing the guards to remove him from the court. My heart broke as I turned my head towards Margery. I could not watch him go. For I knew that I would never see him again and that was a horror I was not willing to face.

George would not be hanged, drawn, and quartered; nor would the other men. They would be beheaded. Beneath my window where I could hear their pleas for mercy. I would look out and see all of them lose their lives. I refused to look away as each of them faced their fate. I was responsible, so I would watch as my sins were paid for in blood. I did not sleep with any of them, but I did bring them into my world. George was unlucky enough to be my brother, and I cannot even explain the pain of watching him lose his life. It was like my heart had been torn out of my chest. I screamed as the axe made its connection. As it took the last breath from him. He was someone I was supposed to look after. I am his older sister; I am supposed to protect him from the world. I would do anything to sit with him awhile.

There are no words to describe how it feels to lose not only a brother but your best friend in this world. He was the angel on my shoulder, guiding me in this life and now he had been snuffed out. The pain is too much to write about. There are no words to tell of the feeling that overtakes you when you see a loved one destroyed. It was like all of the joy had been removed from the world. Up until that point I had thought that I could still be saved, but as my brother spoke his final words and laid his beautiful head down on the block I realised it was over. This was the end. I would go to my grave tomorrow. I would be welcomed by sweet George. At least I would have one friend to guide me to the next place. I watched as life was wasted. As a young man was cut down too soon. I wondered what my mother and father thought now. They had pushed us up in the world, and now they would receive the news that one of their children was dead. I hope that they hate themselves. I hope they are filled with guilt. I hope that Norfolk had heard the news and felt as the weight of what he has done knocks him off of his feet. I pray that George is at peace.

At this moment I would like to lay tribute to George Boleyn. He was my life and soul, and I will love him for eternity.

* * * * *

After the trial was over I sank to the floor in my room, the reality finally hitting me. The betrayal dealt from someone I loved so dearly on me like an open wound. I had done nothing but love Henry. And loved him with everything I had. And how had he repaid me? By murdering my brother. By murdering my friends. And by murdering me. He may as well swing the sword himself. It may as well have been he who removed my brothers head. For it is he who has done it. With his twisted and bitter lies he has removed the only woman in this world blind and stupid enough to love him. He is a cruel man. He does not know the meaning of real love, for if he did he would not injure me as he has. More than anything I am sad and I am cold. I am lonely and I am wretched. I have lost every last thing that meant anything to me. I have had my heart ripped out before my own eyes. I lay here now an empty shell. Abandoned by the person who gave me a life. The person who promised me the world but snatched it away at the snap of his fingers. I am in ruins.

CHAPTER TWENTY-FOUR

19 May 1536

Now my tale is done. I have bared my heart and soul for you in these pages. I hope that you have read this well and with kindness in your heart. I hope that you have managed to make it to the end. I pray that you do not judge me too harshly. For my sins are many. My mistakes in full view. There may be points where you thought me evil, stupid, perhaps naïve. But it is my wish that you all have seen my kindness, my love, my bravery, and a side to me that you were told never existed. You will have seen that I was much more than a mistress who overstepped. I loved deeply and without shame. I thank you, dear reader, for staying the course with me. For not giving up. For feeling the things I have felt these years and still making it to the end. Thank you for giving your time to me.

The hour of my death draws closer now. It is closing in on me, and I can do nothing more than sit and wait. The night is fading away, taking with it my final moments in this world. The day begins to spread warming the night sky. It will be a beautiful day. The bright light of the sky will shine as my light fades. The sky will be blue and the air warm. As I fade, the day will bring with it blessings of the summer to come. I feel the time ever so keenly now. There is a stillness that comes towards the end.

I sit and wait for the time to come, for my ladies to rush in and ready me; to sweep my hair away from my neck and leave it bare so that the executioner may make his mark. To dress me in my dark gown, and place my necklace around my neck, one final time. They will talk with me awhile and distract me from the day. Then I will hear the key to the door turn and in will come Kingston and I will be directed to follow him out of this room down out of the Tower.

I will be offered some prayer for my soul and will be led up the steps onto the scaffold. There I will pay for my own death, and I will bid my final farewell to the world. My ladies will remove my headdress and take my necklace from me. They will weep and weep, and they will not want to part with me. But they will have to go. I am grateful enough that they will be there at the end. They will leave me. The executioner will ask me for my forgiveness, which I will willingly give. God save his soul. Then he will tell me to ready myself. Then that will be it, over in nothing but a few moments. In one final moment of weakness,

I have written a note, to be given to Henry. I know not of the effect it will have if any at all. However, I would like to leave something with him, for him to know that it comes from a woman who he himself has condemned. I would like him to read it and to know that I choose to use my final moments writing to him, thinking about him even. I would like for him to think about what he has done. If but only for a moment of his time.

"Commend me to the king, and tell him, that he hath been ever constant in his course of advancing me: from a private gentlewoman he made me a marchioness, and from a marchioness a queen; and now, that he hath left no higher degree of earthly honour, he intends to crown my innocence with the glory of martyrdom."

I hope he knows how he who raised me so high, has also lowered me, six feet into the ground.

What was that? No. It cannot be now. I am not ready. I thought I still had time.

My ears are alert to every sound. The birds chirp away as if this is a happy day like any other. I imagine for many it will be a happy day. Babies will be born. People will marry, be with their loves, their families. Far away from the dark cloud that will sweep my world today. Far away from

325

London and its cursed walls. People will be rejoicing. Happy in their own little homes. Many will know what happens today. Many may note the hour as the bell chimes to announce my death. Many will not care at all. Some will be happy to be rid of me, and some will be sad at losing me.

What faces will I see in the crowd today, I wonder. Will my family come to see me off one final time? To look upon the daughter they have ruined? Will my sister take pity on me in my last moments and come to share one last moment of sisterly love? My uncle? Who did cruelly pass the sentence that got me here. The one who ordered my death, would he like to say goodbye to me? To watch his sentence be carried out?

Well, what is the use in dwelling on it now? I have some happiness at least. My daughter will be far away from here. She will be too small to know of today's tragic circumstances. She is young still and will have no idea that as she plays and laughs the day away, her mother's life is being stolen. One day when she does know, I will be nothing but a distant memory from long ago. Not a mother at all. Just a figure in her past. A faint image at the back of her mind. She may not weep over my death, as I weep at the loss of her. She may not feel the pain of a mother ripped away. And for this I am somewhat thankful. She will not feel the tear in her heart that our separation has caused me. The unbearable hole that I feel growing bigger the longer I am away. I just pray she knows how deeply I love her. With all of my soul and every part of me. If only for a short three years, she was the absolute joy of my life. My reason to fight. She was my red-haired beauty. And I will go to my grave clinging to the image of her.

To lose her has been the hardest part of this. It pains me more than the thought of death. The thought that my daughter must believe I have abandoned her. She does not know that I was ripped from her arms. But perhaps with this, now she will. If this is destined to reach my little Lizzie, just know that I will always be your mother. Forever. And that I love you with love so fierce it will be felt long after I am dust.

Good reader, I feel this must draw to an end soon. The bells chime the early hour, and the sun begins to brighten the sky. The birds' chirps grow more incessant as they call the day ever closer. I hear the Tower busying around me. People are at work ready for the great event ahead. The swordsman is here from Calais. My last gift from Henry. Practicing, readying himself to make the brief swing of his sword that will kill a Queen.

The excitement is in the walls, as a day that will mark history comes ever closer. My blood will mark this day forever. My tears stain the pages in history and my sobs, the ears of the people all around.

If these are going to be my last words, then I choose to say goodbye. Goodbye to this room that was both my beginning and my end. Goodbye to this Tower whose walls have held many tragic men. Goodbye London. My home. Goodbye this world that I have called home for such a short time. Goodbye my child, my husband, and family. Be well and be happy. I will miss all of you and hope that you too will miss me in one way or another.

What time is it? Is the time now? It must be around 7.30 in the morning. Will it be now? Will my door swing open now? I feel less prepared as the moment creeps closer. I feel panic knowing that I have less than an hour to live. I am tired now and have nothing left to say. There is nothing more to say. All words have been used up. I have told my sorrow, and I am now exhausted with the pain of relieving my darkest days.

I hear footsteps outside. They seem to match my beating heartbeat as it picks up. I feel the bile rise again in my throat. My head pounds with anticipation. I feel I have already been cut off from this world. I do not want to die, please God, save me from this fate, forgive me, I want to live. I want to go on and live. They are here. Why have the hours gone by so quick, why is my time gone? I cannot stand this.

Lord, help me, please. Look upon me kindly and save me from the torment ahead. I cling to my book of hours, as if this object may be the thing to save my life, as if by some miracle, my holding it to my heart does keep me here a little longer. I cling to life for a while longer. But a silence falls. A silence that calms me. I am left with an emptiness. A longing for this to be over with one way or another. I am sad and tried. Death appears to me almost as a peaceful rest now. Where I will be with my dear George and my sons forever.

They're here; they bang down my door as they come to drag me away to force me into my death. The thieves are here at last ready to pounce. The wolves at the door, like beastly hellhounds, they scratch away at my sanity and request that I go along quietly. They have come to take me down to my doom. Come to take my light and snuff it. There is no turning back. Nowhere to run. I cannot hide. I can do nothing but follow them. God, please, forgive me and accept me into your kingdom of heaven. Lord protect me. I take a breath and...

EPILOGUE

Two years later....

They cleared out her rooms after she was gone. She owned hardly anything after she was decrowned. The jewels were taken, ready for the next queen. Queen Jane. They would pay Master Kingston for her belongings from the tower. As he by rights owns anything she may have left behind. And now I believe they plan to remove her entirely. Like she never existed. They do not want history to remember her. They have taken her life, and now they wish to destroy her legacy.

They found nothing but some clothes, and a few personal items. William Kingston came to me a few days after her death and revealed that he had tucked a few things away. He did not want Anne to be erased. I believe that he felt for her in the short time she was in his keeping. I imagine he loved her as his queen and was shocked and saddened that such a thing could be done to a woman crowned before God. I was given her beautiful pearl B necklace to keep with me at all times. And these papers. I have read them well, again and again hoping each time to discover some new truth from the pages, to find some source of happiness from them. I wish to understand her, and I know that these pages are straight from her heart to mine. Now that I have read them, I feel like I understand her more. I can see why she did the things she did and why she acted in a way I could not support at the time. She was not a manipulative woman striving to step on everyone. She was a normal girl who fell victim to a man's advances and suffered in a world that was created just for him.

I watched my queen die on this exact day, two years ago. I watched as she left this cruel world. Two years since we lost such a beautiful bright mind, a wonderful mind that was her downfall. Her intelligence and fierce passion were her own great enemy. She was naïve and sometimes stupid, but she was brave and strong. She took this world by storm, and she left a permanent mark that will forever be written across the ages. She will not be forgotten. I will not let her. Elizabeth will know her. On that I swear. Elizabeth will one day hear about the woman who would give her life to save her daughter. A woman who loved with no boundaries.

Even as she prepared to die, she held her head high as the queen she was. She took command of the crowd, and she made them hear her.

I will never forget the words she spoke on that day. I remember them like it was just yesterday. They will ring in my mind for a long time to come.

"Good Christian people, I am come hither to die, for according to the law, and by the law, I am judged to die, and therefore I will speak nothing against it. I am come hither to accuse no man, nor to speak anything of that, whereof I am accused and condemned to die. But I pray God save the king and send him long to reign over you, for a gentler nor a more merciful prince was there never, and to me he was ever a good, a gentle and sovereign lord. And if any person will meddle of my cause, I require them to judge the best. And thus I take my leave of the world and you all, and I heartily desire you all to pray for me. O Lord have mercy on me. To God I commend my soul."

She then knelt, ready to place her head on the block. And she repeated this over and over until the fatal swing took her. She started by crying this out, and it soon became a gentle whisper as she prayed that God accepts her into his kingdom.

'To Jesus Christ, I commend my soul; Lord Jesus receive my soul.'"

Only at the very end did she break and weep and the fear shone in her eyes for the first time. She looked at me. Her eyes met mine, and I saw her fade from this world, as the sword connected and thus ended Queen Anne Boleyn. She stayed true to herself and her love right until the end.

The strongest woman to ever have lived among us. After the horrendous deed was done, it did not take long for everyone to realise that no instructions had been left for her body afterwards. There were no burial instructions. No coffin. Would Henry really display her head on London bridge? He clearly wanted to destroy her. He wanted everyone to believe that he no longer loved her. But I know differently. He never looks at anyone else the way he looked at her. He kicks himself every day for his crimes. He misses her. You can see the sadness in his eyes and the hate he bears Elizabeth for the fact that she reminds him of her. She has Anne's strong will and fight. She will never be walked over. When she smiles, it is Anne he sees, and I hope that it torments him. I know he cries out in the night for Anne and I enjoy every moment of pain he feels.

Her other ladies had run to her and thrown a white cloth over her sad face the moment it was removed from her shoulders. Henry loved this woman with his whole heart not that long ago. And now he has just left her to rot on the ground. He does not care if she be accepted into heaven, or if her body be buried in consecrated ground. He doesn't care what happens to her physical body or her eternal soul as long as he be rid of her.

Her ladies and I, still loyal even now, took a length of cerecloth and wrapped her carefully in it.

"Lady Margery, what shall we do? It feels cold and cruel to place her into the ground like this." One of them asked me, tears streaming down her young face. These ladies had served Anne for a number of years now and had grown to love her as I had.

I looked around me, searching the faces for an answer. The nobles come to watch had already begun leaving. They did not care about what happened next. She was gone. They had gotten the show that they wanted. They had their entertainment for the day. Now they drifted off to carry on with their lives as if it was yet another day. It was William Kingston who finally came to our aid.

"I have sent some men to the armory. They will find something there. We will bury her in the Tower chapel. Do not worry. She will rest in peace in consecrated ground."

"Thank you, Master Kingston. Anne would appreciate your loyalty." I nodded at him.

Within moments the men came back carrying a crate. They had told us that it had been used to carry weapons into the armory. They placed it down and then they ever so carefully lifted my dear mistress, sweet Anne, into the crate. She was wearing nothing but a shift. She had stripped off her grey gown to give to the executioner as part of the payment for his gruesome job. The crate would not fit her petticoats as well as the cerecloth, so her ladies and I removed those as well. What a way for a queen to go, undressed and headless. It is a sad end to such a magnificent woman. The crate was only just big enough to fit her body in lengthways, I picked up her head, refusing to look, but wanting that closeness to a woman who was as good as a sister, one last time. The last time I would ever touch her. The last memory I have of her is her lifeless body being stuffed into a box because no one bothered to arrange what would happen after she was murdered. I say murdered, and I mean murdered. Anne and George were murdered. Henry wanted to be rid of a problem, and he got rid of the problem and did not care who went down with them at the same time.

I placed her head under her arm. The crate did not have the room for her to be placed in the way she should have been.

We then followed as the guards carried her carefully from the scaffold to the chapel, St Peter ad Vincula. (St Peter in chains) which is ever so appropriate. We followed to the front of the altar where they dug a hole, and placed her in, next to her little brother George. They will rest peacefully together I hope. Side by side, as they were in life. I pray that George was there to welcome her in heaven. I pray that they will be up there laughing and singing like when they were children. I hope that they are carefree now, far from a world that destroyed them. The weight of this life's troubles far behind them. Nothing but love and warmth to surround them. I will join them one day, but until that moment, I will remember them. In my heart and my soul, they will live within me for as long as I shall live. Then when the clocks stop for me and my life is up, I will join them up above, and we be reunited again.

Goodbye and may God go with you as you read. Please, remember our dear Queen Anne. Take a moment from your day to remember your queen, but most of all, remember a woman, a kind, spirited, happy, young woman. Whose only mistake was to fall in love.

Margery.

THE END

ACKNOWLEDGMENTS

There are so many people to thank for helping me make this book. I would like to thank each and every person who has supported me along the way. I would like to thank my family, my mother, and my Grandfather who have each individually offered me guidance when needed.

Thank also my brothers and sisters, Courtney, Chelsea, Lucie, Jacob, Sophia and David for being the wonderful siblings that they are.

I want to thank my best friend Ashley for being there for me always, through thick and thin, supporting me on every one of my decisions. He always knows how to make everything better.

To Cara, who always has my back and has been there for all of my lowest and highest points.

To Helen who is a crazy Libra like me and I can never get bored of our afternoons watching Harry Potter or screaming High School Musical at the top of our lungs.

To Jade who has come back into my life and has become like a sister to me. I have the most supportive and caring friends that anyone could ever wish for.

To Linda for proof reading and aiding me in making the book the best that I can.

To Jenna for saving the day when things were not going to plan.

To Laura and Kim who were always on hand with advice even in the early hours of the morning.

Most importantly I would like to thank my publisher and friend Kathi. You saw my book from the moment it was nothing but an idea in my jumbled head and you believed in it. This book would not exist if it were not for you.

And finally I would like to thank my grandparents. They took me in and they cared for me. They supported every decision I ever made whether it made sense to them or not.

My nan was the greatest lady I have and will ever meet and I like to think that I am at least a little bit like her.

Holly-Eloise Walters
October 2019

O Death, O Death, rock me asleepe,
Bring me to quiet rest;
Let pass my weary guiltless ghost
Out of my careful breast.
Toll on, thou passing bell;

Ring out my doleful knell;
Thy sound my death abroad will tell,
For I must die,
There is no remedy.

My pains, my pains, who can express?
Alas, they are so strong!
My dolours will not suffer strength
My life for to prolong.
Toll on, thou passing bell;
Ring out my doleful knell;
Thy sound my death abroad will tell,
For I must die,
There is no remedy.

Alone, alone in prison strong
I wail my destiny:
Woe worth this cruel hap that I
Must taste this misery!
Toll on, thou passing bell;
Ring out my doleful knell;
Thy sound my death abroad will tell,
For I must die,
There is no remedy.

Farewell, farewell, my pleasures past!
Welcome, my present pain!
I feel my torment so increase
That life cannot remain.
Cease now, thou passing bell,
Ring out my doleful knoll,
For thou my death dost tell:
Lord, pity thou my soul!
Death doth draw nigh,
Sound dolefully:
For now I die,
I die, I die.

— Anne Boleyn, 1536